To Iren

May God bless you

as you read

"May God Really

Bless You as you

Read

"Martyrs of the Cross

Passion for Christ"

Larry Shelf

1-17-15

MARTYRS

OF THE

CROSS

Passion for Christ

Larry Skelf

UPWARD BOUND PUBLICATIONS

Soddy Daisy, Tenn.   2005

Upward Bound Publications ®

Skelf, Larry

Martyrs of the Cross...Passion for Christ

copyright © 2005   Upward Bound Publications

ISBN 0-9768072-0-3   Library Of Congress Control Number 2005926388

Martyrs of the Cross ...Passion for Christ, is a registered trademark ® of Upward Bound Publications

Printed in the United States of America

Biblical quotations from KJV King James Version Holy Bible, by permission, Cornerstone Bible Publishers © copyright 1998,Nashville, Tennessee.

Quotations from Micheal Minor-by permission

Quotations from Wayne (R.D.) Wallin- by permission

Quotations from Dr. Ron Phillips- by permission

Partial editing by Jeremy Reece
Partial editing by JCW
Partial editing by LES

Martyrs of the Cross, Passion for Christ is a novel of fictional content, and should be considered expressly so, except for certain key direct references to current events and/or public figures, or historical or religious places or persons. Any other similarities to persons living or dead are purely coincidental.

UBP Upward Bound Publications ™

Special Thanks and Acknowledgements:

Thank you, my beautiful, loving and encouraging wife, Debbie, without whom I would not have been able to have the tenacity to complete this book, (or the audacity) to even complete the first page.

Debbie, you had the insightfulness right from the start, to know it's uniqueness held many challenges, but also held the possibility and the hopes for being used as a tool to help win souls to Christ.

Thank you so much!

Also special thanks to the many friends and family members who encouraged me all the way.

Thank you to my children, Kasey Cahoon, Kris Cahoon, Shannon Skelf, Stacey Smith, and Sheila Skelf. They all have helped me grow in Christ by teaching me life-lessons they probably weren't even aware of. Strength in Christ comes often times at unexpected times, in unexpected ways. It is true ...our children are indeed miracles from God!

Thank you to my grandchildren, because yes...even they can teach us and inspire us so much in the Lord!

Thank you to April Cahoon, a very dear friend of mine and Debbie's, and mother of two of our grandchildren, for the fabulous photography on the cover of this book!

Thank you, my pal Jeremy Reece, for your abilities and using them for the computer imaging on the front cover of this book, and for designing and engineering our web site, and for his help in partially editing the book. Great job, April and Jeremy!

Special thanks also to Jeremy's mother, Kaye Reece, for helping in the design and layout of this book cover.

Also, thank you my beautiful daughter, Stacey Smith, for being the model for the front cover of this book, and the plays and ongoing promotions of them!

Thanks to Gospel Baptist Tabernacle, in Rossville Georgia, and their pastor, David Thompson, for your support and encouragement and for participating in the very first Martyrs of the Cross play, without which I doubt this book would exist!

Thanks to Wayne (R. D.)Wallin, for his support as my pastor and for allowing the second Martyrs of the Cross play.

Thanks to my mother and dad, Hazel (the miracle woman) and Robert Skelf for their upbringing and teachings and examples. (Hey mom, hey dad, you were right about all that stuff you taught me...now I'm trying to teach my kids and grandkids!)

There are thanks due directly to many other individuals, you know I love and thank everyone of you!

Mostly, mostly, mostly ...I thank my Risen Savior, Jesus Christ! I'll be in your presence soon, and I'm looking forward to it!

Remember...this life is not our home ...we are to tolerate it ....but look forward to the next!

Thou Shalt Love
The Lord Thy God
With All Thy Heart, And
With All Thy Soul, And
With All Thy Mind.

Jesus

Matthew 22 : 37

Martyrs of the cross- Passion for Christ, is a work of Christian Apocalyptic Martyrology, bringing together fiction and non-fiction in it's world of reality, probability and possibility ...this same world we now live in!

In doing so, it incorporates a unique blend of *special effects* to cause the reader to not only read and relate to the book, but to enhance the realism of actually being an integral part of the book.

It focuses on the critical need to become a Christian...a real Christian, empowered by God's Holy Spirit and with the willingness to pray for, then submit to and do God's calling, no matter what the consequences.

Life and death for this life, and Heaven or Hell for Eternity, hang in the balance for more people than ever before in history!

Right or Wrong ...or just Right Justification in this impending Pre-Raptured day and age of constant *gray areas*...how Eternally significant are those decisions we make on life's Dailey tests and challenges, both for us and for others?

Is much of the subject matter about a state of radical liberal governmental domination and chaos fiction or fact?

This book invites you to take a look around ...in your "own back yard" and globally, then decide for yourself.

It invites you then, if you come up with the same hard-hitting answers the book does ...to act on them, in your strong witness and educating others through Christ Jesus. our Lord and Savior.

Contents

Food for thought...

"Be careful how you treat the people that witness to you...you could be the next one witnessing!"

"Don't just play church...the church needs Kingdom Builders."

Excerpts from a sermon by Michael Minor (October 2004)

"When is the last time a tear touched your pillow for the empty pews in your church?"

Excerpt from sermon by Wayne (R.D.) Wallin (March 2005)

"Continually be aware there is another kind of passion Christ has for his children, the deep passion He has for all of us to have a burning, passionate, committed, involved and working love for Him. This book is about that unselfish love for Him and our fellow human beings. This book is about our becoming and staying grounded in a deep 'Passion for Christ.' Talk is cheap; this book is a wakeup call to action!

Quotes from Dr. Ron Phillips, Pastor Abba's House, Chattanooga, TN

The battle...rages in this present world. Our earth has been plunged into disaster, and disasters are often due to Satanic control. Our world is littered with the casualties of satan. We are in an awful struggle for the minds and hearts of men.

Live Jesus, Love Jesus, Be passionate about Jesus.

God is so madly in love with you - He sent the Sweet Holy Spirit to you - He loves you, He loves you, He loves you!

From Heaven's perspective, Death looks good!

T-MINUS ONE DAY AND COUNTING
_____The Spectacle of the Last Day

Some Child of God, caught up "in the twinkling of an eye," once wrote:

Never has the glamour of the Earth been so blessedly beautiful. Like a blind person who suddenly gains sight, everything is so awesome. The mountains and the valleys, in their endless array! How could all this have come to be?

It's as if, in hindsight,(being 20 / 20),she was putting on her best dress, adorning her hair, the excitement of her life placing her into the highest of high anticipation!

Adorning of the Caretaker - Story and a Poem

Nature's splendors and wonders magnified . . . and you didn't notice a thing!
Time came, and time went.
Too busy, you!
Too sad . . . too busy you!
No man knoweth when the Son of Man cometh, except the Father!
He shall come as a thief in the night!

We knew that the Earth was a most crowning jewel to the Word, and in being created, not like we were created, but also . . . as -we were created. Her splendor, her majesties, her mysteries, her numerous powers, known and enjoyed completely only by her ever watching, ever loving omnipotent Hand of Mercy!

The blessed children that she has kept as much as possible, in tender loving care, while it would appear, she eagerly awaits the masterful Creator of all, including she and her trusting inhabitants in Christ.

Not to be worshipped, not to be revered, but to be admired in all it's wondrousnesses!
Could she breathe, might she say, "Don't bow to me, but enjoy to your fullest, my millions-fold sparkles of spectacle!

Eat of my tasty bounty, keep my blood veins-my rivers-clean and pure, and drink the coolness thereof and quench that part of your physical thirst! Breathe me, unpolluted. The oxygen of the air is sweet!

Contain yourself not! I am all in wonder to enjoy, even as a loving horse enjoys its rider, strutting in pride to boastfully exhibit for all to grasp in sightful, exuberant longing!

13

Come, look what I have in my entrust!
Worship not me!
Worship with me!
Of all creations in the magnificent universe, the Creator visits me!
Of all creations in the universe, the Creator comes for **you***!*

Are my locks of hair, the clouds, adorning my beauty, my blue cheeks, my skies?
Do they gently tease upon my breasts, my mountains covered with foliage, trees
and snow ...and the mothering of the wildlife, the clothing I display in all pride!
Does the dew trickle upon my face, moistening my skin, the green grass of my
fields?

"Did I do well?" I ask.
"Did I do well?"

But to only ask . . . oh please to only ask . . .
And even my rocks and stones would fall down and worship You!
But to only hear You speak . . . that I could obey your command, and my rushing
seas and mighty winds and storms would with heart pounding in excitement . . .
obey!

Even the very twinkle of my eye ... the hand of time itself ...
Requires no skill ...to be mastered by You!

It is the whim of your fancy, your desire, Your imagination!
Visit me, oh my love, visit me!
Come to me that my pride is filled!
Come reap thy sweet harvest!

Did it, we not see?
You should have been taking-better care of me!
My needs, my cares . . . too few the great.
You need! You want! Sad mankind . . . it's your trait!

You were too busy . . . taking care
Of the thousand some-odd things, that threw you in despair
Time was, now time is, and every knee shall bow
I should have, but didn't...in time...not until now!

So sad, for you, that on that day,
When your Savior was told-He could be on His way.
He came, as He said, like a thief in the night.
Now, and now eternally...everything enjoys His Bright Light.

Too busy, you!
Too sad . . . too sad . . . too busy you!

14

In a word…in a single word…this book is about . . .

Commitment

Luke 12: 2-3

"For there is nothing covered that shall not be revealed; neither hid, that shall not be known. Therefore whatsoever ye have spoken in darkness shall be heard in the light; and that which ye have spoken in the ear in closets shall be proclaimed upon the housetops."

Luke 12:8-9

"Also I say unto you, whosoever shall confess me before men, him shall the son of man also confess before the angels of God. But he that denieth me before men shall be denied before the angels of God."

Luke 12:4-5

"And I say unto you my friends, be not afraid of them that kill the body, and after that have no more that they can do. But I will forewarn you whom ye shall fear: Fear Him, which after he hath killed hath power to cast into hell; yea, I say unto you, fear Him."

Romans 12:17,19-21

"If it be possible, as much as lieth in you, live peaceably with all men."

"Dearly beloved, avenge not yourselves, but rather give place unto wrath: for it is written, Vengeance is mine: I will repay, saith the Lord. Therefore if thine enemy hunger, feed him; if he thirst, give him drink: For in so doing thou shalt heap coals of fire on his head. Be not overcome of evil, but overcome evil with good."

Luke 12:6-7

"Are not five sparrows sold for two farthings, and not one of them is forgotten before God? But even the very hairs of your head are numbered. Fear not therefore: ye are of more value than many sparrows."

Daniel 12:3

"And they that be wise shall shine as the brightness of the firmament; and they that turn many to righteousness as the stars forever and ever."

Preface

It's almost unbelievable how things came about, how rapidly they happened. Many now say that they saw it all coming, but they didn't think it would really happen, or that it would be so bad. Deep inside they knew the truth was out there . . . and they could have prepared for it all.

This book is not about Ruby Ridge, or Waco. It's not about Columbine or Y-2K, or even 911. It's not about anything else that may be defined as non-fiction, government intrusion or conspiracy-as horrible as they all were. The latter may have been a fabrication that allowed the rich to get richer or maybe control us with a cruel joke

I'm not saying we should forget those events, and I'm not saying we should stop discussing them. We should keep seeking the truth about them. We should always seek the truth about the terrible events that befall mankind.

That said, this book is about martyrdom for Christ, and the strength, resolve and perseverance that go with it. It takes strength and a surrendered soul to be an "overcomer for Christ." It takes grace in abundance to face the challenges and adversity in a world hostile to Him and His word. Nevertheless, it is about putting Christ first . . . no matter the consequences. In First John 4:3 - 5, we are told:

> "And every spirit that confesseth not that Jesus Christ is come in
> the flesh is not of God: and this is that spirit of antichrist, whereof
> ye have heard that it should come; and even now already it is in the
> world. Ye are of God, little children, and have overcome them:
> because greater is he that is in you, than he that is in the world.
> They are of the world: therefore speak they of the world, and the
> world heareth them. We are of God: he that is not of God heareth not us.
> Hereby know we the spirit of truth, and the spirit of error."

Looking at the mood of the United States, our nation is filled with and ruled over by many that are led by the spirit of antichrist. God's standards are quite clear when it comes to such things. Look at First John 2: 22-23:

> "Who is a liar but he that denieth that Jesus is the Christ? He is the
> antichrist, that denieth the Father and the Son. Whosoever denieth
> the Son, the same hath not the Father: [but] he that acknowledgeth
> the Son hath the Father also.

While some would even define Christianity as another conspiracy, this book is about your reaction to the current condition of the world. What would be your reaction as a Christian or non-Christian in light of life altering changes in the system? Are we the victims of off-kilter checks and balances? Is there something we can do to change things? May you be challenged and inspired as you seek answers to such questions.

Perhaps, it would be best to start with Y-2 K, an "invention" of a few in the federal government to keep tech sector earnings high. Some were scared out of their wits that computers around the world would all crash as the millennium changed. Many, however, scoffed at it, saying that nothing would happen and nothing would come of it.

Y-2K demonstrated how easy it is to control society in both mind and deed. If nothing else, we learned how easy it was for a select few to sway our perceptions of reality through the mass media. Control of the masses by the power brokers is not new. It should be noted, though, that those who seek to control us are very skilled at what they do. Never short change their need for power and their willingness to achieve their goals. We probably all know people who are talented in this area and who understand the "cause and effect" method of controlling human behavior.

The deeper questions revolve around what drives them to control the masses. While some might call them subversives who place themselves at a point and purpose, reality points to them being placed there with the backing of powerful, behind-the-scenes forces. They are, quite simply, backed by the power of numbers-by others of similar mind and heart. They will use any given tragedy to advance to the next level their pre-contrived plans, a momentum gaining entity. Once the beast they create is born and grows to adulthood, it picks up speed and power of its own.

The deed-holders to this power play use this method. To this end, these power brokers are very good at picking and choosing the events (as they happen). It is those events they use to their advantage. In other instances, they create events, or pieces of the puzzle, though this method places them at risk. It's far easier to go with what happens naturally than to create an illusion of innocence or ensure a cover-up.

One clown case of this was Watergate, which was a classic example of an event on which the opposition capitalized. Few people remember that President Nixon was one of the most popular presidents in history, and did a lot of good during his term of office. He brought the Vietnam War to a nasty end after years of mismanagement by two liberal administrations and their "masterminds" at the Pentagon. This was a murkey quagmire, and there was to be no simple end to it ...but end it must ...and end it did!

Whether or not he was directly involved in the Watergate break-in, his need for re-election was so intense, he compromised his own ethics and summarily destroyed his own term in office. His conduct after the fact ran through the veins of America like ice water.

The next point, while maybe not popular to discuss, because of the "mystical' illusions we were guided to buy into, contains yet another monumental government failing. This is one that no individual, family or group should ever be forced to cope with, because the government is not supposed to embrace or appear in any way, to be involved in vigilantism.

Randy Weaver and Ruby Ridge also revealed the government's insistence on controlling the minds of the masses. Evidence revealed during the lawsuit he brought against the federal government proved that Randy Weaver was set up by federal agents to saw the barrel off a shotgun. Weaver did so to earn a few dollars to support his family, during financial difficulty. He then was arrested on federal charges and released on bail. To further cripple him, he was given false and misleading information by the court with regard to the date he was to appear in court and the disposition of his bail and his property.

He missed his court date, which allowed the government to spread lies and inflamed allegations against him throughout the intelligence network. The rumor mill proved deadly for Weaver's wife. Vickie was shot straight through the face by a government sniper, while she was inside their house holding their baby daughter, Elisheba. She was killed instantly. It also proved deadly to their fourteen-year-old son, Samuel, who was shot in the back while trying to run to his dad. The government responded with a cover-up. Weaver was labeled a white supremacist, a radical, and separatist. The cover-up worked until the lawsuit in a federal court. Weaver prevailed and did incredible damage to the reputation of the FBI.

The next administration was no better than those that preceded it. Waco, Texas was another example of the government inventing a story that would sell to the public. David Koresh and his followers were labeled Christian Radicals who were in the gun-smuggling business. While the truth remained hidden, the White House and the media spun stories of misinformation to control the minds of those who paid attention to their words.

We live in a nation that guarantees religious freedom. We may not like what others believe, but they are still free to believe as they choose. Conversely, we are equally free, as Christians, to believe, read, and share the gospels. We are free to look upon the Ten Commandments and not have them hidden away from us because a few are offended. While Muslim calls to prayer ring out in major cities as part of their religious freedom (often likened to the sounding of church bells on Sunday mornings), the freedoms of Christians has been slowly and systematically removed from this nation.

While our martyrdom for Christ is lightweight at this present time, compared to the suffering of brothers and sisters in other nations, this nation is based on the rule of law-and those laws as written by our Founding Fathers were based on Judeo-Christian truth. It is wrong for the government, individuals, or other entities to refuse us the right to religious freedom. The Christian view of "In God We Trust" is not about the worship of pagan gods, but about faith and trust in the God of the Bible. Those fundamental values and principals should not be denied or reinvented by our government, especially our courts.

Forget the skeptics, the agnostics, and atheists who have a sick-soul view on such matters. Truth is not determined by majority votes; it stands on its own. This nation *was* founded on Judeo-Christian truths and values. During times of tragedy, both personal and national, many turn or return to God. This was the case after 911. God becomes, however, a matter of great dispute during calmer times. The falling away increases when the focus is not on the "brevity of life."

We live in a day and age that will very possibly bring about the Rapture of the Body of Christ. That's the foundation of this book-that wondrous event, and those that were prophesied to follow, and we think it will happen soon. However, only God the Father knows when the fullness of time will take place.

Please understand ...it is common knowledge that there are many variations of interpretations of how and when the Rapture will occur, in regard to the Tribulation, or Great Tribulation (the last three and a half years of the seven year Tribulation period). There are also many interpretations of when Christ's Great Appearing will occur. This book specifically addresses one such interpretation, the one that the author of this book feels led to believe to be the most accurate.

This is not to say that this author is a *gavel banging, my way or the highway* type person. There are mysteries in the Holy Word that will only be known for sure by man when the fullness of time is complete. Until then, we can debate until the cows come home, for the sake of argument, and bang that gavel all we want-that we know for sure how it will all play out, but this author can tell you one thing with all assuredness...only God the Father knows for sure, no matter how compelling anyone thinks their argument is.

Again, for the sake of this book, this author takes a stand, the stand that he feels is the most likely, according to his studies and discussions on these Biblical apocalyptic topics. This author wishes to advise you, don't get hung up on his interpretation of those events and times. If your interpretations are different, that's alright, as long as we agree on the Deity of Jesus Christ and the need for forgiveness of sin. There are many vitally key issues brought to light in this book, and hopefully, some enjoyable reading for you. This author prays that if you are or are not deeply imbedded with the significant meanings in this book, you will be moved and stirred to greater meaning and God-filled purpose in your life. Read this book, and take from it what God has in it for you, on an individual basis. From what this author has observed, most people do not exit the end of this book the same as when they entered reading it, they usually come out motivated to some form of Christ driven action, compelled to take a stand on a cause!

Some of the underlying premises of this book are:

We believe, first, the "dead in Christ" will be Raptured and then "we who are alive" will "meet them in the clouds" before the start of the seven-year Tribulation. Christ then comes again in the Glorious Appearing to defeat Satan and cast him into the hell for a millennium, after which, he will be set free for "a season", then he will be cast into the "Lake of Fire".

During the end times, as has been for more than two thousand years, there will be

martyrs for Christ. There will also be martyrs for Christ after the Rapture and up to the return of Christ at the Glorious Appearing. Satan is then defeated and the Millennial Kingdom will be set up with Christ ruling in Jerusalem.

Today, there are alarming numbers of martyrs for Christ, an average of about three hundred thousand per year. The media sweeps that truth under the rug, allowing the masses to conjure up erroneous reasons for the wars and skirmishes that dot the earth. Most people tend to deny or ignore the truth, especially in nations where they think persecution is limited to hateful words, such as ours. However, the truth is that many thousands of Christians are imprisoned and murdered every year on every continent.

If we are truly a government of, by, and for the people, then our government is as fragmented as our culture. We are divided on morals and values, which is reflected in our electorate. To the extent that God raised up this nation to preach the gospels in all the world, He also made us aware of those who are suffering for their deep faith in Christ as their Savior. Acts of government and media propaganda can spawn atrocities by hate groups or radicals-even neighbors, family or "friends." They inflict severe pain and suffering on God's people through wrongful religious imprisonment, torture, and death. This book does not ignore those issues, as it depicts scenarios in which government and society run amok, its checks and balances totally out of kilter, as we see many signs of the beginnings of these as realities. As George Washington once said, "Government is not reason, it is not eloquence; it is force. Like a fire, it is a dangerous servant and a fearful master."

Many have spoken on this issue. Nick Begich once said, "Overreaction by the government is a greater threat to democracy than those posed by real or imagined threats." Max Stirner said, "The state calls it's own violence, law, but that of the individual, crime." Double standards flourish in corrupt societies.

Remember the events that made you run to God. Remember Columbine High School, and the young people who refused to deny their faith in God and suffered death. Never forget 911 and the attack on our nation by those who used God's name to justify their evil deeds. And never forget the judges who spit in God's face when they removed the Ten Commandments from our schools and from the public square, and are even now continuing to do so, as they work to turn this Judeo-Christian nation into a secular nightmare.

If we come to terms on what true martyrdom is, we realize that it must be for a true end, a purpose that is true. Martyrdom involves sacrifice and suffering, including the possible or real loss of life. True martyrs for Christ give willingly. They do not attempt to take life, they are witnesses for God's truth; they do not take freedoms, they show how God's sets us free, they do not take property, they give freely from the heart of all they have. Listen to them. They bear witness to the truth of God's Word.

Larry Skelf ...Martyrologist
November 2004

Understanding This Book

The prophet was speaking of the anti-Christ in Daniel 7:25. "And he shall speak great words against the Most High, and shall wear out the saints of the Most High, and think to change times and laws: and they shall be given into his hand until a time and times and the dividing of times." Three and one-half years were determined.

This book is different. Like most novels, it contains separate chapters, but each chapter contains its own story, until all of the chapters are tied together at the end of the book. Think of the last chapter as the hub of a wheel and each chapter as a spoke. All of the spokes are needed to make the wheel turn around the hub. That's the beauty of a mystery grounded in reality, both spiritual and physical.

I started the story in our world, someday soon, and included many events that are current time realities. Even *time* is addressed as a major issue, as it is has been calculated and guided by the largest event in the course of mankind-the death, burial, and resurrection of the True Savior. Only Jesus was capable of accomplishing this astronomical task of boundless love.

Evil cannot abide this outcome. It tries to undermine everything accomplished by God.

It minimizes the significance of Christ as God, the events that took place during His ministry, the meaning of the crucifixion, His death and burial, and His rising from the dead on the third day. This is only part of evil's design to destroy humanity. Even in defeat, evil has been on a quest to separate the souls of mankind from God.

According to Daniel 7:25, there is a distinct possibility that the anti-Christ will divert the inhabitants of earth by changing laws and time as we now know it. However, there is nothing evil can do without God's permission. Satan has no power over time, but he may use the anti-Christ to change the way it is calculated or at least its wording. Evil will not allow the continued use of terminology that relates to the time after Christ death, burial and resurrection.

Logically, why would he allow the continued use of terminology or the graphing of time, in a way that always leads right back to the one event that doomed him to defeat and snatched the most monumental prize away from him, the prize of separating every man's soul from God for eternity.

(UPDATE)...Remember the Christmas 2004 season *Indonesian Tsunami* that killed hundreds of thousands of people? That occurrence happened while this book was being edited.

Note! Scientists say that event was so powerful, it changed the rotation of the Earth. It would be logical to deduce that this also changed time as we would calculate it. This was done only through God's great power! However, for what things God has, satan has a counterfeit! Could it be that it is now time for the fruition of that particular deception?

I wish for you to know, that this book is a witness for Christ, which forces the reader to acknowledge the total defeat of Satan. Credit does not belong to the enemy, nor do we wonder about the identity of the anti-Christ. Our hope is in the resurrection and the imminent return of the Lord Jesus for His own. While Satan's show of power is acknowledged by his changing of mans perception or calculation of time, the source of that power is still God. Satan is not equal to the Creator, he is a creation without equal power to God. To further reveal the extent of God's power, we refer to this time calculation change in a way that humiliates evil. We use the reference of BCR (Before Christ's Return for the believers) and ACR (After Christ's Return, or After the Rapture of the Church.).

At the time this book was written, for the record, there currently is a powerful grass roots movement under way and gaining support and momentum, to change A.D. to C.E, or "Common Era". (Now why in the world would the powers-that-be want to do that)? This author sincerely doubts this will happen, mainly because Common Era does absolutely nothing for satan or the antichrists vanity. Power, show of power and vanity are what it is all about for these monsters!

If you're wondering where you fit in, I must explain that you and the unknown narrators have missed the Rapture because you were not redeemed. You may be a Christian. I praise the Lord if you are! However, it is quite probable that everyone you know or come in contact with is not a Christian.

Laying aside that issue, the truly redeemed man interacts quite personally with his Savior. For that reason, this book is intensely reader interactive as it weaves a trail in and out of fiction and non-fiction. Your own imagination will help you see the possibilities as real situations which are woven into the feasible.

For example, many have been martyred for Christ over the centuries since He walked among us. This year is no different. Imagine the pain, suffering, loneliness, agony, and bloodshed of the martyrs who stand for what is right in a world that is against God. A world where man thinks he can do as he pleases without consequence.

Look at the cultures where Christ is denied and notice that God has turned them over to their enemies. Will they succeed? Will Christians lose hope through fear and despair in these horrendous times? What would you do and how would you feel if you were going through all this as they are? Our hope and our prayer is that you will get some sense of actually being there, being part of the book, as it goes from person to person, setting to setting.

It is also my hope that this book will help you choose God and God's ways, and recognize that He has a calling in your life. May you have the strength and resolve to surrender your life to Him so you can stand victorious for Christ regardless of the obstacles or consequences. Writing this book has been a blessing for me, and I am in much prayer that it will be a blessing to you. *It is not easy reading*. Martyrdom and sacrifice are difficult and do not spawn pretty pictures of human interaction.

To this end, this book is not meant to scare you but to help you see some of God's reality and help you act on them in your life. *Graphic illustrations are deliberate*.. There is no other way to portray through fiction or non-fiction the nature of martyrdom for Christ.

The story begins with the voice of an unknown narrator who is unwilling to reveal his identity or whereabouts. He is a Christian who was saved after the Rapture. Other narrators follow. Some are willing to reveal their identities; none will reveal their locations. The first narrator discusses events in his life that lead to his post Rapture salvation. Characters tell their own stories, including the circumstances of their lives that caused them to miss the Rapture. Try to put yourself in the life of each narrator. Would you do things differently or the same? If you are a Christian, you will not be subject to much of what takes place in this book. If you are not, may this book help you make the decision that will place your name the Lamb's Book of Life for eternity.

Chapter 1

One Year Before Christ's Return (BCR)

Narrator: Twenty-two-year-old young man telling the story of events that occurred
when he was just sixteen. His whereabouts at the time this was written
are unknown. The location of the topic is The Little White Church. He is
remembering the past.

You had better put this book down. You can't handle reading what's inside. Don't frustrate yourself by thinking you can. Just set the book down and back away. This book deals with restricted, outlawed, and forbidden topics. If you're a Christian reading this book, you've been made aware that the Rapture has occurred and you were not included.

Don't ask me my name! Never ask me my name or I will never talk to you again! I will tell you what I want you to know. And let's get something straight . . . you are the reader and I am the narrator .. . . at least for now. You just sit there and read . . . and I will do the talking. If we can't agree on this, just close this book and go away.

Shouldn't be too hard for you. You're good at running away, of not facing up to the truth, of taking the easy and popular way . . . of always thinking of yourself. Oh, yes, you put your selfish little head in the sand and pretend everything is "good to go." Well, you're wrong. Everything's not okay and it hasn't been for a long time. For centuries before Christ returned for His own, things were getting worse and worse.

My part of the story starts back when I was just sixteen years old. I was as innocent and naive as any normal, backwoods country kid could be-at least that's the way I see things now because I've had to do some quick growing up. Some people were prepared for what was coming. My mother took that approach. Some of those folks were right with God . . .. and those that weren't were caught off guard. I guess it was smart to be ready. I sure wish I'd been prepared before the Rapture. Heaven knows I had every opportunity.

Well, Christ came for His own and you and I missed it. Things really get heavy on my mind as I reminisce about what started it all. It was about a year before the Rapture. I remember the service that took place the week before the big play we put on at the little white church I attended. We were starting our drive down the street toward the church that day . . .

I heard the grinding and light roaring sounds of a few lawnmowers. It was time to go . . . always been told hurry this . . . hurry that . . .. wait here, wait for that. I had to get used to it . . . it would be that way all my life. There was no time to think about that stuff now. I was gonna be late . . . I know, I know . . .

I smelled the fresh cut grass from that guy's house . . . the one everybody just called Lester. He was the one with the really big dogs that always get loose. They tore things up, terrified other animals and scared the pants off the people in the neighborhood. Little kids and old people feared those dogs the most. I just rolled up one of my newspapers or grabbed for a rock or a stick or something . . . did that since I was seven or eight . . . maybe nine.

Not all the same dogs . . . well, some yes, some no . . . the ones that were the same were pretty old, but they still ran faster than people and nobody complained to Lester . . . much too mean . . . some say even meaner than his dogs! Everybody says that the look on his face told it all . . . I thought so too ... I thought. He came up with several nick-names in the neighborhood, mostly among the kids. Grownups were too scared or smart for such things. Name that sticks out with me the most is "Big Dog", 'cause we all thought he was the biggest and ugliest of the pack.

We were gonna be late. We got in the rattletrap of a car . . . reverse . . . forward . . . and then waited for the transmission to catch up with us. I know, I know . . . it slipped and then backfired . . . ducked down behind the seat . . . embarrassed like always . . . laughed about it and waved as we passed Mr. Canube. We moved very slowly down the street so I could see and hear it all.

Mr. Canube carefully placed fishing rods and tackle boxes under the seats of his fishing boat before he hooked it onto the ball on the back of his late model SUV. He wondered if he'd finally catch the real thing, the greatest of fighters, the prize of prizes of a fish. That's what it's really about, isn't it? It was the one he knew would give him years of bragging fish stories to tell.

Two little girls and a little boy laughed and screamed as they played in the kids' wading pool. Their mother finally came out wearing headphones and dancing like she probably did last night at her favorite Saturday night hangout, seemed oblivious she wasn't still there.

The kid's eyes lit up as a car pulled into the driveway. They teased their mother.

"Ken's here, Ken's here!" I can still hear them calling to her.

The man inside the rust bucket leaned toward the woman. He spoke as the man he really was; something like"Hey baby, dump the rugrats and let's party."

Silence two houses on the left and four houses on the right.

Expletive, expletive- exploded from Tina Harks' house, just like they did every Sunday morning. Sam stormed from the house like a flailing quail about to experience its last few moments of flight. Tina came slashing out a second after him, talking trash like . ... you know who. Well maybe you don't, but it wasn't pleasant. It never was. Her words were bad . . . very bad.

Folks wondered if she'd kill him this time. Then they wondered if he'd kill her. Maybe not, maybe Who knew...who cared? Nobody I knew After all, he cheated last night, she cheated a couple of weeks ago-he accused her, she accused him. Right or wrong . . . like I said, no one knew and surely, nobody really cared. Those who heard them just wished they'd both shut up.

The bald-headed gentleman was very different from the Harks. He seemed like such a nice man. Every Sunday morning he had the same big smile and high-masted, high-in-the-air wave of his hand-the same hand that held his Bible is the one that was high in the air. He was going to church. No one knew where, but it was good he went there. I was sure of that.

Mrs. Murfrey was ducking in and out of her house, working on her

31

flowers, vacuuming, and cleaning her windows. She was halfway up a ladder . . . still going . . . still going, because there was no cleaning job too big, no repair too high for her to reach. Mrs. Murfrey never rested-during the day, at night. Never! It's never happened before, and it's not gonna happen now. Everyday was the right day for getting' work done . . . and Sunday was even the better.

I could finally see the cars in the parking lot of the small, wooden, white church. Half full, half empty ...depended on how you looked at it. There was a big steeple on the roof, just like on most churches. People were talking their "good to see you" and "good to see you toos". The men in the parking lot were discussing, among other things, the parking possibilities for the following Sunday morning. They thought it might be so crowded, the lot would be filled to overflowing . . . or nearly that full. If you had passed by, you'd of known it was because of the play.

Inside the vestibule, teens and a couple of adults made plans for their parts in the upcoming play-they all wanted to be in it ...and the outing next month. Teens were bein' teens. It was this thing or that thing they do. Most of it was foolish to the adults, but they said they understood because they were that age at one time or another.

I *really* doubted that! Never was much chance of that for most of them! Their faces were much too brittle and it showed . .... even if they didn't think it showed.

Anyway, some cast members wanted changes, some wanted to improve, and some wanted others to improve. Some wanted lesser parts and some wanted greater parts. All seemed to want a little more last-minute practice. You can understand all that, I'm sure.

Carlton Hempter was in charge of general promotions. He did a fine job. He had some flyers printed and put them on a couple of school bulletin boards. He even put a few on bulletin boards at three convenience stores and the big supermarket! And if that wasn't enough, eighteen or twenty commercials ran on the Christian radio station. Mr. Hempter took his work seriously. He even got us a mention or two on early morning TV. Everybody wanted a lot of people to be there, but mostly they wanted some souls saved. At the time, I knew it just might

32

happen.

The men were in their prayer group, the women in theirs. Why weren't people here-in the house of the Lord-especially on this Lord's worship day morning? I remembered the chatter from the groups.

"Who needs prayer? Who has kinfolk, a friend, an acquaintance, or an acquaintance of acquaintance that needs prayer? For those unspoken requests of the Lord, we bow our heads and raise our hands! Let's also remember next week's drama in our prayers," someone said.

Everybody was talking to the Lord all at one time! I couldn't really make out much of anything anybody was saying! It was pretty much that way, at least every Sunday. I'm sure there really were different prayers, though . . . you know . . . from Sunday to Sunday.

Granny Wilton brought Preacher Janus some of her homemade *Chatalga stew*. The preacher's wife, Mrs. Betty, as most everybody called her, took the hot stew and thanked Granny dearly. She told Granny that Preacher Janus and the kids would enjoy it immensely as they always did all the special treats Granny brought to them. Mrs. Betty told her she's one of the sweetest people she has ever met. Granny told her pretty much the same thing. I know they were both right . . . and both were really smart, each in her way, mostly.

Granny could sew real well, and she could cook a meal out of nearly nothing and still make your mouth water before you've even tasted any of it. I think Mrs. Betty was completely book and organizing smart. If it could (and sometimes maybe couldn't, it seems) be done, she was definitely the person to do it! Even though she was so smart and kind of acted like a teacher, all the kids and teens loved her with all their hearts!

So, then it was time for the meeting and announcements to begin before Sunday school started. Mrs. Betty helped Granny into the church. Her glasses should have been replaced three or four years ago 'cept she couldn't afford them. I heard at a church business meeting that they were going to take the money out of some kind of special fund at the church to get her

Granny sent you her recipe for Homemade Chatalga Stew

Here it is…she hopes you'll enjoy it!

(go back to www,MartyrsoftheCross.com)

for recipe.

eyes checked and buy her a new pair of glasses. I also heard some of the men were a little upset because they felt the church should have shown her this kind of love much sooner. That's how I remember it.

Preacher Janus was acting a little strange-kind of peculiar and quiet-and very prayerful, but almost secretive about praying. It's like there were things he only wanted God to hear. Afterwards, he was in one of his stern, somber moods. I hadn't seen him in a mood like that for a long time.

Sunday school ended and the worship service began with a much longer praise and prayer time than usual. All I remember is something about man and his sin nature, instead of letting God's nature take control. After prayer, there was great singing . . . as always.

Everything was very enjoyable, even though it seemed some people were still a bit sleepy. It was a long week with a lot goin' on and a lot of problems for most of the people (or so it seemed). When the offering was taken up, people were a bit lazy in their tithes and offerings . . . as usual, know what I mean?

Pastor seemed a bit distracted, thinking about the secret meeting he knew he had to attend the next day. He got up and started the preaching message about service to the Savior; how it took effort to get ready and come to church after a long and difficult week. Then he said that it was easier to say you're a Christian than to live like one . . . but we had to give of ourselves more and not forsake the assembly of the brethren.

Folks never seemed to forget the other things they considered pleasures, though. I guess this meant the church-ours very much included-needed to double and triple its efforts to visit those in need and to pray fervently. He continued on about not bein' afraid to do right by God during very perilous times. He said that perilous times were just one of the signs God told us about; you know ...a sign of the (very soon) second coming of Christ and the beginning of the seven years of Tribulation.

At the end of the service, Pastor Janus requested that all keep him in prayer for a very disturbing meeting he had to attend. Then he told us that, Lord willing, he would continue preaching from the Books of Daniel and Revelation during Sunday morning service week after next. He said we had to learn more about the meaning of "wars and rumors of wars" 'cause those wars were about more than just country against country.

He asked us if it could mean family against family, community against community, this group against that group, or even this church against that church. He also asked us what could cause such confusion and divisiveness; and told us to pray about what we could do about it.

"Think about it," he said. "Can anything be gained in such a world? Is it safe to even think along these lines?" He lifted his hands and yelled, "Rumors and babblings!"

I guess we had all kinds of things to ponder on until the Sunday morning service week after next. You see . . . yeah, you do see that Pastor Janus always left us with something to think about and consider until the next service. After Pastor's "food for thought," he requested that we all pray hard about the upcoming play . . . I mean, he really wanted us to pray for God's biggest blessings.

"This will be a world shaker, at least in our church," he said, then laughed. We all laughed a bit with him . . . 'cause it was the right thing to do.

~

Fifty-one weeks Before Christ's Return for the Church

It was Sunday morning, the day of the play, *Martyrs of the Cross,* and excitement filled the air. Several church members, and some that are not members, invited other people to come this Sunday. I guess I believed they'd come because they heard about how the church put lots of effort into getting' the play together. I know that at least Sam and Tina Harks, and Mrs. Murfrey and Mr. Canube were invited because I invited 'em. They all said they would try to be there and sure enough they came!

Sam and Tina Harks were sitting in the very last row, and you could tell they were not happy. I'll bet they were fighting all the way to the church; they looked like they were still fighting . . . but mostly under their breath.

I came to find out that Mrs. Murfrey had a niece in the play, and she wouldn't miss seein' her . . . even though it was really hard for her to sit still. She was sitting there, fidgeting, and I thought she was probably wishing she could just spring up and maybe even shout a rousing "Glory Hallellujah!" Nope, I knew she couldn't sit still for one more second. She must have had a really hard time sitting for so long.

Mr. Canube seemed a bit befuddled. I wondered if something was wrong with him. Fact was, he seemed downright confused, sort of like a fish out of water. I remember thinking that I should go talk with him to make him feel more comfortable. I don't remember if I did that or not. . . maybe I did?

Carlton Hempter was in a side room giving last-minute instructions to a few of the cast members.

"Remember, this is a play that you really can't mess up," he said and they all laughed at him. He put his hand over his face as if he knew he had just put his foot in his mouth. He was laughing and shaking his head, which meant he was extremely embarrassed.

"You know what I mean! You can't mess up because basically we all studied the basic structure and basic thought of the play. We also basically created the framework and learned some basic lines to build from." He sighed . . . and then said, "The play is basically and fundamentally impromptu-you know, you can just improvise-which means you just basically can't mess it up."

I *basically* couldn't stand to hear him say, "basically" or "basic" even one more time . . . *basically* speaking, of course. I just had to leave the room when he started fussing over a particular young teen-age girl who happened to be his daughter.

"Be sure to say your lines loudly and clearly," he told her. "Oh, and remember to look at the audience and the other actors at the same time as much as possible!"

Her neck was gonna hurt if she did it his way . . . it was gonna hurt real bad . . . or badly, whichever word means she was gonna hurt from trying to look two places at once. While I thought about the future condition of her neck, I noticed five nicely suited men. I didn't think anybody knew them . . . but they were at the church all the same.

It was great to see them, but it seemed everybody was talking about them, or would be when they found the time. If some people didn't talk about them, I was sure they'd have at least looked at them a lot. Their suits looked very fine, indeed, which made people talk . . . that's for sure. Well-dressed strangers always brought out the kind of talk that maybe shouldn't have happened in the church-or anywhere else-but always does.

Although the little white church was not a big church, it was not a really small one either, so for some reason those men stood out like *Nanna's homemade punkin' bread in a big city bakery baking contest*.. There was just something really different going on, about

Recipe for Nanna Debbie's Homemade Punkin Bread
It's really good. It's called punkin bread, but doesn't taste like punkin's!

(go back to web site www.MartyrsoftheCross.com)

Those nicely suited men I mean, that made folks glad they came to the church that day. Word had it they came from other churches, or maybe some big church organizations, to sort of scout out the play. I thought they'd ask our group to do the play at other churches. I was excited just thinking about that idea!

Church started with only the singing of *Nearer Christ to Thee* as the congregation and visitors not inside the church came in to be seated. We could hear the echo of church bells ringing from the Prespeterian church downtown, which was less than a mile away. Anyway, with the doors shut, you couldn't really hear anything except what was going on inside our church 'cause the acoustics were real good. Pastor Janus sometimes told us we should have an open-door service so the community would know we were alive. I think he was throwing us some hints that maybe we should do visitations more often.

That thought made me think a bit more about all the folks we should have asked to come worship the Lord with us. I wondered what the people in all those quiet or silent houses were doing. I knew for sure that they were gonna miss a really good play.

Seemed like just about everybody in church invited 'em. I know 'cause I was there when they were invited. I guess I used to think too much about things that happened. Didn't matter. Pastor Janus was about to speak so I had to stop thinking and do some listening.

"Good morning folks, it's very nice to see all of you here this beautiful Sunday morning!" Pastor Janus said with lots of joy in his voice. "I want to thank you all for attending our play, *Martyrs of the Cross*. This is the very first time we will have put on this play and we're real excited about presenting it to you. Our cast members have worked very hard to make this morning both realistic and entertaining. In fact, it's so real, that I have to tell you not to be surprised by anything you see after I tell you the play is beginning. Some of the scenes are quite disturbing. They are meant to be. We pray they are thought provoking and stir you up inside."

Pastor Janus wasn't finished speaking. There was something important he had to say and I knew he'd speak from his heart. He never pulled any punches when it came to preaching the truth.

"If the Holy Spirit visits you in your seat-or overcomes you-don't be alarmed. Let the Spirit of God do it's work on you. And if one day this week you give your heart and soul to our Lord and Savior, Jesus Christ, or find yourself doing more for Him after the play is over, then we shall rejoice with you! The play is beginning . . . lights off, please! The play is beginning now!"

Chad Eurto was picked to narrate the play.

He was a distinguished looking, older gentleman-probably about forty or fifty years old. Maybe older . . . but I don't think so. He had gray hair, but that didn't mean he was old.

He said it's 'cause he had kids and somehow they made his hair that way!

No matter why his hair was gray, it just was. Nearly everybody said he had a nice baritone voice and missed his calling in life by not being a Christian disk jockey at one of those local Christian radio stations. He was really a nice man . . . always laughin' and kidding around, 'specially with the kids and young people.

"This is the part about Stephen, the first person in the Bible mentioned as a martyr for the faith . . . a Christian martyr," Mr. Eurto said as John Williams entered from the back of the church.

John played the part of Stephen, the man in the Bible we learned about in Sunday school. He was wearin' a robe, sort of white, but not really extremely white like bright white. In pictures I've seen, it looked kind of similar to what they wore in those days. He also had a frayed rope looking thing around his belt line. I think that made it look more real, too. Mr. Eurto started his narration.

"Stephen was a man that today might be considered comparable to a deacon. He was among the smartest men of his time and was considered to be a very important deacon that helped the early Christians in many ways. Stephen was a preacher and . . . a miracle-worker. He also was an extremely outspoken man . . . one not easily dealt with because he preached and taught that the Old Testament laws had been fulfilled through Christ. That one got him in terrible trouble with the Jewish leaders. Some folks still get in trouble for that one even today!

"Powerful people among the Jews believed that Stephen had blasphemed against God and Moses, and was hostile toward traditional Judaism as a whole. They would have none of Stephen's type of teaching. He was arrested and brought before the Jewish council, the Sanhedrin.

"Stephen didn't take it lying down. He accused the stiff-necked Sanhedrin of killing the Christ, or Messiah, when they allowed the Romans to execute Jesus on the cross. He also charged that they were not keeping their own laws because they murdered an innocent man. All this drove the religious leaders to almost insane anger. They were terribly self-righteous and wouldn't take criticism from anyone or even debate their beliefs. It was their way or the highway . . . you might say."

Mr. Eurto continued, "As I said, Stephen was very astutely outspoken. There wasn't one person who could win a debate against him. Even those powerful and scholarly religious leaders and politicians just couldn't argue him down. When they tried, they couldn't win, so they resorted to biting and hitting Steven. This did not silence him. He was truly a Godly man of great principals, who was willing to speak the truth even if it meant suffering torture and death."

Mr. Eurto's words had an effect on the audience. I saw a few folks squirm in their seats. "And Stephen *was* put to death for the "sin" of preaching the truth . . . for the sin of sharing the message of salvation with his countrymen! But that didn't stop the Lord from raising up another. At Stephen's death, there was another who would become a great man of God . . . a man that was very much to be used by God when the time was right.

"No, he wasn't Gods man yet . . . in fact, he was one of the people who participated in the execution of Stephen. Who was that man? It was none other than the man who held the coats for those carrying out this barbaric task. His Hebrew name was Saul. His Roman name was Paul."

All this was narrated as the actors came in from different doors and took

their places for the reenactment of the stoning death of Stephen.

~

Off to the side, one of the nicely suited men was speaking to Pastor Janus. Did they like the first act? Maybe they didn't. Pastor Janus seemed upset. He got up and walked to the pulpit.

"Frank and Sandy, would you please get up and turn the lights on?" They did as instructed. "That's right! All the lights in the whole house please!" Then Pastor spoke to the congregation right in the middle of the play.

"Ladies and gentlemen, I'm sure you've all noticed that we have some visitors with us today. I'm not talking about the majority of our visitors; I'm talking about the finely suited men seated here in the front row. Well, folks, I need, at this time, for you to know that I was forced against my will into a meeting with those men. Last week, they told me this play shouldn't and couldn't be presented today. They told me that if it were presented, there would be dire consequences. They told me there are new laws in place that prohibit religious meetings and that includes religious dramas."

Pastor Janus bowed his head and then raised it, as if in some kind of prayer. He wasn't gonna to take any of this . . . he would stand up for righteousness for sure.

"Folks, those men said that from here on, these meetings are considered *assembly without permit*, and that we can't get a permit because no permits are being issued. They told me there are newly enacted federal laws and . . . well, you should know that our government 'of, by and for the people' has just authorized the use of all means available to quash all 'unauthorized' religious meetings. They specifically took note of our play.

"Ladies and gentlemen, there's something about Jesus Christ and martyrdom for Christ that must terrify our government. I can't think of any other reason for them to be in such a panic over our little assembly and our little play. My fellow believers, take note, take heed! There are many forms of martyrdom!

"Yes, there are many forms of martyrdom, but the one true form of martyrdom is for the sake of the name and work of our risen Savior. When it comes down to it, folks, it's what you do for the Lord and in the name of the Lord that you take with you when you leave this world! Nothing else! Nothing else!" he shouted. "Nothing else!"

Pastor Janus was so filled with the Holy Spirit, I thought he would be taken up to heaven in a chariot, the way Elijah was taken up back in Bible days. He spoke again with what had to be the authority of the Lord.

"Live for the Lord, witness eternal salvation that none should perish but have everlasting life through Jesus Christ our Lord. Remember John 3:16, hallelujah, hallelujah, and if need be, or if required of you by our Savior, then die for the Lord! You don't have to fear. He *will* receive you into heaven as He received Stephen. If you die witnessing for His awesome glory, His awesome power, His unbounded infinite creativity, and above all, His absolutely limitless understanding and love. The cause is worthy, the cause is worthy!"

There was shouting all over the house! Arms were up high in the air all over the church as people were praising Jesus!

"Thank you Jesus, thank you Jesus, thank you Jesus!" could be heard throughout the sanctuary.

"Folks, I don't know about you, but all I have to say is, continue with the play! If they don't like it . . . they can just arrest me! I'll gladly go to jail for my Lord! Gentlemen, you can either sit back and enjoy the play, or hit the door! We pray you will get your lives right with Christ before this service is over!"

Somebody in the back of the church whistled really loudly.

"Amen...amen...amen!" Pastor Janus said in praise to God. "This is what a Jesus worshipping service is supposed to be like! At least as much energy and heart as fans rooting for their favorite team at a football game!"

The congregation was up on its feet, praising God, and clapping loudly. Some people were even whooping and hollering. Some of the men and about two of the women yelled things out loud like "go ahead, preacher, tell it like it is," and "preach on brother, preach on!"

So, we finally found out what these men were doing there. They were there to add realism to the play! What a great idea our pastor had .. . . and he didn't even let the actors know about this part of the play until now . . . what a powerful message!

"Mr. Janus, you just sealed your fate!" snarled the medium sized man as he huffed toward the pulpit. What a stupid thing to say!" He didn't even have the decency to call him Pastor Janus. He just called him *Mr. Janus.*

Then, two of the other nicely suited men stormed toward the pulpit and fanned out to cover a larger area, probably about fifteen feet wide. They all just suddenly stopped dead in their tracks about four or five feet from preacher Janus like on cue . . . like they were waiting for somebody else to say their lines.

All three stared intensely at the preacher but he didn't back down. He stared back at all three just as intensely. His head was going side to side, slowly, man to man, then back again. As soon as three of the men were in place, the last two-by far the largest of the six men-went toward the two exit doors. One went to the back doors through which most of us enter and exit the church. He looked rough, like the biggest linebacker I had ever seen! Even with his nice suit, he still looked awkward . . . as if his body wasn't built for wearing a suit. When I first saw him, I thought he was a new convert so I readily accepted him in my mind as not being so out of place. Right now, though, he was starting to look intimidating, partly because there wasn't a man in the whole church even close in size to him. I sure was glad this huge man was a Christian and this was just a play!

Even our church member, "Big" Fred Handley was a good four inches shorter and fifty pounds lighter, and I thought Fred was about as big a man all round as I'd ever seen!

The last man seemed a little sneaky. He was big but not quite as big as this "Tiny" fellow. Tiny wasn't really his name, or at least I don't think so. It was just a nick-name some of the teens teased him with behind his back. Not very Christian of us, but it was meant in fun. None of us dared say anything like that to his face. We were joking amongst ourselves that teasing him would've been too much like suicide, and we all wanted to stick around planet Earth. . . at least for awhile!

Anyway, the sixth nicely suited man, the sneaky one, hurried through the exit door of the church near the choir area. He was gone for about two and a half minutes. I know how long it was because Paul Plank told me. He was my best friend. I always thought Paul was a little strange because he timed everything. So, it was only two and a half minutes, but it sure seemed like he was gone for ten or fifteen minutes because the congregation started getting a lot calmer and I didn't really like that part. How long could Pastor Janus and that nicely suited man just stand there and stare at each other?

It seemed like there should've been something else acted out during that time. It was almost like somebody forgot his part or something. I sighed a big bored sigh . . . I wanted to yell at somebody to do something! I looked around and saw several other people squirming in their seats. The play was really good and the Spirit was "in the house" up 'till now, so it seemed everyone wanted more of it.

Just then, when I was sure everybody was out of lines, Pastor Janus spoke.

"I'll tell you again, this is our church! You can't come in here like this and tell us what we can and can't do. We *will* worship our Savior as we wish to. Do you want to give your hearts and souls to the Lord? Will you join us and become our Brothers in Christ?"

"The questions are for me to ask, pastor man!" the man smarted off, then made it clear he wasn't finished. "My dear Pastor, if one could legitimately call you by that title, have you lost your mind? Did you think we were kidding about our warning to you? We *will* carry out our duty to the government to the fullest, and I can tell you it will be my personal pleasure to do so!"

"Wow!" I thought. "This guy is pretty good! I think I'm gonna like this

44

part of the play!" I just wondered when they got together to practice this part . . . and I didn't even know it would happen this way? No more time for thinking or wondering. The play was definitely gonna progress rapidly from here.

The other two nicely suited men lurched forward and snagged hold of Pastor Janus just as the sneaky one came racing through the side door with a half dozen military dressed men and one military dressed woman. Other military dressed people flashed inside the church just as fast and secured the other exit doors.

Pastor Janus seemed to be wrecked with pain as the two nicely suited men grabbed him.
One had him by the hair, the other had him by the throat and was squeezing with all his might. The third man was hitting him first in the face and then stomach, face then stomach. Pastor Janus was yanked back and forth, up and down, then twirled around. They never did let go of his hair. One of the men let go long enough to push his knee into Pastor's right arm. I heard a loud popping sound, which scared the heart out of me.

"Arrest you? I never said anything to you about arresting you!" the smart mouthed, medium sized man said.

Mrs. Betty, the preacher's wife was screamin' and running toward the choir area where most of the play was being acted out.

"Please no! Please no! Please no! Don't do this! Don't hurt him please!"

Three of the military dressed men tackled Mrs. Betty, which caused her to hit her head against the back of a pew. It was all so real! They must have practiced this part of the play for weeks without anyone knowing about it! You can be sure that if they didn't practice a lot, Mrs. Betty would have been hurt really badly . . . what with that fall. I mean, they even made it sound like she really hit her head on the pew! The three men got off of Mrs. Betty, jerked her around and rushed her through the door on the right that was nearest to the pulpit. She was sobbing uncontrollably and screamin', even though she looked dazed and out of it.

Then the nicely suited men grabbed hold of Pastor Janus again! Oh those screams! Pastor Janus was gurgling and spitting blood and just screaming,

45

screamin', screamin'. He just wouldn't let up praying for them.

"Oh, God! Help these men! God help them to know that what they're doing is wrong. They don't know what they're doing. Lord, protect this little church, and Lord, protect my precious wife. Please don't let them hurt her anymore."

They'd hurt Pastor Janus so badly-had beat him up and knocked all the wind out of him. Most of his last words of prayer had been whispered.

It was a whisper that was so faint, yet so loud . . . it must have been delivered to each and every person in the congregation directly by the Holy Spirit! With all that commotion, there was no other way we could have heard him. I was stunned deep into my insides. Man, those men could act! This was more real than anything I'd ever seen . . . and it was a whole lot better than what we'd been practicing! All that fake blood and those sound effects made it look so real! I didn't see how we could carry out our parts when this act was over! I mean, how could we follow something like this?

Just then, the sound of two loud bangs exploded from the side room, followed by an immediate thud like somebody falling dead to the floor. Then there were two more, just for spite or maybe just to show they could do whatever they want! I heard the men laughin' hysterically and talking to each other.

"Man, did you see that?"

"Nothing to it!"

"I could sure get used to this."

Those were the words I heard. Then, one of the nicely suited men pulled a large military looking knife out of his suit jacket, grabbed Pastor Janus by the hair again, and put the large knife to his throat. The whole time he looked at the congregation and laughed . . . as if killin' our Pastor would be a great victory for him.

Preacher Janus looked toward Heaven and said, "Dear God, unto you I commit my spirit!"

Within seconds, the laughing' man in the nice suit slit preacher Janus's throat . . . he slit it long and deep, from ear to ear! Preacher Janus was dead before he hit the floor! Blood spewed from the hideous wound in his neck all over the new carpet!

Just then, Granny got up slowly with help of her cane. She just stood there and suddenly began to sing. In the middle of all this . . . our play . . . she just started to sing.

"'Amazing Grace, how sweet the sound,'" she sang *"'that saved a wretch like me! I once was lost, but now I'm found, was blind but now . . ..'"*

The military dressed woman ran from behind and cracked Granny in the back of the head with her rifle. I could hear the pop, the crack, and the thud as Granny slammed into Mrs. James and then hit the floor. She was unconscious and her blood was goin' everywhere. The military dressed men were laughing uncontrollably."

"We need a new law now that prevents people from becoming so old. Birth control? Death control! Abortion? Just call it late term abortion . . . very, very late term abortion, for the one that almost got away!"

Even the nicely suited men laughed at that one! They dragged old Granny to a side window and heaved her up. She started stirrin' up a little as they lifted her up.

"Lord Jesus, I love You," she weakly said as her killers laughed.

"'I'll fly away, oh glory, I'll fly away! When I die, hallelujah by and by, I'll fly away!'"

"Old woman overboard!" they screamed and laughed as they got ready to push her through the second floor window.

"No, please, please no!" several cried. It didn't do any good. They threw old, weak Granny out of that window. I remember how I felt. I prayed, "Dear God, what's goin' on?"

"Are there any other martyrs for Christ?" the middle sized, smart mouthed, nicely suited man asked.

I finally realized it was for real! The play had changed! Now it was the play they were persecuting, trying to quash the Lord's work by quashing the play! They had become the play and the play had become real! Those men were supposed to be from our own government and all they did was bring martyrdom

47

for Christ into our *Martyrs of the Cross* play! We should have seen it coming, but we were too busy to notice.

I looked around and saw nothing but chaos . . . people were screaming, crying and huggin' each other as if there was no tomorrow. It was as if the church were a giant jetliner controlled by foreign terrorists. The plane was gonna crash and no one could stop it; but our enemies weren't foreigners, they were Americans who hated God and were enemies of God and the cause of Christ.

I snapped back to an even harsher reality. This wasn't an out of control plane, this was a defenseless little church. Those nicely suited men and military dressed people wouldn't lose their lives! They weren't fighting *for* religious freedom; they were taking ours completely away! I wondered what happened to the Bill of Rights and the Constitution of the United States. I wanted to understand, but it wasn't the time or place for seeking answers to the many questions that popped into my mind.

I knew it was time for some to die as *Martyrs of the Cross,"* and some to stay alive to fight the cause of Christianity. Many would forget the cause and run for all they were worth so they could stay alive and in one piece. Others would see the cause as a very bad habit or worse. They would never take up the cause because they knew it might be their last. You know they were right. If you take it up, it could be your last.

Chapter 2

You're Busted

Narrator: Powers-that -be
Subject: You!
Location: Where are you? Don't tell us...we know where you are!
Time: ...NOW!

"You're under arrest!

Step away from this book!
Put your hands behind your back!
I'm going to cuff you now!

Anything you say can and will be used against you in a court of law. You have the right to an attorney. If you cannot afford one, one will be appointed to you. You have the right to have an attorney present when questioned. Do you understand these rights as I've given them to you?"

"Why am I being arrested?" you ask.

"Obstruction of justice," you are told.

"What have I obstructed? What justice have I obstructed? What have I done? What's going on here? You can't do this . . . you can't do this! Somebody call the police! Oh no . . . they are the police!"

You feel so helpless; you want somebody, anybody, to call your lawyer. *"I want a lawyer!"* you cry out to your oppressors.

"Shut up or I'll beat you to a pulp! Bet you've never been so humiliated in your life? Well . . . well then, we've got something in store

49

for you!"

Your mind is spinning rapidly through a series of thoughts. You believe that someone at the police station will make sense of all this. After all, you were just reading a book. The ride to the police station is terrifying. The police won't protect you.

"I was just reading this book," you tell the police sergeant. He doesn't care to hear a word you have to say.

"Did you make out a report yet?" the police sergeant asks the arresting officer at the precinct.

"Not yet, no rush . . . narcs were right, drugs everywhere, mini mobile meth lab, pot, crack, you name it! Resisting arrest, obstruction, fleeing to avoid prosecution, and attacking a police officer!"

"My God!" you cried. Question after question floods your mind. "What's going on here? Are they talking about me? Why is everybody looking at me laughing? What is so funny? I just want to go home! Get me out of here! Everybody must be worried sick about me! I'm so humiliated! Why are they doing this? I have things to do . . . let me go! I need to go home or call someone, somebody please listen to me! What's going on here?"

The Sergeant leans over and pretends to whisper, "The perp was reading that book, huh?"

"Yeah, oh yeah, the snitches were right. That idiot had that outlawed book, *Martyr's of the Cross,* opened up to the beginning and was obviously reading it when the bust occurred. It was definitely a righteous bust!"

"Stack the charges to the ceiling!" the sergeant whimsied, his smile more a sneer that reveals the contempt in his heart.

"Hey perp, yeah you, ***reader*** . . . you want to go home? You know you've been caught dead to rights reading this book. Don't you wish you had burned it like you were ordered to? You shouldn't have opened this book. Now we're going to *throw the book* at you!"

"But . . . I . . ." you say, unable to finish the sentence.

"There you go with the 'But . . . I' routine! Don't even try that stuff with me! You heard all the formal charges against you! ***Now we're going to make an example of you!*** You didn't think this could ever happen, especially to you!"

You thought all this kind of thing and the way they are talking to you could only happened to people in the movies or in books!

Think again! This is not a movie and it is not a book. It's for real, and it's happening to you!

"Toss this *'reader'* in the tank and throw away the key! And by the way, no, you don't have any so-called 'rights!' Your rights don't exist! You threw them away when you opened this book and started to read, continued to read, and for some strange reason thought you could read even more. You'll pay dearly for that bad choice!"

You are speechless. What can you say? There is no one to help you. All you can do is listen to the ranting of the Sergeant.

"You know that all religious materials must be legally approved before being read . . . by the way, do you have the tracker? If you don't, one will be applied to you whether you like it or not!" Hey, show this perp what happens to those who don't willingly accept the tracker. Let the perp look out the window!

"Oh my God, oh my God, oh my God, oh my God!" you cry aloud. "But I just started the book and I didn't get very far . . . I promise, I didn't get very far! Can't we work this out? Keep the book . . . take it . . . it's yours . . . you can have it!"

"Yeah, well . . . sorry, perp, I can't do that! Now about that mark . . . uh, tracker."

Chapter 3

Angrin speaks...you'd better listen!

Narrator: Angrin Boodman
Sometime Between One BCR - 0 BCR
Location: Mr. Boodman has located you, reader, right where you are!
Status: He is not at all happy with you

"Sorry we interrupted your little panic attack, reader, but other people have problems besides you, you know. I'm afraid this book will run out before I have my say. Nobody ever listens to me, and I have a thing or two to say that you need to hear."

You watched him pause to collect his thoughts so there would be no confusion about the words he spoke. Fear ran through your veins.

"My name is Angrin Boodman

I'll try to explain what just happened to you when you were caught reading this book and how it affected the rest of you life. Before I share all that with you, I want you to know that I'm not afraid of any man or anything else. Don't even start your mouth with me. When you got in trouble, and when you get in trouble-and you definitely got in trouble and will continue to get into trouble if you're a Christian type person-you were supposed to remember my name."

Angrin wasn't finished. He had far more to say, even if he didn't say it as eloquently as others might have said it. His words shattered you.

"You weren't up to speed on the changes yet, were you? You were asleep in your own little world . . . huh? Well, things changed partly because you slept in your oppressed little world and didn't see it coming. My fuzzy headed disgusting reader-wake up! You might have slept and not noticed the moral decay. Inch by inch the disgraceful became acceptable; but that didn't stop them from instituting each part of the moral decay . . .first one speck, then many specs . . . over and over they made the despicable legal and the righteous illegal . . . and now, here we are! I'm one of *them* and I will make your life a living nightmare!"

"I did as I pleased, when I pleased. I made you get out of my face with your religious nonsense because I wanted to turn you in. I told you to close this book and deny you ever opened it! You were not man or woman enough to take and absorb what was in this book and I personally wanted you to know that I watched you and saw to it that you wished with all your being that you did not continue."

The warning was late and you knew it. He was honest about his hatred toward you, and toward God and His people.

"Martyrdom . . . martyrdom . . . You? Yeah, right! We had nothing to fear from the likes of your kind. What do you know about the Bible? What do you know about being a Christ-like person? You went to church . . . or at least you thought about it? Whoo wee, whoo wee!

His laughter made you feel worse. Angrin knew that wouldn't be hard to do. You knew it, too.

"Example one: You said that you listened to the preacher? What did he preach about at the last service you went to? No! Really! You have nothing to say? That's exactly what I thought! You don't have a clue, do you? Of course not!"

You don't want to hear him ranting and raving any longer. You are tired and frightened. There is no place you can go. You are trapped and you have to listen.

"Example two: When was the last time you witnessed verbally to someone . . . anyone? Who was it . . . when did it happen . . . and where? Correctamundo! You don't know, because you didn't do it! Quick . . . who was the last person you lead to the Lord? Tick-tock . . . tick-tock . . . tick-tock . . .. "Hah, you don't remember because you never witnessed to anyone. You thought it was the preacher's job, didn't you? When was the last time you were so excited about the Lord you couldn't help but talk about Him and His amazing goodness?"

The shame you feel must be overwhelming. He is right. His laughter fills the air!

"As a so-called Christian, you were about as close to *us* as you could possibly get!

Did you really give your heart and soul to Christ? Really? Couldn't prove it by me!

Go back to sleep! You might not have been one of *us,* but you sure didn't act like one of His, either! If you weren't going to *actually be* one of *us,* you were just where we wanted you, anyway! Asleep! No fire . . . not even a spark. I know, because if you had read your Bible, studied it, felt the love of Christ in your life and prayed fervently, you would have been a strong witness for Him, and you would have done it naturally. That's right . . . through the natural love of God, nothing would have silenced you! His fiery radiance would have been all engulfing in your life and you would have shared it because you had to share it!"

Your soul is in pain. It reels from his attack . . . from the truth you heard.

"My good friend, don't change that spark plug, because . . . . if you don't work *for* Christ, you work for the *other one*.. That makes you just what we always wanted . . . as bendable and pliable as putty in our hands. Remember, ***dear reader***, ***if you don't stand for something***, ***you will fall for anything*** . . . so you were easy! I know you . . . you won't stand for anything except keeping your own little world safe, tidy and comfy! You don't have to be one of "us"to be our cohort! **Hey, we used you anyway! We were your friends!** There was nothing wrong with being what you were, and still are! It's okay that you didn't let anybody change you! Besides, you have always been safest the way you are!"

You know he is right. Now, he is speaking even more truth about you and it makes you sick inside.

"Society changed more and more. It became sophisticated and you knew you couldn't buck it! I would have taken care of you if you did, and it wouldn't have been a pretty picture! I *would not* let you make me look bad in those changing times! If you didn't like it, you should have kept keep your mouth shut, which you did! I knew you would! Everything was always the easiest way you could find. ***You, reader***, have always been such a pushover!"

Wait! Your mind finally focuses on his words and you realize it is happening . . . *now!* His words are being spoken now, not just when you took the easy way out. He who rejected and still rejects God's truth is speaking the truth about *you* now!

Why are you just sitting there right now, reading what this person is saying to you and about you? Why are you taking all this from an unredeemed sinner?

(***Reader***...you don't have to take this ...he isn't right ....is he? If he isn't right, you really don't have to take this kind of verbal threats and abuse...do you?)

"Close this book now ...and forget you ever opened it!"

"Go ahead and mess with me and see what happens! As times change, you *will* change. You're a conformist! That's what you are! **You will adapt to whatever we say is right!** I don't even want to hear a whimper out of you! Whimper? *You are too scared to even take your next breath!* How could you whimper?"

But you do . . . whimper, that is. Your insides are churning as your soul realizes what you knew all along. You were . . . perhaps you *are* a fraud!

"You don't want trouble, do you? You don't want to be in trouble, do you? Take a deep breath, ease up and join the world society thought circles that are tailored to fit you! Relax! Oh, I almost forgot, you're so relaxed now that you're almost in a deep spiritual coma!"

The air seems to move. You are deeply struck by his words . . .

words that attack your soul . . . _**you**_ ...the one you thought was saved.

"Now, to stay alive, and I know that is your utmost priority, you'd better pay attention and play the game. Society is changing and there's nothing you can do about it! Oh, but maybe you wanna be a hero? Maybe you wanna be a Martyr? No problem! On *the first sign of physical* or *emotional pain and you'll choose to obey*! You're *not* Martyr material! You're no Paul Revere! If you were, you wouldn't be in this position now! Haven't heard a word I've said, have you? That's fine; after all, it's **your neck** we're talking about here, not mine!"

Oh, the rightness of those words. What will you do? Will you repent for real?

"Snap to attention, reader! If you're going to be dumb enough to keep reading, I might as well fill you in on a little of what's in store for you! Remember just a few pages back . . . after your arrest, at the police station when they checked you for the mark? Well . . . the mark . . . no, it's not the mark that reveals which side you're on . . . good or evil. This mark is a registration mark . . . and implantation reserved for certain individuals such as criminals. They say it's for obvious reasons. High ranking government officials, from the highest to the most local leaders-mayors and city council members in small cities and towns-have the mark."

You wonder at the two groups who have the mark . . . or tracker. You ask yourself if there's a reason for this. Then you wonder if it really matters.

"You now have the mark, or tracker, which means you're tagged like wildlife. They can now track your every move-every place you go-everything you do. With remarkable ease, they can find out more about you than even you know about yourself. Of course, house arrest with the ankle bracelet is no longer necessary.

You're not allowed to hold any cash currency. If you're caught with it, which will be easy to do, you will be instantly thrown into prison. I say 'instantly' because you are being tracked 24/7. We know everywhere you go and everything you do."

The sickness in your soul is so powerful, you can't think straight. You're afraid to think because the tracker may allow *them* to know even your thoughts.

"If you're really bad, they'll put a 'necklace' on you! You've seen them by now, though you probably didn't know what they were. They're quite abundant because the government has total control over the people. They even promote them in many different styles-with gold, diamonds and other precious stones, metals, and settings. You do remember now, don't you? I thought so! Neat aren't they? Maybe you'd like to have one? I'm sure they want you to have one and will probably see to it that you get one before very long! You will have to earn one of the really nice ones though!"

The necklace! How could you tolerate a tracker and then a necklace that made you nothing more than government property?

"You really are something! What rock have you been hiding under? You think those necklaces are the latest fad in personal jewelry attire? *Duh- de-duh- de duh!* Yeah, well, you can just wiggle yourself back under that rock! *And don't get serious with me all of a sudden!* It's not my fault you were so sheltered all your life! And now you've been busted reading this book! You know, *Martyrs of the Cross.* How stupid could you be?"

Your mind is now on overdrive. It is just a book! What's wrong with reading a book? You wonder if Angrin can read your thoughts already. **If you read this book, your thoughts are being read as you think them!**

"Since you so rudely insist, I'll tell you the rest that you need to know! That mark they put on you is a Replicating Nan Tracker! Once they chemically injected it into you and activated it with **enzymatis**-that patch they placed on you and required you to wear for thirty minutes-you quickly became a walking, integral part of their living computer system. The way it works is different from anything they ever dreamed up before. They are not exactly tracing *you, they are tracking the part of the living,* *chemical, and nano cells that their mega computer is missing.*"

You appear a bit safer than you thought, but you know he's telling the truth because you were warned over and over again that it would be this way. You listen . . .you had better, because you know it's true.

"Where were we? Yes, the nano thing! Well, this 'colony' does indeed multiply to the point that the recipient host, which is you, is the host-home to a mark about the size of a refined birthmark-or about an inch and a half in diameter! First, the patch was installed. It then took up to thirty minutes to complete the 'conception' process of nano-fertilization and growth. This, of course, depends on your sub-atomic molecular structure, which is your DNA and such, and your specific body metabolism. *You're just lucky that I majored in the sciences so I can help you understand the process*!

Don't expect to understand it like I do. I mean, I don't understand it all, but I did do my thesis in college on its developmental stages when the technology was in its infancy."

You shudder because again you know he's right. You heard all about it . . . read about it on the Internet. Still, you thought you would escape it. You thought you'd be taken out of this mess in the Rapture!

"We live in a day and age when man's knowledge is increasing exponentially. Yes, indeed, that X-factor, Y-factor and Z- factor produced a bonanza of exponential development! Now, back to English . . . you want to know what this means? What it means is the technology goes well beyond the ability to track a person. It allows the computers to become part of a person. They just about know what a "tagged" person is going to do before they do it! In fact, it tracks uncontrolled will and controlled will simultaneously!"

Your soul is terribly grieved . . . your spirit, too. You know your life is over . . . as least the life you once had. You are no longer a free person, but a part of something sinister . . . something hideously evil.

"Of course, this technology shall become more and more useful as our wicked world becomes out of control and more chaotic. The citizens of this world are begging for some way, someone to control the madness. World domination is enticing to some .. . . fear grips and dominates. **Control is the only answer.** How can anyone save this world as it is? Mayhem, madness, murders! All will be subdued into submission when the one the people are looking for arrives . . . it has to be . . . it has to happen because otherwise, this turbulent world cannot continue except into extinction."

The words hit you hard, especially the word *extinction!* Would man really doom himself to his own demise worldwide because of sin? You try to remember all that you learned . . .. you try to remember the end of the story.

"The technology is here and in place, the mind set has been created-the completed digestion of the propaganda that allows the *one* to walk onto the world-scene and take control! They said mankind did this to itself! They said man's sins took away the freedoms given by *your* God. Well, what did you expect them to say? Now *they* tell us we need *their* protection or we will die. That's what they said!"

You weep inwardly thinking about liberty over life or life over liberty. You know you must choose. They answered our call for protection . . . and we made our decisions. What do you say now?

"Reader, why were you busted? You were reading this book? Do the smart thing and destroy this book! Hide it where it will never be found! Remember your RNT-your Replicating Nano Tracker? Remember the necklace? The necklace those hardened criminals get? Well, you'll get yours soon! It's an actual transmitting device that's a multi-directional camera as well! It gives them a bird's-eye view of everything you do in real time! If they have any suspicion that you may be doing anything their mind- controlling **nano-tracker** would prefer you not do, they know it and see it instantly! They don't have to see all things at all times, just when you stray in any way."

Stray? Where could you stray now? You have no way to stray from

60

them and their ever watchful computerized "eyes."

"Here's just one example. You don't have to be doing anything you would consider to be wrong. Maybe you want to try paying for something with cash. You lost that right when you were busted for reading this book . . . or other similar offenses. You are banned from using cash for the rest of your life. *It is never to cross your clenched fist again!*"

You remember the debit and credit cards you used to use with little or no thought about the consequences. Do you remember the feel of money in your hands?

"Your RNT alerts them and tells them exactly where you are and how to find you! Your necklace has recorded your *transgression* and instantly they become witnesses to your crime. You will be immediately apprehended because you have nowhere to go. You'll serve your time or *suffer well-deserved torture or death.*"

You think about the children growing up in such a world. In their quest for freedom, they became slaves . . . just like you!

"What about the kids? They're growing up in a society that now teaches them that they can never get away with anything. They know they must be in agreement with the new mindset; they must be in submission at all times to the quickly emerging New World Order! They must be in submission to the *one* who will lead! The "man's" gotta have control! Mind you, this *punishment,* this *control* is not necessarily a bad thing . . . that is, if you don't buck it! Think about it! No more serious crimes and no more right wing conservatives moralizing and telling us about our sins! Well . . . well, there are a few, but they won't last long!"

Are you one of them? What will you do? He reads your thoughts!

"What are you going to do now that you know? Live or die? Will you do something worthy of your mentality and become a liberal or a moderate, or will you continue as a radical conservative? You really are stupid . . . aren't you?

Chapter 4

Brother Danny and Sister Brenda

Narrator: Unknown
Location: Unknown
Six Months BCR

Doing the wash . . . cooking . . . cleaning . . . taking care of family. **A gain and again,**
Again, and again,
Day in, day out. Normal . . . huh? Used to be normal, that is!
Not today!
Different day today is.

She woke up this morning, sore, aching a bit both from age, and the intensity and strenuousness of her daily, "work around the house" ritual. Grandkids come to visit. What a day . . . what a day! Rowdy .... sweet ...hey, kids are kids, right?

Sister Brenda and Brother Danny were considered two of the sweetest God loving, God fearing and God serving people in the Body of Christ. For Sister Brenda, it was real; but for Brother Danny, it was just show-the impression he wanted people to have of him. Oh, well. Every story has a sub-story and every plot has a sub-plot. This story is no different. How could it be different when it's about people? I guess what matters is the story.

Her life was short, this sweet soul, and she didn't even know it, but that was okay because her Lord wanted very much to see her.

Kids went to work, leaving a grandkid or two, to be watched by no one better qualified than their grandmother, Sister Brenda.

Workday over, the kids came, the grandkids left, and a little tear always came to her eyes, it seems!

They'll be back; she'll see them again. It was Friday, so she'd have to wait until Monday to see them again. That wasn't good . . . but it would have to do. Besides, she was very good at busying herself-you know, being a good housewife and all.

Then there was Danny, her husband. I don't know if I should be telling you about all this or not. Danny wasn't quite what he was cracked up to be! Come to find out, Danny had quite a temper, and was quite the sneaky one!

All fun and games!

Yeah,

Uh huh,

Sure,

Right!

Oh, but I forgot, you thought a lot of him, didn't you?

Well, I'd better stop here 'cause . . . I mean . . . I don't want to bust your bubble or anything.

Yeah, you knew it! I can't keep my big mouth shut. I know, I know! If I tell you anything bad about Danny, you're going to think I'm just making it up! Well, think what you want. I'm going to tell it like it is, because it's the truth!

Brother Danny and Sister Brenda were living modestly all those years, as you know, scraping by at times . . . and occasionally the Lord would send some sweet financial blessings their way. They both served the Lord in their own ways. The part you don't know is that Danny was one of those preachers who was so afraid of losing his job that he would tell anybody anything and bless (as if he could) everything! How do you spell *wishy-washy*? Okay, so you know that it starts with a **"D", then an "A", then an "N", then another "N!"** You get the picture, don't you? When it came to taking a stand for what was right, jellyfish have more backbone than Danny did.

I guess you can tell that I'm just a little bit ticked-off! I should be. Like everyone else, I also thought the world of Sister Brenda. Not only that, but I'm also a little vengeful! I can't stand to see this degree of wrongdoing go unpunished! It probably will, though!

What was his problem that he couldn't work it out some other way? From what I've heard, he was afraid to lose his retirement benefits, so every week he preached the same weak message, "Don't worry, God loves you," and "You can make the Bible say anything you want it to, and ***blah-de, blah-de, blah!"***

Watered down and overflowing with fluff, he preached fluffy, "don't sweat it" messages. Oh, yeah, he told his flock a pile of lies.

"We've got God in our pockets! We've got the upper hand here!" he would tell them. "We've got eternal salvation, right?"

Guess again! I mean, wait just a minute!

Whoa baby, whoa!

There's just one itsy-bitsy, teeny-weeny little problem with that kind of thinking and preaching! What Brother Danny was afraid to preach, afraid to teach, and afraid to even talk about was what frightened him the most-the lack of his own salvation and the future of his own eternity! He should have told the truth. Heaven is real, hell is hot . . . and if you're a Christian, your life will reflect your faith! He didn't have the courage to say that and he's not around to answer for what he didn't do!

Well, maybe and maybe not.

Danny really was a lousy shepherd, wasn't he? Works do not save us "lest any man should boast." We've all fallen short of the Glory of God, but when you're truly saved your words and works should bear you out. You just can't hide His light under a bushel . . . no, you can't!

Okay, so I'm ranting and raving a bit, but everything I'm telling you is true, and it's what Danny should have told you! He should have told them that God works through your life in numerous ways. No matter what's happening in your life, He will work on you at the same time. You can't out run Him, you can't out-think Him, and you can't hide from Him! He's always there! Jesus said He would talk to your heart, even if you backslide. He'll talk to you!

There was so much Danny could have and should have said. He should have told you that if you're a Christian, your time is short and precious. Sister Brenda knew that we must use that time prayerfully. Don't you see? All you have to do is ask the Lord to speak through you! Danny should have told you that, too! You're one of His vessels for delivering His divine word, for preaching His word. Ask Him to help you so you don't stray from the truth-so you say exactly what He wants to say through you!

Christ said, "I will be with you always, even unto the end of the world." He sent His sweet Holy Spirit to be a comforter to the Christians and to beckon the non-Christians to repentance. Now that's love!

"Read Romans in your Bible!" Sister Brenda would beg Danny. "Read it and teach it!" she encouraged him. "Danny, it explains so much of the rest of the New Testament that the people need to understand. If you preach and encourage people to read, study, and pray on Romans, they will have a sound base for their understanding of the Holy Word of God, especially the New Testament."

She didn't stop with those words because she wanted desperately for her husband to know God and preach the truth. She prayed for the right words to share with him.

"Danny, read the gospels of Matthew, Mark, Luke, and John to learn even more about the dynamic impact Jesus had on all of mankind! Read First John and you'll see His great plan for humanity. The people in First John were unsaved people; the ones who remained unsaved because of their unwillingness to accept Jesus as their Lord and personal Savior. You need to teach them that believing in God and praying to God is not enough, they must be born again by the redemptive saving grace of Jesus Christ."

Was the truth so alien to Danny? Sister Brenda believed it terrified him. She knew that "all our works are as filthy rags" compared to the holiness, righteousness and power of God. She believed that we are commanded by God to live holy and righteous lives by studying and obeying His Word. She even told Danny that not knowing His Word and not reading it doesn't water it down, dilute it, or make it less real or significant. And, she told him that the commandments in it never change. Sister Brenda knew that everything God wants all of us to know is compacted into one book-the Bible.

Yes, she had it right. The only way man is worthy is when man repents and is covered by the shed blood of Christ. I knew she was begging Danny to see the truth. She desperately wanted him to know and love God .She wanted Danny to feel Him, anticipate Him, look forward to Him, and always feel His presence.

"Danny, don't just teach these people to pray to God and have them believe that He knows and will understand if they have some misunderstandings about Jesus. Don't tell them it's okay to leave Jesus out, to hide their belief in Jesus as the Son of God, or to not accept Him as being the one and only intercessor between them and God for confessing their sins. They can't say, 'I just don't know how I feel about that man, Jesus! I pray to God, and that's enough.' It's not enough, Danny! Our flesh is corruptible and only when we die does the perfect man live on-the man inside the carnal flesh who is made perfect through the blood of Jesus, that part of us, that perfect spirit lives on as we go to be in the presence of our Lord."

She didn't hold back a bit. Those who refuse to repent, she told him, will be held accountable to God at the Great White Throne Judgment. She begged Danny to teach them about such things. I remember her words. I heard them!

"Danny, don't fail to teach them, whether they want to hear it or not. Your time behind that pulpit is precious, and people's lives are depending on what you say. Their eternal souls are depending on you to do this!"

Sister Brenda, sweet Sister Brenda! She was just trying to help Danny to be the soul winner he should have been. Oh, don't get me wrong. I know the truth. He'll have to answer for all the misleading he did-some call it poor shepherding-and is still doing in the name of Christianity. He'll have to answer for his part in what happened to his wife' and all because she "nagged" him relentlessly! He'll have to answer to God if he did what he did for position, power, prestige, or money. I mean, was he really saved or not? Is he saved now?

I can't judge his heart, but based on what I've seen and heard, I don't think so! I'm not The Judge and I don't know all the answers; but I do believe that Sister Brenda was just trying to lead him right . . . towards what he already knew but was afraid to tell people about!

Oh, well. This world had already become about as wacky as one would ever think it could! In fact, most of us couldn't even believe it had become so bad. It was just more than we could handle. After all, they were years from using the guillotines again, or so everybody thought . . . everybody but Sister Brenda! She knew the truth better than any of us knew it!

Yeah, it was too much . . . I mean the way they came in on her that day. The grandkids wouldn't be back until Monday. She was going to go do some grocery shopping when BAM! The door flew open followed by all those folks in nice suits.

I don't think I ever want to see another nice suit again in my life! Sure was a nice car they threw her in and slammed the door without making sure it didn't crush her arm! You know that had to hurt! It makes me hurt just to think about it!

"Witnessing, huh?

Witnessing, huh?

You were witnessing?" That's what I heard them ask her.

They talked so rude to her that day!

Well, that's all right! God will get them for that!

So, then they took her to some place that only the "nice suits" knew about and were allowed to go to. I don't exactly know what happened next, but I think torture was involved. What I do know is that they thought they had her head securely in place before the blade came down; but she was looking squarely into heaven when man's evilness separated her from this life and sent her straight to her loving Savior! Praise, God, she was smiling all the way!

She was even singing . . . singing a song she wrote! She started singing it in this life and kept singing it the next as she was on the way to Jesus! She had sung it at least four hundred times if she had sung it once! I seriously doubt that her trip to Glory will be her last time singing it, too. I hope she's there singing that song when I meet the Lord. It goes something like .. . .

"Does anybody care . . . does anybody care . . . does anybody really, really care? As I recall in days of old, people really seemed to care." Gosh, I wish you could hear the music . . . beautiful music!

"They cared about the poor and destitute. The old folks were never forgotten and unborn babies were not murdered. Families knelt in prayer every night. But as time has come and gone . . .Christians have lost their vision . . . Souls are perishing without a Savior.

Oh, that wonderful Sister Brenda could sing it . . . and your heart was rent . . . just wide open for the Lord to do a powerful work in you!

"As souls are perishing . . . and the churches are dying . . . we can read of One that really, really cares . . . for he was wounded for our transgressions . . . and He was bruised for our iniquities and that surely by his stripes, we are healed."

Such a simple chorus . . . such simple and true words came from Sister Brenda's heart through her music!

"Yes my friend Jesus cares . . . yes my friend Jesus cares . . . Yes

Jesus really, really, really cares . . . He still cares."

I've heard many times the phrase, "Oh, she sings like an angel!" I'm sure I now know what that means and I can now bear witness to what the angels sound like when they sing. Sister Brenda recorded that song one time. I wish I had a copy of it so I could share it with you . . . the way it really sounded, but I don't have a copy and she's with the Lord now. All I can do is shake my head and wonder about what has happened to mankind. What on Earth are people thinking? What on Earth are they thinking? What's happened to their hearts that they should turn from God?

"Enjoy this life, it's short . . ."they always say, don't they? Then why do they live as if there's no end to it? If they were really so concerned with the end of this life, wouldn't they be preparing more for the return of the Lord or for the Great White Throne Judgement? That's what Sister Brenda was all about. That was what she was completely about.

Now wait just a minute! You've got it wrong I do believe! She lived life. She lived life in love. She loved God and knew He loved her. And that love flowed into everything she was and did. She lived life in love with her husband, her children, her grandchildren, and even the family pets. She loved the daily life of being a wife, mother, and grandmother because she was filled with the joy and admonition of serving her Savior.

Did she enjoy serving her church? Yes indeed, it was a joy. She loved not only being involved, but also the drama and passion of the message she brought to "the flock" . . . the sheer love of it-not for brownie points! You see . . . in her heart, Sister Brenda knew that to love Christ was to know Him; and knowing Him came from reading God's Holy Word. She studied and witnessed because it was proof of her love for Him and His love for her. Sister Brenda loved God so much that she wanted everybody to be with Him, in Him, and into Him! That love, she knew, would bring Godly obedience, not ungodly rebellion. Love . . . real love! I mean, heart-pounding, pure, Godly love!

She figured out long ago that you could have a glorious, overfilling, abundant love for people, as Christ does, while living life at the same time. Oh, for sure, Christ doesn't love or even like many of the things that people do. I'm sure that much of who we are and what we do breaks His heart; but He still loves us.

Well, back to Danny . . . at least for a moment. How will God deal with Danny? He's a Christian, isn't he? Maybe not! He participated in the massacre at the little white church, didn't he? Sure, he was just following orders, but he helped throw that little old granny out of the window.

Oh, I forgot! I didn't tell you about that . . . did I? I think that maybe I should explain it the right way. Remember the story in the Bible about Stephen being stoned to death? You must remember that he was the first person in the Bible to be referred to as a martyr for the Lord. Remember about the man who held the coats? That man was Saul. Saul of Tarsus. Saul was a mean man with a lot of power. He was on the road to Damascus to persecute Jews who accepted Christ as their Savior when God struck him blind. It didn't take long for Saul to repent and turn his life over to God. The Lord changed his name to Paul, and then used him in more ways than you can imagine.

Point being . . . you think the Lord can't use Danny and the things he has done in a powerful way? Who are you to belittle the Creator of the universe that way? Yes, Danny joined the ISD (Internal Security Department) as a left wing Christian-hater. He blamed God for his own shortcomings. Come to think of it, that's how most people deal with their sins and faults. They find all kinds of "creative "ways to explain or excuse them . . . or they blame God for them!

Was Danny really a Christian? Was he ever a Christian? Well, if he ever had been, then he still is. So, what about his cruelty and meanness? Okay, so I have my doubts that he ever was truly saved, but I'm not the Judge. The Bible says that it rains on the just and the unjust . . . and I say that people are people . . . it's up to God alone to deal with Danny's soul and the possible turmoil he might face for the rest of his eternal life. Yes, we all have eternal life; just depends where you want to spend it.

Sister Brenda is gone. How I miss Sister Brenda. I miss all the Sister Brenda's of the world that this evil New World Order has dissolved from our realm of existence! I praise the Lord for the Earthly death of Sister Brenda because lots of lives were changed when folks saw what happened to her. She understood martyrdom better than most of us could or would. The fact is . . . truth is . .. . I can look up to heaven and almost see her smiling down at me with all that love in her heart!

Chapter 5

Mass Insane

When: Unknown
When written: Unknown...Thought to have been written shortly A.C.R.
Narrator: ...Unknown...Thought to be a young preacher, deacon,
evangelist or missionary ...unsaved before the Rapture

> *Worship...*
> *Don't worship...*
> *Worship...*
> *Don't worship...*
> *Your choice...yours alone...*

It used to be so easy, but I can't say it is now. Used to be times when there was such a thing as a "Bible Belt" in this country. You didn't have to live there to worship, though. We had the freedom to choose to worship as we pleased, or not to worship.

Most chose not to worship. They didn't believe, were too tired, it wasn't convenient, it wasn't mandatory, or we could all do pretty much as we chose to do as long as it was legal. Most people worked 8-40-40- eight hours a day, forty hours a week, forty years of their lives. Their lives seemed like mine. You know the drill: you woke up, worked, went home, relaxed and then slept, looked forward to the weekend for whatever was considered pleasurable. Life's pleasures were limited though. Let's see . . . you went where you wanted, watched television, read books, talked on the telephone, visited friends, went bowling, swam, camped, and took vacations to get away from the stress.

Life was so basic for you. You talked or just chatted about pretty much what you wanted and pretty much when you wanted to. Gossiping, spreading rumors, taking about politics; you know, playing the game. It was all right, because there were no repercussions . . . except for the occasional lost friendship or spoiled business relationship.

You picked your clothes, your friends, your house, your car, including the color. Letters were written, bills were paid, e-mails were sent, and games were played on your computers. Sports or no sports, it was your choice. It didn't matter which you chose because you thought you were the one in control of your life.

Morals were another thing altogether. Do right, do wrong, feel bad, or don't feel bad. You could listen to your conscience, obey the Holy Spirit, or live your life according to the "dictates" of Sigmund Freud …the Id, the Ego and the Super Ego! Any philosophy that explained human behavior was acceptable-you know the stuff that explained why we did the things we did, and how we felt about the choices we made . . . or you might say, *what made us tick.*

What did I start this conversation with? Oh yeah, I remember! Worship or not to worship, it was your choice! Well, not anymore! Doesn't really matter whose choice we're talking about now, does it?

Lazy Christians, even if they were in church . . . still …many lazy Christians! What matters? Nothing! Nothing! You were on fire for Christ? Yeah, I sat there and felt all warm and fuzzy for about an hour or two on Sunday mornings. I did my weekly, church-going duty and I was all *"Christianity"!* Did I read my Bible? Yeah, I have one . . . somewhere. I read it . . .. no …come on ... really ... I always read my Bible! Well, I did!

Are you catching my drift here? Will things ever go back to the way they were? Can we ever just go back? Will this world ever allow us the freedoms we used to take for granted? We saw it coming . . . be honest with me . . . didn't we see this New World Order barreling down on us? Why didn't we put the brakes on it before it took over?

Did we go **mass insane**? How could we let this happen? How could we allow the theft of our God-given freedoms, *in the name of anything whatsoever*, . . . I mean to the point that we slowly, then more and more quickly, sank into the irretrievable abyss of never more, never again! This truly must be the literal living meaning of *tyranny and chaos.*

Thank you for joining me in a world many said would never happen! It's a world mankind created or allowed to be created. What a deal! We did little or nothing to stop them from creating a world in which the Honorable Roy Moore, a former Alabama Superior Court judge, was martyred for Christianity. Did we stop them when the state power brokers threw him out of office for holding firm to what he knew in his heart was true and right? They just couldn't stand that he held his belief in God and God's Word so dearly in his mind, soul, and heart . . . so much higher than his faith in man and man's government. We sleepy cowards did little or nothing at all to stop the lie of "separation of church and state," and the liberal activists won that battle.

Didn't they realize that what was important in this life . . .. is not this life? What's important in this life is the next life and doing all we can to help others to get to Heaven with us. Things *in* this life were important . . . don't get me wrong . . . but they were just not at the top of the God-fearing man's priority list. If you don't believe me, I just wish you could talk to those who've already tasted the irreversibility of death and understand what it means to them.

I wonder if people will ever get out of their "mind bubble of superior intellect" long enough to see what effect their decisions have on them in this life . . . and forever. All those tens of thousands of people . . . if not millions . . . seem hermetically sealed in some anti-sacred place of denial.

Well, such is martyrdom for Christ! What did we expect? Too little willingness, too few patriots for the cause, too much apathy was what took hold of us. It's so sad that it happened this way. After all, where else would there be a greater call, a greater need for Christ's inspiration and guidance than in our alleged halls of justice? Oh, but they didn't want the "Christian zealots" to regain even a toe hold because they believed, that humans are independent and have no need of God-no need to rely on a Superior, Supernatural Being, that, in fact, even created us from the very dust that He made! The ultimate Potter who used His clay to form us had made us imperfect so we would seek His perfection, His love . . . and most of all, His forgiveness.

The battle raged as to whether it was lawful for the state to sponsor and pay for abortions, prayer was taken out of the schools and replaced with "diversity" and multiculturalism teachings. The Ten Commandments were ripped from the public square, and people removed from government positions or fired from jobs because they didn't conform to the secular way of doing things. The people of Alabama voted Roy Moore into office. He should never have been removed from office for taking a stand on the Ten Commandments monument issue-for taking a stand on what should have never been an issue at all!

It should have been a given that our government was allowed to continue the course of guidance by God that it was originally intended to have. I remember Billy Graham's daughter, Anne Graham Lotz, saying that it was "funny how simple it is for people to trash God and then wonder why the world is going to hell. Funny how we believe what the newspapers and television talking heads say, but question what the Bible says." You know all about this though, don't you?

Dr. Benjamin Spock told two generations of parents more things about raising children than we needed to hear-and he was wrong about everything he advised. He didn't think we should demoralize the children and warp their personalities, didn't think we should make the children lose their self-esteem by spanking them when they misbehaved. Love of God and God's love for us was not part of Spock's teachings. Ironic that his own son committed suicide.

The Godly foundation and fabric that formed this country and contributed greatly to the civilized world just withered away because of rotting moral decay. This rot, this fibrous withering, grew out of apathy and an overdose of liberalism that was mixed with an unsafe dosage of anti-involvement. You should take note that we're now reaping what we sowed.

To some, it sounds like what they used to call activism. They told us not to buck the system or get involved. They told us to keep quiet, which is what they say when they want to win the battle with the least amount of opposition or resistance. Imagine what would happen if they banded together in like-mindedness! Get the people on your side and you can rule the world! Sell them your worldview and they'll help with the brainwashing, overwhelm the majority with an acceptable mandate, and the rest will have no choice but to accept it. In other words, if it's done properly, the opposition will fade away, the new ideologies are locked in and society must adapt to the new rules.

I know I've been rambling, but please indulge me. **Thank you!**

It was sort of like the military officer who gave a bad order to an enlisted man. The enlisted man knew it wasn't right but he had to obey or suffer the consequences. What was he to do? It used to be called "a moral dilemma," but now, the few who chose to reject this relatively new way, The New World Order, soon became the "Roy Moores" of the world. The new counterculture wasn't liberal anymore; it was Christian and conservative, just like in the days when Christians lived in the catacombs to avoid capture by the government. How many were caught and thrown to the lions? Too many . . . too many!

How could we have let our God-fearing society turn into this hellish shell of its former self? How could we have let this happen? Didn't we see this coming? Didn't we care? Weren't we brave enough, smart enough, strong enough, vocal enough, willing enough to experience the honor of martyrdom so it wouldn't happen? What happened to us? Life without the sacrifice of battle and the rewards of that sacrifice, and of enduring persecution, is too easy! We just didn't get it, did we? We either didn't know or didn't have the courage to accept what Christ said in Matthew 5: 10-15. Do you remember the words? I do . . .

"Blessed are they that are persecuted for righteousness' sake; for theirs is the kingdom of heaven. Blessed are ye, when men shall revile you, and shall say all manner of evil against you falsely, for my sake. Rejoice, and be exceedingly glad for great is your reward in heaven: for so persecuted they the prophets which were before you. Ye are the salt of the earth: but if the salt have lost its savor, wherefore shall it be salted? It is thenceforth good for nothing, but to be cast out and trodden under foot of men. Ye are the light of the world. A city that is set on a hill cannot be hid. Neither do men light a candle, and put it under a bushel, but on

a candlestick; and it giveth light unto all that are in the house. Let your light so shine before me, that they may see your good works, and glorify your Father, which is in Heaven.

Our lives changed so fast. Going to school, going to work, home life, society, friends and family, and the ability to have anything became totally different. Again, how did this happen?

I remember 9-11. It was a horrible day for the nation, perhaps for the world. Just part of the tool, or was it a message from God? We were too safe, too smug, and too secure. We were attacked here . . . right under our very noses! Those Twin Towers were an icon and thousands of lives were lost when they came down. The Pentagon was also attacked and greatly damaged, and hundreds of wonderful lives were lost. Attacks on Capitol Hill and the White House were part of the plan. No telling what would have happened if some brave passengers on Flight 11 hadn't stopped that last plane from reaching its destination.

You felt pain for a short time, prayed a bit more, and then you moved on. Perhaps you shuffled it under a rug with the label "another event in history that won't happen again," but I can assure you, there are tens or hundreds of thousands of people whose lives were irreversibly changed that day. No, it didn't just affect Americans, it affected the world-a world that looked on with sadness for the dead and joy that we were brought low. It changed the lives of people in Afghanistan and Iraq, altered the political landscape of those regions, and put America's foreign policies under a microscope for the world to examine and condemn. The left-wing liberals didn't wait to spin their propaganda, and the foolish believed them.

Chapter 6

Brother Tiny goes to Chattanooga

Narrator: Author of this book
When: unwilling to reveal
Timeframe of this chapter: Four months BCR

The connections on short-wave radios were the only way Christians could talk to each other. Codes were used but were changed on a very regular basis for fear of decoding by the enemy.

"TNY 1 ears, any mrtr 4 Hm , wakeup, wakeup!"

"Wrk , Wrk 215 N uwevwdwltq M.A. 10 Chtn pmeh."

"WBT hv > c . . . h . . ."

"Grt, cudn."

"Listening . . . listening."

"Tina, come here!" Sam Harks yelled.

"Whassup?"

"Whassup? You're just about the goofiest person I've ever met! I do love your goofy self, though, from head to tiny little toe!"

She put her arms around him and teased at his ear!

"Well, What is up, Mr. Harks?"

He laughed almost uncontrollably!

"Love of my life, you can be the love of my life in a few minutes, but I need to let you in on an rsh e-ml I just got!"

"Things are so hyper fast paced these days. Why can't they be like they used to be, back in the days of snail e-mail?" she cried. "Now everything's abbreviated, we have to rush this and rush that, and everything is coded for secrecy. This person is against that person, this group is against that group. It's making me crazy!"

"You know that firewalls have always been overcome! There had to come a day in the battle for privacy and secrets that the war against the hackers had to be won or lost."

Somebody was going to go as far as he could in the battle for privacy or the hackers would get the final victory with virtually no bloodshed. A victory without a real battlefield was hard to imagine, but it happened that way. It really did!

"We were so stupid. The government really fooled us by telling us they were against the hackers!" Sam said.

"Ha! Really funny! That wasn't true. Not since the entrance of the new government, and most likely long before that, the kingpin hackers- the masters of the masters of hacking did their thing and invaded our privacy," Tina replied.

Sam knew she was right and added his own comment. "Oh, they were the best of the best of the best because guess what? We were duped again! Now those people spend their time figuring out encrypted codes for the government!"

Sam Harks knew the codes. "TNY 1 ears mrtr 4 Hm, wakeup, wakeup . . . Tiny went by TNY 1, and ears mrtr 4 Hm meant he was standing by waiting to find out if there are others willing be martyrs for Christ. The important word was 'listening.' I figured that one out! It means to be wary because 'Big Brother' was listening. 'Wakeup, wakeup' meant we had to pay urgent attention because . . . because MA 10 Chtn really meant 10 a.m., in Chattanooga, Tennessee."

"The message is clear, Tina. There will be an intense showing of *Martyrs of the Cross*, as signified by 'wrk, wrk.' The address is not 215, but 512, not north but south. 'vwevwdwltq is harder. We simply back up three letters per letter and we have the street name of Substation. It means we have to get everybody possible to meet at 512 Substation South Road at 10 a.m. for an intense showing of **Martyrs of the Cross.** It has to be tomorrow because there's no date."

Sam explained the last part of the message to his wife. "WBT hv> c . . . h . . . means Carlton Hempter will be there and promises to bring a lot of "untaggables" with him!"

"But what does grt cudn mean?" Tina asked, a bit confused.

"I don't have the foggiest clue! It must be a new one!" he replied. "I think we need to get busy, we have a job to do. We must keep the cause alive. The play is a thorn in the side of the I.S.D. and a catalyst for us! You call Quick X and I'll start trying to get in touch with Rag Tag!"

"For the last six months since "The Bethlehem Church Project " started at that little white church, all I've heard from you is how important it is for you to do work for the Lord."

The knock on the door didn't startle them, but it did cut their conversation short. They were expecting a visitor who would only add support to Sam's efforts. Brother Tiny was no stranger to the cause and his visit signaled that something big was about to happen.

"Come in, Brother Tiny! It's so great to see you again! Let me take your coat! We've sure missed you!" Tina said, fluttering around their welcome guest.

Great to see you again! "Sam added, shaking Tiny's hand. "Tina, why don't you get Tiny some coffee, please!"

Tiny was touched by the reception his dear friends had given him. His heart swelled with love for those who were deeply involved in spreading the truth about Jesus Christ under dangerous conditions.

"Sammy, Sammy . . . and Tina . . . it's really good to be back in your home again! This 'New World' sure is wacky, isn't it? Nothing really makes sense anymore, does it?" Tiny said, his questions requiring no answers because they all knew the answers.

Tina brought Tiny a hot cup of freshly brewed coffee and placed it on the table near the armchair so Tiny would be comfortable. He thanked her with a smile that crossed his entire face and then settled in to get them up to date on the news.

"Good things happened after the "The Bethlehem Church Project" . . . like you two working things out with each other and getting right with God! Who would have thought that would have happened? Everybody used to say they'd lay odds on which one of you would kill the other, what with all that daily cussing and fighting and all. Now you've dedicated your lives to Christ and are working for Him. That's a miracle!"

Tiny stopped and reflected back to the day everything changed . . . the day at the little white church when the massacre broke loose.

Thank God, thank God you two weren't at the church that day a few months ago! I'm sure glad it wasn't in God's plan for you to be there!"

"We were there, Brother Tiny, but we hid in a broom closet until all the bloodshed was over and Scontee and his men were gone."

"Do you really still think about those days?" Sam asked Tiny. "Oh, sorry . . . that was a stupid question."

"It's okay, Sammy. There's nothing you can ask that I'd consider stupid, my brother. I'm just so sorry for the loss of all those wonderful people that day and wish I had done my part. I might have been able to save more people. I mean, it's not like I'm blameless you know! Tiny replied. "I was following orders, but that's definitely not an excuse. I also took innocent, beautiful lives, and I should have done something to help stop the slaughter sooner, even if it cost me my life! I'm just so glad that nobody hurt you or Tina."

"You saved many lives that day. Since then, you've done much more to prevent the loss of innocent lives," Sam added. You know, brother, I believe we're involved in the End Times right before Christ returns for His children. Who would have dreamed the world would become so evil and dangerous so quickly?

"We just thought real life, politics, and religion were in turmoil. We just couldn't imagine, even when people turned to their own sick desires and pleasures, and were morbidly cold towards Christ," Tiny replied.

"Look at Tina and myself. Look where our lives were," Sam added. "We were arguing and fighting all the time. There was no purpose in our lives except our own selfish lusts. We had no interest in anything except what we thought made us happy! So sad, so, so sad . . . all that wasted time!"

Tiny comforted Sam. "But look what Christ did for you! The world was about to nosedive into total abomination, which is where it is now. It's the perfect time for the grand entrance of their precious antichrist! I know we've heard this for years, but I don't look for the evil one. I think of the Rapture, then the Tribulation period. They're near ... . so very near! I'm really excited . . . at least about the Rapture! We'll be gone from all this, my brother and sister!"

Tiny couldn't help but think again about his earlier role in persecuting the Christians. "I do hurt that I was part of the start of the enforcement of this chaos. You two at least were not part of that, thank God. "It's a movement now and you're at the helm. *Martyrs of the Cross* is your 'baby' now. I'm so grateful to Him that you've seen the picture as it's developed!"

Sam was stunned that so much responsibility fell on his shoulders. "Many, many lives will be lost to Satan, but, in the end, many others will be won for Christ-even if it's at the eleventh hour!" He sighed and then said, "The physical bodies of those won to Christ may be lost because of evildoers, but their souls will go to be with the Lord. They will stand for righteousness and be the real martyrs . . . the ones who hold a very, very dear and special place with our Savior!"

"Praise, God, you are part of God's divine plan through what you're doing. Stay strong in the faith, brother, no matter what, and remember . . . my prayers are always with you!" Tiny said.

"Thank you, Tiny. I will remember your kind words for the rest of my life" Sam said with watery eyes.

"And *I* want to thank you also, Tiny, from the bottom of my heart."

Tina said. Having heard the special words from their dear friend, she swelled with gratefulness and godly pride that the Lord was using her husband in such a powerful way.

"Tina, you two have really got something special. No matter what lies ahead, don't lose what you have, which is easy to do in a world where nothing matters but oneself." Tiny added.

"Thank you, Tiny. We'll keep God first in our lives and keep each other second, the way it's supposed to be," she replied.

Tiny had so much he wanted to say to his dear friends. He bowed his head for a moment and spoke the truth. "Friends, time's coming up for a very important meeting-the one tomorrow. Brother Carlton Hempter is presenting another *Martyrs* play and we need to let other true Christians know."

He took another deep breath and continued speaking. "We can't and must not let Satan's works and atrocities go unchallenged. We're in God's army now, and He wants good soldiers. We must use all God has put at our disposal to help bring as many souls as possible to the Lord."

The three friends prayed. They knew it would be hard to make many people comfortable, but they wanted to spend as much time and effort as possible reaching out to others so they understood what was happening. If they could reach others with the truth, they would understand why things were happening the way they were and would know what they must do about it.

"This world is in chaos. Every soul is precious. Christ died on the cross so every soul could be with him throughout eternity, if they will only believe in Him," Sam said. "This cause is worth dying for a thousand times. We should be willing to give up our very lives just once to win souls to Christ. We have to help them realize that they in return may also be asked if they're willing to sacrifice their lives for the Lord."

Tina wondered how many were willing to sacrifice their lives to see others saved. She wished she could ask each brother and sister in the Lord, "Are you willing to sacrifice your luxuries, your comfort, your freedom for the glory of God?" She knew that many martyrs for the Lord were not immediately killed. Many were tortured or greatly sacrificed in some way in Christ's name. Either way, they never gave up the faith.

"I don't know how many people will die or suffer in Christ's name, but I do know their numbers are in the millions," Tiny said. "Truth is, there will be millions more who will be strong in the Lord, on both sides of the Rapture-before the Tribulation and after the Great Tribulation is over.

"I know they will cry out to the Lord for Him to avenge them, and He most certainly will when all who will gain martyrdom for Christ, have done so," Sam responded, his heart heavy with what he knew was true. "Then, He will most certainly avenge them and they will be given a white robe that has been washed in the blood of the Lamb. He is *just* in all He does, and His vengeance is awesome and mighty. Those who oppose Him will receive every ounce of His wrath because they made the wrong choice!"

Tiny shared that after the play the next day he would honor an invitation to preach on the beauty of Heaven . . . on the joy of being with Christ in the presence of Almighty God. "I'll preach on being in that state of consciousness, on earthly reality versus heaven's reality. I want to tell them about the likeness and the differences of being in a holy state-not a holier-than-thou-state-rather than this carnal state.

Sam said, "Brother, Tina and I can't wait to be there! I always enjoy hearing about the Lord, and although I've never had the honor of hearing you preach, I can't wait to see the play once more and hear you teach the word of God!"

"Brother Tiny, we have a room ready for you. You'll be our honored guest tonight," Tina said.

"Thank you, Tina. I'm very grateful. Tiny would never get used to folks treating him with such love and respect. It was still so new and he had no idea how to accept it. He lowered his head and blushed a bit . . . and he remembered what life was like before he gave his heart to God.

"I'm overwhelmed by the love in this home."

"Well, before we do anything else, Tina has prepared a wonderful supper for us," Sam said. We both hope you like it, we made it. in honor and loving memory of Sister Granny, Tina has cooked up a special batch of *Chatalga Stew*.. We know that nobody could make it like Granny, but I helped and we did the best we could!

"Thank you again my brother and sister in Christ. *Chatalga Stew!* What a most certain, special surprise! I hope indeed that you fixed plenty! It is one of my very favorite special meals that I enjoy greatly!

After this I will engage in my nightly devotions and then get ready for bed," Tiny added. "By the way, tomorrow I have a stop to make on the way. I promised an old friend that I would pick him up early. His name is Brother Tom Aglar.

"You're right, we all need to get our rest. It's a couple of hours drive to Chattanooga, so we'll have to get up about six a.m.," Sam said. His heart was filled with a deep sense of God's glory and a touch of foreboding.

Chapter 7

Crazy Tom's

Narrator: Unknown ...thought to be the mother of Carla...
Where: We feel the narrator of this chapter knows where this occurs, but
all we know is, there is mention of a sandwich shoppe.
Four months BCR

Crazy Tom's Sandwich Shop was always abuzz with activity. It's central location, albeit a side street in the city, made it a favorite stop for workers in the downtown area. Today, Tom was on alert.

"Man, I wouldn't miss the play for anything in the world," he said to one of his patrons.

"Will you have to close the shop?" asked a man with a neat haircut tucked under a baseball hat.

"No need to close up. I've got it covered. Carla said she'd cover for me, didn't you, Carla?" Tom added. The small restaurant owner had far more going for him than just making sandwiches for hungry patrons on this day; and Carla would prove to be a tremendous asset.

"Yeah, you go ahead with your plans! I don't have anything to do anyway," Carla responded, then lapsed into her usual ruminations about her work. It didn't matter if anyone heard her speak as long as she could vent now and then.

"One sandwich, then another, then another. I've done it nearly everyday for about a year, so why would I mind now?"

"You're an angel!" Tom said as he prepared to head out the door.

"I know, I know! Now you and "Mr. Summers" go ahead and you can tell me all about the play when you get back," she added.

She wanted to go with them, but she knew everything had to look normal. Nothing could look out of the ordinary . . . like the restaurant being closed for no good reason. Christians had known for some time that the government was watching them, to see if they might be subversives . . . some of those religious wackos.

"Tom, do you want to take your car or mine?" asked the man in the baseball cap, as they were walking towards the parking lot.

This was a man who for some time had tried his best to travel incognito . . . a man known as "Mr. Summers," for all practical purposes. Most Christians, who knew him, knew him as Brother Tiny.

Inside the restaurant, the telephone rang again. Carla could handle the pressures of her job, but the constant ringing of the phone unnerved her more than usual.

"I can't answer this phone every time it rings and keep up with all the other things I have to do. I've only got two hands and one brain." Carla grumbled aloud. It was going to be another great and crazy day at Crazy Tom's Sandwich Shop. The sarcasm defiled her thoughts.

"Hello? I mean . . . it's a crazy day for a sandwich at Crazy Tom's! What kind, what do you want on it, and how many do you want?"

"Is this Carla Aglar?" the caller snarled.

"Absolutely! How you want your sandwich?"

"No sandwich today, Carla, just some lifesaving advice." he mused.

"O.K., so you're serving up **a plateful of funny** today, huh?" she asked, snapping her question.

"'No, Carla, I'm afraid I'm serious. My name is Mr. Scontee. I'm with the Internal Security Department. I'm sure you've heard of the ISD, haven't you, Carla?" he asked.

"Oh, I'm sorry sir . . . yeah . . . I mean, yes sir, I've heard of you," Carla said as she started to shake with fear.

"Well Carla, it seems we have a little problem. You see the ISD. has recently discovered that your boss, Mr. Edwars, is participating in illegal activities-very serious ones I might add."

"I'm sorry, but . . . but . . . uh . . . why do you want to . . . uh . . . talk to me?" Carla stuttered.

"Because, Carla, we need to know where he's going."

"Where who's going? You mean, Tom? That I don't know," she replied, hoping she'd convinced him and he'd leave her alone.

"Carla, you do know about Rule Six, New Government Annotated, don't you? We have the authority to use any and all force needed-or that we wish to use-to get any information we deem necessary for the security of this country, the world, or this administration," Scontee said. "I'm five seconds from deciding to pay you a visit to enforce those powers. Five, four, three,"

"Hold it, hold it! Wait a minute!

I'm looking for the address! I know he left it here somewhere!" she screamed into the phone.

"Two . . . .one. . . times up, Carla . . . but being a nice man, I'll give you one more second!"

"Wait! I found it! I found it!" she cried, her heart pounding.

"Where's he going, Carla?"

"Okay, he's going to 512 Substation Road South, in Chattanooga, Tennessee!"

"Thank you Carla! You've been a real angel," he said, laughing at her.

"I wish people would quit calling me an angel. It's starting to give me a bad feeling about my future." She tried unsuccessfully to joke with Scontee. "Hey, you sure you don't want a sandwich, Sir?

Scontee didn't respond. All Carla heard was a loud click as he hung up the phone. She wasn't happy about the call to begin with, especially the way he frightened her. Hanging up on her was the last straw.

"He hung up on me! At least he could have had the decency to just say no, like everybody else!" she said aloud while trying to regain her composure. Then it dawned on her what had happened.

"Oh no, what have I done?" She suddenly screamed to herself.

What she had done was reflected in a conversation between Scontee and one of his underlings.

"Whadya want, Boss?" a rough, ragged looking man wearing a nice suit asked, looking stupid as he spoke. It was his normal look whether he spoke or didn't speak

"Go to Crazy Tom's Sandwich Shop. Here's the address," Scontee replied, handing him a piece of paper with the appropriate information. "When you get there, flip your badge at this Carla person. **Then do the world a favor and slice her throat, like she slices the rotten meat she puts on those sandwiches she makes**.

Drain her blood on everything that looks like a sandwich or anything that could be used to make a sandwich!

The thought of torturing Carla was actually pleasant to the man whose mind was numb intellect and numb of love and who worshiped evil. His stupidity made him easy prey for those whose hearts were filled with malice . . . and now he had the pleasure of doing its bidding.

"When I called that miserable excuse for a sandwich shop, I told her I'd give her an extra second to answer the question I asked her, but I've changed my mind!" Scontee added, a touch of evil radiating from his eyes.

"It'll be my pleasure, Boss!"

"And the next time you call me Boss, cut your own throat! That's an order!"

"Y . . . Y . . . Yes, bo . . . I mean, yes Sir! I'm on my way, Sir!" His crossed eyes almost bulged inside out from fear.

Chapter 8

Mr. Lands' House

Narrator: Thought to be the same as in the previous chapter
Where: Somewhere in Chattanooga, Tennessee
When: Thought to be sometime between two and a half and five months BCR

"We made good time getting to this house. We should have plenty of time setting up for the play, don't you think, Tiny?" Tom asked.

Tiny was a bit lost in some thoughts, but he responded with a flurry of words. "Everything is fantastic! This should be one of the best showings of the play! Thank God for brave Christian men like Mr. Lands who will take chances and allow the performance of *Martyrs of the Cross* in his home . . . and at great risk to himself and his family!"

"I agree with you completely, Tiny. Do you remember the house number we're looking for?" Tom asked.

"Yes, 512."

"Here we are at 520 . . . 518 . . . 516 . . . 514."

"Wait! I think this is it! Yep, no cars and it looks like nobody's home!" Tiny eagerly said.

"I would say we're here!" Tom said in agreement.

"Now, we have to circle around so we can find a way to park and not draw suspicion about what's going on here. There! That cul-de-sac right there will work," Tiny said.

"Yes, I think so. There's only one house and one car. We should be able to do this and not look too suspicious! If I'm right, the house was just over that little rise on the other side of that tree!" Tom added.

"Sounds about right to me! What do you say we go find out?" Tiny asked.

"I'm with you!" Tom almost couldn't contain his excitement.

They knocked on the door, their tapping a code . . . they knocked to the tune of *When the Saints Go Marching In.* A Southern "good ol boy" type older gentleman answered the door.

"Good to see you boys! Glad you remembered the secret knock. Come in, quickly!"

The two men entered the house and were amazed at the number of people who were there. It took Tiny and Tom a few seconds to catch their breath.

"Wow! Look at all these people! Are they all here to help with the play?" Tom asked.

"Yessiree, Bub! Ya'll come over here! There's a coupla fine fellas I want y'all to meet, if you haven't met 'em already!" Mr. Lands said, half-laughing "All right now, Brother Tiny and Brother Tom have both got such testimonies, I have to just tell y'all about 'em! Wait a minute! What am I doin'? They're here, so I'll just let 'em tell it all by themselves!"

Tiny said, "Thank you, brother Lands! It's so good to be in your home to break the Bread of Life with you and all these saints! Let's start with a show of hands! Everybody, raise your hands toward heaven and thank our wonderful God and Savior, Jesus Christ, for allowing us to be here to breathe in all His mighty goodness today!"

The group took a few minutes to pray and offer praises to their Savior. With their heads bowed, they prayed the prayers of those who understood persecution. When the prayers were over, Tiny stepped up to speak again.

"That was awesome! Now, did anyone bring a visitor today?" he asked and then counted the number of raised hands. "Great! I counted at least twenty-five. Oh, and is my brother Carlton Hempter here today?"

The group clapped as Carlton Hempter went forward to shake hands with Tiny.

Tiny continued speaking. "This is what we're so encouraged to see, Brother Carlton! People whooping and hollering all over the place about their Savior can't wait to serve their Lord, and participate in this wonderful drama. They came here at great sacrifice or at great risk to either be a participant or a spectator! Either one is fine by me, Praise the

Lord Almighty!"

A round of "Praise the Lord" could be heard throughout the room. Many were grateful to be there to see the play.

"I want each of you to know that if you don't know Jesus Christ as your Lord and personal Savior, it's my prayer that you surrender yourself to Him before the night is through," Tiny said. His heart was overwhelmed that the Lord had placed him in such a serious, yet joyous position. "It is so, so very important that you do! Your entire eternity will be decided on what you sitting there, or you standing there, decide to do today!"

He continued with more truth. "Heaven is more awesome, more wonderful, loving and beautiful than anything you can imagine . . . it's so much more than anything you have here. And, lest you still don't get it, hell is so much hotter than you can imagine, so dark, so lonely! Imagine if you will, boiling some cooking oil to fry a basket of fries. O.K, now, turn up the heat just a little! Now just a little more . . . and a little more! Now, ease up to the oil carefully with your fries. Slowly, put the fries in the boiling oil one or two at a time. Be careful. Be very careful! You can be burned badly! That would hurt for a long time if you were splashed with less than one drop! Uh, oh! Did we have the heat up just a little too high? Did it burn your fries? Well, reach in there and take the fries out so you can start over!"

Folks in the room began to shudder at the thought of placing their hands in boiling hot oil. They cringed as Tiny took a breath before finishing his description of hell.

"What do you mean, am I crazy? Go ahead! Imagine the container is larger. It's large enough to contain your whole body! Wait a minute! Just hold on there! Before you take that dive, you're only at about four-hundred-and twenty-five degrees Fahrenheit. That's not high enough! It will just never do! Let's crank it up a bit . . ."

"How's this? Six hundred degrees! No? How about if we turn it up to eight hundred and fifty degrees? Can you smell the smoldering oil . . . the stench of it is everywhere! Fried potatoes burned to a crisp and disintegrating the very second they touch this caldron of hot oil!'

Folks began to squirm and a few began to cry. That didn't stop

Tiny.

"Now it's getting more like you probably enjoy your oil . .. . now come on now, you know you could really get used to this as soon as you jump in! What did you say? I'm certifiably crazy? Look at this face! Look at it! Does this look like the face of a crazy person? Just a minute, don't answer that just yet, please!"

Everyone started to laugh. A few got the picture . . . others weren't sure what he was up to, but they wanted to hear more.

"How about two more times? Just two more times now . . . come on . . . let's turn up the heat! Oh, but this time, turn it up to full blast! What do you think full blast is? This includes you, reader! What do you think full blast is? Is it two thousand degrees? Is three thousand or four thousand degrees full blast? Try five thousand degrees! Can you imagine being invited to take a swim in that? If it were the dead of winter and a swimming pool a block away from your home was that hot, I assure you, you'd never have a heating bill for heating your home! That's right, jump right on in there! Oh, wait, you're not going to? Gee, I must be crazy for even suggesting this! Maybe you don't believe in this type of nonsensical talk or the picture doesn't work for you. Fine then! Let's crank it up seven times hotter!"

The picture was clearer to those listening. The future for those without salvation was not a pleasant one . . . and Tiny was sure his description would at least make folks think.

"The container has grown. It's as big as the Atlantic Ocean and you're not there by invitation! It's pitch black outside and you don't know where you are. Now, the most terrifying, frightening, powerful, horrible beasts imaginable have grabbed you, and you can't get loose from them! There's no escape! No wrestler has ever been strong enough to get free from just one of them. No complete wrestling team or group could ever outwrestle just one of them. I'm not talking about tag-team style. I'm talking about all of them all at once against just one of these horrible beasts! He'd whip em all, in no time flat!"

Folks in the room began to wince out loud. It was as if they were feeling everything Tiny was describing. Some looked away while others

94

bowed their heads. Still, they listened.

"Even that little three hundred and forty nine pounder running for his life down through that field over there! Okay, you guys pretend with me for a moment there's a field over there and not just Mr. Land's beautifully painted wall!"

Everyone started to laugh, even when they knew there was nothing to laugh at.

"Now back to reality! Does everybody remember how hot the burning oil is? I think it was around five thousand degrees times seven, right? Something like thirty-five thousand degrees and the fries will cook up easily at about four hundred and fifty degrees. Kinda makes you wonder, doesn't it? I mean, how many of you would voluntarily choose such an outcome? Well, the oil is hotter than before and there are more horrible monsters than Hollywood has ever dreamed up. Those ugly creatures are way bigger and far worse than anything I've ever seen. They're worse than all the atrocities I've ever committed in my whole life . . . and now they have you firmly in their grasp. You're not going anywhere they don't want you to go . . . however . . . you'll go exactly where they want you to go!"

A few who were listening could be heard crying. Some had to wipe the tears from faces. A few began fanning themselves as sweat poured from their brows.

"Now you're . . . shall we say used to the idea of this ocean of extremely overheated oil, but you're still stumbling around in the dark. You're terrified and lonely and . . . well . . . those monsters get you out towards the middle of the ocean . . . and you're more terrified than you've ever been in your whole life."

Tiny stopped for a moment to let the truth sink in to each unrepentant heart. He asked each person to picture him or herself in the dark with an ocean of hot oil waiting for each of them. He asked them to imagine that monsters are just waiting to toss them into the hot oil. "Imagine yourself terrified and screaming at the top of your lungs for someone to save you!" Then he yelled at them at the top of his lungs. "Stop screaming! I said stop screaming! It won't do you any good! It

95

just delights the monsters that much more! Nothing on Earth can or will save you now! How do I know? I know because you're no longer on Earth! Nobody can do anything to help you . . . there's no escape! I mean absolutely no . . . no . . . *no* escape! No one cares about you! There's no one to care! It's just you, the awesome heat, the darkness, and those ferocious monsters! Oh yeah, did I forget to tell you, about the oil? No? I didn't think so!"

There was a sudden silence and then Tiny raised his arms as if lifting a person over his head. "In you go! That's right, all of you . . .and you . . . and you, too!" Tiny yelled. Some in the room began to scream at the thought of being thrown into the hideously hot oil

"What are you screaming for? Too late, too late, *too late*! It's just you, the darkness, the super hot oil, the loneliness, the eternal separation from God and memories of chances you've had . . . and a tragic eternity!" Tiny took another deep breath before he continued speaking. His heart was heavy with the picture he'd created.

"Now I asked you a couple of things. One had to do with me being crazy, and the other had to do with me being nuts. Have you figured it out yet? I'm not the one that's crazy here! I'm not the one that's nuts here!"

The room was enveloped in total silence. One could almost hear a pin drop as listeners were forced to face their futures. Tears could be seen gently flowing down Tiny's face.

"Between you, and me, I'm not going to be dealing with that horrible place. I'm not going to be dead . . . and you're not going to be dead no matter which side you choose! Contrary to some popular beliefs, we're going to live forever in either heaven or hell! I'll be living the life of luxury in the presence of the Lord! I know because the King of kings has gone to prepare a place for me, and that where He is, I might be also,' and I'll guarantee you folks, it's definitely not a shabby, shoddy place! It's a place of beautiful, wonderful love and life! Streets of gold so pure they are as crystal glass! Pearls so fine, and so big they make gates of some of them! It won't be hot there, or cold. The weather will always be perfect! There won't be any turmoil, no fear, pain or suffering, for our Lord will 'wipe away every tear.' It's all there . . . . in your Bibles.

Chapter 9
Governmental terrorists

*T*he command was simple. Tiny had no time to waste.

"Everybody here at Mr. Lands' house . . . ***and you also, reader*** . . . pick up your Bibles and read them! It's all there in black and white. ***Go ahead…right now…read your Bible***…I didn't make any of this up and the writers of the Bible didn't either. You say you just don't believe this part or that part? Well, that's really just too bad for you because it's true! It's all true, and what I just told about is in there! In the last chapter of the Book of the Revelation of Jesus Christ, it clearly says, 'woe to the man that taketh away from these words.' If you don't believe it, then you've done just that . . . taken away that part of the Bible . . . taken away from His words."

Tiny was so filled with the Holy Spirit, he almost fell over backwards. He had so much he wanted to tell them. He knew in his heart that he had to tell them that not believing God's Word, in whole or in part, didn't change the fact that it was true and real. It didn't change the fact that God's plan would play out soon, which meant in the very near future.

"I challenge you to choose today before it's too late! By the way, to not choose is to make a choice! This is Satan's world, or haven't you noticed? God has allowed him to rule the world system. Therefore, to not choose is to walk away from the Cross of Calvary, straight to hell. It's choosing to jump into the dark, blisteringly hot lake of fire! You've been told, 'now make you this day . . . your choice!'"

People were shouting and clapping their hands, rejoicing in the Lord, singing "Glory hallelujah, somebody touched me, glory hallelujah, somebody touched me! Must have been the Hand of the Lord . . . ."

"Folks, there's never been a better time to give your life to Jesus! Christians, let's help those who need us to help them get right with God! Let's hold hands in brotherly love and pray for the lost to get their life right with Christ and to help us to spread the Gospel of Christ that they might not go to that awful place someday, but will meet us there in God's Kingdom!"

Several people were already praying and repenting. Tiny knew it was probably the last chance for some. He knew the world was in chaos. One only had to look at the changes that had come about in the United States-the massive loss of God-given freedoms and the government-given freedoms that were a direct attack on everything holy and decent. Many would not live until the Rapture of the Church. He prayed for all unbelievers present to pray the sinners' prayer.

"Pray the sinners' prayer now! For it is assigned once to man to die, but after that, the judgment. People, this is the judgment of those who didn't repent. Christ Himself will judge you if you have not given your heart to him!" he cried as he looked around and saw people still praying. "We'll start the play in just a moment, but let's give everyone a few moments more to pray this eternally important prayer."

(If you happen to be reading this book and you've just given your life to Jesus, take a moment to thank God for saving your soul and changing your life. As soon as possible, tell someone what Christ has done for you! Right now might be the best time. The Bible says that "he who is not ashamed to confess Me before men, I will not be ashamed to confess him before My Father.")

Tiny was finished. It was time for all to see the play. "Thank You Lord for another opportunity to witness "Thank You so much! Now folks, as they say . . . on with the show! Right now I am going to turn this portion of the service over to my fine brother in Christ, Carlton Hempter!" Applause resounded as Carlton Hempter stepped up to the front of the room.

"Thank you so much, one and all, for coming today. I realize the risks involved with being here because as we all know the government is viciously involved in the ultimate destruction of Christianity. Multitudes have been martyred for Christ in this country-more than ever before in our nation's history. We all know that a large part of it started in a small white church not so very far from here!"

Tiny held his head down in shame. Were it not for God, he would be one of "them" instead of a being the Godly man the Lord had helped him become.

"Brother Tiny, please don't feel guilty. If not for you, I would most certainly be dead and in hell awaiting the second death . . . the lake of fire! I was a leader in my church, that little white church, and what many in the church and community considered to be a pretty good guy. I was willing to help anyone I could, but nothing I did mattered. It was as a 'filthy rag to the Lord' without His precious blood of atonement for my sins. Sure, I was active in the church and community, but I never made that move! Very few people knew it! I didn't really talk about it. People just assumed I was saved because of my deeds. Regardless of what I'd heard or read, I never made the move. Yes, I prayed. I just never prayed the sinners' prayer."

Carlton Hempter's words were a surprise to some, but those who knew him well were not surprised. There were many churches that were filled to overflowing every Sunday . . . and many so-called worshipers filled those pews who didn't know the Lord.

"I didn't pray the sinners' prayer because I believed in God and had no trouble with regular praying. But I never confessed my belief in Jesus Christ as the one and only intercessor between man and God, the Righteous One who took my sins on His shoulders. He shed His perfect blood on Calvary's Mount for the redemption of mankind's sins. He bought each of us with a price when He shed His blood and laid down His life for all humanity. We only had to ask His forgiveness."

Again, silence filled the room. It was a strange silence . . . the kind that comes when hearts turn toward God.

"But, He didn't stay physically dead! During those first three days, His spirit went down into hell so I wouldn't have to, if I only would believe in Him and ask for forgiveness for my sins. He went to hell and preached to Satan and his angels. They didn't have any choice but to listen. He then captured the keys to death, hell, and the grave, and He took away the sting of death! Remember the song that goes something like, 'Grave, where is thy victory, and death where is thy sting?' He then went to a place that was called Paradise and retrieved all the souls of people waiting there for Him. He rose physically from the dead of His own free will on the third day, as proof that He was God's only begotten Son. He brought those souls with Him that had been in Paradise and later ascended in the air to be with God the Father. We are His witnesses!"

Words were not slow in coming for those called by the Lord to preach. Carlton Hempter was among those called for His purposes. "You know, dear friends, Christ predicted all these things would take place. The ones relevant to that time period happened just like He said they would! All of them did; and the rest have all been coming true. If you know the Bible . . .. then you know there's more that will come to pass as it was predicted. We know the materials are in place for the building of The Third Temple in Jerusalem!"

A chorus of praises to the Lord resounded through the room.

"We know there are several red heifers. One will be sacrificed to the antichrist. Three and a half years into the Tribulation, He will defile the temple when he sits on the throne and declares himself to be God! This will mark the beginning of the second half of the tribulation called the Great Tribulation. There will be many martyrs for Christ in those days. In fact there will be millions and millions who will be martyred! If you think things are rough now, just wait! Those who don't give their lives and their souls to the Lord before He comes again to meet us in the air will have to endure seven years of horror. The ones who give their lives to the Lord after the Rapture will have to endure untold hardships, because they will be the ones who do not fall for the great lie!"

Carlton had so much material to cover. He knew the Lord had prepared him for this moment.

"Most likely, those saved during the Tribulation will either hear the preaching of the two witnesses in Jerusalem or the witness of one of the one hundred and forty four thousand Jewish preachers-the ones sealed by the Lord to be His witnesses during the Tribulation. The Lord will seal those Jews with the truth, and they will spread the Gospels around the world. They will tell the people of the world to not believe in the antichrist and warn them not to take his mark! People who listen, take heed, and give their lives and souls to the Lord at this time will have to endure untold hardships, because they will refuse to receive the Mark of the Beast. They will not be able to buy or sell. They'll also be hunted down like wild dogs and forced to take his mark or be beheaded! Things are tough now. I mean they are really, really tough. No one can dispute that for the Christian, things are extremely tough. What I want you to realize though, is that things are the good life now, compared to what they will be then! Please, please take heed!"

He almost begged them to take his words seriously. "If there's anyone else here who has not given his or her life and soul to the Lord, please, please do so right this very minute! Don't wait another second! Tick . . . tock . . . tick . . . tock. Every tick and every tock could be your very last! Okay! If at anytime during this play or afterwards you decide to submit to Christ, please do so. Either by praying where you are, or come to one of us Christians and we will be glad to pray with you! Oh, and remember, folks, this play is not for real! It's only a play and anything you see after I tell you the play is beginning is not real. It's only a play and only for dramatization! Thank you folks. The play is beginning now!"

Two men who were sitting up front rose from their seats. They were dressed in garments similar to those worn by the Jews in the days after the crucifixion and resurrection of Christ. According to the Scriptures, Stephen, a Jewish man, was the first martyr for our Lord.

Mark Smitford, played the part of Stephen and came down the aisle next. They played out their roles . . . to the part when Stephen was stoned to death. Then they played out a new twist in the story that hadn't been part of the play at the little white church. They elaborated more on Saul becoming Paul, about God blinding him, his conversion and how he started preaching to the Gentiles. The audience echoed a "thank God for that"! How wonderfully God used that great man of God in his death for the advancement of Christianity among the Gentiles!

They were showing God's infinite wisdom-how He used martyrs for Christ so their very act of sacrifice was not in vain! The improvisational format of the play always kept it fresh and different. It was such a blessing for those who had seen it before. And, in order to help with the historical aspect of the play, they added another period when Christians were murdered for their faith. Those very real people are resting in Christ right now!

For the next part of the play, the scene switches to the very real act of *governmental terrorism* that inspired the great spread of it more than anything else, the massacre at the little white church while presenting the play ***Martyrs of the Cross***

Brother Jacks went forward pretending to be the pastor. With Pastor Janus gone to be with the Lord, someone had to take his place in the play.

"Everyone, we've decided to stop the play! Instead, we're going to go

101

back to preaching the Word because the government has told us we can't do this play anymore! Everybody turn with me in your Bibles to Matthew 7:28 and let's begin reading.

Just then, every head in the building turned as Andy Jones and Frank Fripps went forward dressed in very nice suits. "Wait a minute, pastor, haven't we had a talk about this?" Andy asked. Didn't I tell you not to meet in this type of assembly again? There were to be no more unlawful church-type assemblies again!" Frank railed.

Brother Jacks answered, "Well, yes sir, you did, but all we are doing is putting on a little play. What harm can come from that?"

"It's unlawful! That's what's wrong with it! You've broken the law and for that you must die! Frank screamed.

Andy pulled a toy knife from his belt and pretended to stab brother Jacks! Right after that, Mrs. Talbrey started playing "Nearer to Thee, Dear Lord!" Two young teenage girls came in and pretended to take Brother Jacks to Heaven to receive his martyrs' white robe, washed in the blood of the Lamb!

As they crowned him, another scene was beginning. It was the scene of the storeowner witnessing to a customer. A young man came in demanding money and the cross the storeowner was wearing around his neck. The storeowner told the young robber that he would gladly give him the money *and* the necklace with the cross on it. The store owner told him about the saving grace of Jesus, about Him dying on the cross for the young man's sins, and for everybody's sins if they would only believe in Him.

The young man seemed rebellious at first, but changed his mind. He told the shopkeeper he didn't believe that way. He then pretended to shoot the storeowner.

Mrs. Talbrey then began to play the piano again as the young teen-age girls came like angels to take the shop owner to Heaven to receive his Martyrs' white Robe. Next, Sister Sompras came to the front of the room. She and another lady, Sister Bakewell, were sitting in chairs talking about their work as missionaries when Pete Clark and Bill Freemont pretended to break in and kidnap the two ladies. They pretended to torture them, asking if they were really Christians, every so often. The ladies kept saying yes until

Pete said he was going to kill them. Right then, Sister Bakewell changed her mind about being a Christian! She stood right there and denied Christ! Pete and Bill let Sister Bakewell go free but pretended to kill Sister Sompras! Mrs. Talbray began to play again as the two young teen-age girls led Sister Sompras to "Heaven!

Brother Tiny came forward and declared, "There is nothing pretty about being a martyr for Christ! There is much suffering and much pain that goes with it, not to mention the worry, imprisonment, and fear! Not to worry, though! The Lord is with you always and the cause is mighty and worthy!"

~

Just then, very loud booming sounds could be heard coming from several directions. Military dressed men and other men dressed in very nice suits came barging in from almost everywhere! The place where Tiny had pretended there was a hole in the wall now had a real hole in the wall!

"Hit the floor you scum!" one of the nicely suited men screamed. "Hit it now and hit it hard!"

Guns and knives were drawn on everybody! The military people were wielding guns, rifles, and shotguns, and the nicely suited men were waving knives around. Then, an official-looking, nicely suited man strolled in like he was right at home. He was swinging one arm and holding his other hand wide open behind his back, like he was about to smack somebody.

He eased over to the TV and turned it on. As he was changing channels like he just couldn't find the station he wanted, another nicely suited man came up to him and whispered something in his ear that seemed to please him greatly.

"I'm so happy today! I am so pleased to announce to you all that today is such a very special day for me! Before I came here I wasn't so happy, but now my mood has changed! My esteemed associate has just given me some incredible news! It seems there was-and I do mean to emphasize the word "was"-a person who *was* not much different from most of you who chose to lie to me and deceive me deliberately!"

The man shuffled his feet a bit as he took a few steps forward. Then he said, "She's not deceiving anybody right now and will never deceive anyone ever again! She's . . . let me think of a nice way to put this . . . oh yes .

. . she was very brutally tortured and killed!"

He shuffled closer to some in the room. "Her name?" he asked. "Does anybody here know a young lady by the name of Carla Aglar?"

Mr. Summers screamed. He was in shock and heartbroken with immediate grief.

"Well then, so much for the overly polite niceties and the reasons for my little visit!"

The official-looking, nicely suited man swiftly swung his arm from behind his back. This time it didn't appear empty. Instead, there was a gun in his hand! He aimed and shot once . . . and it was all over for Mr. Lands! He never knew what hit him; he just fell to the floor with a loud thud.

"You'd have thought he had a bull's eye drawn on his head with the little crease between his eyes as the center mark!

Before the sound of the gun being shot reached his ears, Mr. Lands was on his way to the loving arms of Jesus. Short journey, between here and there...if you know what I mean!!

"Now that you all see that I, and I alone, have all power over life and death, I want to talk! We all have so much to talk about! Who wants to talk to me? Huh? Nobody? Yes, I'm sure somebody wants to talk to me! I know because I'm in such a good mood! Look, see me smile? I can smile from ear to ear! Do you know why I can smile from ear to ear? Because I have this great big smile cut right across my mouth!"

He pointed to the huge scar on his face. "See this huge scar? It goes across from ear to ear so I smile all the time! When I'm happy, and when I'm not so happy, I just keep right on smiling!

Everybody was lying perfectly still on the floor. No one dared to budge even a fraction of an inch.

"Nobody is answering me! I guess I'll have to just tell everybody why I'm so

happy ...it's because . . ."

He yanked one of the young teen-age girls straight up off the floor by her long brunette hair. "I'm happy because . . . are you saved little girl? Do you know Jesus Christ as your Lord and personal Savior?"

The girl was sobbing violently and pleading, "Please don't hurt me, please don't hurt me!"

The nicely suited man put a long knife to the young girl's throat, smiled and asked her the question again. "I just asked you a question, a very good question! Are . . . you . . . a . . . Christian?

Just then Pete Clark jumped up and lunged forward. He was trying with all his might to get to the young girl. As he ran a couple of steps, he screamed, "Don't hurt my daughter! No! No! You can't, you can't hurt my daughter!"

Just then, the shots from a gun were heard. Brother Danny! The man who used to be Sister Brenda's husband before he had her beheaded, shot Pete Clark dead in his tracks! His body slumped loudly to the floor and he was gone . . . he could no longer protect anybody, nor could his body express love or kindness anymore! He would not hug or kiss his daughter again, he would not go to work the next day! No, it was all over on Earth for Pete Clark's Earthly life! In that very instant, he was with the Lord! He was now witnessing the awe and spectacle of the Holy Hereafter!

"Young lady, look what you made us do!" the man in the nice suit said instilling more fear in the young girl. She was screaming to the top of her lungs, as were most everyone there! "Just for that, I'm going to show you what I was going to do! Now answer me! Are . . . you . . . a . . . Christian?"

The young girl sobbed as she answered. **"Yes! Yes! Yes!"**

"Okay, then!" The nicely suited man had drawn his arm back, then forward. The crack and thud was deafening as he stabbed the young girl right through the head, temple to temple, with the long stiletto! The young girl became deathly silent . .. . except for the sound of the nicely suited man holding her for a moment then allowing her body to slam to the floor!

Everyone was stone cold silent . . . like the silence of death!

"I'm sorry people, but I asked her a question, and I only ask once! Oh, I would have killed her anyway, but now at least I can feel right justified! I mean, I did give her a chance, now didn't I? I don't hear any answers coming my way!"

He snickered at the people as he looked around. Most of the people were trembling like dead leaves in August-a time when a gust of wind blows them off the trees.

"Change of subject. Well, sort of. I'll tell you what, let's watch a DVD!"

The nicely suited man slid a disk into the DVD, player. However, it was no ordinary movie. The military dressed people and the other nicely suited men seemed anxious and nervous, as if they are expecting something good, but something very active, just the same.

The movie started outside a little white church. It showed the church being surrounded by most of the people who had "invaded" Mr. Land's house.

"Watch closely, I don't want you to miss a thing!"

The movie showed those people storming into the church and methodically brutalizing, torturing, and butchering the people inside. The people were being massacred. They screamed as all the military dressed men and the nicely suited men massacred them! The nicely suited men, including . . . Tiny! He was one of the nicely suited men at the little white church that day!

The nicely suited man stopped the DVD at an awful place. He stopped it just as Tiny was gouging out the insides of one of the church people. Who it was caused everyone watching to shudder. Tiny was gouging out the insides of Big Fred Handley! Big Fred didn't stand a chance against . . . against . . . Tiny! Even in a fair fight without weapons he wouldn't stand a chance! The huge guy was just too much for anybody there!

Most of the intruders were smiling and massacring-just having themselves a good time greatly enjoying what they were doing! Tiny wasn't smiling.

The nicely suited man backed up the DVD. "Oh, did you see this part closer to the start of the movie?" Yes, ah, this is it, the part where I am arguing with that preacher man. I think his name was Janus or something like that! I'm going to forward it just a bit. Oh, see this part? This is where the preacher gets his throat cut! Beautiful! I really, really love that part!"

The nicely suited man was ecstatic. He was so gleeful! But that was not the case for those who came to see the play. They were so quiet you could almost hear the elements in the air.

"Oh, let me forward it to where we left off! Here we are! And there's Mr. Fabulous himself! Our very own . . . your very own, Tiny . . . as you call him! He has just killed that man, that big guy, and there's a young teenage boy talking with him as he is about to send him out of this world! They keep talking . . . they keep talking . . . they are still talking!"

"Now, Mr. Tiny was falling. He fell to his knees. What was Mr. Tiny doing? Nobody wants to answer me? Mr. Tiny was praying. He was doing that stupid thing you idiots do! He was praying! Now he must have thought he really did something, because . . . watch this! See that? He jumped up and killed three of my finest men! He threw weapons to the other people, and he got those weapons from my men and the soldiers he needlessly murdered!

"Now look at this fight! We didn't stand a chance! We were outnumbered three to one! Your "Christians "kept shooting at us! I lost a lot of really fine men that day!"

The nicely suited man looked sad for a moment.

'"Now let me forward it just a "Tiny" bit more, yes, pun intended! Okay, here we are!

Let's watch this part! I wouldn't let you see this but trust me, you're not going to remember it anyway after tonight! This is it!"

"Tiny caught me off guard! I was his boss . . . I mean his superior! There he is! He slammed me from behind and tried to cut my throat! I was just about to elbow him in the ribs and turn around and kill him with my bare hands, man to man, but when I moved, he cut me across my mouth . . . and now I have this really big smile!"

He paused from his rage for a moment. His anger was growing with every word he uttered . . . especially toward Tiny.

"There I am! I fell helplessly to the floor! That's probably what "saved" me. Oh, pardon this pun! Tiny and the rest of those Christians that were left alive probably thought I was dead! The rest is history, but let me fill you in on a few of the details! For the last six months since what you people illegally did to us at that church, we've been eliminating you! You are the resistor elements that operate all around the country. You're getting slicker at this, though! You know you're wrong to go against what *we* believe is right! To each his own, live and let live! Life is too short to intrude on another person's rights, and if you don't believe it, we'll just kill you!"

Another pause and then he started ranting again. This time, he revealed his identity.

"Oh, by the way, my name is Mr. Scontee. Since the incident at the little church-and the ones subsequent to that-I've believed it was my honor and privilege to introduce myself just before I turn the floor over to my esteemed colleagues. Well, I've introduced myself, but I do have one more request. I want Tiny to please come up here! I know you're here and I have a little present for you, you traitor!"

"Would it be me you're looking for, you little weasel? Tiny teased!

He was hidden behind a large drapery panel. Five of the military dressed men grabbed Tiny and pushed, shoved, choked, and kicked him all the way forward until they got him right in front of Mr. Scontee. Mr. Scontee seemed to shutter just a bit, as they firmly held Tiny, his chest almost hitting Mr. Scontee.

"Hiding again, huh, Tiny?"

"Oh yeah, you think I would ever hide from a hideous face like yours? Well, I might. It's so dangerously ugly!"

This seemed to us so to be so out of character for our beloved brother!

"Tiny, Tiny! I have so much vengeance to vent, and to think, I owe it mostly to you!"

"Scontee, you don't owe me a thing! You were who you were long, long before I ever met you! You've always been mean, and you have the right job with the right position for your personality and disposition!"

"Tiny, I have just one thing to ask you before I kill you."

"What's that, Scontee?"

"Why didn't you come out when I was offing the girl and that weasel, her daddy?"

"I wanted to, but I thought you probably didn't know I was here. Chances were, you wouldn't kill anybody if you didn't know I was here! I guess I'd forgotten how cruel you really are. After all, you did effectively brainwash all these men and even me into doing your cruel assignments and those of the government!"

"I'm not cruel, I'm a patriot!" Scontee screamed.

"Now, Scontee, I have just one thing to ask *you*," Tiny responded.

"Okay, okay! I'll break the rules one time. Hey, I can do that! I made the rules! I can break them if I want to! What's your question, Tiny?"

"Scontee, have you given your heart and soul to the Lord and Savior, Jesus Christ?"

All the military dressed men and nicely suited men all bellowed out laughing! When Scontee finally quit laughing, he motioned for everyone to settle down a bit.

"Now, Tiny, that was a great last question to ask me! I will answer your final question honestly, something I very rarely do . . . especially as a political type in this new environment and age that we now live in! *No! I have not given nor will I for the rest of my life give anything to your God or Savior or whoever you idiots think He is!*

"I'm sorry for that, Scontee. I truly, truly am sorry for that!"

"Don't be, loser!" Scontee sneered

Then he gave a look to his men and everybody in the house knew what that meant! Tiny's years, days, hours, minutes, even seconds on Earth were to stop . . . right here, right now!

"Kill him now . . . the coldness of death must enter his body . ... permanently!"

Who were they trying to kid? That was a joke . . . to think they had the capacity or manpower to draw Tiny's life from his body! Big Tiny dropped to the floor alright, but not because of their murderous designs. This now was his stage, the thing he had previously given his entire life to perfect! Before he reached the floor, he already had in motion a three-hundred-and sixty degree leg sweep, stretching as far as it would reach, instantaneously bringing down everybody anywhere close to him! His moves were so quick, so swift . . . you'd think he never had to make the move from vertical to horizontal at all! Men started falling and rolling like tumbleweeds! This man hit that man and that man hit this man! Tiny was using Ju Jitsu, and combinations of Aikido to make the men fly through the air as if they were weightless! Oddly enough, they never hit a Christian. There was pinpoint accuracy as those people slammed into each other! Bodies crashed everywhere! All of them were trying to find Tiny but they couldn't until *he* found them! He was like the eye of a hurricane! His moves were cold, practiced, and calculated!

Guns went off! Yes they did indeed go off, but only accidentally-like when a man was hit mid air as he was flying through the air and collided with another! All of a sudden, they both found gravity and slammed down on the floor! They were out cold! There must have been fifteen to twenty men flying through the air at any given time. In fact, all air traffic controllers must have been on strike because there were mid-air collisions all over the house and even in the yard. How it could have moved into the yard I will never know . . . I will just never know!

It was unbelievable! Tiny did some kind of crazy looking belly flop roll-over-roll with one man, that slingshot his body weight like a missile! He was going so fast that he snapped his head so hard when he hit the banister, his head was just limply hanging like a chicken that just had it's neck wrung!

Tiny was trained in at least ten forms of martial arts including karate, judo, boxing, and Kung Fu. This was awesome enough, but how did he use them all at once? There is only one way I know of! God must have sent the spirit of Samson to help Tiny. There never has been a man as powerful or as unconquerable as Samson. I don't know if Samson could have done a better job at destroying this enemy than Tiny did. If he could have done a better job, it wouldn't have been by very much. I truly believe this, because surely God was with Tiny that day!

Chapter 10

Great Day in the Morning ...AKA G.D.M.

Narrator: author
location: not revealed
Three Months BCR

"***J****esus* Christ will get them for this!" G.D.M. Turnkey shouted

"Oh yes He will! He is no respecter of persons and His judgment is sure and swift!" It was unbelievable, almost incredible to see him all fired up like this! Oh, he often times was seen getting "worked up", but not like this. He didn't totally lose it though, and he came back to the same strong, wonderful charismatic extremely likable preacher and person that he was!

"There are walking dead people all around us, oh yes there are! Folks, you'd better wake up from the dead! Christ is alive and well, and He doesn't expect us to be dead either!"

"The blessed Spirit within us is alive, hallelujah... hallelujah!"

"These people walking around us with their spirit so dead that you can just feel the death as you get near them!"

He paused and for a moment, and things got deathly silent as the congregation was pondering on the things he said.

"A walking dead spirit is one that has no life! Life is animate! Life is ...*moving*! Some people's spirits are just sleeping. Even in sleep, there is some movement!"

"Is your spirit sleeping, needing to be jostled . . . needing to be prodded . . . needing to be shook up a little bit, so it will wake up and show life . . . show that it isn't dead?

Do you remember that old saying, "Wanted . . . Dead or Alive"? Well, if your spirit is dead . . . it needs a resurrection, and if it's asleep .

111

. . it needs to be all shook up! If it is on "mosey", just barely shuffling around . . . it needs all shook up!"

As G.D.M. preached, he was extremely excited! He couldn't be still! The excitement of God's spirit was on him so thick that you could almost see it! This was the anointing that brother Turnkey wanted everyone to feel. He was twisting around and shouting hallelujahs and praises to his King. He hoped he would be heard and felt for miles around. "Let's be alive for Jesus! Let's praise His Holy name and be strong in Him! He loves us, and that ain't no little thing to be light about! That's a heavy thing! God loves me! Everybody shout it! *God loves me*! God's spirit seemed to radiate from him!"

"Great day in the Morning, we will have a great and wonderful day, God's Children, in the morning! Somebody shout it! Shout it so everybody can hear it! Come on brothers and sisters! Let me hear you now!"

Maybe reader . . . you should turn your head if you don't believe in the charismatic feeling that God instills in those who accept it, because I'm about to tell what happened just about then . . . and believe me, it was *very* charismatic! (By the way, don't you find it strange that in times of great need for God, we often open the door to the room in which we've had Him "locked" away? Then we finally allow Him to blanket us again in His warmth and love, and we can even feel Him as our spirits cry out and bubble forth with the Holy Spirit!)

Well, they all knew what the preacher wanted to hear. This was his coined phrase, his identification, and his passion; and they all shouted, "Great day in the Morning, we'll have a Great Day in the Morning!"

G.D.M. was attached to that phrase. He didn't even know when it all started. He just felt what he called "goose bumps and Holy Tingles" every time he said it or heard it. Even his initials in his name came from it! Somewhere along the line, people started calling him G.D.M. or "Brother G.D.M." People respected and admired him because they just felt so "tingly" when they were around him!

"Just let me hear it one more time! Hallelujah, praise His sweet Holy name, oh yeah, say it now, "Great Day in the Morning" . . . and shout it like you mean it!

112

"Great . . . Day . . . in-the . . . Morning!" they all shouted.

It was always so wonderful to be with G.D.M. He was always smiling big, always happy. He didn't care about the color of your skin, didn't care if you were a man or a woman, rich or poor, tall or short, attractive in outward appearance or not. He didn't care what you had done in life-whether it was good or bad-or even what you were doing with your life when you were with him. No, he just didn't care. That man loved everybody unconditionally! That man knew how to love his fellow man! He knew the meaning of giving his coat to someone in need! He knew because he had done it . . . many times. He knew the meaning of giving his shoes to someone who needed them because he had done that many times! He knew the meaning of giving someone the very shirt off his back, because he had even done that!

That man was downright amazing in his reflection of our Lord Jesus! He knew the feeling of going hungry so someone less fortunate could eat. And he knew the face of Jesus because he did those things we are commanded by Him to do. G.D.M. didn't do those things out of any selfish motive whatsoever! He did them because it was who he was! God richly blessed him many times over for his genuine nature-which was more Christ like than most folks!

G.D.M. Turnkey liked his last name, too. He believed it was a blessing from God to have such a remarkable last name. For years, he believed it was his responsibility to help the homeless. He knew that when buying a house, the term "turnkey" meant that everything was out of the way in the purchase process. When all was said and done, "turning the key" was the sign that it was a done deal and the home was yours! It seems that God probably allowed him to have the last name of Turnkey to confirm his calling to help the homeless.

And he didn't stop there. He helped the poor keep their electricity turned on, and he organized inner city childcare for the poor so they could go to work. He helped people to get the assistance they needed and inspired them that God would help them if they would trust Him and do their part as well. God blessed him to be able to help and love them and gave him the ability to inspire the down trodden to help themselves and even others, as they got "on their feet." He was spiritually blessed in ways that you and I can't imagine. We can't even start to fathom the depth of closeness this man had to God and his fellow humans! I mean, his flock was one happy group of people. Wouldn't you be if you had a pastor like Brother Turnkey? No? You really wouldn't? Come on . . . you really would . . . wouldn't you?

It's funny, you know. Not only should we be proud to have a pastor like G.D.M., but we should also pray for the Lord to show us how we can minister to other people in their afflictions. We should minister to them in their poverty . . . in their low self-esteem .. . . in their grief . . . in their poor spirit. We should pray for the wisdom and ability to help those people, for in them we see Christ.

Remember the story of how the person asked to see Jesus. Brother Turnkey also taught on visiting the orphans and widows. He told us that we're commanded to do so in James 1:27. He read from his Bible when he told us that "'Pure religion and undefiled before God the Father is this, to visit the fatherless and widows in their affliction, and to keep himself unspotted from the world.'"

That was a different day, though. Things changed and you would get into trouble for helping people or visiting them in the spirit of brotherly compassion. The general belief of the day was that those people had become a nuisance and an encroachment on society.

Everybody in the congregation of the Brave and the Free/ Everybody Invited Church on the Hill felt they had taken about all they could take. There was talk of revolution and insurrection, the kind that might have, and probably would have, worked in the past-like in the 1960s and 1970s. You know . . . the kind of person-to-person, everyone-is-equal kind of changes that are brought about by great leaders like Abraham Lincoln and a century later, Martin Luther King, Jr.

Those movements have to start somewhere, and they necessitate the need for great internal leadership with a drive, a commitment, and a compassion for equality of individual freedoms for mankind. Oh, not the alleged freedoms that government gives and takes away, gives and takes away. No, those weren't real freedoms. Real freedoms come from God and G.D.M. knew that . . .so much so that most at his church agreed he had a gift for "swelling the spirit" of other Christians and freedom lovers.

G.D.M. wanted to lead, and he thought that with a struggle, he could possibly be of a useful service, at least here . . . if nowhere else. This movement was being attempted, like the earlier one, on untested ground, and there wasn't a leader who had risen to the top yet. This wasn't a racial or ethnic battle, it was a religion and freedoms struggle . . . one that the people at this little predominately black church and others like it was still in its infancy. They wanted the chance to be able to openly rejoice in unison-all Christians of the world, in harmony-and to be able to witness with impunity, like it used to be!

Just for the chance to pass out Christian literature! Just to be able to openly have freedom of religion, to have the opportunity to meet openly, worship together and express that it's the Risen Savior they adore, that all honor and glory should be lavished upon Him! To be able to determine their church's itinerary, its form of worship and witness . . . oh what a blessed relief, oh what blessed freedom! Pastor G.D.M. Turnkey continued to preach . . .

"We just didn't know what we had . . . we just didn't know what we had . . . until we and our fellow brothers and sisters worldwide lost it! We had it all and just didn't see it! We didn't exercise our freedoms to the fullest . . . we didn't use even a fraction of what we should have! There should never have been the drama, *Martyrs of the Cross*! There should never have been the need for such a play! Spooky isn't it? To think that the play was written and produced at various churches and other venues as the truths of the play were unfolding in real time! We just didn't look around . . . in time .. . . and now there's no time, there's no turning back to the way things were yesterday. There's just yesterday . . . and there's tomorrow . . . whatever the will of God brings!

If we could just go back to a new future . . . turn back the hands of time so we go forward into something great . . ." he lamented. "I can't stop wondering why we didn't pay attention. Why didn't we do something? Why did we take it all of our freedoms for granted? It was as if our spirits were sleeping and our freedoms were drudgery instead of blessings from God! How could we allow what He gave us to be taken away so easily by men whose power was nothing compared to Him?"

He preached that there are no guarantees in life but death and taxes. We sure heard that one all the time; but he said there was another guarantee . . . the guarantee of the non-stopping change. There is a guarantee in life that nothing stays the same. It just doesn't!

"No, dear friends, it just didn't stay the same! We should have been alert; you should have awakened well before now. We all should have prayed to be in God's center, to be in the center of His will! We would have found that to be in His center would have been to witness, witness, and witness! We found out too late, that the reason for the play . . . was the meaning of the play, what it was and still is about . . . getting in the center of God . . . the center of His will and letting Him into the center of *our* lives!"

His fervor for the Lord was glowing through him. It showed on his face as a tear or two rolled from his eyes.

"What happened to diligent, fervent, inexhaustible prayer? If you were going to be granted one wish, and one wish only, what would that wish be? The answer is to wish for more wishes! Pray each time as if it's the one and only time you will ever be able to talk to God! What will you say to Him? How much will your heart be in your prayer? Would you ask to know Him better? Would you ask to know Him fully and have Him impart His wisdom to you? Would you ask him to place you in the very center of His being, of His will? You *must* ask Him boldly to reveal what that means so you will know it with all your heart for the rest of your life. Would you ask Him to fulfill you through His strength as He blesses you with the power through Him to do those things He calls you to do? What will you find out?

G.D.M. wiped beads of sweat from his forehead. He raised his hands to heaven for strength to keep going.

"Witness! Through the good times . . . witness. Through the bad times . . . witness! In you actions and deeds . . . witness! In your prayers .

116

. . witness! In your mind and through your mind with full memory of His Holy Word…witness! At work, at school, at play or leisure, at home, at the store, witness in deed, with your life and with words . . . not unspoken . . . but with the holy boldness He will give you. If they pretend to not hear you . . . that's acceptable! If they pretend to turn away . . . that's acceptable!

"Don't harp at them; be direct and to the point with a few loving words that pass through the ears into the minds, hearts and souls of those with whom He puts you in contact. And don't fail to let your life be a witness in whatever fashion He allows it to be at the time. Be willing, in all humbleness, to do what's necessary to take a stand for Christ! Don't be a willow that bends and loses its leaves every time a strong wind blows!"

He stood and stared at us . . . his face aglow with the Holy Spirit. Who could we miss it? We didn't!

"Don't be afraid or ashamed to admit you're a child of God, a joint heir with Jesus Christ! Stand up! Stand up, for Jesus! Put on the whole armor of God! Lead that others might follow, and serve that others might be fed the Word! Form a coalition of prayer warriors who are like minded and of one accord in your quest for God! Stand strong against the wiles and temptations of Satan and of man! Be strong and do not succumb to the intimidation of man! Never be afraid of what man can or will do, but take care to fear what the eternal God can and will do. Man can only take the body, but God can take the unrepentant soul and banish it to the lake of fire and brimstone! Man can only reward or punish during this life, God can reward or punish in this life *and* the next!"

He wanted to shout a chorus of hallelujahs to the heavens! He wanted them to see the heavens part and the Lord smiling down on them. He prayed for wisdom.

"Be faithful to always do your part, and be assured that God is always faithful to do His part according to His divine purpose, His divine plan! Always keep in mind that all things work together for good to them that love the Lord! Be prepared even to give as He did, your heart, your mind and, as He did for you, your life . . . in service to Him . . . or in death . . . in martyrdom for Him! These things He has taught us in his Holy

Word! These things He showed us in His Holy Life! These things He commands of us, giving in all humility, compassion, and bravery . . . as He did!

For those reasons, they considered Christians . . . and among other things, the play . . . to be dangerous! But they didn't and couldn't understand! They wouldn't . . . they shouldn't dare!
The fun they were having . . . like a ball rolling downhill, one major victory, then another and another and another! Soon, two's and three's and more at a time! It was and is all right! All of it is . . . it's our "trial by Fire! We cannot, we must not, and we will not stop!"

There was shouting in that little church on the hill like you never heard before! No one showed fear, no one showed shame, and no one looked funny at someone else for worshipping the way it always should have been . . . happy in the Spirit . . . happy in the presence of the Lord!

What would happen when the ISD (Internal Security Department) found out about this? They didn't seem to mind that eventuality, and they did know it would probably happen sooner than later. I could tell you, and probably should, but this book is not the proper place to go into the rest of that particular story, so be sure to read this book's sequel. I'd be proud and honored to have you join me there!

For now though, please keep reading . . . if you dare. Well, time waits for no man, and there's so much more to learn about what was happening all over the world during those times. Not to say that those things aren't important, because they are; but the escalation of those types of events and far more atrocious ones were gaining momentum exponentially. You'll learn more about what happened soon, but now we need to know of the massive, almost countless numbers of martyr's for Christ who answered bravely to the call of the witness. The Army of Christ! They thought they would annihilate that zealous-(they called them cult-like)-bunch of fanatics, that kept growing in righteous numbers! The world had tumbled into something that had to change. "Oh please God, everything is so crazy, so senseless, so out of balance " was the cry of the day. "Even so, come quickly, Lord Jesus " became the saying and the greeting of God's saved children, and believe me, they meant it!

Chapter 11

Sam and Tina Harks .. . . Missionaries

Narrator: Unknown...thought to be author of this book
location: Place known only as "The Islands"
When: three months BCR

Rat-a tat tat!
Boom . . . Boom
"Incoming!"
Kapow . . . Kapow!
"Everybody, hit the deck!"
"What's going on?"
"Tina, the insurgents!"
"Gotta go! Now!"
"My stuff, my papers, gotta have my things!"
Boom . . . Boom!
"Forget your things! We're going . . . *now!*"
"You're not going anywhere!"

What seemed to be a full squadron of soldier type men rushed into Sam and Tina Harks' tent!

The man spoke with a slight accent, the kind that reminds you of a person who speaks several languages, or one who can't decide which accent to put with which dialect!

"You're American, aren't you?" Sam asked

"Shut up! Take them to the Rovers!" he barked.

The men smacked Sam squarely in the forehead with a healthy

size piece of brittlebus, (the charred remains of what the locals call *Te' ke undanato*), a local tree type tropical bush that holds heat for a very long time without burning up completely. It's sizzling inside but cool to the touch on the outside until the last moments before becoming extremely hard and brittle.

The hit left a long gash on Sam's face. It was bloody and raggedly dirty, the kind you know should be cleaned immediately and medicine put on it. No medicine for Sam though, because now his and Tina's lives were no longer theirs. They now belong to these men, and it didn't look as though it was going to be pleasant! The men grabbed Sam and Tina, tied them up using knots similar to what a rodeo steer- roper would use and " escorted " them to a waiting Rover!

The drivers all spun out trying to get as much distance as possible between themselves and the now burning tents and huts!

"Sam . . . Sammy, what's going on?" Tina whispered as quietly as possible.

She was crying but trying to be as coherent as possible, not an easy task under those circumstances!

"Unhh . . . " Sam said as he was trying to gain some semblance of consciousness. "Shhhh, pray!"

Tina got quiet and through her tears she prayed, "Heavenly Father, Sam and I need You! You know all our needs, but right now we're in special need of your blessing of freedom from fear. And if it be Your will, please release us from this pain and bondage."

She heard Sam praying very quietly. "Lord, we your servants humbly come before You and ask You to keep and preserve us in this hour of our desperate need!"

Sam looked at Tina and whispered "I love you Tina. I want you to know that I always did love you. Even when we were fighting so furiously, you were my beautiful, wonderful everything. I hope everything turns out okay for us., but if it doesn't, I promise I will look for you in Glory. I promise you that!"

Tina continued to cry. She was shaking and sobbing! "I don't want it to end like this! Oh, Lord, I just don't want this to be happening! Something has to stop this! Sam, I love you, too! What's going to happen to us, Sam?"

A burly and extremely ugly man jumped back in the back of the Rover and backhanded Tina with all his might. He had a ring on his hand that had a skull cut into it, and it was perfect for cutting a face when it hit the soft flesh. Tina moaned out in agony as the impact of the hit felt like a sledgehammer and the ring felt like a hurling stone. Blood gushed from her once pretty face.

"No! Please don't hurt me!" Tina begged

"Oh, I just love it when they beg! Don't you worry! Big Dog won't hurt his little lady! I won't hurt you to death, anyway!" he smirked "But I do love to watch the fear and pain on the faces of you imbecile little Christian girlies when your judgment smacks you in the face . . . and that happens to be me!" He laughed uncontrollably.

"Me and you, we got plans! Oh, by the way, who's this other "man "here?" he asked right after squeezing Tina's face so tight in his hand that she thought he was going to crush it.

Tina was crying and shaking so uncontrollably from fear and pain she couldn't catch her breath. She felt like she was having a severe asthma attack! **"P . . . P . . . P . . . Please . . . Please don't! Please doesn't H . . . H . . . H . . . Hurt us?"** Tina kept begging.

"Ugly" smashed her again, this time with his elbow. Tina's face immediately swelled up with what doctors would have described as massive trauma to the cranial-facial area causing major lacerations, contusions and major bruising to the left cheek next to fractured nasal cavity, with the pending various possibilities of aneurysms occurring in the near future. Her prognosis was high for death or severe mental impairment if she survived. In other words, he knocked the living daylights out of that precious young lady for the sheer enjoyment of it!

"You're not much of a protector, knucklehead! " Ugly" then scoffed at Sam. "I know the both of you. You used to live down the street from me and my dogs when we lived near that little white church that got all busted up that day! Didn't any of my dogs ever bite you two? Not gonna answer me, huh? Well, they musta not, cause your blood woulda probly kilt 'em!

By the way, let me introduce myself, I'm the one everybody, especially my friends, call "Big Dog". You may consider yourselves to be my friends, and I'd be honored if you'd just call me "Big Dog" too!

"Hey, knucklehead, you've been with my woman for some time now, I expect you to protect her, and this is what I find? I look at her and she's all beaten up. What kind of a man are you? Oh well, she'll probably clean up okay. I've got a bunch more of these Christian gals, you know? They didn't have anybody to protect them, either! Big Dog takes care of them, though! They make for some great entertainment when my boys and me aren't engaging in camaraderie! You know, we have to have some kind of distraction from the drudgery of whipping you fanatics into shape!"

You would think Sam was dead himself. Bleeding, swollen, his hair dirty and matted up with dried blood. Sam was tied up and unconscious. Or was he? Unconscious he wasn't! You see, these men weren't exactly disciplined military men, and one of them had left his "hardware" in the back of the Rover . . . and it was within hands-reach of Sam.

Sam had never been in the military, either, but he was learning some of the basics of New World survival as he was living it. Miracles do happen, you know, and even though we don't always get the particular miracle we're praying for with the snap of a finger, all things do work together in God's perfect timing!

Sam had been in no position to help either of them, but with the distraction of Big Dog beating Tina and talking garbage to her, Sam had been praying. He didn't just pray a little prayer, he prayed one of those lengthy heart-to-heart-with-God-through-the-Holy-Spirit prayers that one could never experience except in a situation like this! Sam knew that Jesus understood this kind of praying, because it must have been very similar to His own praying in the Garden at Gethsemane!

No man and no woman could have an inkling of what was about to happen-though, for Sam and Tina, it was nothing like what Jesus did some two thousand years earlier. Could they understand that He *knew* He was about to take on the sins of the whole world through His personal sacrifice? Could they understand that he endured horrible torture and an agonizing and grueling death while being unjustly mocked, humiliated, and ridiculed?

Sam knew and acknowledged that Jesus was, and is the Christ, the Messiah, the Savior of all mankind, the Redeemer, and His sacrifice on the cross would provide the once-and-for-all redemption (or purchasing) of men's souls. There would be no further purchase price required or accepted thought history. The only thing any man, woman, boy, or girl would have to do is believe Him, repent, and ask for and accept His forgiveness. You see, without belief, a person will not ask for that forgiveness. And if they don't ask for it, they can't receive it.

His was a horrible personal sacrifice for my sins, Sam and Tina's sins, and the sins of you, dear reader. He died for all the wrong things we did or will do. Satan stole our souls at the moment Adam and Eve ate the fruit from the tree of the knowledge of good and evil in the Garden of Eden. God told Adam and Eve that they could eat all of the fruit except the fruit of the tree of the knowledge of good and evil. He said that if they ate of it, they would surely die.

Satan said they would not surely die, and that they would be like God, Himself. This was Satan's ambition . . . even when he was still in Heaven. He was kicked out of Heaven along with a third of the angels, and when God created Adam and Eve, Satan skillfully used that same sales approach on them.

Oh, sure, Eve was fooled by the devil to eat that fruit; and she convinced Adam to do the same. Eve blamed the serpent, but Adam blamed the serpent and Eve for his own sin. Then he blamed God for giving him the woman in the first place! An eternity of bliss with the Lord was changed at that very moment. Their offspring, you and I, would be born with a sinful and carnal nature from that day forward.

Guess what? When man fell for the same thing that was the downfall of Satan, the same thing happened to him! What Satan did was sin and what man did was sin! Sinful . . . carnal . . . doesn't that sound like we're already in the grip of evil? We've often heard the phrase, "You can sell your soul to the devil." But you can't sell him what he already owns!

God cannot look upon sin, for He is perfect and righteous in all things. This wasn't an emergency plan created by God. He knew, in His foreknowledge that man would sin. It was the planned before the foundations of time that He would redeem us from our sins. Loving us with perfect and pure love, which only He can do, He created an atonement, or covering, with perfect blood. It was the way to make right our sinful selves and provide us with the gift of salvation!

Imagine that atonement could be only through perfection, itself! God had to send His only and uniquely born Son to shed His perfect blood for us in sacrifice. Such a horrible sacrifice for God! What a horrible sacrifice for Christ! What a Love, what a Love! What a wonderful gift to us! Now we're free to accept this gift! Satan cannot bind us or hold us to our deserved future! After this walk of life is over, and to some degree while we're still living it, we can resume where Adam and Eve were before they lost man's souls with that horribly wrong decision!

Believe . . . don't believe. Believe . . . don't believe . . . Believe . . . don't believe!

Eve believed Satan and Adam believed Satan *and* Eve, thus damning men's souls forever. That means your soul! Oh, is it stranger to believe in the miracle of being born twice than to believe in the miracle of being born once? There is death from this life. Is that not a strange and unexplainable occurrence? We don't understand it except as a phenomenon that all things on this Earth, including human beings, experience death.

We don't usually like for it to occur, especially if it's to a fellow human being we love. We see part of what it entails, but we don't grasp what it's all about. When it's a person's time to go, they are going at the appointed time. Again, I say, they are going to go! But where will they go? Well, that's the big question! We can't stop death when it occurs at the appointed time, and we can't understand the phenomenon of the birth thing, except from a very limited perspective. It's a "well, I sort of get it . . . I kind of get it" mindset.

Some biologists think they have a handle on it, to some degree. But do they? They understand (somewhat again) the dynamics of the laws of nature that God has given this universe, such as when certain things occur by Gods laws and with His blessing and power, cells will reproduce. Did man make the cells reproduce? Let's try a resounding *no* to that question! The stage was set, the environment of God made, even though maybe man mixed or somewhat controlled specific elements in order to allow for the cells to enjoy the ability to reproduce themselves. You see, man did not make the first cell, he did not make the second cell or the third or fourth. In fact, man has never made a single cell, nor will he ever be able to make anything from nothing. Only God can do that, and only God will ever understand the miracle of birth, the miracle of life, and the miracle of death! Only God could have arranged for the miracle of the second birth and the miracle of eternal life . . . whether it's in heaven, or on the new Earth, in hell, or in the lake of fire.

There is way too much knowledge for any man-or group of men-to even start to understand one itsy bitsy piece of information about the realities of life, death, and life after death. Folks, my suggestion is to do what the Bible says in John 3:16 and just give it all up and believe in Jesus Christ as your personal Savior. Then just leave the technicalities up to God, because they are all in His able hands, and His alone.

Sam and Tina knew those things were true. They had heard brother Tiny preach on those and many other deep philosophical subjects several times before his death. But this was another reality, one that would certainly send Sam to be with the Lord very soon and Tina into some

125

of the most horrible tortures imaginable. In fact, without God's divine province and intercession, Tina might very well be in the presence of God before Sam! It was completely in God's hands. Was He ready for Sam and or Tina (or maybe both) to die as martyrs for Christ, or did He have other plans for either of them?

Sam had been playing possum, praying, connecting with God in a very quiet way that few men ever enjoy. God had told him to be still and he would receive his answer very soon. When God is ready to make His move, no man, no beast can deter Him from accomplishing what He sets out to do.

Did you ever notice just a bit of how complex God is? When we do something or make a move in a particular direction, isn't it almost always for more than one reason? Really now . . . isn't it? At first you may think of one reason, but then you realize that there's more than one reason that sends you on the path of doing or saying those things. Well, weren't we created in God's image? How much more multi-purposeful is our omnipotent, omnipresent God? He knows all things yesterday, today and tomorrow! If He helped Sam and Tina, what purpose would it serve? We can't begin to see all the things God can see! Sam had prayed, and part of his prayer was that if God chose to save them, they would not be vengeful. Either way, he had prayed that they wanted to be in His perfect will and in His perfect plan!

Sam was still basking in the warmth of prayer with God. He thought their time was very near. Instead of killing Sam at that moment, as Sam though he would, Big Dog leaned forward over the seat and started talking on the radio in the Rover. He told the drivers of the other vehicles to go straight ahead at the next upcoming fork in the road. He said he had personal business to attend to.

The lead vehicles went straight, as did the vehicle behind the one containing Big Dog, Sam, and Tina. However, the Rover veered right a little sharper than anticipated, sending the driver and Big Dog jostling up and down, left and right, and back and forth! It also sent a long knife

126

sailing into the back of Sam's head! No, it didn't send him flying straight out of the Rover and into Glory! It didn't even hit him with the butt of the knife, which might have knocked him out!

God sent Sam that knife in such a miraculous way so he could wriggle a certain way, with almost no difficulty, and grab the knife. While Big Dog and the driver were laughing and still trying to get their composure, Sam cut his ropes, lunged forward over Tina, who was badly hurt and unconscious in the back seat, and butted the driver in the head with the back of the knife.

Driverless Rover coming through!

The driver was sprang from the driver's seat like microwave popcorn! When he was between the here and there, a tree limb positioned at just the right place ...or the wrong place, which depends on if you are the narrator of the story or the driver of the Rover just about to get nailed with the nasty thing, did what it was created by God and divinely put there to do . . . it nailed that idiot! That felt good! I think I'll say it again. It nailed that idiot!

The driver had a face-to-face, not too pleasant talk with God at that very instant! I can just hear it now! **"Uh . . . well uhh . . . well uhhh . . . yes, I was going to hurt Your children, but, but I . . . but I . . . *oh no! What have I done, what have I done?"***

Well, you get the picture, don't you? It goes something like: "So much for that driver! God's judgment is now upon him!

Just as all this was happening to the driver, Big Dog lunged forward as if in sync with the driver's body motion, and took control of the Rover. This put Sam squarely in back of Big Dog, and he took full advantage of it, believing this opportunity to be a miracle from God! Sam had him tightly around the neck with one arm and he had the knife at his carotid artery in his neck with the other. You never heard the likes of Big Dog's whining, begging, and crying in all your life! When it came to his own life, Big Dog was no more than a helpless puppy! He acted like he didn't know the seriousness of what he had done, but he was sure his was

127

an innocent life.

Sam had a lot to think about, and he didn't have much time to do the thinking. What was he going to do with Big Dog? Sam knew he was very dangerous alive, but he figured he was more dangerous dead, because his gang would probably hunt them down and kill them for sure if he killed him.

"Ohhhh!" A pained sound came from the back seat! Sam looked toward Tina for just a moment and saw her stirring just a bit.

"Tina, baby, we're all right, just stay calm, honey. I'll get you medical treatment right after I kill this coward!"

Big Dog screamed like a two-year-old child. He screamed, cried, yelled, and whimpered so much that it would make anyone wonder what that blowhard was really about. It was extremely hard for Tina to talk, because her face was so badly injured, but she managed so get out something like "No Sam, you can't kill him! It's not the Lords way!"

Sam thought about it for a second and quickly decided. He told Big Dog to slow down (slowly) and barely pull over to the right side of the road. Never did anyone obey an order with such swiftness. Big Dog just kept saying, "Yes sir, yes sir, yes sir," as he gingerly pulled off to the right side and eased to a stop. Sam told Big Dog it was probably the first time in his life he ever did anything "right" . . . or maybe "rightwing"!

"Yes sir, yes sir, yes sir, yes sir" That was all he still could say. Sam knew that Big Dog's fear came from something other than the knife he wielded. God's miracle was still very much in play! He also knew Tina needed immediate medical attention. Deep in his heart he believed God would bless his efforts to save the life and preserve the mind of his precious Tina!

"Dog!" Sam commanded! "Where's the nearest place to get medical assistance, extensive medical assistance, the kind you'll need if you lead us into an ambush . . . so think very hard before you answer!"

Big Dog didn't hesitate. He wasn't about to ruffle Sam's feathers any more! He knew someone else had the gameball now, and he thought it was Sam. Sam thought differently. Oh, he knew the ball was in his court, but he knew it was God who had it! He had always had it! Sam prayed beneath his breath, "The situation is in Your hands, Lord! Your will be done Lord! Use this situation, Lord, in whatever way it pleases you. Use it, please Lord, that the outcome might bring people's souls to you!"

Big Dog did know a place. It was a very safe place where Tina could get help . . . a very close place. He knew it because he and his coward commando comrades had, a time or two, thought about attacking the place. It was a small, hidden compound just about two "clicks" to the east. They knew it was rich in supplies, including fuel and food. They didn't attack, though, because they were always afraid there were hidden guards dressed like ordinary people who would spring, at a moment's notice, into action and decimate them all. Numbers weren't important. They could destroy them all no matter how many of them there might be at the moment.

Surprise, surprise! They're wrong! Ridiculously wrong! There were no guards and no weapons . . . except maybe a surgical scalpel or two . . . nothing! They had nothing to fear except fear itself. I wonder where that came from? The fear, I mean, not the saying! God has many tools at His disposal to use as He sees fit! Assuredly, Dogs men won't attack this place! It's under God's protection and watchful eye!

Sam and Tina received top-notch care and their health rapidly returned. There they met Mrs. Saaths, who took excellent care of them. They told her they had heard of the ordeal she and her husband, Bill, had gone through.

Mrs. Saaths already knew about the little white church in the United States. She had heard about the masquerading that went on there that day. She also knew how quickly things had escalated into mass hysteria throughout the world as other churches were systematically wiped out.

She knew about the efforts of *EASES-the Ecumenical Atonement Spiritual Eradication Services*-Christians one by one and two by

129

two being systematically wiped out. The ones that disobeyed their government's direct orders to not put on *Martyrs of the Cross* were the first to be wiped out! She felt she had indeed found friends in Sam and Tina Harks, and was amazed to learn that they were survivors of the Little White Church Massacre, as Christians around the world called it!

Sam and Tina filled her in on the power that God bestowed on the play, the lives that were saved at its showings and the great fear and paranoia the governments had for it. They told her the government officials were furious that the play, through God's power, was being used in to save souls and band Christians together. It inspired them, they said, to get busy for the Lord and not be afraid or unwilling to stand for the right things!

Then they told her of their lives before going to the Little White Church that day. They shared their long story about fussing, fighting, and using violence toward each other. The play in the church that day completely changed their lives for eternity!

Mrs. Saaths and the others, who by now had joined her, were so inspired! They didn't know exactly what the play consisted of, but they said they were *dying* to find out! Sam and Tina shared its basics, and Mrs. Saaths and the rest were hooked! They insisted on Sam and Tina directing. They were going to put on the play!

Chapter 12

The Villages

Narrator: This books author
Where: Narrator in hiding ...location of events, The Islands
When: Three Months BCR

*T*he two women approached their sister in the Lord hoping she would go with them.

"Sister Mary Tams and I are going to the villages in the morning. Do you care to come along?" Sister Mary Martha asked.

"I think maybe we'd better stick around here. There are so many people to attend to, but maybe when you make the trip in another month or two we can take time to go. I don't know, maybe not even then . . . we'll just have to wait and see." Mrs. Saaths replied.

"If you're sure?"

"Yes, quite sure, thank you!"

Mrs. Saaths was certain all right. She and several British people were missionaries to those Islands and were holed up in a compound that seemed out of reach to anyone but God-and they knew full well that He was always with them.

Besides, a lot could be accomplished in the six to seven days it took to make the "rounds." This was what they called the trip they took every-other-month-or-so. Each trip gave them a chance to do some hands-on work at all the surrounding villages. They also found their way into the rest of the villages on the island, except for maybe a few that were considered hostile.

Those rounds were for their missionary work and for survival, dangerous, as it seemed. There were no malls, huge department stores, supermarkets, or even mom-and-pop grocery stores at which to purchase their supplies. They couldn't even get everything they needed in one village. They had to buy or trade goods at several villages scattered around the island to meet their needs.. Even then, they could only secure all the supplies they needed when they were available on the island, a rarity at any one given time.

They sometimes joked that it would be great if someone would come up with a way to have one-stop shopping in one of the villages-a place where they could get everything they needed at one place. "It would be just like shopping at home?" one or the other would say.

They knew full well that they would still visit the other villages, at least every other month. It was important for them to keep in touch with the locals who God had placed in their witnessing care and, to some degree, physical care. Missionaries were scarce, especially in this remote part of the world. They would have to make do and depend on God to provide.

Often, they would talk to each other about waking up one day to find newly repaired and paved roads, and a Range Rover to get wherever they needed to go and get supplies. It could also act as an ambulance. Maybe someday God would bless them with those needs, but for now, an old, worn-out horse and rickety cart would have to do. This was their beloved mission field, although their workdays were extremely long and arduous. Simply put, their tasks were primarily witnessing and survival.

What? You thought missionaries only study, teach, or preach? No! Oh, no! They must survive. Yes, it's true that we must all survive, but there are more than a few differences. We must survive the circumstances and lifestyle we're accustomed to-work, home, weekend, air conditioning, heat on command, appliances that make our lives easy, more enjoyable, more luxurious, and which produce more leisure.

We have a car, or I should say that we usually have more than one car to choose from. The roads are mostly well paved, save a few potholes. We don't have to feed our cars. We just have to keep them well-maintained and put gas in them when the tank runs low. And we can go wherever we want to or feel compelled to go.

Clothes are easy to come by, even at a moment's notice. We just go to our favorite department store to buy them-and many of those stores are open 24/7. We can spend whole days shopping for our needs and wants. Sure, we sometimes have to battle the forces of nature, but we still have our own or public transportation to get us to our destinations and back.

Oh, and we do have to eat, don't we? We need food. Well now, that's a tough one! It's such a chore to go to the supermarket or one of our favorite restaurants and choose from the hundreds or thousands of options-steaks, seafood, chickens, pork, something else. It's tough to choose, huh? I mean, right down to the spices and various ingredients, some of which we learned while watching our favorite cooking shows on TV. Not all, though! Some we learned during visits to a sister or brother's house or while visiting a best friend, who lives at least twenty minutes away!

How about TV? Now that's certainly a tough one! Which station should you be watching? Oh, I know, there's always everything good to watch or nothing good to watch, even with hundreds of stations available with just the push of a button on a remote control.

We can choose to read, talk on the phone with friends, or go to our favorite chat room on the web! That's right, because there's at least one computer in almost every home. The choices are astounding! Think about it! Don't most of us live pretty much like spoiled kings and queens in comparison to "the old days?" What more can we ask for? What more do we want? What more do we need? How strange and "spoiled" our little worlds have become; where man's mind has expanded in ways unimaginable, even to the very ones who created those things. How strange that enough is never enough and good enough is never good enough! With all those conveniences and opportunities, there's never enough time, and never enough money.

Mostly, there's never enough time to thank the Creator of all . . . the Creator of us! There's never enough money to tithe or to give the first fruits of the money He puts in our hands. We don't even take note, much less acknowledge, that it's all His anyway and He can distribute in any manner He chooses-by need or by repayment for faithfulness, or by what ever desire He has!

Mrs. Saaths and the other missionaries were quite another story. Their world was a different world. They chose to follow God's calling and knew they had a mission to accomplish, no matter what! It is the "no matter what's" that are the catch! They don't have to be in this environment, their mission field, but to not be there would be in direct violation of God's plan for their lives.

We don't even think about them, much less support them? Are our churches doing God's will? Do they support those missionaries? Do they talk about the missionaries, who are suffering in His name, to witness Christ in word and deed to a lost and dying world, no matter what? They serve God in the face of perils and dangers, with little or no support from those who have trouble getting up to go to Sunday school and church because *we've* "had a rough week!"

Careful about supporting the missionaries! They might just come out of this with a profit! Why, they might even make more money doing this that they could have at a regular job earning a "comfortable living!"

Baloney, hogwash! Do we squeak when we walk, or what? You wouldn't dream of living their lives or walking in their shoes for one instant! You wouldn't leave your comfort zones! Tell it like it is! Would you even dare to raise your hand in praise in worship unless the pastor requested that the entire church do so in unison? Well, now be honest! Would you? This isn't something we do for the preacher, this is something we do in response to an urge from the Holy Spirit, and we ignore it! What a sad bunch we are!

"Quench not the Holy Spirit," God's Word says!

Mrs. Saaths and the other missionaries, now that's another story! Their lifestyles regressed, if you would call it that, to the lifestyles, customs and, for a large part, the mannerisms of the people to whom

134

they minister. They have no clean water coming from the sinks in their beautifully decorated kitchens. They have wells or streams. They don't have TV, they have a small radio, which sometimes picks up a station or two! They have no supermarkets or fast-food restaurants, no cars and no paved roads, and the dusty, dirty roads they have are filled with huge potholes!

They have no favorite department stores. Clothes come in through occasional donations, but they do come in. Whatever money they have (or get), they spend on fuel for the generator they use sparingly, on food, medicine, or other needs to help those living in desolation. The ones they help don't even know they need help because they've lived in hopeless, helpless situations! The rest of the money goes toward visits to the States- to their sponsoring churches and organizations, trying to drum up the support they so desperately need.

Why would anyone begrudge them the money? Why do they almost have to be coerced into letting it go of so little of what they earn? Many don't want to give without knowing where their money is going and whom it will help. "How will it be spent?" they ask before opening their hearts and wallets. Gosh, those missionaries might have fun with *your* money! Poor, poor pitiful you! You want to see where every measly cent goes? Go do the job yourself!

No, I didn't think you'd want any part of that! It's still too hard for you to get up on Sunday morning! I'm sorry. I didn't think you'd want that brought up again! We'll go back to the money issue. Your church can't be a co-sponsor of a missionary because it's just squeaking by, because people don't want to use it for that purpose, because we have so many things we need here, because we're already stretched too thin! What about the cost of that huge new church building? What about all the things we need to do to satisfy this committee and that committee? Keep going! Keep going! I could probably write a book on reasons not to support missionaries, but there's one major reason why you *should* support them … God said we must support them!

What else do you need? Why wouldn't God want you to support those who are doing His work? Those people spread God's Word throughout the world, even in these difficult times-and yes, that work involves meeting the physical needs of those people as a method of witnessing. You got me side-tracked! I was trying to tell you about Mrs, Saaths and I got side-tracked! You kinda have to watch me like that!

Well, Mrs. Saaths wanted to go with Sister Mary, but that just didn't seem to be a possibility. Someone *had* to stay with the people, because this primarily served as a medical complex for the community-the community being everybody on that island of about a hundred square miles or so. There were several other people there to help Mrs. Saaths so she wouldn't be alone, figuratively speaking, that is.

Mrs. Saath's husband, Bill, had been with her until about two and a half years ago. Rebels kidnapped them both for ransom and things were really bad. They had to do exactly what the kidnappers told them to do at all times, including torturous hours of hiking . . . almost daily. They were in danger from poisonous snakes and insects, other wilderness animals and all manner of vile things! She became accustomed to those things because she had lived in that environment and among those island people for some time.

However, when she was in the compound, she didn't have to watch every step. You need to remember that Mrs. Saaths was an American woman. She grew up in the United States. Well, she and Bill married when they were both in their mid-twenties, and four or five years later they heard and obeyed God's call to the mission field.

Living on the island with those varmints didn't change the way she felt about them, though. She reacted to them much like women in the civilized world would; she couldn't stand them.

During their ordeal with the kidnappers, their physical needs were no longer in their own hands. Instead, they were at the mercy of the rebels, and each day they remained alive was an extension of their kidnappers' desire for ransom money. This, Mrs. Saaths often said, was the longest two months of her life. The constant fear of their captors was in complete conflict with the humiliation they suffered because of their dependence on them. Personal privacy was a thing of the past. Their inability to control their own destiny caused minute by minute frustration. They functioned in a state of bewilderment as they wondered if God had turned His back on them. If that were true, they wondered why.

She thought her time-the ordeal itself-to be long and hard . . . she had just thought. But there was no way could she anticipate the horrors awaiting her, no way she could foretell the future for her precious Bill! The government had grown weary of such kidnappings and had done nothing to stop them. At least that was the way the government felt about them at that time.

Confirmed and intricate intelligence came to central headquarters about the rebels' movements. They prepared for a multi prong attack to rescue the couple. When dawn broke, the raid on the rebels' camp took place. It wasn't supposed to go down like the way it did, but the incalculable sometimes happens, especially when God says it's time for one of His children to come home.

She and Bill awoke to the sound of rapid gunfire and heavy mortars! She was afraid to move, but Bill, being the protector he was, jumped up and started dragging her to safety behind an old, rusty tractor. He thought that another rebel clan had attacked and their lives were in greater danger. Besides, he thought the situation might present an opportunity for them to escape. He didn't know that all he had to do was let the government do its job and they would be all right. Really? No! God called Bill home and he was going to go, regardless of what he did or didn't do. Bill caught a bullet in the head and became another martyr for Jesus.

On some occasions, Mrs. Saaths suffered from depression and loneliness due to Bill's passing. Sometimes she thought she would never smile again, but God always brought her back with one of His miracles. Sometimes it was something as simple as some surgery they provided for one of the island people. Other times, it was something far more complex, like meeting vast needs at the compound.

Now was one of those times again. She had to be available to sacrifice for the Lord, which meant she had to stay there with the French missionary lady and a few other men and women. Together, they would keep things running smoothly and try to meet the needs that trickled or sometimes flooded into the compound. She had no problem doing what the Lord commanded-what He spoke to her heart to do. Everyone at the compound knew that; and the needs did come as expected. That one needed medical attention, that one needed food and water, another needed instruction in good behavior in marriage, yet another needed an inspirational song. One just needed directions to another village, another came for medicine and for a long splinter to be taken out of her hand which she'd gotten when cutting the fields with a scythe.

Mrs. Saaths was now more content. She was much needed and much blessed in her work. Oh, she often wished Bill was still with her, but when she thought about where he was, she didn't want him back on this corrupt earth for anything. She felt her meager needs were blessed and filled by God abundantly!

God has been good to us all, don't you think? And God has been good to Mrs. Saaths. She found peace in her life . . . peace and joy. At least for now she wasn't depressed and she was far too busy to be lonely. She had hope for nothing but to be of service to her Lord and Savior.

Remember? Do you remember about those saints of God that Big Dog and his men captured right before his own capture? You could add to that the brutalizing and kidnapping that never stopped. It was time to right some of the wrongs that Big Dog had done! By now he should be a man, and step up to bat and do the right thing!

While the people, including Soul Winner, prepared for their very first presentation of *Martyrs of the Cross,* Big Dog was preparing for a precisely planned insurgency. However, this time the insurgency was on the insurgents themselves! Big Dog, or Soul Winner, as he became known by those people, was totally briefed on exactly where his men were located, and how to get there! He knew how many there were, and understood their strengths and weaknesses. He knew when, where, and how to strike with the least amount of resistance and the least possibility of casualties.

His men were not soldiers, though, not even for distraction. He prayed again, only this time for the holy boldness to be able to inspire the men of the compound to participate, and his prayers were answered! The men and women banded together, knowing they might die in their rescue attempt of those wonderful women of God.

A week went by, and life went on as normal as possible. Of course the pleasant exception was practicing for the play and, oh yes, the preparation for the attempt to rescue their colleagues in Christ! Time was drawing nearer and nearer!

Something greatly troubled them all. Sister Mary and Sister Mary Martha had not returned. It had been about three weeks since they left for their rounds and they should have been back almost two weeks ago. Why they weren't back? Had they met with foul play?

Everyone prayed for the best, but was afraid for the worst! They were afraid that men from Big Dog's former unit had captured or killed them. Their concern for the two women gave them even more incentive to be part of Soul Winner's plan! These two saints of God, and quite possibly others, had to be rescued. Again, he prayed for the Lord to give him strength and the ability to succeed. Everyone prayed for and with him.

The time had come . . . it was time to strike . . . the time was here! Please forgive me if I take a short break here . . . at least for a few moments. I get all torn up inside when I think about what happened during the attempted rescue. It gives me "cold chills" inside to think about it. I'll get back with you in a minute ....
....
....
....

....

Chapter 13

Rescued? (or not)

I think I have my composure back now!

Okay, I'll tell you about it, but if you need to stop reading for a moment, to shout, pray, to thank the Lord, or to regain *your* composure, trust me, I'll understand. I'll be right here waiting to tell you what happened when you pull yourself together . . . again!

Well they took off in the Rover that Soul Winner had promised to give his brothers and sisters at the compound . . . if they survived. That was the fulfillment of a desire, of fervent prayer-God meeting a terrific need they had at the complex.

Do you remember how much they needed a new vehicle like the Rover? My, how God answered their prayers! The same Rover that was used for evil was now a vehicle to rescue God's people. It was a vehicle of hope in an integrated plan to help those helpless women out of their imprisonment, which brought with it agony, despair, fear, and torment!

The plan was simple, Those evil men knew that Big Dog (a.k.a. Soul Winner) was their leader! They were afraid of him and respected his cunning, cleverness, and coldness! That's why they often times called him, "The Big-D with the three C's!" Anyway, Big Dog would traipse in with Sam and Tina and say they were bushwhacked while the others set up special jungle traps the way he'd taught them. He would inspect their bounty, the captured women and supplies, while the others completed their traps. He figured it would take a couple of hours to complete that part of the mission before he revealed the surprise. Big Dog would have Sam and Tina put in "storage" with the others, unharmed. He would tell them that Sam and Tina's big surprise would come in the morning, at which time Sam would be gruesomely drawn and quartered right in front of Tina and the others!

Big Dog would then distract them with great stories of conquest about which he wanted to brag! Meanwhile, guns that were hidden in the Rover would be smuggled in and given to the three or four women who knew how to use them. Sam would also get one, and he and Tina would carry the bulk of the ammo.

Big Dog would fully arm himself in preparation for an impending battle! He would have all the men hooting and hollering over his stories- yes, indeed, those men would carry on and have a big time listening to Big Dog brag! They'd all be in the same place and the doors would be silently wedged to they couldn't be opened from the inside.

There was no police or any kind of law enforcement to worry about within about four hundred miles-not that it would do anything but bad to them. They would just have to tie them up and hope for the best while trying to make their escape. Bad plan or good, this was the plan, and it was what they had. But it didn't end with man's plan. They knew better and joined together, as "the joining together of two or more in His name," in fervent prayer the way they had done many times before.

Now ...the execution (of the plan) you probably want to know if the plan was successful. You know . . . did they pull it off? Well, if the truth were known, it all went down just as planned . .. . until the drinking took its toll. Sam and Tina were safely in the detention cell where, to their great relief, they did find Sister Mary and Sister Mary Martha who were in relatively good shape. Oh, they were relatively unharmed, except for the "smacked around faces," that made those men "famous."

All the men were hooting and hollering in the designated part of "the big house," as they called it, while the guns were smuggled into the cell area where the detainees were imprisoned. Big Dog distracted them well. In fact, he really had those guys going, all right! They couldn't wait for another of his stories! I guess he didn't lose his knack for storytelling! Anyway, when he thought the time was right, he went for a beverage. While he was in the kitchen, he thought he heard a noise. Maybe, he thought, his "cohorts" outside were a bit too noisy. He didn't know was that the "gang" from the compound hadn't blocked the front door yet, so they weren't ready for the next step in the plan.

Fortunately, they hadn't even started yet. They had just arrived at the side of the house and were about to block the door at the exact time that Big Dog had gone to the kitchen. That's when four of the men decided it was time for a "10-100", which is also known as a latrine break . . . uh . . . they needed to relieve themselves.

Do you understand now? Oh, it's not that important, so don't even bother with that part of the story!

Anyway, Big Dog had two canisters of sleeping gas with him when he went to the kitchen to get something to drink. He came out prepared to toss the canisters. The worst case scenario was that he would also go to sleep. He hoped the chemicals would work fast so the men inside wouldn't figure out what was happening. The last thing he needed was too much time passing. They might think it was a joke or something, and *"pull a round or two"* on him. If they were already asleep, they wouldn't be able to shoot him.

Well, it's like I said. Things didn't go that way. Instead, those four men went outside and the plan went in a whole other direction from there! It was almost hilarious what happened next! If you don't mind, picture Big Dog standing there with no "juice" from the kitchen. Instead, he was standing there holding two canisters of sleeping gas . . . for everyone to see! The looks on those men's faces! That was worth this whole story!

Hold on a minute. I still can't stop laughing . . . .
....
....
....

Okay, I think I'm back now! Here we go . . . back to the story.

So . . . the door was wide open and those men were staring at Big Dog like he was some kind of an idiot or something! Well, he took advantage of the situation, with help from the front door's "ghostly" closing! The four men went to the latrine and would probably be gone for several minutes. The gang outside knew this was their only chance to act .

. . and they had to be quick and silent!

They closed and jammed the door, and figured they had about a minute and a half left before the first man got back. They still had to set up something that wasn't pre-planned-the appropriate way to neutralize any aggressive response from the men outside. They also hoped that Big Dog would be able to safely pull off his end of the set-up. They knew this would be hard because he'd be subjecting himself to the same gas he would use on the other men.

Of course, Big Dog was a bit of a smart aleck and comedian, so he stood there holding those canisters when the door shut and the bewildered men turned around. Big Dog said, "Boo! What's wrong, guys, booger man gonna getcha or something?" Those men all thought they were real macho and started their "tough guy" talk, shooting off their mouths with a bunch of nonsense!

Just then, Big Dog started belly dancing and singing, "We'll kill 'em in the morning, they're goin' to the sweet bye-and-bye" over and over, while pretending to juggle the canisters. Oh, and he didn't stop his act with just a bit of singing and juggling. He even acted like a drunken man when he pulled the pins out of the canisters and the stuff started going everywhere. Those men were incredibly stupid! They still didn't get what was going on!

Yeah, they tried to get to the doors and when they tried to open them, they thought their knucklehead buddies outside were playing tricks on them! None of them even pulled a weapon much less fired off a shot! Within seconds of Big Dog releasing the gas in the canisters, there was total silence inside the room. There was also no indication that things were all right with Big Dog (who, you recall, is also Soul Winner)! The others had to work quickly to accomplish their mission, and there were still four men outside who could turn even the new plan into a terrible disaster!

Everyone got very quiet as the four men got closer! It looked like none of them had their guns! Unbelievable! The "gang" got a clean drop on them! They didn't know what hit them! Oh, they were cussing and swearing and all that, but there wasn't a thing they could do! Glory hallelujah, all four were taken alive without a single shot!

Big Dog was one of the first two men inside the hideout to wake up. The other men didn't take much longer. When he awoke, Mrs. Saaths helped him up and gave him a fresh cup of coffee that she had brewed for those who wanted it.

"Praise the Lord!" Big Dog said, and he rejoiced! "This went well, don't you think? Now, for the next step of the rescue!"

"The next step?" Tina asked.

Sam looked puzzled.

"Guys, you didn't think it would just end like this, did you?" Big Dog asked. The rest of the "gang" was curious . . . well, he had gotten them suspiciously interested in what was to happen next.

"O.K., you didn't think I was planning this and riding along with you for nothing but this, did you?" he asked them.

What did he mean by that? There is just no way that Big Dog could be a traitor, especially with the anointing God had poured on him. The idea that Big Dog (a.k.a. Soul Winner) could be a "Benedict Arnold" terrified them. The men they captured sensed it, too, and it created a playground in their minds of what they would do as soon as they got loose. They realized those people thought Big Dog was on their side, and they also figured that he was "playing them like fiddles".

"Soul Winner" sensed what was on their minds and it hurt, although, with his mischievous sense of humor, he was able to play it into humor.

"Come here!" he barked at Sam

Sam had a terrible "de-ze-vois, or we've been here before" feeling. He knew God had helped them so far and prayed deep inside that "Soul Winner" hadn't gotten a bad case of "backslide-itis."

Chapter 14

Mrs.Saaths (Lord, deliver us from evil)

*M*rs. Saaths suddenly called out, "Lord...deliver us from evil!"

Mrs. Saaths and the rest of the "gang" knew this could be devastating because it appeared that whoever he was, he now held the key to their freedom. It was as if they were at a fork in the road of the plan with little or no guarantee the right road would be chosen. Nobody but Big Dog, or Soul Winner or whoever he was .now had a gun or any weapons. It was up to him to choose the outcome of this ordeal.

Would Sam and Tina continue in their missionary work that they had begun not long after the massacre at the little white church? Would they live to have children of their own-children they could raise in the fear and admonition of the Lord? Would they now suffer horrible physical abuse and probable death because this "should have been foreseeable" judgment call of trusting a man whom had been a monster?

"Sammy, Sammy . . . go over to old Carl there and give him one of those great big Christian hugs you people are so famous for!" Big Dog said with a wry grin on his face.

Naturally, Sam hesitated. The man Big Dog, referred to had his hands tied behind his back, but Sam didn't want any one from the "gang" to get that close to the "opposition. You and I know how bad those men really were, how they would brutally hut and kill you in a heartbeat! Sam knew it too and he just wanted things to be like he thought they'd planned in this "rescue."

Those men started laughing and making fun of the "gang." "Yeah, Sammy, come here and give old Carl a great big Christian hug!" He mocked Sam, then they all started catcalling and mocking him. Sam knew the saving grace of Jesus Christ; he knew that he would go through and endure much persecution in the name of his Savior. At that moment, He gained favor in God's eyes, as he submitted to the holy boldness of the

"Spirit of the Lamb." Sam smiled and bravely walked up to the man, then hesitated for a moment as the man suddenly stopped his nonsense and his blood ran weak in his veins. Sam immediately stretched out his "welcome to the fellowship" arms and hugged that man-yes, he showed Carl love the way God loves us!

Everybody knew what that meant. The opposition got deathly quiet. There were no more jokes, no more catcalls, no more "terror darts" coming from their mouths!

The ones making noises now were the Christians, who were shouting and witnessing, and praising the Lord! There were no hard feelings, no anger or bitterness, because they knew now that God had shown them how, "All things work together for good, to them that love the Lord and are called for His purposes."

The men knew that all manner of meanness was out of their hands, and submitting to an unknown future was the only thing they could do. They looked at each other, and those "other people", but didn't utter a word. They couldn't!" Were they tongue-tied by God?" Did he ever do this before . . . like in Biblical days?

Well, there was no rush! They thought they had all the time in the world so why would they hurry? God worked miracles and wonders to bring this about! They would show kindness and love and mercy to these men. They would witness to them about their God . . . and the way they knew Him personally. They would speak of his proven power!

Wasn't this just the most amazing event unfolded for them by God? To have this opportunity, which for some Christians would have been a disaster. They wouldn't have had the spiritual strength to see this situation for what in a divine way, it was-another powerful blessing and gift from God! Again, He had proven that He controls all things.

God now reminded them that, had the events turned out differently, they still would have had their purpose in His will. It still would have been for His glory, not for us to demand an answer from Him as to why and how!

They fed the men food for their bodies and food for their souls. They gave them water to quench their thirst, and preached that Christ said to "take of the Living Water, and you will thirst no more." And they did preach the "living water" to them. The men listened, and listened well! The Holy Spirit visited this little hideaway and Soul Winner won the name he had given himself when he was at the compound. In fact, he had just won rewards for himself in Heaven and was recognized by Christ in His Kingdom, as a soul winner and a good and faithful servant! Soul Winner knew this and was split between feeling proud to be on the winning side, and remorseful for all the wrongs he had done. Above all, he wished there were a way to erase those things. Sammy and Tina stepped up to bat for Soul Winner.

"You just don't know how many times I felt the same way!" Sam told him. "Before Christ enters our hearts and our lives, we don't stand a chance! I was never good enough, but even if I'd been a model citizen, without God's amazing grace, all my goodness would be "as filthy rags" before the just and worthy God! We are not worthy. Oh, we are not worthy! Only when we repent and ask His forgiveness, are we made worthy and our Spirit-filled deeds acceptable!"

Sam said it was time for Soul Winner to stop whipping himself for the past. "That's just the devil harassing you! He's telling you that you're not worthy to make you remorseful-he wants to you to lose your joy, your confidence, your zeal, and your fire for the Lord, which means your effectiveness for Christ!"

Sam shared with him how the Lord sent a preacher to help him understand those things not long ago. That preacher's name was Tiny. "That was his name in his mean days," Sam said. "And if you think you've lived a rough and mean life, well, let's just say, you simply ain't gonna believe how bad that bad can really be! Fact is, you don't know how mean, strong, and tough a man can be! As mean and as bad as Tiny used to be is how kind and how good he is now! His strength used to flow through his size, muscles, physical strength, and his combative abilities. Now, his strength lies in his love and knowledge of God and the anointing of the Truth on his life"!

Soul Winner's heart was filled with the Holy Spirit. It was all he could do to keep silent, but he knew the Lord wanted him to hear the rest of what Sam had to say.

"God forgave that man and tossed his sins 'as far as the east is from the west.' I know that if God forgave him, and God forgave me and removed my faults and weaknesses, He has forgiven you! Just keep asking Him to help you because God is "just and faithful to forgive us our sins! We're all in the same boat, Soul Winner. 'None are righteous, no not one!'"

Sam took a moment to pray and seek the Lord for more wisdom. As he did, a greater anointing of the Holy Spirit fell on him.

"None of us are righteous through our own abilities. It takes atonement from the heart; it takes knowing that the spilled blood of Christ is the only way to make our spirits righteous. Lots of folks say they're "good people," but they might as well hang up that idea. None of us can live perfect, righteous lives in these mortal bodies. God knows this. He cannot look upon sin. As Christians, we're sinners whose sins are covered by Christ's blood. Our once broken relationship with God is restored through repentance and the shed blood of our Lord and Savior. By accepting His sacrifice, we can approach the very Throne of God in prayer and speak to Him as our Holy Father."

Soul Winner opened even the pores of his skin to let those words from God absorb into his being-all the way to the core of every bone in his body. He had just had a Holy Spirit awakening and knew he was finally "good to go" with the Lord. Now, he wanted to help his former comrades in the opposition see the Light!

The witnessing went on into the night as did the gospel singing and showers of mercy and kindness! When it was all over, over half of the men had received understanding and a new direction for their lives directly from God. And it didn't end there because each acknowledged Jesus Christ as his Lord and Savior. One by one they asked Him humbly, willingly, and in all sincerity to come into their hearts. They wanted God to lead and direct their lives in all matters. They wanted to live the way He wanted them to live. They wanted others to see Him in all they said and did.

Chapter 15

Time to make a change

When: T-Minus one week and counting

*T*he man looked around and rubbed his eyes. "Where's your army?" Grunt asked

"What army?" Tina replied with a question, not a real answer.

"You know, the army that was all around this fortress!"

Tina looked at Grunt in a quizzical, confused state. She had no idea what he was talking about . . . no idea what he was asking and why.

"There was an army of a thousand, or maybe ten thousand camped all around this place. They were camped so thick that we couldn't get within a couple of miles of the outer perimeter of this compound. It woulda' been suicide to even try!"

Grunt was serious! Indeed, he had seen many guards, and he had seen an army protecting the complex, but it wasn't exactly the type of army I can accurately describe!
They were not what you would call your regular army . . . no, these weren't from any earthly military or militia! God sent them, and only certain key people were allowed to see them!

These were special times, and God sometimes honors special times in a special way. His power is without bounds, His glory is in excellent abundance! He's the Creator and Master of thousands upon ten thousands of angels, each with a different description, purpose, and glorified tasks! Grunt and his men knew they had seen something, and it was large and powerful . . . . whatever it was!

"We saw them! We all saw them! We can't go into the compound! We'll be captured and arrested!" he railed.

Well, reader . . . it's a reasonable assumption . . . wouldn't you agree?

"Nothing's going to happen to any of us-at least not to those who've given their lives, hearts, and souls to Christ-at least not from what you saw,

Grunt!" Soul Winner said.

"Huh?" Grunt grunted out . . . sounding strange when he said it. Grunt always talked in a very abrasive manner. His voice always sounded really weird, with a rough quality to almost every word he spoke. This "huh" sounded rougher, but somewhat musical . . . although off key.

Tina wasn't by herself when she started laughing hysterically.. She made quite a spectacle of herself! Grunt started smiling, then laughed roughly, himself! You know how it is . . . one person does something silly, another person starts laughing, and pretty soon almost everybody starts laughing.

It's taking a while to tell you about this, because I'm laughing so hard I can't think straight! Give me a minute . ...

......I believe I can go ahead now, without breaking out laughing again.

Okay . . . well, basically speaking, Grunt didn't know how they were going to get into the compound, invited or not. The men who gave their hearts to Jesus *were* invited into the compound, and were more than eager to go! They'd repented of their sins and asked forgiveness of them from the Savior. And they did more! Just as Big Dog was converted to Soul Winner, they repented of their evil ways. They begged with all their hearts to be forgiven by God, and those people they'd harmed. In fact, they wanted forgiveness from the many they had repeatedly tortured and abused

My God is a big God! He is a really Great Big God! And He forgave those men.

How those people forgave them, I'll never know in my human carnal mind. Thanks be to God that my spiritual mind is far larger than my carnal mind! Those rough, mean, vicious men who had tortured and abused God's people were now part of God's army!

It's always amazing when God transforms wretched people and makes something of them . . . like he did me. *He's the potter and I am the clay.* Say that, reader! Pray that and say that until it soaks into the center of your life . . . the very center of the marrow of your bones! **He is the potter and I am the clay! He is the potter, I am the clay!**

Mold me, Lord. Keep me strong, Oh Lord, that I might face the obstacles, challenges, trials and tribulations in my life! Help me to withstand *all* tests of my faith that I might grow stronger in You. Make me a shining example of Your glory and honor, as I witness for You. Let those I meet along the way and those who see me in my daily walk see the strength and commitment, joy and overwhelming gleefulness in enduring all trials and tribulations. Let me endure with honor and be even stronger for them in my life!

I know this story is getting more than its share of interruptions, but I just needed to stop for a moment to pray that prayer! I just pray that you will pray a similar one now, or at least very soon, it really feels good! Go ahead and try it! God is strong, and He will bless you with His strength!

....

....

....

....

Perhaps you want me to tell you more about what happened. Well, I will because I really think you should hear the truth. I mean, it's pretty amazing what you're about to find out.   Those men vowed to be patient in their quest for new lives in Christ! They didn't know how God would work through them, they just trusted God that He would! It was really amazing! They didn't get just *one* Rover . . . they got *five* Rovers! That's where Tina came in and shared more truth with them. When they were nearing the compound, she explained that they were just trying to obey God and do His work . . . whatever it is and whenever it's given to them.

"Soul Winner saw things, like a special protective army from God, that we didn't see. I have to admit these are pretty amazing times, and especially so when God's protection is manifested before our eyes . . . the very protection He promised we'd have! And that's not all He doing for His children, it's just one example!"

She was more excited and on fire for the Lord than she'd ever been in her life!

"Let's face it, these are strange and perilous times. The whole world is upside down from where it used to be because mankind let its guard down and let evil enter. And you can bet your boots that Satan was right there to take advantage of it as mankind is spirals more and more into corruption and meanness everyday. Christians in this world who want to do right are on a "tiny little island" that's rapidly sinking into oblivion . . . but for the hand of God!"

"I know you're right, Tina. We are on the mission field, knowing that life is extremely rough and forbidding here! It is here though, that we are still spreading the gospel, as best we can," Big Dog finally said. "It's not just happening in the United States, it's happening all over this 'Tower of Babel' world. Evil just grabbed hold of this world it spread like a cancer throughout the planet."

"We might be a little late about feeling the pains of decay, but it reaches us all the same," Tina added. "We do have one "benefit" though! As of yet, the government hasn't attacked us, as they have our brothers and sisters in other parts of the world. For the most part, they've either chosen to ignore us or just haven't gotten to us . . . yet. We do expect that to change, we just don't know when. For now, God has kept us safe from their attacks, but we still face danger everyday. We have no 911 we can call for help, even for medical emergencies. For us, He sent his protective angels, and manifested them visibly to the ones who were meant see them."

Soul Winner saw God's response to those perilous times and said, "Tina, the whole time I was at the complex, I felt that none of you guys saw what I saw! I found out real fast that what I suspected was true! I can't explain what happened to me the day that Sam got the jump on me. I just know that it was a lot bigger and stronger than Sammy was . . . and it was sweeter to my soul. In fact, it was a lot bigger and stronger than fourteen armies of bad guys ever was . . . you know, like this bunch of hooligans I used to command could ever be!"

Soul Winner explained that when they arrived at the compound, he was terrified.

"I was totally scared out of my wits! There I was in the midst of a powerful army from which there was no escape! That army surrounded the entire compound and kept all of you alive . . . I mean, it protected every one of you from the men I used to command! Now, you all need to listen up, including you, Grunt, and your men! There's nothing to fear! I believe that army was sent by God. They were angels sent to protect those people from the likes of us, at least the likes of what we used to be!"

Finally, Mrs. Saaths spoke up. "I wonder what's happening with other missionaries around the world? I've heard of the brutal and savage persecution that's fallen on many of them. Whole villages and compounds have been wiped out . . . and it seems nobody cares anymore. This world is not my home! It used to be somewhat tolerable, but now . . . well, were it not for God's grace, I wouldn't be able to tolerate it anymore!"

Tina consoled her, "Sister, it's a wonderful thing you've done . . . and for such a long time. Remember, the Bible teaches us to rejoice in our suffering. We must keep our faith strong no matter how much we have to endure. It's worth it, Sister! Whatever we go through, He is always with us to comfort us, and eventually they will get theirs and we will get ours! God *will* avenge the martyrs!"

As they were driving through the gates of the compound, the Rover stirred up dust when they went around a couple of small curves in the dirt road. Tina spoke up again and said, "Hey, what about that play we decided to put on?"

Sam excitedly agreed, "Yeah, let's show God's glory as well as the resolve and strength He gives us. Let's give it a week and glorify God with the play!"

Sister Mary and Sister Mary Martha both agreed. "Yes, that's exactly what we should do! "Brother Grunt, could we possibly borrow one of your Rovers and make our trip? You know we didn't complete our "rounds" this last time . . . ran into a bit of trouble, you know!"

"No sister, you may not *borrow* a Rover from me or my guys!"

Sister Mary looked down, as if hurt and disappointed. She hoped she didn't upset the big man. She was totally unprepared for what he said next.

"Sister, the Rovers are not mine to lend. They now belong to the compound! We gave them to the compound freely, no charge, no strings attached! I don't know how those other people see it, but in my opinion, the Rovers are yours to use at any time-whether it's for personal business or God's work! In fact, some of my men and I would consider it a great honor if you'd

155

let us come along, to help you out in any way we can. We're very interested in your work and there is so much we can learn from all of you!"

"Brother Grunt, I don't know what to say! I guess we'll have a new role as your teachers, won't we?" she said, feeling more comfortable with him now. "Of course I would be honored to have you escort Sister Mary Martha and me! With those vehicles and your help we should be able to cover the Island more effectively and in less than half the time. We'll be able to get supplies without rushing . . . and we'll be able to talk with the people we visit about attending the play!"

"Thank you. I really mean that, Sister. Thank you! This trust means the world to us! We're honored!"

There! It was set. There would be a lot to do to put on the play at the compound! They were all running on nervous energy and couldn't wait to get started. They also had to catch up on their chores and see the people who came to them for medical, psychological and spiritual help . . . the latter being the best cure they knew for anyone's troubles. They decided who would play the various parts and thought it kind of funny and fitting that Big Dog, alias Soul Winner, would play the part of Tiny. Brother Grunt was cast as Scontee. Sam and Tina would direct the play and would also handle the roles of, Brother Janus and his wife, Mrs. Betty. Some of Grunt's friends would naturally play the "nicely suited men" and the military dressed people!

Sister Mary was not really very old, maybe fiftyish, but they decided that she should play Granny! One of the other men in the "gang" from the compound would play Steven. It took almost no time to fill all the parts in the play. They practiced quickly and within days they were ready to put on an excellent and stirring production.

Word came in that the people on the island were excited and eager to attend! Grunt said he was glad he didn't see the angelic army surrounding the compound anymore. He hadn't seen them since they returned to the compound. He didn't know where they had gone, but he was certain there would have been a major seating problem if they were there! Besides, he wasn't completely over the "heebie-jeebies" they had given him!

Chapter 16

The Question For You ...

*T*he night before the play, the cast and crew got together one last time to fellowship and praise the Lord. They thanked God for His goodness and mercies, for the joy of serving Him. Then they asked Him to bless the play and use it as a witness, that souls might be won to eternity with Him!

Sam and Tina were up very early in the morning. They sat together watching the beautiful daybreak! It was incredible! They had never seen such beauty and majesty!

"The Lord is happy with this showing of *Martyr's of the Cross*," Sam whispered to Tina!

"You bet He is, Sam! I just wish Brother Janus, Sister Betty, Sister Granny, and Brother "Tiny" could be here to see it! Maybe I'm being selfish, but I wish they were here!

"They're in a better place than this, rejoicing eternally with the Lord. They're actually in His presence, as we will be . ... someday soon!" Sam assured Tina.

"I know, oh yes, on this beautiful, glorious morning, I do know that, Sam."

Sam was totally awed by the beauty of the morning, the bird's magnificent singing, and the freshness and the crispness of the early air! To share this beauty with his wonderful wife, Tina, made the experience even more miraculous. He didn't know how to describe what he was feeling, but he knew he was extremely humbled. In a strange way, he saw himself as very small and insignificant, and yet, ten feet tall at the same time. They snuggled together, and rejoiced that God allowed them the opportunity to be each others closest friend other than God. He allowed them to be life-mates, their hearts intertwined together and with

Him! They hugged closely, soaking up and basking in God's beauty and goodness!

How wonderful to be here with you! How wonderful, reader, to enjoy this moment, this beautiful sunrise, with me, Sam and Tina! Well, I do need to tell you about the play . . .don't I. Okay, here we go .. . .

Missionaries around the world, as well as Christians in city after city heard of the play. They knew the power God blessed it-version after version-every time it was shown in city after city, town after town, village after village. Many pastors started the play by informing their congregations, "You don't have to go to Broadway to see a good production! The secular world doesn't have a lock on all the great plays and dramas! We have a few of our own! In fact, we have something they don't have . . . as you may see tonight! We might just receive a good, old-fashioned, heavy-duty dose of the Holy Spirit's Power tonight!

Some especially charismatic preachers called on the Holy Spirit to rain the fiery passion for Christ upon the congregation, and if it were His will, to use this play as a tool in doing it. It happened too many times to count. It did exactly what the governments thought it would-it worked to help wake the people up, to make them re-examine their freedom of religion, and how it was being stolen from them in the name of tolerance and ecumenism. They started to watch and pray, and they paid closer attention as adversity increased. They came to understand how precious true freedom was and how tightly they should guard it

The new governments put it all together very quickly. They knew the only way they could institute their New World Order policies and laws was to obliterate this movement and similar ones that would jeopardize their plans. They thought that verbal intimidation would frighten the masses into submission, especially when they raided a few showings of the play and made public examples of them with a show of force.

It didn't work! If anything, it had the opposite effect! It made those who ordinarily wouldn't take a stand on any issue or go head to head in any confrontation, band with others of like-mind. They felt empowered to work with others and became even more protective of their religious freedom, freedom of religious expression. To them, it was a sacred institution.

Don't get me wrong. The governments didn't want to create martyrs, but they did just that. And in doing so, they created their own worst nightmare. To create a martyr is to create a never-ending quagmire. However, once the New World Order government got started, it became so power and success hungry, it just wanted the evil 'high" of victory to continue, which meant destroying all obstacles. They were on a roll, without so much as a speed bump in their way . . . or so they thought!

Their major speed bump was more like a stone wall-the waking up of Christ's children from a deep spiritual slumber! The diversity, adversity, and strife within the Christian community slowed to a trickle among those who already were strong and those who became strong! The others just withered, as expected, into their own little "yes men" world. They believed everything they were told and did everything they were told to do. They didn't fight back and they didn't bother to witness for Christ, something they didn't do well from the start. They backed down at the merest hint of a battle, be it legal or in other debate forms, and the government's snowball of victory started on it's growing and bulging descent.

The time to confront this was at the top of the hill, as tough as that seemed to be, before the snowball started its descent. As it came downhill, it became too big. All we could do was chip away at it, slow it down, or force it to melt.

Well, maybe man couldn't stop it, but God was, and still is, in control. He knew this would happen, and He knew when it would happen! Like those tormenting moments in the Garden of Gethsemane, when Christ asked His disciples to watch and pray with Him because the hour was at hand . . .. they slept! A little wine and celebration at that final Passover supper made sleep a welcome friend. It was not in their nature to stay awake and talk to the Father. They were not keenly aware of what was going on all around them.

We should have been awake to do the work of our heavenly Father at a time when steadfastness and awareness are so much needed, and toughness and bravery in the light of personal sacrifice is required. Imagine the joy, fulfillment, and contentment of submission. Imagine knowing the honor and privilege of being selected and even allowed to do that work . . . chosen by the Creator of the universe!

Christ knew *they* were asleep; He knows that most Christians are asleep. He knew what Peter would do. "Before the cock crows twice, you will deny Me three times!" He knew that before the dawning of His return for His children. **Many will be caught sleeping, and when they wake up and are put to the test, they will deny Him instead of accepting the consequences of acknowledging Him.**

Denominations in the church denied Him! The government denied Him and tried to get rid of Him and everything to do with Him! There were extreme repercussions for not denying Him and for continuing His holy work!

You see, the government was so afraid of creating a martyr for God when they crucified Jesus, but they were more afraid to let Him live. He was dangerous to their legalistic and powerful hold over the people, not to mention their compromises with the Roman authorities. What would happen to their religious system, which the apostle Luke referred to as "old wine skins" if they didn't do away with Him? In their eyes, He was a danger to their stiff-necked religious system and the government feared his power over the people."

Nothing they believed was true. Jesus didn't come to overthrow any government, He was here to show His people what God really expected of them . . . to show them what the law really meant. His Deity, faith in Him and the Father, and taking the sins of the world on His shoulders were all part of God's plan for those who would listen, repent and have faith in Him.

I guess if we really understand the play, *Martyrs of the Cross*, we already know those things. And we know that history always repeats itself. Yes, there's a new cast of characters, and the patterns may vary a little, but the basic theme is always the same-a mirror image that shows us it all happened before.

That brings up an important question. Would we allow our Christ to be put to death again? Would we be caught sleeping again? Would our Christianity be so lukewarm that we allow our witness to be hindered by bickering and internal strife within the Christian church and community? Just as bad, would our lives in Him be just a passive experience or one filled with surrender to Him?

Jesus commanded (there's that word, commanded) us to do certain things. If we trust Him as our Lord and personal Savior first, then we will be with Him eternally, but that's not enough. Our faith must bear fruit . . . and that fruit is revealed in how we follow His commands.

He commanded us to live our faith, to let our light shine, to not hide that God-given light where it cannot be seen, to tell the whole world about Him and to pass on the truth of His Saving Grace. Impact as many, in loving kindness, as you can…and expect the miracles of His harvesting of souls! Trust and obey! What you sow…you will reap, as told by our Lord, Jesus Christ, in…St. Luke 6:38, "Give, and it shall be given unto you; good measure, pressed down, and shaken together, and running over, shall men give into your bosom. For with the same measure that ye mete withal it shall be measured to you again.

God blesses the seed of faith! God blesses the seed of witnessing, why wouldn't He? That is the very center of His Will! That is the purpose of this book! That is the purpose of *Martyrs of the Cross*, the drama-to have faith in God's willingness and ability. Our faith must produce a belief that He will bring in a bountiful harvest, We must believe that both have and will continue to plant seeds of hope, strength, and courage in the face of adversity. Through the roles we play, we have and will keep spreading and administering hope and faith in Christ!

Notice I said "faith" a lot! Christ said that if it was difficult to have faith in Him when He was here, how much more so it would be with Him gone. In the Gospel of John (20:29), it is written, "Jesus saith unto him, Thomas, because thou hast seen me, thou hast believed; blessed are they that have not seen, and yet have believed. Then there's the word penned by Matthew (17:20), "If ye have faith as a grain of mustard seed, ye shall say unto this mountain, remove hence to yonder place; and it shall remove; and nothing shall be impossible unto you." In the book of James (2:20), we were told that faith without works doesn't show very much real faith. "But wilt thou know, O vain man, that faith without works is dead?"

Faith in our eternal salvation, as in John 3: 16,17 and 18, "For God so loved the world, that He gave his only begotten Son, that whosoever believeth in Him should not perish, but have everlasting life. For god sent not His Son into the world to condemn the world; but that the world through Him might be saved. He that believeth on Jim is not condemned; but he that believeth not is is condemned already, because he hath not believed in the name of the only begotten Son of God."

We must have faith and we must acknowledge His commands. We are expected to work diligently for Him and we must rely on His strength when we are weak and face opposition. We are to be awake and aware of things that occur around us, "fight the good fight," keep the faith and continue to spread the Word, no matter the consequences!

The play and this book, *Martyrs of the Cross,* **asks us the question of** how awake we are and how willing we are to do His work in a world spinning out of control, in a world that is gaining in unchecked chaos. How strong and how willing are you? When adversity comes, how fast do you fold? Adversity comes in many forms. It may simply be getting up on Sunday morning, and getting ready for church to fellowship with the brethren! It may be when you're asked to teach Sunday school because you don't feel equipped or knowledgeable enough for the task. Don't worry! Pray and study to prove yourself worthy and He will bless you with the things you need to do the job well!

He may ask you to make the sacrifice of coming out of your comfort zone and praying in public. This is not an easy thing for some folks to do, but if He asks it of you, He will give you the grace to get it done .. . . and the prayers to pray. It doesn't matter how many people are around you or how many can hear you. God always hears prayers that come from your heart, so pray to Him! Obey Him!

Remember that it's not easy to sacrifice something, especially your life. If it were, everybody would be doing it. You may be asked to give more financially to your church, to someone in need, or for some other purpose. You may be asked to sacrifice more of your time. Give it joyfully!

Remember the key to your sacrifice, though. It must be *intended* to be done in secret and come from the heart. Never brag about it and never do it for any recognition. If you do, you'll get your reward here, but when it's done in secret, He'll be faithful to reward you in His time and in His way! What you do may be seen here-maybe there's no way to hide it-but don't do it for recognition or honor or praise. Put it in the bank . . . God's bank! God will not forget it. We may, but God never will.

Do these things from the heart, not for the reward here *or* in Heaven. Do it because you love God, love people and mankind, not because of any reward.. God loves a cheerful giver and blesses them as He sees fit, according to His riches in Heaven . . . and believe me, that is no small thing.

You may be asked to give your life for Him . . . in work, deed, worship, or maybe with your freedom. Your sacrifice may require that you endure adversity with all long suffering, or those who revile the correct and righteous stand you take for Christ may take your life from you. Would you be willing to obey even if it meant losing your life? Okay, get over yourself and remember that He gave His life for you! Now, will you give your life for Him? If and when you have to choose, will you choose compromise and life or will you choose Him regardless of the consequences? That doesn't mean you have to be stupid about sacrifice for the Lord, but if the situation presented itself, what would you do? You may never be asked to make the ultimate sacrifice, but you may be asked to do difficult work in His name. Will you do it?

I was just thinking about how we, the redeemed, are to live. We've been commanded to live Christ-like lives that others may see Him in us. Are you doing it? Are you living God's will for your life, are you letting your light shine, are you a witness to the unspeakable wonder, peace, and joy that comes from being God's child?

You're right. I'm not laughing now. It isn't funny! You may be asked to make a variety of personal sacrifices, and let me tell you that I know it's tough . . . very tough . . . for *all* of us! Some sacrifices demand more of us than others, but with each one comes the joy of victory-the satisfaction that we have obeyed Him, done His will, and passed another of His awesome tests.

He may ask you to come out of your "safety zone" and participate in a play, through acting, directing, or doing another job connected with the production. He may want you to be in this particular play, *Martyrs of the Cross*. He may want the play performed at your church or some other place in your community. If so, do it! Then, watch Him bless the play, the people in it, the people watching it, and the community! God moves and in mysterious ways!

I'm sorry if you think I'm rambling, but I'm doing His will. My heart is filled with these words and it's impossible for me to remain silent. We've been silent far too long!

Whatever God tells you to do, pray for guidance. Make sure it's God speaking to your heart. If it's of God, obey! We've often thought God was telling us to do something . . . and sometimes we've been wrong. God has a plan and a purpose for your life. Pray about it and He will guide you.

I'm almost finished . . . I promise to wrap this up. God often reveals His plan and His truth to you through the confirming words of others-a friend mentions something you've been thinking and praying about, you read about it somewhere, or it's part of a television program. That's the time to seek His face and pray more. When you're sure it's from God, obey and do as He asks for His honor and glory.

If a man gain the whole world, but lose his own soul, what has he prospered?

I'm done! I've said what was on my heart . . . what I believed He wanted me to tell you. I'm sure you want to hear more about the play that's about to be performed at the compound!

Chapter 17

T-MINUS ONE DAY AND COUNTING
_____**The Spectacle of the Last Day**_____
_____

Some Child of God, caught up "in the twinkling of an eye," once wrote:

Never has the glamour of the Earth been so blessedly beautiful. Like a blind person who suddenly gains sight, everything is so awesome. The mountains and the valleys, in their endless array! How could all this have come to be?

It's as if, in hindsight,(being 20 / 20),she was putting on her best dress, adorning her hair, the excitement of her life placing her into the highest of high anticipation!

Adorning of the Caretaker - Story and a Poem

Nature's splendors and wonders magnified . . . and you didn't notice a
thing!
Time came, and time went.
Too busy, you!
Too sad . . . too busy you!
No man knoweth when the Son of Man cometh, except the Father!
He shall come as a thief in the night!

We knew that the Earth was a most crowning jewel to the Word, and in being created, not like we were created, but also . . . as -we were created.. Her splendor, her majesties, her mysteries, her numerous powers, known and enjoyed completely only by her ever watching, ever loving omnipotent Hand of Mercy!

165

The blessed children that she has kept as much as possible, in tender loving care, while it would appear, she eagerly awaits the masterful Creator of all, including she and her trusting inhabitants in Christ.

Not to be worshipped, not to be revered, but to be admired in all it's wondrousnesses!
Could she breathe, might she say, "Don't bow to me, but enjoy to your fullest, my millions-fold sparkles of spectacle!

Eat of my tasty bounty, keep my blood veins-my rivers-clean and pure, and drink the coolness thereof and quench that part of your physical thirst!
Breathe me, unpolluted. The oxygen of the air is sweet!

Contain yourself not! I am all in wonder to enjoy, even as a loving horse enjoys its rider, strutting in pride to boastfully exhibit for all to grasp in sightful, exuberant longing!

Come, look what I have in my entrust!
Worship not me!
Worship with me!
Of all creations in the magnificent universe, the Creator visits me!
*Of all creations in the universe, the Creator comes for **you**!*

Are my locks of hair, the clouds, adorning my beauty, my blue cheeks, my skies?
Do they gently tease upon my breasts, my mountains covered with foliage, trees and snow ...and the mothering of the wildlife, the clothing I display in all pride!
Does the dew trickle upon my face, moistening my skin, the green grass of my fields?

"Did I do well?" I ask.

"Did I do well?"

But to only ask . . . oh please to only ask . . .
And even my rocks and stones would fall down and worship You!
But to only hear You speak . . . that I could obey your command, and
my rushing seas and mighty winds and storms would with heart pounding in
excitement . . . obey!

Even the very twinkle of my eye ... the hand of time itself ...
Requires no skill ...to be mastered by You!

It is the whim of your fancy, your desire, Your imagination!
Visit me, oh my love, visit me!
Come to me that my pride is filled!
Come reap thy sweet harvest!

Did it, we not see?
You should have been taking-better care of me!
My needs, my cares . . . too few the great.
You need! You want! Sad mankind . . . it's your trait!

You were too busy . . . taking care
Of the thousand some-odd things, that threw you in despair
Time was, now time is, and every knee shall bow
I should have, but didn't...in time...not until now!

So sad, for you, that on that day,
When your Savior was told-He could be on His way.
He came, as He said, like a thief in the night.
Now, and now eternally...everything enjoys His Bright Light.

Too busy, you!

Too sad . . . too sad . . . too busy you!

Chapter 18

The Visit

Narrator: Unknown
Location: On trip towards home with the kids
When: ---

"*M*ommy, Mommy, Trisha keeps bothering me! She keeps calling me names and poking me!"

"No I'm not mommy! I'm wookin' at the cows! Mommy, when will we be there? I'm sweepy!"

"You girls behave now. Daddy will be surprised to see us, won't he? Bonny, try to stay awake honey. Daddy will be so happy to get a big hug from his little angels. Hey girls, look, more cows!"

Sarah and the girls had been to Atlanta to see her sick mother. The doctors didn't give her much hope. Well, actually, they gave her no hope of her spirit staying on earth for very much longer. It was a bittersweet visit because Sarah hadn't seen her mother for quite some time.

As is often the case with most families, problems came up that tore the family apart. The wonders that bind families together eroded in what seemed to be only a moment in time. Mix a little distrust and miscommunication and Mom became someone different. She just wasn't who she always seemed to be.

Sarah and her mother were both Christians, but they didn't heed God's word and the wounds festered. They didn't even try to come to terms with the problem until it was almost too late. Now, with so little time left, they regretted the loss of precious moments. Memories of old wounds gave way to a sadness that was unbearably real to them both.

Sarah's mother loved her very much. She loved her adorable granddaughters. When everything went wrong, she knew her loss would be great. She wouldn't just lose Sarah, she would also lose those loving little girls. At the same time, Sarah lost trust in her mother. She just didn't, and still couldn't comprehend the reason for the loss of trust.

Had she taken a good look at her own heart and wrestled with the demons that trespassed her thinking, she would have understood why her mother had done the things she had done.

There were good and logical reasons, not selfish ones. Well, that's the way Sarah's mother saw things. Even when she tried to understand what happened, in her heart she didn't believe she had done those things out of selfishness.

Quit asking what happened, because I'm not going to tell you! Quite frankly, it's none of your business! It's a family thing and your opinions, judgments, and debates about it aren't necessary. You just stick to reading and I'll make sure you know what you need to know, and when you need to know it. Anything else I could tell you would just satisfy your lust for gossip, and I'm very well aware of that! It isn't what happened that you need to know, it's what happened because of the thing that happened that you need to know about.

That's the point, it isn't what happened first, but what happened next in the sequence of events that matters …isn't it usually that way …especially in family situations?

This also you really need to understand ..that we can call these types of events time, and we all know that our time on earth is short. Like vapor, it's here today and gone tomorrow. You absolutely <u>must </u>take care of time!

If you ask a dying person about their life, they will tell you how short life was for them and how they can't believe it's almost over. (Inserted in memory of this authors Mother, Hazel Skelf, who went to rest in Christ's loving arms July 5, 1994, who was this authors most important Earthly guide to obedience of the Holy Spirit in giving his life to the

Lord, Praise God and thank You Lord !) They may be a Christian and ready to go, but something inside them wishes for a little more time . . . perhaps to do things better or fix something that needs mending or in some cases, because they want to be with the Lord, but also feel an impending upcoming separation from their loved ones here.

We're all going to die or be taken to meet the Lord in the clouds at the Rapture. Some will go sooner than others will, but we're all on our way and there's no stopping the inevitable. Perhaps we should pray for God's wisdom in using our time here wisely, *what do you think?*

Well, I guess I should get back to the story. I'm sorry I go off on tangents, but there's so much the Lord has laid on my heart that I must share with you. Okay, here we go again . . .Sarah and her mother lived as if time apart would heal their wounds-as if there was all the time in the world. Wrong! What were they thinking? Had either of them seriously considered how short time really is? Fervent prayers from a few very close friends and relatives were heard and answered by God. But did they really turn this problem over to Him as soon as they should have? I mean, did they turn it over to Him completely . . . with all due haste? Who knows?

If I were asked my opinion, I would have to say they didn't! But then, who can say for sure, and which one of us really knows the mind of God? We know He tests us and we know He challenges us. He tests our faith to strengthen it, to make us understand ourselves, to help us understand Him, to show us both natural and spiritual realities.

He also tests us to help us grow in ways that go directly against our human and carnal natures. What binds us to God-what repairs the broken relationship with Him-is repentance, salvation, and faith!

Now, I know that God never forgot Sarah's situation with her mother. He never took His eyes off it, never lost focus of it. Enough said? He was ever present in their hour of need just as He's always present in our hours of need. Just like Sarah and her mother received God's comfort, so we sometimes receive His comfort and realize that we're in His strong and all-capable hands. Sometimes He chooses to bless us with more, but whatever He chooses to do, we must remember that He has it all under His control. He can and will use our afflictions to His glory if we let Him!

Fortunately, Sarah and her mother realized this before it was too late. It didn't stop Sarah from crying tears of both sadness and joy! Understandable, wouldn't you say? She and her mother missed each other so much, they didn't know if they could continue tormenting each other with silence let alone not seeing each other. Only through God's love were they able to suffer through their prideful and self-imposed separation.

Sarah's daughters felt the pain, too! They knew their grandmother's warmth and her loving kindness for the short time she was part of their lives. They loved their grandmother, and no matter how much they heard the adults talk about her, they loved her with a childlike and Godly loyalty. There's just something about a grandparent that's more fun, more wonderful than any words can express! Sarah's mother was no exception to the rule . . . or was she? The fun things she taught, the joyous times together could never be forgotten and were always longed for by those little girls.

And so it was with today's visit. The girls wanted more time with their grandmother, but it was time to leave. Sarah was a wife, and her husband, Abel, was waiting for them at home. Sarah didn't know if she or her daughters would ever see her mother alive again-but she knew for certain that she would see her mother in Heaven one day. What a blessed reunion that would be!

How could she tell her mother goodbye, especially after all the time they'd lost? How would she explain it to her little girls? What would she say? After all, hadn't this cost them too? She would have to tell them the truth if they ever asked, **and you know they will!** Did Sarah have the right to witness to her husband now that he had learned the truth, about how unscriptural all this heartbreak had been? Had she lost her witness to him forever? Her deepest prayer was to see her husband and daughters go to Heaven someday!

Sarah's thoughts moved to their return home. Her daughters would run up to their father with hugs and kisses, and chants of "I missed you, Daddy!" He would hug them and kiss them and tell them how much he had missed him too. They would unpack their suitcases and Sarah would tell Abel all about the trip. She would tell him how excited the girls were to see their grandmother . . . and she would finally tell him about the extent and seriousness of her mother's illness. They would discuss it at length, and then they would talk about healing their mother-daughter relationship! She would then pray for him and witness to him, as she had never done before!

"Abel, time is short. Time is so very short," she would tell him . . . again.

"You must give your heart to the Lord. The girls and I want to be with you in Heaven someday! Oh, time is running out for us all! Please pray, Able, please pray!

She just knew that on this wonderful, beautiful, and glorious day, he would heed the tugging in his heart-the call of the Holy Spirit. He would humbly, fearfully, gladly, give his heart and soul to Jesus Christ. She just knew he would. There was something extraordinary about today. Her heart was singing as joyfully as the birds because she knew today was the day!

She started to enjoy all God's handiwork as they drove along toward home. She marveled at the level ground and the hills, and she thought about how all those wonders looked to her little girls. How did they see them? What fun it must be for them to see the cows and horses grazing, the squirrels and birds playing and working. Sarah also smelled the sweetness in the air-how crisp and fresh it smelled and how regimented the trees looked today! She mused that they were the color guard about to parade to the cadence.

The girls were now quiet, and they respectfully said "yes ma'am", when Sarah asked them if they were still awake. She saw beautiful scenes, just before the car topped each hill. It's as if we could keep going and drive straight through the air into The Father's loving arms in Glory! "I can just see it now", she thought to herself!

As they rolled down another hill, Sarah noticed that all the animals seemed preoccupied, as if they were in some deep thought or tuned into something far greater in power than the simple dominion man had over them. The car chugged up the next hill to reveal a spectacular view of the sky. How beautiful! She had never seen such gleeful and perfectly white clouds set against a bright and bold blue sky. It almost took her breath away.

"Almost home" she thought. "Thank God we're almost home . . . just past this last hill and we'll be home!"

And then it happened.

At that moment, just as the road crested the magnificent sky, Christ's "twinkling of an eye" occurred! The driver's seat and the girls' booster seats were empty. The seat belt that usually protected Sarah or her husband held no one in its safety!

Christ's rapture of the Church had just occurred. Sarah, Trisha, and Bonny were on a lightning quick ascent to meet Christ the Redeemer. Out of the corner of their eyes, they saw brothers and sisters in the Lord racing through the heavens. Then they saw Sarah's mother. They knew their grandmother saw them . . . and she also saw the Savior of mankind! They would all get to Heaven at the same time . . . and there would be no more separation for any reason! The excitement, the love, the thrill of their lives was to be in the presence of the Lord;

But what about Daddy, what about Sarah's husband, Abel? Oh my goodness, what about Able?

Please, dear God, what about Able?

Chapter 19
Lori and Mrs.Tobles

Narrator: Unknown
Location: The Compound
When: time of the play, Martyrs of The Cross

All of the wickedness and cruelty of those man-beasts slowed to a trickle, as if to place the righteous souls on high defensive. It was unusual not to hear news of atrocities on the Christian frontline. There was no news of any shift in policy. Did they think the battle had been won? Did they think now was the time to ease up on those they referred to as "the few remaining enemies of the state?" Did they honestly believe those "enemies" would simply and suddenly accept the new system, or did they want them quickly flushed out like a forty-eight-hour virus that finally dies off? Perhaps the Christians on this island did not hear through the grapevine about the continuing evil that wanted to destroy them-an evil they might believe was subsiding like floodwaters after a tidal wave, hurricane, or other tropic storm.

Well, in all honesty, there was no time to dwell on such thoughts. There was a drama in the making and, realistically speaking, they hadn't been given much to work with as far as talent goes! Two weeks ago, no one could have believed Grunt would participate in a play, much less a Christian drama. And who could have imagined Big Dog, alias Soul Winner, having a role in the play?

Those men had been rogues, rough hewn and bristling with hate and anger-men filled with vile meanness and given to treachery. They tortured or killed at the drop of a hat. Now they were working for Christ. They helped around the mission . . . and they prayed that God would get their lives in order so He could use them. They had so much to learn and so much to teach . . . and so many wrongs to right. The only tool at their disposal was the play . . . and they hoped and prayed that someone's life would be touched by it!

Everybody involved with preparing for the play was busy! Village people were from all over the island gathered at the compound. It had been years since some had seen each other and their reunions were joyous. Everyone was excited as they talking about the upcoming play. They knew what it was about, at least in vague generalities, and couldn't wait to see it. While they waited, they gathered in small groups and listened to believers share the love of Christ with them.

Everything that was pre-planned was completed. People had been arriving for two hours . . . well, really since last night, if you count the Jahannsons who arrived just after sunset. There were sleeping quarters available, and they were invited to stay. They even offered to help in any way possible, and the "gang" willingly took advantage of their offer!

Carts and horses were everywhere! Parking was mess, if one could call parking horses, mules, burros, and carts a parking situation. Several of the men helped tie the horses off. Others fed and watered the animals.

At ten o'clock that morning they were ready to start the play. As if was at the little white church, this would be a morning showing of the play. Everyone seemed to be in a good mood. Tina and Sam had been shaking hands with everyone they possibly could. Then, Tina went to the front left pew as Sam went forward to the antique pulpit.

"Welcome, everybody! Thank you all for coming to this miracle, this miraculous performance of *Martyrs of the Cross!*" Sam said. "We want everyone to enjoy the play and have a good time, and we pray that each and every one of you will get a special blessing from this drama. We pray that it will show each of you how strong you are in Christ. May He reveal to you the extent of that strength and courage that can only come from Him. The Christians at this compound believe time is short before Christ's return. We want to thank Him and praise Him for what He did for us so long ago. He took those awful beatings, those awful stripes, and suffered the humiliation and shame for us . . . all of us. He shed His blood for us, died on that old rugged cross at Calvary for all of us! He died for you! He died for me! Will you now believe in Him and believe Him? Will you now give your life freely to Him? Will you give your life in His name? I mean . ... really give your life?

Sam took a few steps and then looked out at the people whose faces radiated God's love. He saw the faces of those who were on the verge of turning their lives over to Christ, and the ones that still weren't completely sure which way to turn.

"Will you live a Godly life? Will you witness for Him? Will you stay strong for Him in the little things and the big things? Will you bridle your tongue and not use it for gossip, but for clean, pure, Christ-filled, and faith-filled conversation? Will you walk the walk and talk the talk? Even if you think nobody can hear you or see you, will you show you are in the center of God's will by keeping your speech and works clean and holy? Will you find creative ways to discuss Christ with other people? Will you stay strong even in the face of stiff opposition? Will you freely sacrifice to others for their well being and for the good of their souls . . . as a witness of Jesus in your life? Will you commit to show Him proudly in your everyday life? Will you stand for Him . . . no matter what?

"Those questions are the subject matter of this play. Indeed, He has a passion for you! Do you have a passion for Him? Do you have a burning fire for Him? Do you buckle and tremble at every hardship or do you stand strong in Him? Do you have faith only in what you see, hear, and touch? Christ said that it's easy to have faith in what you can see; but the blessing comes from having faith in that which you cannot see, but know in your heart!

"This is what this play is about! The strength and faith to witness, the strength to endure, the resolve to help as many people become Christians as you possibly can in your lifetime, so they can be part of God's glorious kingdom throughout all eternity!

"Yes, I've asked you good questions, and they are hard questions to ask yourself. But questions need answers . . . demand answers . . . and your answers cannot wait!

This world will demand those answers! Will you bear His Cross? Tell me .. . . will you? Will you be His good and faithful servants? Will you be with Him . . . to the end of the journey, as He is with you even to the end of the journey-the end of your days on earth?

"Will you stay strong for Him in these perilous times, as He was strong for you in the perilous times in which He lived among us? Will you rejoice in the face of tribulation? Do you have the faith to do as He asked you to do?

"Folks, we will start the play a little differently than it's been started in the past. We will start with a segment that we have titled, 'The Decision!'"

Janice Jonsen entered from a side door on the left. She was singing a rock song she knew. Lori Tokel came in from another door, singing a song she'd heard, "Does Anybody Care." It was Sister Brenda's song, which had become popular on Christian radio stations a few months back.

Just as Lori finished singing the song, Jenny started singing as she entered from front and center. Billy Budroe came dancing in from the front door. He was swaying and humming to the tune that Jenny was singing, a catchy little "worldly" song! The two girls pretended to not see each other, as if they were in different rooms.

As Billy was coming up front to the girls, he stopped as if to make a decision. What would he choose? Did he want the influences and attractions of the world, or did he want to become a Christian, set his sights on Christ, and pay attention to the preparedness of his soul? Billy went slowly from Janice to Lori . . . then he hesitated. He seemed very inquisitive. Then he slowly leaned towards Janice and she started singing the same song again! Billy got into that! He started singing with her!

Just then, Bobby Samps came in and went over to Lori. Janice and Billy stopped singing and watched Lori. Again, Lori sang about what

Jesus' death on the Cross meant to her. When she was finished singing, she looked at the other three and started witnessing to them. She told them that she hopes and prays they are Christians . . . then told them how to become a Christian. She told them about an experience that influenced her life so strongly, that when the Holy Spirit beckoned her, she responded.

She told them her life wasn't a rose garden before becoming a Christian and that it's still isn't. If they gave their lives to Christ, their lives wouldn't be ecstatically simple and trouble free.

"No, it doesn't work that way. Being a Christian means you could have the peace that comes from God, and eternal assurance that you will never enter hell when you die," she told them.

Billy, Bobby, and Janice listened to Lori. When she was almost finished talking, Bobby broke in and said something like, "Hey Lori, I thought you was one of us! This stuff is not cool, and I thought you were cool . . . we all thought you were cool like the rest of us. We though we knew you; but all this Christian stuff . . . what happened to you? I thought all that was an act to keep your folks off guard! Actually, I thought it was pretty good! I thought about trying to fool my folks with some of that Christian stuff just to throw them off my trail!"

The others stood in agreement with Bobby. Lori's sadness was evident on her face. Oh, she wasn't sad because of what they said; no . . . she was sad because she felt sorry for them . . . sorry for their souls . . . sadness that they might miss Heaven in all it's glory! She desperately wanted to reach them with the truth! She knew how much they could do with their lives if they gave them over to Christ . . . how much they could accomplish. She wanted to tell them about the things that are truly important . . . the things that are eternal, like witnessing and influencing the lives of others so they would ask Christ into their hearts, too. She tried to relate it to them with words she prayed were from God.

"I don't know exactly how to explain it. In a way, it's as if you were on this island for a long time, and wanted desperately to leave for a while . . . and . . ."

The others started laughing!

Lori became very quiet and embarrassed, and then laughed with them. Then she hesitated for a few seconds so she could get her thoughts in order . . . you know, back on track, in greater focus!

"Well, that was fun, but it's not enough," she said "Listen, what would you do if you knew you'd be going to a really great amusement park next month? And what if you knew that you'd have to stay here until it was time to go? Because you were really excited, you told all of your friends about where you'd be going! Then, you invited them to go with you at no cost to them. They'd get to go for free because a very kind and loving person had paid their way so you'd all have some fun."

Billy, Bobby, and Janice were very interested in Lori's example. Now, they wanted to know more.

"There's a catch, though! Your friends don't believe you. They've never heard of such a place and certainly haven't been there. What would you do if they told you they were too busy having their kind of fun to go with you? How would you feel?"

Everyone started laughing again . . . mostly because of the way she said it!

"Now I'm not saying that you've been to a place like that before, but at least you could imagine it! You could at least picture it in your mind . . . you'd have some idea how great it would be . . . but your friends couldn't. They've never even been off this island, so how could they imagine another place that's so extraordinary . . . .so incredible? How could they imagine the fun of going to a fabulous amusement park when all they know is this island?"

The room became very quiet as folks pondered Lori's words. This young girl was onto something that many of them, including the adults, just didn't understand. Would she be the one to help them see the big picture?

"Okay, so your friends didn't go with you because they thought the whole thing was ridiculous. So when the day arrives, you go without them, and it's too late for them to change their minds! You go to that wonderful amusement park and have a great time, but you wish they'd come with you! You know how wonderful it would have been if they had accepted your invitation. Just think how they would feel if they received postcards from you with 'wish you were here' all over them!"

Again…the congregation laughed . . . .oh, that Lori . . . there was something about her that was so likeable. People just loved to see her ham it up! They were terribly surprised by the sudden reaction of the other three teens. Billy, Bobby, and Janice started jeering at Lori. It was one of those "we're too cool for this kind of stuff" moments. Then they insulted her with nasty remarks about Christian girls. As they walked off laughing and ridiculing her, Lori spoke up and said, "I'll be praying for you! I'll pray for all of you!"

"Don't pray for us!" they yelled back at her. "We don't need that garbage, we don't need your prayers; and stay away from us and everybody we know from now on!"

Bobby pretended to push her so hard that she fell down! Janice sassed her and pretended to smack her. The three of them walked toward the back of the church where the doors are, together, still laughing and making fun of Lori. Lori was crying . . . and praying for them . . . and telling the Lord how much her heart aches for their souls and lives.

The narrator broke in telling everyone to pray for those who despitefully use us, and about loving people even though they hurt us, and to pray for those who cannot see the way to salvation. "We know that you've heard about this play, *Martyr's of the Cross*. Many of you are aware that there have been violent scenes *in* the play, and that violence has occurred because of the play.

That violence was directed to the congregations who were watching and participating in the play. Although we cannot guarantee your safety, we want to express our appreciation to each of you for coming here. We hope that before this play is over, you will all leave as Christians, sure of your eternal salvation! We pray that this night will otherwise be safe and uneventful for all of you!

"There have been several versions of the play and, at this point, we believe you've seen and heard enough cruelty towards Christians-like tales of the Crusades when Christians fought to take the Holy Land back from the Muslims and the Turks of the twelfth, thirteenth, and fourteenth centuries! We know you'd like to see a kinder and gentler version of the play, if there is such a thing, but we want you to understand that there is a Holy purpose to martyrdom for Christ!

"Some of the martyrs die, often suffering very cruel deaths. Some are imprisoned, and still others suffer without the imposition of death as the ultimate sacrifice. All, however, are witnesses of Jesus Christ, who was a witness of His Father, our Father, Jehovah God!
Let's now get on with the play!"

People started laughing because, as the narrator, Clancy Mac, was saying this, the people in the second act had already started coming out. They'd mixed up the cue they and came out a tad early! Well, I suppose, under the circumstances, those people probably needed a good laugh!

Clancy acted a little embarrassed, like he had done something foolish. It was pretty obvious where the mix up came from, though! Clancy scurried off center stage and the play continued.

Junior Hampton, who played the part of Mr. J., entered through one door, acting as if he was a big time businessman. Mrs. Jackie, who played Mrs. Tobles, came in through another door, twisting like she thought she was really something!

"Mrs. Tobles, would you please bring me those reports we've been working on?" Junior asked.

"Yes sir, Mr. J." Mrs. Jackie said. She pretended to hand him some files.

"Mrs. Tobles, this is not right. Have the temps not completed these files yet?" Mr. Hampton asked.

"Well . . . apparently not, sir," she said.

"This will never do!" he barked.

He then continued, "Well, that's going to mean more overtime for you! You'll have to come in on Sunday and work all day to complete this! I need it by next week, so make sure it's ready!"

Mrs. Tobles was in shock. How could she tell her boss the truth?

"I mean no disrespect, sir, but this is not a seven-day-a-week job. It's not like those other jobs, and there's no urgent need for it to become one. I always try to meet the requirements and deadlines of this job, but this time I can't. I must tell you that I prefer not to work on the day of the week I go to church to worship the Lord!"

"The choice is not yours!" he snapped "You will do as you are told! Now, like I said . . . be here on Sunday!"

She acted nervous, and said, "Mr. J., I like this job and I need the money, but I must take a stand. I cannot and will not come in on Sundays!"

"You must not like your job all that much . . . and you must not need the money your earn here all that much, either! There are people standing in line to get your position in this company, so I'll give you one last chance. *Be here on Sunday!"* he commanded.

She acted petrified. The participants in the play became very quiet . . . as if to give the audience time to contemplate what they would do in a situation like this . . . then she looked up and said, "Again sir . . . I cannot do this. I will not do this!"

"You're fired! Pack up your stuff and get out of here . . . and don't use me for a reference!" Mr. J. screamed.

She didn't rush to obey his hideous command. Instead, she told him that she wanted to pray for him. He ordered her *not* to pray for him and-using a barrage of shocking epithets-told her to leave. She told him again that she felt the need to pray for him . . .. and she started to pray.

Mr. J. played his part well . . . as if he was furious. Then as the new scene called for, he contacted corporate security officers on his intercom. It didn't take long for two burly men to arrive at his office. As soon as they entered, he told them to arrest Mrs. Tobles for refusing to leave and for harassing him.

She acted scared out of her wits, then prayed again for God to grant him wisdom over his business and over his decisions. She prayed for God to take control over this situation and help her at this time. And, she prayed for Him to give her peace that the situation was in His hands and in his control.

The audience loved her . . . they almost clung to her . . . as if they had bonded with her! Some were seen praying for her, even though she was just a character in a play.

The men acting as security officers pretended to arrest her. They escorted her off the stage, but that didn't stop her Christian heart from its assignment.

"I will still pray for you! I will pray for you to get your life right with the Lord! I will pray that whoever you replace me with will be a strong Christian who God will use to lead you to Him!"

Mr. J. snorted and fumed about having to get a replacement. How would he ever find someone as moral, ethical, honest and willing to work as Mrs. Tobles. He knew that most workers had no values and no core beliefs to keep them honorable on the job . . . or anywhere else.

"I hope I can find someone as good as Mrs. Tobles," he said aloud, playing his part to perfection. "She's a hard one to replace." He put his head down and ran his hands over his face, his anger gone and replaced with exhaustion.

As he tried to figure out how he would replace Mrs. Tobles, a woman entered his office hoping to get the now-vacant position.

"Hey, Mr. J., I want that job!" she said in a demanding tone of voice.

The acting was excellent . . . far better than anyone expected it would be with so little time to rehearse.

Desperate to replace the good woman he just fired, Mr. J. hired the woman who just walked into his office . . . a woman who was very bossy and crass. After a few exchanges between the two, Mr. J. knew she would make his life miserable. Mr. J. began to mumble again about something Mrs. Tobles said to him as she was leaving with the security officers.

"The last thing Mrs. Tobles said to me was from . . . Romans 12:18. He raced to his massive bookshelf and pulled the dusty Bible that had been there for years off the shelf. His fingers turned the pages in search of the verses she had cried out to him. Then he found them and read them aloud.

"'Dearly beloved, avenge not yourselves, but rather give place to wrath, for it is written, vengeance is mine: I will repay, saith the Lord.'" Then he remembered something else she said. "She said something about 'if your enemy is thirsty, give him drink' . . . and something about 'heaping coals of fire on his head.'"

He looked at the congregation, as if worried or puzzled. They looked at him and laughed! He looked at his new secretary, then back at them . . . back and forth . . . it was certain that everybody got the picture of what he was thinking. The congregation laughed even harder!

When things died down, he dropped to his knees and begged the Lord for forgiveness, asked him to enter his life . . . and asked for extra forgiveness for what he had done to Mrs. Tobles. Taking a stand for the Lord and doing what she knew was right in God's eyes, Mrs. Tobles was a martyr for Christ. The circumstances weren't important. Mrs. Tobles suffered humiliation and a job loss . . . and the hardships that go along with it.

The narrator broke in with, Luke 12:6 and 7. "'Are not five sparrows sold for two farthings, and not one of them is forgotten before God? But even the very hairs of your hear are numbered. Fear not therefore, ye are of more value than many sparrows.'"

The congregation was touched by the Holy Spirit, they praised God and shouted and thanked Him! Their praises went on for several minutes and the play stopped. There was no way anyone would interrupt a move of God from the Holy Spirit.

When the play resumed, it went extremely well. As each scene was acted out, people in the congregation were saved, while others fought back believing they still had time . . . time to get it right . . . someday . . . later.

That was a bad mistake! It was a very costly and eternally bad mistake!

It is wise never to procrastinate and it is just as unwise to turn your back on the Holy Spirit! Don't turn away from God's voice!

Chapter 20

Attack !

Narrator: Unknown at this present time
Location: The Islands
When: Little Time, BCR

*T*here was unexpected movement outside the compound that got closer and closer to the chapel where the play was being performed! As the seconds ticked away, the sounds grew louder. *The folks watching over the burros and horses outside were the first hit!* Well, no matter for the attackers because they didn't care about anyone!

They didn't have any loved ones there; I doubt they had any loved ones anywhere!

Those insurgents were not like you and me. They burst into the church as if this was the hide out of Billy the Kid or Jesse James! Oh, they were too late to stop the play . . . .too late to prevent the salvation of some members of the congregation. Those folks gave their lives to Christ. "No man can pluck them from the Father's hand."

There was a lot of human devastation on that island that day; the kind of carnage no one wants to think about . . . .the kind no one could believe one man would wreak on another!

Did they spill the blood of the innocents? Yes, there was a lot of blood spilled that day. Were believers tortured . . . was there intense suffering and agony? Yes, there was an abundance of that! Were lives shattered physically for most, and emotionally for the rest? It was short-lived, but when a person is brutalized even for a moment, that life is still shattered.

Most people went through the physical, mental, and emotional agony of seeing their loved ones tortured and killed. What greater torture could mortal men or women endure?

Were people poisoned? Yes, poison was used on some of those folks and it wasn't the gentle type of poison! No, they forced them to take the horribly painful stuff!

Then there were the beheadings! Men . . . women . . . children . . . . yeah . . . with no exceptions!

Hands ...eyes ...fingers ...legs ... arms ...burning skin ....nothing was exempt!

No, it was no big deal to those who tormented them.

People who were alive, breathing, and praying were flung from a cliff. Their screams were hideously shrill . . . but now their mangled dead bodies lay at the bottom of the cliff!

So still ...so still ...

They were mocked as they were forced to climb to the top of the cliff . .. . and as they were hurled headfirst into eternity. "It's not the fall that'll get you . . . it's the landing," their attackers mocked them time after time!

I could go on and on, but why? You get the picture!

Reader, if you want to read about all the gory details of what happened that day, you must be pretty sick!

From the beginning, I told you to close this book. I told you not read it! Now, do you think I'm going to tell you all the horrific things that happened to those fabulous brothers and sisters in Christ, that day? Forget it!

Not happening!!!

Like I told you before, I'm the storyteller . . . you're the reader!

You and I missed the Rapture, so I'm stuck here writing and you're stuck, where you are, reading and trying to figure out what happened-all of which I'm not going to tell you.

I will tell you that we should have paid closer attention, but we didn't. So

. . . here we are, and you want me to tell you about how evil things were. You want to know the minute details of the horrible pain inflicted on the *martyrs*?

Is that what you really want? Well, I'm **not** going to tell you! I know I could, but I'm not going to!

I was there! I saw it all! They couldn't hurt me, even though they wanted to. There were two reasons they couldn't hurt me. Do you care to know what they are? Well, of course you want to know!

The first reason they couldn't hurt me is because I'm the writer of this book, so they know that I'm off-limits. They knew that, and as bad as they wanted to get to me, they couldn't! Someone had to be left unharmed to tell the story . . . I mean the truth about what happened.

The second reason made it easier to pass me up, to ignore me, notwithstanding the first reason. More importantly, reader, I wasn't a Christian at the time so there was no point in torturing or killing me. That's why we weren't harmed . . . because the torture and killing of those other folks was about the eradication of the Christians, not the unbelievers. Oh, some non-Christians got it that day …wrong place …wrong time!

Oh, I forgot to mention that there's a third reason. You see, I was petrified out of my wits. Now be honest, wouldn't you be scared senseless? Come on! Tell the truth, now, I know for a fact that you would be scared to death just like I was!

So the third reason came down to the fact that I ran like wildfire. I ran so far and so fast that I nearly ran the souls off my shoes! I ran so hard and got so lost that *only* God could find me! Before I got the clear opportunity to run, though, I did see a lot of things I wish I hadn't seen; and I started to realize a lot of things I wish I 'd realized much, much sooner!

Now, I'll tell you that our Brothers and Sisters in Christ were not all that lucky . . . or maybe they were! Their pain and agony lasted for an eternity . . . at least it did to them. Trust me, it didn't last that long. Eternity lasts for a long, long time. In fact it lasts longer than time. The thing is, we weren't created for time, we were created for eternity. Only our human bodies were created for time!

I also think you should know that the play wasn't the reason all those people were hurt and killed. No, not at all! It was the need for control by those who rebelled against God!
Think about it! Weren't we always their pawns, even before all the violence began? Didn't the alleged powers-that-be, the "elites" of the world, believe they had the "right" to rule over us? That's exactly how it was, but even when they did all they could do to us, our souls are in the hands of our heavenly Father, alone . . . exclusively!

Come to think of it, maybe I should tell you some of the things that happened, because you probably need some inspiration. I know I need it! It's the kind of inspiration that will help us make it through these days of tribulation, this Time of Jacob's Trouble-with the full knowledge that it will be over soon. We can count the days because He told us that number!

Also, in retrospect, I think it would be unfair not to tell you! I mean, since you've read this much of the book, it would be unfair of me to keep it all to myself. It's a fair deal. I'll get to talk about some of those events with someone who shares a joint interest, and you'll understand what really happened. Maybe it's not that you're nosey, maybe you just need inspiration just like I do!

How could we make it through the rest of the Tribulation and Great Tribulation without hope?

Love,

Faith,

Hope!

Each has its own characteristics, but they are all intertwined. They work together in so many ways. Please don't ask me to baby you so much that you can't figure that one out for yourself. Okay, so right now, hope is a lifeline for us-a major component of the inspiration we need to keep going!

You do still have hope, don't you? Even the people at the

compound had hope! Even as they endured the horrors they went through, they still had hope! They knew God was with them, even unto the end . . . even unto the beginning of their eternal lives in His presence! So, I'll tell you the things of hope and to help inspire you! Listen closely, because I won't repeat this story unless God gives me sufficient grace to do so!

Many of the town's people that were visiting started to get sick. They were vomiting suffering with diarrhea, sweats and flu-like symptoms that were similar to the flu. They started convulsing to the point of near death? Who could they call? 911? No! There was no 9-1-1 there!

The compound had a couple of doctors, seven or eight nurses. There were also seven or eight other people who were not trained in medicine, but they assisted the doctors and nurses from time to time. One of the doctors and several of the nurses and helpers were among the first to get sick. There was no one who could handle the situation!

No wonder! Counter surveillance and infiltration teams had tainted the pre-play banquet food with botulism or something, and had dusted half dozen choice sites with trace amounts of rat poison of some kind. They were clever! They dusted that stuff near the wash stands and in the out house facilities.

Almost everyone visited those locations before the play began! ISD figured most visitors to the compound and those who lived there would be so weak by the end of the play, there would little or no resistance to their attack. And that's exactly what happened. Those nicely suited men and military folks barged in to find a community starting to get very sick. All they had to do was mop-up work! Then, they had their "fun"!

It went according to their evil plan! By the time the people at the compound realized what had happened, it was way too late to do anything to stop it! Only God could have stopped that lethal attack on His children!

Mercy? You want to know if they showed those folks any mercy? Don't be ridiculous! What did they know about mercy? They were nasty men . . . and nasty women! Their hearts were hardened worse than the big bully you ran from throughout your childhood! Either you took a stand

and probably got hurt or you didn't take a stand and you *did* get hurt! What could you have done under such circumstances?

Well, in this case, you didn't do anything! Wait a minute… yes, in fact, you did do something. You prayed! You prayed for safety, or you prayed for His comfort so you could endure the trial! Yes, that's what you did . . . and you were right to do as you did!

Of course, those ISD folks didn't give anyone a chance to escape, let alone survive. Their cruelty had increased to the point that they considered all the people at the compound *guilty by association..* Anyone who was there was considered a radical Christian and dangerous. They were not to be taken alive. They were to be snuffed out, with no exceptions!

Chapter 21

ZZZZZing

Narrator: Not sure, possibly someone on the Island, or this books author
Location: "The Islands"
When: Shortly BCR

I guess I didn't tell you that some people did escape from those ISD killers that day and became fugitives from justice. None escaped the compound without a scratch, even if the scratch were deep emotional pain from losing loved ones or dear friends. It was a terrible time of grief for those poor souls. I'm sure you can understand how devastated they were, can't you?

Okay, so you've figured out that I've left out something big. Well, you're right, but this isn't the time to tell you about it. I'll tell you in a few minutes, so promise me you won't race ahead of me . . . like the little oxen in the yoke, you have to let the big oxen lead so you get it right. In other words, slow down! You're lucky I've told you anything. I almost didn't! And sometimes I think I shouldn't!

In a way, I feel especially sorry for the visitors that day, especially those who didn't make it to the altar to repent. Many died in their sins and are now crying out in agony a billion times worse than those men could inflict on them. Now, their pain comes directly from hells' flames. At the end of the Tribulation, they'll be sentenced to the Lake of Fire to burn forever!

If they'd just had the opportunity to see the whole play, if they only had a little more time, they might have repented! It never happened! Who knows? Maybe they would have gotten their lives right with God, maybe they wouldn't have!

Still, I can't help but believe that a few minutes would have made all the difference in the world . . . and in heaven . . . .for those folks! Oh, I know you agree with me . . . .I just know you are all too aware of the difference a few minutes, even a few seconds can make in one's life. And, just a few minutes might be all it takes to change eternity for you! You might not make it to the end of this book! You might not make it to your next breath! It's possible that we're all one breath away . . . one heartbeat away of losing this life and entering the other side of eternity!

So here's a morbid fact that might make you sit up and take notice. You will die . . . and go straight to hell . . . unless . . . you accept Jesus as your Lord and personal Savior. That's right! You are bound for a hellish eternity unless you get right with God . . . .now! You might make it to the Glorious Appearing, but what if you don't? Are you willing to take that chance as an unbeliever? Might be better to try to make it through as a Christian . . . a totally forgiven child of God. I know, because of what happened while I was at the compound that day.

The two girls, Janice and Lori, had been poisoned and were dying. One of the mercenaries came up to them and decided to do them a favor. He asked them if they were Christians. They both claimed Christ as their Savior, knowing that it might be the last time they would have a chance to make such a claim

Well, that merc told them everything was fine, dandy, and all right. He was going to help them out of their suffering whether they were Christians or not . . . but their professions of faith made it a little easier for him. He pulled his machete as far back as he could and swung down so fast that the blade whistled as it sliced through the air!

Sweet little Lori hadn't seen it coming and never had a clue what hit her! She never heard the loud thump it made as it disengaged her head from her body! At least there wasn't time for the screams that a lot of people made that day, as their decapitations took place. There were no guillotines, so many were beheaded with dull knives. Those were the same dull knives the mercs used to destroy dense foliage on their way to the compound. There was no reason to use clean knives. Those folks would be dead anyway, so there'd be no chance of infection from a dirty knife!

Poor Janice was also a beautiful young lady. She just happened to be at the compound that day by chance. Her mother was a traveling missionary on another island in the area when they heard the play would be performed at the compound. Her mother had always wanted to see it, from the first time she had heard of it! This was their golden opportunity!

Janice had always been the studious type. That girl was unbelievably smart! She and her mother arrived two days before the day of the play, and Tina Harks asked her to fill in for a girl who couldn't play her part because she'd gotten sick. Well, Janice loved acting and jumped at the chance!

When the attack on the compound started, the sick girl escaped into the jungle, but Janice didn't. No, she was next in line for the machete that sent Lori to heaven. At least the blade they used on her was sharp . . . there was no slow torture.

At some point leading up to the second half of the Tribulation, I'd often heard how wretchedly vile and unmercifully cruel the powers that be were to their "prisoners." I'd heard that the Christians would never know who the antichrist is, because they would be caught up in the Rapture. What I didn't know was that the world was getting ready for its acceptance of him long before he stepped into his evil role.

What was I thinking? It was all around us! It had been for more than a century, and suddenly things moved quickly, and it started to get worse by the minute! We didn't accept the changes, so they forced them upon us until we got used to them. After all, change can be good in a modern world. Many believed there was no point fighting it because it was all part of God's plan. There was nothing they could do to stop it or slow it, was there? That's what they believed and nothing would change their minds or get them to stand up against evil.

Again, I hesitate to tell you all of this. Still, I have to ask you again if your motives for reading this book are . . . correct . . . sincere? I can't force you to answer that question, but you might want to think about it for a few minutes. Why are you reading this book? Why? You maybe should take a break and search your heart for an honest answer.

Now, I'll ask you to be even more honest. Are you reading this book because you like to read horror stories and because you're glad Christians were persecuted? Instead, maybe the reason is a better one-to build personal strength so you can make it through the Tribulation without taking the Mark of the Beast.

Actually, your motives are none of my business. If your reason is because you like to read horror, that's just great. You should continue to read. You've already missed the Rapture, but maybe you'll see something in your future that will scare your socks off; Maybe you'll be scared enough and wise enough to give your heart and soul to the Lord before that option is lost forever.

Chapter 22

COREST

Narrator: Through research we have figured out this was definitely written by this books author
Location: "The Islands"
When: very shortly BCR

If you're a Christian, then you became one after the Rapture, otherwise you'd be with the Lord right this minute! If that's the case, read on and pray that you will not take the "mark." Pray that you will make it to Christ's Glorious Appearing! I know that prayer works and it will help you gain strength to make it through . . . and to read this chapter!

Grunt saw what was happening. He was well aware of the nature and workings of cruelty; he just had no intention of participating in it ever again! With the poisoning of the people at the compound, Grunt moved into protection mode, but it was too late! There were no rescues by Grunt that day! His time was cut short.

The arrow sailed through the air with a forceful zing. The shooter didn't miss his mark. The arrow hit exactly where he wanted it to hit- about two inches from Grunt's heart before it went through his body!

Grunt never had a chance! He had run into people as mean as or meaner than he had ever been! As soon as they recognized him, they murdered him to keep him from killing them. Oh, it didn't end there. Those mercs wanted him to see what was going to happen next, so they didn't aim exactly for his heart. No, they wanted him totally incapacitated, but not quite dead yet!

Obviously, some of these men were former associates of his! Perhaps it has always been true that there's "no honor among thieves." Well, it certainly rang true that day for Grunt.

Big Dog, alias Soul Winner, was next. About ten mercs tackled him all at once! They were cowards, even when they strung him up in a tree! Oh, they were so wretched toward him. They tied his hands together and threw the other end of the rope over the high limb of a tree. Then they raised him about ten feet in the air. No, they didn't hang him from his neck, they hung him from his arms and they didn't leave it there. They tied his feet and knees together, rolled a big rock under him, and stretched the bottom rope tightly around the rock.

They told him he was poisoned in such a way that he would have to watch the others, as they were tortured to death. They told him that in a little while, they would "draw and quarter" him! There was nothing he could do to protect those he'd come to love so much.

Big Dog and Grunt must have been very confused. Where were all the guardian angels that had been camped around the compound just a few days earlier? Where had they gone? They had kept Big Dog, Grunt, and their men away; so where were they now? Both men wondered if this was payback for all their meanness. Surely not! Surely the Lord wouldn't allow all this to happen just to get even with them!

I'll tell you a secret…they never learned the answer to that question until they were in heaven. At the time, though, it drove them nuts, even through their own physical pain. What they really wanted to know more than anything in the world was the status of their relationship with God. If they were truly right with Him, they could endure everything that was happening to them.

I know . . . you want to know, too! I'll tell you, pretty soon. Just hang in there! I'll get to it in a little while!

Well remember, people were getting sicker and sicker by the minute. Some were already dead from the poisons. Others were mutilated. No, I will not go back into that . . . there's no need for that! Paint your own ugly picture of that scenario. I will not tell you about it! I don't feel good about telling you about this, anyway! Take what information I'm giving you and be satisfied with it. Besides, I think you're a little on the pushy side anyway! Here goes . . .

Big Dog and Grunt's men were in shambles. Almost all of them were ambushed and killed quickly, or they were captured and experiencing the same fates as their former bosses. Men and women, stretched tightly like guitar strings, were hanging from trees all around the compound. They hung on every tall tree with a limb high enough and strong enough to hold the weight of a person!

It was a really strange scene. I often think about it . . . like they had created some hideous stringed instrument. I don't know, but it looked as if some huge person would play a song using humans as strings. Yes, that scene was utterly horrific! And talk about a captive audience! Anything the mercs wanted to do or say, was seen and heard by all the people they had strung up!

It hurt! It hurt like crazy! Blood didn't flow through their arms like it normally did because circulation was cut off at the wrist by those ropes! Rib and chest muscles ached to the point of pulling loose all the way up the arms! Their legs were stretched to the ground, which made it even more painful . . . more horrific.

Hard to breathe! So hard to breathe!

What's the matter? You don't like reading about things like this? You don't like knowing that things like this happen? Well, I tried to warn you that the truth is worse than fiction! I truly hope you don't have nightmares! I hope you have sweet dreams tonight even though you know what happened.

You do realize that even worse waits soon for you if you don't take the mark of the beast, don't you? Oh, and you do know that it will be millions of times worse if you do take that mark! Remember, you missed the Rapture, so how will you survive the Tribulation without taking the Mark of the Beast? What? You don't want the mark! Well, what will you do to make it through to The Glorious Appearing of Christ?

In the days leading up to the Rapture, cruel acts like these occurred all over the world. One huge company took over the lion's share of those operations. The newly elected Vice-President of the United States owned it. Wouldn't you know that money and politics would be involved, even to sponsor such horrors? Anyway, it was and is still called COREST, which was an anagram for Christian and Other Religions Eradication Services Technologies.

Their primary mission was pretty obvious, but they also had a secondary mission. It was based on the Revolving Population Theory (RPT), which was first made popular by Adolph Hitler. It didn't take long for it to catch on among other ruthless tyrants.

At the heart of the theory was the eradication of those people terminally ill-those brain damaged, but still alive.

You do remember Terri Schiavo don't you? The courts sided with her husband and ordered her to die by starvation and dehydration, which she did on March 31, 2005, in a Florida hospice. The courts took away all the parents rights to keep her alive, and her husband who had been in a relationship with another woman for nine years, wouldn't even allow them to be with her as she died! Then, when she did die after thirteen days, he had her cremated, which goes against her Catholic faith. He then reportedly, took her ashes to an unknown, "secret" place somewhere up north, where her loving, protective parents could not ever know where they are and could not ever visit the site of her ashes!

Way to go, Florida courts that made the ruling against her parents, and doomed Terri Schiavo's life on this Earth! Even the Supreme Court of the United States wouldn't intervene!

(About six months earlier, a Florida court ordered a man to serve six months in prison for starving his dog to death. What he did wasn't right, but isn't a *human life* more valuable than a *dog, even taking into consideration the special circumstances?*)

There were many other disturbing aspects to this mind boggling event, but needless to say, Christians by the droves were arrested, men women and children, for trying to save the life of this precious woman, her life ordered snuffed out in a torturous, slow process by the same courts that protected her husband with police snipers on roofs of buildings close to the hospice she was dying in. (Kind of reminds you of a possible lead up to similar tactics used at the Little White Church by the I.S.D., and COREST, doesn't it?)

Question. …what is the difference between the way they killed her and lethal injection? The only answer I have is that lethal injection is the way a great many dangerous, hardened criminals are put to death. It is "humane …so they don't suffer.

Terri Schivo's crime? She collapsed while on the verge of anorexia while trying to stay thin, I would suppose probably to be attractive to her husband!

This woman wasn't brain dead! She was brain damaged to some extent. She wasn't a "vegetable". I always heard that state as being one where either the brain is basically dead…can't respond, and the body is still okay, or both are totally irretrievably close to death unless drastic measures are take to extend the persons life. Was a feeding tube "drastic?"

What the public was allowed to see via television was neither. Also, this woman had no Living Will, to tell the courts or medical world what she would want to happen to her if she had become in that bad of condition. She was connected to a feeding tube, but was not connected to a respirator. She was breathing on her own …she just needed help with the feeding part.

Long live the memory of Terri Schiavo!
Long live the memory of what those American courts did to her!
Long live the memory of those brave people who allowed them to be arrested while protesting what had been done and for the other brave people who tried to help, in vain.

(Do you want the fictional parts of this book to come true? Just keep sitting there, doing nothing, not raising your voices in protest dogmatically against atrocities like this, and my guess is, those types of events are not far behind!)

~

The Revolving Population Theory continued with AIDS, cancer, leukemia, and other deadly diseases …from the moment of diagnosis, Phase two of the theory included the eradication of the poor, the homeless, the aged-the latter included those who were sixty or older, and the lesser mentally or physically challenged. The last phase was for those who were considered spiritually incurable. Those who believed in Jesus Christ had to be systematically eradicated as well. Anyone who they believed was a burden to society was fair game!

This is not baloney …it's for real!

Oh, it was all declared legal by the judges! No monkey business for them! They thought it was sport to shoot to kill, or kill on sight anyone who got in the way of the New World Order government. Yes, indeed, it was all approved under the Right Justified Homicide Laws, a subsection of the Positive Movement of Society Initiatives enacted by Congress. It didn't take long for it to be approved by other governments . . . one by one until it was in operation worldwide.

Wake up! Where have you been? Didn't you think this could happen? What rock have you been sleeping under? I don't even know why I'm wasting my ink telling you about this! Oh, sure, you said you wanted to know, but when I tell you the truth, you turn a deaf ear or get upset! Well, get your head out of the sand and face facts! Is it too hard to believe, or do you just refuse to believe?

That does it! I'm going to continue telling you just a little bit more of what happened at that particular place in the world because you have to face the truth! I could tell you a lot of different stories of "events" happening all around the world, but I wasn't there, so I would have been reporting second hand information to you. I was on that island, though, so I can give you a first-hand, eyewitness account.

Remember where we left off? You were hearing about the poisoning, torture, and maiming. Grunt had been shot with an arrow all the way through him, as well as many other people who had been shot close range with arrows or bullets. Soul Winner and many others had been strung up and stretched like guitar strings! Sounds great, like a place you would like to have been, doesn't it?

There were others, also! In loving memory, I feel compelled to list them, instead of just writing their names one by one in a sentence. They deserve better than that, in my opinion!

Sister Mary . . .

Sister Mary Martha . . .

Sam and Tina Harks . . .

Eight other people, with their hands bound behind their backs, were led to the front of a six-foot-high, wood fence that faced all the people who were strung up on the tree limbs. Nine mercs, including a captain and eight of his underlings, formed a firing squad! Sister Mary and Sister Mary Martha prayed as they have never prayed before! Sam and Tina prayed for deliverance from their enemies, finished their prayers and told the others to be brave. "Trust God!" they cried. "He knows exactly what He's doing! Their captors allowed them to hold hands …such a sweet thing they did! Yeah, right! Nothing sweet about these evil hooligans!

Mrs. Saaths, was the next to place her head on the bloody chopping block in front of the man with the machete! At least she wasn't going to have her head whittled off by dull knives, like so many of her dear friends had already endured!

I have to stop here . . . right now! I have to pray . . . I just can't speak anymore . . . give me a minute or two.

Thank you!

Chapter 23

0

*M*y goodness, my goodness! This is so hard to talk about. Martyrdom for Christ is never a pretty picture, even if it doesn't result in death! Still, I often asked myself why anyone would put himself (or herself) in such a situation. Why would anyone have an overwhelming need to talk about such events? Truth is, there's absolutely no comfort-zone here!

If you don't get it by now, you'll probably never get it. I started to say that you're hopeless, but you aren't. By Christ's spilled blood, none of us are hopeless! There's hope for every man and woman until they finally decide . . . to take the Mark of the Beast!

Okay, that said, I think I can tell you the rest of the story now. Remember that I absolutely feel awful about telling you all this, so please pay close attention! I don't want you to ask me to do this again, because I won't!

All eyes were on Mrs. Saaths as she was praying…and telling her late husband that she was rejoicing that she would very quickly now, be seeing her Savior…and also him. She told him to just meet her by the Jordan…as she started to place her head on the blood moist, blood soaked chopping block.

Mrs. Saaths was always the neat and tidy one!

She tried so hard to find a spot on the block to place her sweet head and neck that wasn't drenched with blood. Poor Mrs. Saaths tried to stay neat and clean right up to the end, but it wasn't to be as she planned. The merc with the machete stepped forward and smashed her face into a large build-up of the sticky goo! Her nose started to bleed! Sam, Tina, and Big Dog started to cry for Mrs. Saaths, but her words were inspiration to their hearts.

"Lord, thank you Jesus! In you I place all my trust, as all people living and dying should! Thank You, Jesus, for allowing me this privilege, this honor! Use my death for your glory, Father!" she screamed to the heavens.

Sam, Tina, and Big Dog quit crying and shouted praises to their Lord and Savior. They laughed as the joy in their souls was magnified. The man with the machete just shook his head and looked disgusted. Again, he pulled way back on the swing-arc of the blade, as if he were cocking a gun. It was almost as if it had a rope attached to it that pulled it back!

The merc was anxious to complete his evil deed. Sam and Tina prayed again and looked at each other with deep love. They knew their time on earth was over. Sister Mary and Sister Mary Martha also prayed. Both women had their eyes tightly closed.

The blade came whistling through the air towards Mrs. Saaths' unprotected neck! As it raced closer to her neck . . . commands could be heard,

Ready ..Aim ...FIRE!

The sounds of gunfire could be heard. It sounded like a cannon! The bullets came screaming towards Sister Mary, and Sister Mary Martha, Sam and Tina Harks, and the others, as all the people strung up in the trees watched in horror! The blade whistling so close to Mrs. Saaths soft neck tissue, one hundredth of a second more and it would inflict it's mortal irreversible deed of separation

Their hearts almost stopped! Not because of the sight in front of them, but because of the sight above them . . . in the clouds! At that exact moment, they were caught up in the Rapture of Christ's children!

All Glory to God in the Highest!

The blade of the machete vibrated violently as it hit the chopping block. There was no human flesh on the block to stop it from slamming into the hard wood!

"What in the name of the living God!" the merc yelled as he shook his throbbing hands. He couldn't have said anything more appropriate at that moment!

The sounds of bullets ripping through the air and popping as they hit their marks were unmistakable. They hit the wood planks unopposed! There was no skin, no muscle, and no bones to hit because there was nobody there! I'll say that one more time. There was nobody there!

Those brave warriors for Christ never felt a thing! They were not hit! They were Raptured in a moment . . . in the twinkling of an eye! It happened that fast! Faster than a bullet! Faster than all those bullets combined! Those rifles and bullets never stood a chance! In the name of the Living God, the timing was miraculous!

Sam and Tina, Sister Mary and Sister Mary Martha, and Mrs. Saaths were in heaven with Christ and would soon see their loved ones they hadn't seen for so long! As for the folks who were strung up on the trees, well, some were still there. The only evidence of the Christians who had dangled from those trees was the empty ropes that held each of them in place. Those ropes just zinged and whistled through the air, then gently swayed in the breeze . . . empty!

Grunt, Big Dog, and the men at the compound were with Jesus! No ropes could hold them from the power of the One who loved them enough to die for them . . . the one who loved them enough to come back for them!

They weren't there to tell me this, but if they could, they would have thanked God that the gang from the compound loved them and taught them about God's love and mercy, and showed them how they could have everlasting life with their Savior!

They never did figure out if it had been angels guarding the complex, and if so, where had they gone and why? I was never sure about that either. I have my theories, though. I think it had a great deal to do with Christ's Second Coming, or maybe there were multiple reasons.

I know I think too much, but maybe God decided that His people at the compound didn't need the angels anymore. The Bible tells us about Christ's crucifixion and the hour when Christ needed God so much. It also tells us that Christ felt that God had forsaken him. In case you didn't know, that was Matthew 27:46.

Well, God didn't forsake Jesus. Our heavenly Father cannot look upon sin, for He is Holy. When Christ died on that cross, He took the sins of all of us on His shoulders. He became the bearer of all sin. That, dear reader is what happened on the Cross that day, at that hour! If we repent, we can believe Him and know we're forgiven, or we can keep the total responsibility for our sins and deny what He did for us.

You must want to know the end of this part of the story and how it relates to what I just said.

Okay, those Christians at the compound didn't die for the sins of others the way Christ did, but the sins of others did contribute to their deaths. I also think God called those protective angels away when He did because some of those people were meant to be martyrs for Christ. Those who died at the compound that day and those who were Raptured out before they were murdered all met the Lord in the clouds "to be with him forevermore." They weren't just part of the Rapture, they were witnesses to it . . . witnesses who would be part of the great army that would one day escort the Lord to earth at the Glorious Appearing!

Oh, get with the program, reader! God is a great big God and His purposes are beyond anything we can understand. I just know they're good enough for me whether I understand them or not. Remember, "His ways are not our ways, His thoughts are not our thoughts." He's so much greater than anything we can hope to be . . . Praise His Name!

So I keep coming back to the same understanding of what happened at the compound that day. "All things work together for good, to them that love God." Let me repeat Romans 8:28 so that you really get it this time. "And we know that all things work together for good to them that love God, to them who are the called according to His purpose!" It's sad that everyone at the compound didn't take advantage of his or her very last opportunity to repent!

The bullets that didn't hit flesh went through the wood fence and wounded or killed several mercs on the other side. Several people were still strung up because they didn't turn their lives and souls over to Christ. They were now the targets for the mercs, who were confused and angry that some of their prisoners had "escaped." Their rage knew no limits and it was used against those who failed to repent.

Just think, I was there. Yes, I was hidden, but I was there! I could have gone to be with Jesus like those who gave their hearts to Him, but I was too arrogant, too proud, and too sure that I would have time to repent. Now I am stuck here telling you about what happened. I feel so helpless and stupid.

How do you feel about missing the Rapture?

Helpless and stupid?

Chapter 24

Ground Zero....
Zero Hours . . . Zero Minutes

<u>THIS IS A HEAVENLY ALERT!</u>

THE RAPTURE HAS JUST OCCURRED!

EMERGENCY...EMERGENCY...
EMERGENCY !!!

THE RAPTURE HAS JUST OCCURRED !!!

YOUR FEET HAVE LEFT THE GROUND AND YOU

HAVE JUST BEEN CAUGHT UP IN THE AIR!!!

YOUR EYES ARE ON CHRIST THE REDEEMER!!!

THE PAST IS THE PAST,

15 minutes ago and it's opportunities no longer will ever exist again!

You are soaring on your way towards Heaven keeping your eyes on Christ your King where you will be with Him forevermore with all the Saints of God and all your friends and loved ones who heard about and accepted Christ as their personal Savior!

Your new, Glorified heart is pounding with more energy and excitement than it was ever capable of 15 minutes ago because you are bursting with sheer pure LOVE and   THANKFULNESS.
Thankfulness that someone told you about this moment and the importance of being prepared for this.

Thankful that someone or someones did not give up, that they steadfastly were diligent and persistent in their efforts to bring you to the Lord and diligent and persistent in their prayers that you would become a Christian!

Now, all the wonders of the creator are yours to now enjoy according to His purpose!

This super enhanced reality is so wonderful, you have a tremendously overwhelming desire to tell everybody, because you know that nobody, absolutely nobody should miss out on THIS !!!

Your heart is pounding, your loved ones and friends have got to be here! They and all the people in your life you have ever come in touch with have to be here! You think over and over the same things, "please Lord let them all be here!
Anybody that is not here, let me go tell them!

Please let me tell them!

Please, Please let me go tell them all !!!

BUT NO…

15 Minutes ago no longer exists for you.

All the witnessing you could have done… is past. All your lost loved ones … will never go with Christ in the Rapture… because instead of looking towards the Rapture… YOU NOW ARE GLORIOUSLY CAUGHT UP IN IT !!!

Everything is different now, and will be for all Eternity! How eternally wonderful for YOU!!

But…

15 minutes ago no longer exists for them either……………

THE RAPTURE HAS JUST OCCURRED!!!

Your feet are stuck to the Earth like they are encased in concrete blocks !!!

You have been invited numerous times to participate in this wonderful, miraculous, once in the history of mankind stratospheric event, but you so graciously declined. You had too many things to do, or didn't want to be "embarrassed", or thought it all to be a nuisance or just baloney. You had your own "spin" on life and " the hereafter".

You not only didn't get to go with the Lord in the Rapture.....you didn't even get to ACTUALLY SEE
IT HAPPEN !!!

Fooey! Here is something else now to believe in by faith, but wait a minute, better not do that, because the "powers that be" will kill you a horrible death if you believe in that stuff now!
Problem is, somebody witnessed to you and told you about this, that it could happen- or did they say that it definitely would happen?
Anyway, it appears that it has happened... or maybe it is something else.
Let's see, I can now give my life to Christ and be brutally tortured and probably killed, or I can believe what everybody now is telling me and if those "missing" people are right, I will be banished to the lake of fire by God for Eternity.

I just want to go back **15 minutes**, give my life to the Christ I heard about, then I wouldn't be in this horrible predicament.

I'm really not a bad person, please, please let me go back just **15 minutes**!

I will listen! I will listen, I promise!
Yes, I am the same person that ignored and laughed at you 16 minutes ago, but surely if we can go back

just 16 minutes, you can and will find a way to make me believe and will not let go of me until I believe in Christ !

You just were not quite persistent enough, just a little bit more, I know it would have taken just a little bit more!

I now must endure hell on Earth all the rest of my life on Earth or I will endure literal hell in the lake of fire for all eternity!

All of this because …..

15 minutes no longer exists for me!

If it existed for you, oh Raptured saint, what would you do different?

Would you do anything different for me?

T- Minus FIFTEEN minutes AND COUNTING

Just before Christ's return for His children!

Lord, how long must we wait?
It was the call of the day for Millions of Christians all around the globe!

It wasn't a pleasant, pretty picture for many, many Christians who took a stand and continued to witness and worship.

It wasn't at all like you would think- peace and harmony until all of a sudden, BOOM! Everybody looking up in the air like there was a massive mid-air collision of jetliners or something.

No, that day was like no other in history. It was like being in the eye of a hurricane!

Excuse me please ! Am I getting ahead of myself ? I'm very sorry! Let me take a moment to introduce myself. I certainly don't wish to be like these other people who have been telling all the different versions of things as they know it, but for the best part, they didn't even take the courtesy to introduce themselves until they were well into their discussion.

My name, dear friend is Harvard Harry Hamplin. Please don't bother to ridicule me about my name, as there have been, it would seem, twice as many people to do so as what I have met in this life! (Babies maybe excluded). Very well, snicker as you very well must and be done with it!

There are events to be told of importance beyond the magnitude of which have never been!

As you may have guessed, I was a N.A.S.A. engineer. I helped with what used to be America's space exploration program. I was an Aeronautical Engineer. A rocket scientist to be sure. Oh, very well, go ahead presently with your non-sensical farces about "what do you think you are, a rocket scientist or something," or "hey, this is easy, it's not like it's rocket science or brain surgery or something!"

My, what have I done? I have gotten completely off subject again! I have gotten off subject from the most important topic imaginable since God created man except for the equally important topic of Jesus' crucifixion for our sins.

Now, where did I leave off? Oh, yes, that day was like being in the eye of a hurricane. All the implications and possibilities and prophesies had been filled. We had all been told of this day all our lives. We had been told by many different religions, mostly Protestant, as in Baptist, Methodist, Church of God, and so on and so forth!

We had been told all that " nonsense " so many times that it made these " doom sayers " seem impotent in their theology to the point that if one had wanted to, one would have probably burst out in laughter at the whimsy and absurdness of this abject seemingly ludicrous theocracy !

Whomever you may be that I am currently discussing this subject matter with, imagine if you will please, some gentleman flying through the stratosphere on some cloud (probably cumulus, as the mass of no other would even possibly withhold the weight and per square foot weight dispersion of a human body, unless possibly if they were prone instead of in a vertical position.)

---- I got you!

That was a bit of scientist's humor! ....

....

Well, I didn't expect an overt expression of laughter.

Your expressed sentiments of my thought being non-humorous was quite enough to fulfill my need for acceptance with my knowledge of the verbal skills including my ability to make ones emotions lighthearted for just a bit during these dark days in the history of mankind

We must now continue our train of thought of the occurrences of that day!

You must understand, at that time, I did not believe for one nano-second in anything even remotely religious! Why should I? I was a man of science! An extremely learned individual who based his entire existence on reality. The facts weigh out reality and I was not taught anything different while I was maturing towards adulthood, and probably would not have believed any of it even if I had been exposed n or instructed in this manner, as simply put to you as I know how, I am a man of logic.

Scientific formulas and testing, results, controls and assimilating data and proportionately applying it as best needed to daily applications.

This is who I am...or who I was.

I once heard from a very brilliant intellectual that we all have a bit of this type persona inbred in us. Analyzing situations to the maximum, or if their explanation goes beyond our patience or latent abilities, ignore them as if they don't matter or they will change on their own or they will simply vaporize and go away into infinity !

Well, I do apologize, as I was so very incorrect! There were so many lives possibly I could have reached, so many souls I might have had a bearing or effect in.

What if, what if, what if.....

And now, here am I!

My assimilations of data were so very incorrect!

The laws of physics go so far beyond my scope of comprehension as to make my vast assimilation of knowledge utterly null and void.

I was witnessed to...

I was witnessed to countless over and overs.

I allowed the frontal lobes of my cerebellum dictate what my medulla oblongata mandated reality to be.

There I go again! "Passing the buck" again!

It's not my brains fault! It is no one's fault but my own heart!
The magnificent Holy Spirit visited me! ...... Yes, even me!

I had the choice to not be so "intellectually superior". I could have listened to that "quiet, still voice!" I heard it repeatedly just as I expect everyone on this planet in this day and age did.

.......I did not heed it!
I over analyzed it to the point that I am now no longer a space or rocket scientist, but a broken human being, who has no family left, not job, no home, no hope for anything to the point that I am weakened almost to the point of giving up, of taking the mark so all this will be over soon.

You keep encouraging me not to, you keep telling me of the day of the Glorious Appearing,

So now I will continue my expulsion of the events according to my perception at that general time frame!

Birds were singing more gleefully than I had ever noticed.

As I look back, I think maybe they were relieved that the tensions in the air were calming. In other words, it was as if mans hostilities permeated even nature itself.
Doesn't make sense in a lot of ways, but God created all things in nature to be in a certain kind of harmony.

Even the winds and the seas obey Him, and are in tune to His wishes.

Once the Earth stood still for almost a day and once it even went backwards, at His command.

Now, at the thought of the most sought after event in history about to occur, nature was in an anticipation mode.

Christ was about to Rapture His Bride, raise His dead to receive their Glorified bodies and They and the Magnificent Holy Spirit were about to go to be with the Father in Glory.

What did you ask?

Did I see it?

Well, no.

I can't say that I did.

I can't say that I have ever seen air before either, or radio waves, or sound waves, or microwaves or a whole long list of things.

Have you forgotten whom it is that you are conferring?

A scientist believes in what they can see, hear, touch, this is true.

However, we also believe many times in borderlines… the things we can also prove or that stand the tests of logic and workable reality.

Sometimes these supercede the Earthly or universal laws of physics as we at any given moment may know them to be.

Occasionally we must look into the realm of possibilities, and consider unknowns (to us) as in " think out of the box " type " think tankers " . Sometimes even hardcore facts-only to the maximum scientists are near-forced to think of the consideration of inter-dimensional physic anomalies or abjurations.

Speak English, you say?

Glad to, since I am no longer a scientist, but instead, what you might call a survivalist.

I not only think, but believe with every fiber of my being, that there is something "out there "! I think there truly is something or rather, many something's out there, and mankind was never going to be able to reach it. It had nothing to do with light-years or lack of the ability to reach light speed or space-warps or space-time continuums or life span versus distance traveled or materiel needed.

I assimilated all available data and noted that there was only one solution to the occurrences that lead back to that day!

The Biblical perspective was correct!

So many things in the Bible had already been proven true and Sound!
Nothing in the Bible had been proven bogus or even nill-prospectus! It had been put under a microscope of discernment of validity way too many times and always, the seekers came up empty in their quest to nullify any aspect therein!

That being said, with all the strange happenings of that day and thereafter to this point, I set out on my own Quest for answers.

Guess what? I found them! They are there!

In the Bible! They are there!

I sound excited?

Scientists always sound this way when they make a scientific breakthrough!

There was a great occurrence just about two thousand years ago, and there was a great occurrence at zero= no B.C.R. and no A.C.R.!

The phenomenon of the prophecy of all prophecies being fulfilled had just occurred!

All Glory to God! All Glory To God! All Glory to God!!!

Well…………………………………

If that is so, then where does that leave us?

Well I am sorry to break it to you, but the truth of the matter is, it is not too pleasant what it leaves us!

Now I know you are no " rocket scientist " or anything, " no pun intended ," but this leaves us pretty much on Mars with no return craft, or as you may put it… up the creek without a paddle !

Now, start rowing!

Not going to be fun, is it?

How does the thought of getting your head chopped off after you have been given a choice of keeping it or not, sound to you?

If you keep your head, (literally), then you will sign away all possibility of not being thrown into a burning fire so hot that you might as well blast off from Earth and pilot your craft straight into the sun, except that you won't be able to die….ever!

You may live, though, as I hope at this point of the Post- Rapture and Pre-Tribulation period that I will be able to do.

I first was introduced to this by a fellow that is not with us now. He was taken in the Rapture, but told me about it just about two months ago.

I had, yes, been told many things all these years, but this fellow just told me so very much more. Details, that's me, a man that has to have all the details. This gentleman was knowledgeable, seemed to know more than anyone else I had been talked   (witnessed) to. I do certainly believe in formulating all the facts so as to be able to make a well informed assessment.

He had invited me to go to Sunday school and church with him, in fact he had invited me there for quite awhile. He had told me about "Salvation "and the possibilities for my future. I told him that I was agnostic and just didn't know and didn't care either way.

The interesting thing though, was that he wouldn't quit. That fellow just wouldn't quit!
He insisted on discussing this same subject matter with me every single time he saw me, so one day, I informed him I would just go to his church. There I would entertain these concepts, assimilate, dissect, and prove to these "believers "once and for all how utterly bogus all this "life after death "nonsense really was!

Boy, was that preacher Janus right! Did I say that? Oh yes, He was so very right!
I felt this "Holy Spirit "try to help me! It spoke to me in that quiet, still voice that I had heard of.

That Preacher Janus had told me about people that refused the Holy Spirit, that wouldn't listen, and I had become one of them!

During the service, he had been talking about this very Rapture, and about service to the Lord and about perilous times and a coming tribulation time.

I listened intently, and even though I fought the Holy Spirit, I was still analytical and felt I should remain rational, as all this hooey needed revealed.

The next Sunday, there was to be a play, a drama about the need to stand for Christ and do what He tells a person to do. During the week, there was a rehearsal. I was determined I would be sure to be there even for that, and I did!

During the rehearsal I saw scenes about personal sacrifice and how the Lord looks at that. It told of sacrifice by some even to their death. It told about giving up time and energy that might be used elsewhere, in leisure or work. It showed the lack of commitment on the parts of some people, even if it meant the possibility that some precious souls might not be able to share Eternal Bliss with the Father.

 It talked of so many people that won't come out of their "comfort zone" and do something contrary to their nature, even if the price for this is eternal, both for the lost people and for the non-involved Christian, because that person must answer to Christ, at the Judgement Seat of Christ!

It talked of how awful, to be before Christ, and for it to be revealed that even one person is screaming in hell because of that one Christians inaction...

On the day of the play, I decided to attend, so I could access even more trivia to help me finally break the code to this "mystery.

 As I was sitting there, I thought "what a horrible play, leave these poor people alone." Since I had seen so much of the play already, I felt comfortable to whisper that sentiment to a little old lady sitting next to me.

As it happened, this little old lady said that I inspired her. She said that she thought that watching it a second time might help me to see some things that maybe I didn't see before!

Boy was she right! Before the play got started good, these men in very nice suits got up and started dictating pretty much that they felt the same way that I did!

The bad thing was, they got really carried away!

They killed that really nice preacher Janus fellow right in front of our eyes. I couldn't believe it! They killed him and his wife!

It was just about then that that sweet little old lady turned and whispered to me,
"You did indeed inspire me, young fellow!"

Just about then, she for no logical reason, stood up just as straight and tall as she could and started singing to the top of her lungs, something about amazing grace.
I started telling her to sit down, but she wouldn't listen.

Those men killed her, that sweet little old lady! I couldn't believe it! They hit her and threw her out of a window! She kept witnessing and singing and praising the Lord the whole time! What strength! What courage! What commitment! What passion for a cause!

I didn't think so at the time. I just thought she was just totally nuts!

I want that kind of passion for Christ! I want more passion for Christ than I have fear of death or fear for the kind of death that I may be required to suffer!
I want peace through faith that even in death, everything will be
All right!

I want to know that everything I do is for Christ, and that what I do, every waking moment, is for Christ and for my fellow man to be with

Christ through giving their hearts and souls to Him!

I want to remember that everything I do everyday, is for His Glory, not mine!
He is with me always, even in my death, especially in my death, and I must stay strong.

I was a coward during the play, and all I wanted to do was find the nearest way to safety. I decided very quickly that this was not the life for me, whatever the final outcome!
What a mistake that was! What a grave miscalculation! Now I know by logic and not by the Holy Spirit, that you and I missed out! We should have soared through the air like I firmly believe so many others did!

Oh, for just fifteen minutes before Christ's return, to be mine again!
I wrote a couple of little stories about the Rapture!
Want to hear them? They go like this....

THE RAPTURE HAS JUST OCCURRED!!!

 You just read them a few minutes ago, and now, my agony unspeakable...

How could anybody be so wrong???

How could anybody ever be so horribly wrong???

THE RAPTURE HAS JUST OCCURRED!
        You just read them a few minutes ago! Don't you understand that my agony is unbearable! How could anyone be so wrong? How could anyone ever be so horribly wrong? You missed the Gospel Ship and still you feel the way you do? I wouldn't want to be in your shoes! Don't talk to me about your soul and Heaven and all that stuff! I'm tired of talking to you! Talk to somebody else for a change! Get you history from another perspective! Talk to M.C. I doubt he'll ever reveal his name to you. He knows his time is coming and wants to hang on as long as he can. He's not too smart. If he were, he wouldn't be taking his "right" stand just like you'd better not be doing, either.

Chapter 25

Important Topic: ...Suffering...
Post-Rapture Style

Narrator: Person only known as M.C.
Time: ACR Date and time not known
Location: Unknown

I'm riding out these "good" times. I remember how it was ... chaos ... confusion. Nobody knew a thing until a few years ago. Well, things were getting a little "loose," you might say. The difference between right and wrong became grayer and grayer. What was really right and what was really wrong? Seemed few people were willing to say they believed they knew the difference anymore.

Enough people started believing that right was wrong and wrong was right, it seemed hard to believe in anything for more than a few minutes at a time. Safer not to have an opinion, lest someone come along and tell you your opinion was wrong!

Gotta believe in something, though . . . so you say.

I say that to remain un-imprisoned (not necessarily free), I must believe, or pretend to believe, completely what the government says to believe, and only what the government says to believe.

I sound confused? That's okay! It's safer this way! Maybe I'll keep my head on my shoulders!

It wasn't always like this, though. Some people seem to recollect a time up until about four to five years ago when a certain number of people were considered right wingers (some still are). Somehow, it seemed to work out for them to be that way, and it was just fine for them to state their beliefs!

People didn't usually get violent over things like that. They just each felt they were correct and agreed to disagree.

All of a sudden, so to speak, things began to change like they had never before in American history! The very definition of freedom changed. Was it the rampant use of drugs? They said it was the fact that the government was losing the drug war . . . big time.

It seemed that methamphetamine labs were operating in every other home. Just look around, they said! Is one in your neighborhood? Maybe several of them were operating right under you nose?

"No, of course not! No drugs of any kind here! We're not the kind of people to do that sort of thing," the righteous community members railed. "Prescription-only drugs, nothing illegal. Those are for the 'other people.' You know, the poor or oppressed, the hoodlums, the 'lawless ones.' It's the ones we're always leery of, the really bad people that we should feel sorry for but deal with cautiously, all the same."

That's what they all said . . . and one thing they truly believed was that the cops and courts had it all under control. It had nothing to do with their lives! It was just something for law enforcement to handle-we have the limitless resources of the law, the courts, and police to handle it and keep it at bay!

You were nuts and naive! There was limitless money, resources, and members of the intelligence community to stop this country from becoming another Columbia, like the poppy fields of Cambodia, or like Afghanistan, which was overrun with drug lords who decreed the final "law."

Our country was great . . . and safe . . . and free . . . and under control! Democracy ruled and justice prevailed! Judges and juries made wise and right decisions based on the truth, the whole truth, and nothing but the truth! The law protected us from bad people; and when something happened that they couldn't prevent, they protected us by apprehending the bad people and trying them in a court of law to bring justice.

Yeah . . . right . . . uh huh! Sure! Oh, I forgot

this one . . .

"Our system may not be perfect but it's the best in the world!" they chanted.

Do I sound unpatriotic, or like I don't love this country? **No, no, no!** It's not like that at all! All I'm saying is that you and I weren't caught up in the rapture of Christ's Church! We were *not* pre-rapture Christians, and now, for the sake of argument, we're dealing with this little issue of living (existing) in a totally wacked-out, lawless, and evil world.

Are you with me so far?

Okey -Dokey then!

(And quit feeling so safe in your finite little world! I'm telling you the truth! Try thinking outside the little sphere of your day-to-day world and the things you think make up your "this problem to get past or work through," just to immediately run squarely into "that problem to get past or work through!" You might suddenly have some intense flashes of reality.)

Let's get back to the pre-requisite dialogue. That's fine with you, right? Fine with me. You see . . . I'm trying to help you understand the sequence of events, the near-order of circumstances, the social, political, and individual/personal changes that took place. They arose so fast; but you must understand the general time frame in which they happened in relation to the fabulous-for-some event-the return of Jesus Christ, for His Bride, the Church. When I say, The Church, I mean those who were already saved through his blood. Are you with me so far?

Where was I before you interrupted me? Oh yeah, I remember now. I was talking about illegal drugs, and lawlessness, and corruption, wasn't I? No, I remember now! I really haven't told you about the corruption yet, have I? Hey, in these days, it seems that everybody is at least a little scatter-brained!

Corruption . . . what's that? I hear you . . . you've heard of it, but it doesn't affect you, does it? Yeah, oh yeah . . . it does . . . and it has for years! Remember the TV shows where the good guy won? He'd get hurt some, then he'd come through it all and win…one way or another. Remember? Well honey, this ain't no TV show! Real life is extremely tough . . . sometimes it's almost impossible!

Don't get me wrong! I'm not taking a particular stand and don't accuse me of being a conservative. You know in these post-rapture days, and even two to four years before, the liberals took control and *right-winging* became unpopular, then completely outlawed! (Outlawed to the extent of punishment by immediate death due to the danger to national security that it allegedly presented).

Come on now, you coward! Think back! Remember? You remember how it started! You remember how it started kind of slowly then faster and faster, more and more. Snowballing . . . exponential acceptance . . . exponentially it became easier and easier to sell the masses anything they wanted to sell.

Safety? Hey, I'm not telling you that I have the answers to make people feel safer without taking away personal liberties and freedoms. I'm not the one who is supposed to be the smart one here, right? Besides, I didn't open my eyes until it was already done, and I would've been too chicken to take a stand anyway. Even if I had seen it and had taken a stand, the days of Boston Tea Parties, and the like, were over. This country and this world were out of control . . . and you know it just as I do!

The Christians? Well, from what I've heard, some of them saw all this shaping up, and they prayed. Prayed? Yes, some of them prayed for the safety of this country, and the peace and safety of the world, and Israel especially! Did it do any good? Well, from what I've heard, God gave them peace, because that it was all considered part of the divine plan.

It was the bringing about of the fulfillment of prophecy, or in other words, foreknowing and foretelling of events to come. It doesn't ring true if it doesn't happen, and events that must occur, indeed must occur, or it's not a true prophecy. God will not stand in the way of the fulfillment of true prophecy! Now you understand an inkling of why things in this world, and specifically in this country, came to pass as they did.

Corruption, that's what we were talking about, wasn't it? You thought I forgot, didn't you? There were plenty of pay-offs and bribes, lots of extortion, favoritism, and good-buddyism. Trade-offs, or look the other way if it's convenient, and nailing the innocents to the cross if the personal gains are better for the powers-that be."

Now just chew on that for a minute!

Come on now, you saw it too! Big bucks could get you out of anything unless those with bigger bucks were getting their kicks out of seeing you squirm. It had nothing to do with right or wrong, just power and gamesmanship . . . you know, playing the game!

How did they do it? You've heard of insider trading? Well, this was insider politics! To them, it was always an adrenaline rush, to think they got paid for this-and they got pay-offs for this! They didn't know or care that they were just tidbit pawns in Satan's plan to thwart God's plan and victory. You see . . . Jesus won the war on the cross, but Satan just refused to admit that he'd already lost!

Liberal cops ousted lesser-ranked, conservative cops, who insist the job only remained a job as long as they were free to do it right . . . and do the right things on the job! One at a time, they were picked off! Care was taken to replace them with those who would play the game. They blackballed, blacklisted, or bad referenced those who were newly added to the lists of the unemployed because they wouldn't play the game.

And don't think it was just the cops! No- buddy! More and more people everywhere were playing the games in their respective jobs, or wherever and whenever they wanted to "prosper" in their selfish me-and-mine-only worlds. All it took was one more act of terrorism!

It's true! The liberals used every opportunity, every single opportunity, to advance their whiney-babyisms! Take a look! Listen for a change!

Abortion! They changed the name to soften the meaning of the wholesale slaughter of hundreds of thousands of unborn babies every year. What's the problem here? Couldn't they understand that a woman's body is not just her body once she conceives? Conception is the beginning of a brand new life, one that doesn't exist prior to that magical, miraculous moment that God, Himself, blesses and personally breathes life into the unborn. No other way can it grow, except it has God-given life. How, then, did a woman gain the right to choose-that she has the right to go through a procedure that ends a new human being's God-given life?

Abortions were legalized decades ago. Under this new administration, (as it was called not long ago), however, partial birth abortions, which can be performed up to the very moment of delivery, didn't just become legal, they were state sponsored and state supported!

The slope was really slippery so they continued to change the language and the reasons why it was okay. They said, "It isn't life-a human being-until it's born and is considered healthy by a physician and at least two nurses. Again they changed the rules! Now, if a doctor deems that this just born "tissue" is not healthy, it's legal to do a post birth termination (after-birth murder). There, that sounded clean and sanitary, didn't it? Let's not get all carried away, now!

First they changed the source of all life from God to man. All they had to do was change the belief that life begins at conception to man's notion of when "legal" life begins. Man (the government) had to be willing to give its legal blessing to a new life that has been placed into society. (Note that I didn't say the law refers to the new life as created by God!)

Don't be ridiculous? Come on now, isn't that what society did a long time
ago? What's the difference? Before birth, it isn't breathing? I have recently seen debated by a left-wing "right-justification group, that "evidently God doesn't consider an unborn to be life until it 'breathes the breath of life through it't nostrils'"

How ridiculous! This means that a fish is not alive...ever!

My biology teacher taught that living cells require (mandatory) food, water, and oxygen to live. Oxygen to live. That would be . . . air! Oxygen is the part of air that humans breathe to keep us alive. Now, how could that "tissue mass" grow if it didn't get oxygen through its "mother's" body? The key word this time is "mother."

Biology lesson: a female cannot be a "mother" to "a mass of tissue"!

Now, you think changing the biological definition of when this "whatever it is "becomes a legally recognizable, individual entity with "rights" is absurd and not possible? Check your history! How many times have the Supreme Court and the Presidents changed this definition since Row v. Wade? What kind of kids did our parents and our grand parents raise? How'd we get so confused that we would support or make, such laws? Did we lose our minds, our spirits, and our souls to the demons of convenience? Were we willing to believe any lie we were told so we could rationalize our own decisions about abortion?

You think that many of the things in this book can't or won't happen? Wake up! Oh, wake up! Think for yourself and don't be lead around . . . or rather "miss-lead around! Conservatives don't be found sleeping in your apathy! They've made it so unpopular to take a stand for what's right that it's to the point of fearing prosecution as a radical-like you may go on a terrorist or murder spree, or something!

You aren't going to do anything like that, are you? Of course not! You aren't going to let terrorism and murders within the womb continue without a fight, are you? No, of course not!

You're going to do your part and write your congressman, and you're going to vote at all future elections, not necessarily for the easy road for you economically, but first . . . for the safe entry of those beautiful, little babies to come into this world unharmed.

Grotesque! Not some, but all of the forms of "life-termination," or "problem solving" are grotesque! The cruelties to these tiny little people are beyond the comprehension of the human mind . . . even if it was the murderer himself or herself, being torn apart, it's just, plainly put, beyond the boundaries of human mental and emotional abilities to understand!

If someone were about to crack open your skull or inject poisons into your blood, heart, and brain, even if you were sleeping like a baby in the womb and couldn't defend yourself, wouldn't you want someone to defend you? For the most part, what I'm saying is unpopular because people are **<u>inherently selfish</u>**. *Whinny baby ,whinny-baby...* **waaa...waaa**...*Go suck your thumb.*...At least you were loved enough that you have one to suck!!! Most people want "the good and easy" life. They don't like to be inconvenienced . . . they just won't tolerate it.

Think about the hundreds of thousands of people who would have joyfully adopted and raised those children as their own! But no! The government in all its "last days prior to the Rapture" mentality, said yes to infant murder to protect women from back-alley butchers who performed dangerous illegal abortions. Or they said that parentless newborns need protection from the possibility of not finding the "right" home for their unwanted child! Yeah, sure . . . how nice it would be if that were true. Propaganda is often wrapped in evil intentions. What about those partial birth abortions and the sale of the babies' body parts to laboratories and universities? That's right, they do that because it's all about money and power!

Do you know how long it took to adopt an infant? Over two years on a waiting list, because of all the red tape from government bureaucracy, (more like bureau-crazy!), all the investigations to make sure the "right" people get those children. Solution would have been to use the same money used for abortions, political "running scared-isms," and other available funds to stop legalized abortion and speed up the adoption process. Reduce the red tape! Quit pretending to take so long because of "the process," the unnecessarily long process!

Come on! Give the unborn the chance at life that God gave them. Speed the process. Use good judgement, the "right" judgement!

(Note: That's the way I used to think about things. Now I don't know, or at least that's what I make them think for my own safety! I know I'd better! When the Rapture happened, I wasn't a Christian, so I'm still here, just like you. That was a little over three and a half years ago!)

I was considered a conservative. We learned about one issue at a time, let it drop, didn't push it because more and more people had become more amoral. When we were barraged with liberalism, we were foolish enough to question the "rightness" of right!
Even before the Rapture, it wasn't just unpopular, it was downright dangerous to own up to holding conservative or "right" beliefs. One could become very much dead that way.

"We've got to do something," everyone cried, so they took freedoms away in the name of security instead of creating other safeguards. They took the easiest route they could find . . . the course of least resistance.

You think this would be the toughest way? Not a chance! With a little trial and error, they found the most acceptable propaganda to secure mass acceptance of their messages. Those who don't accept them become the social outcasts, the unacceptable "rebels." Not a problem! They can then be dealt with, especially with the majority now firmly on your side! You are the law, and justice is on your side, remember?

Was it the "freedom fighters", the militia type, radical extremists that were the "splinter to be" of this country? You do know about splinters don't you? Well, when they fester enough, you just wait for them to just come oozing out of the body. If they don't, you just label them with some unacceptable title, apply a little pressure, and watch the infection come popping out. Then just put it on a tissue and quickly dispose of it. Easy as ABC . . . wouldn't that be correct?

Terrorism! We certainly had to be defended against terrorism . . . even at the cost of any and all personal freedoms. And when was the last time we were really free?

Well, you get the picture. The law was heavily imbedded with "crafty" ordinances and statutes. Right, wrong, up, down, backwards, and forwards! The interpretations of the law were sometimes well intentioned or not well intentioned. And how the laws were applied was so befuddled. The same went for the enforcement and "end interpretation" by any and all selfish (left/liberal) entities, that to even proclaim oneself a procurer, processor, practitioner, and protector of right over all became abhorrently intolerable!

You still say you didn't see it coming? Remember that goofy statement, "I didn't inhale?" Remember when you were told, "I didn't have sex with that woman?" Remember how many millions of dollars it took for "them" to agree that he wasn't having illicit sex with her while discussing "world affairs" with the leaders of other nuclear powers, because "they" wouldn't decide if what he did was really having sex! What did they think he was doing, composing a symphony for the Philharmonic?

Well, tolerance was fine (even though God told us not to tolerate the very things the government said we had to tolerate), but not to the point of accepting another person's wickedness. Oh, they did such a good job making us feel we were wrong to express our views and to reject government-mandated silence in the face of those great wrongs.

It is, simply put, individuals addicted in their minds to something they believe they have an inalienable right to do--satisfy their sinful desires and their carnal flesh with no retribution. In other words, either they have not been taught that it's wrong, or they don't care because they believe they can get away with it (or think they can).

God sees it, and God is not liberal! He's a righteous God, a just God, and He sees in the dark places where man cannot and will not look! You now justify it by telling me I should not judge because I'm not The Judge!

Careful now, in these dangerous times, what I said makes me sound like an outlawed right-winger, and what you said makes you sound like a person who believes in The Judge. **Christian** or not, we could both be beheaded immediately for such innuendoes!

Anyway, change of subject! Remember the next liberal, "wanna look moderate," election? That was the straw that broke the camel's back! This country, followed by the rest of the world, was in for a down-the-toilet transformation! You saw it happen, didn't you? Did you like it?

Hey, wait a minute, please! I want you to meet a few friends I've made. They'll tell you more of what you need to know. Maybe that will bring you to a point of reevaluation after you assess of what you hear from them. They, and I, may become your closest friends, or you may attempt to "exit" us from this world. Are you a friend or a Judas? Which will it be? I guess we'll see, won't we? Either way, meet my friend, who was a teen-ager when things really started changing. His story started . . .

Chapter 26

Retrospect and Regret: The Forty Two-Month Partners

Narrator: 21½-year-old male (Same narrator as at beginning of book. He was sixteen years old at the time.)
Location: Unknown . . . in hiding
When: Three and one half years ACR

Strange to think that what happened at that little church that day never hit the TV or radio news. It didn't hit the national, state or local news. A year or even six months earlier, it would have been big news.

The world was going through so many changes, some major, some big, and some small. Some were big but seemed small because of all the rapid-fire events that would lead to this day, this event.

Event! What a minuscule word to use! It makes the brutal torture, rape, kidnapping and murder of that day sound similar to a little old ladies charity auction; almost like saying, "Don't miss the great buys to be bargained for! It'll be so much fun!"

It was minuscule, though. The things we didn't know . . . the things we didn't know! Why, just a few months earlier, the country elected, for a large part, a "new administration." Well, that "new administration," that far-left, liberal government was so far left, they thought they were far right.

They were so "anything goes," you had the right to do anything you thought you had the right to do, and if it offended anybody else, it was their problem. It was absolutely nobody's business what you said or did because it was your total right to do it!

If anybody spoke up, it was no longer "cool," except when it came to organized religion. That indeed became unpopular very fast. The people at that little white church didn't know anything about what had started, or at least to what degree. They probably just thought that the political and social climate would blow over in a year or two.

Not true! They hadn't even seen the tip of . . . the tip of .. . . the iceberg! In just a few short months, the far radical right, the right, and even the moderates were forced to change, pretend a great lie, or flee into some sort of contrived safety. This led the far left-the "anything goes because I have my rights" type groups-to go full circle and behave as if they were the radical right wingers. And who would disagree?

Those "shielded little communities" didn't know, though. It made them the perfect places for examples to be made.

Could anyone imagine the power of such rapid social change? The president and his cabinet, the vast majority of the congress, and the liberal courts worked in conjunction with governors and other state officials from a majority of the states-a band of like-minded, "all in one accord" politicians with no checks and balances in place to stop them!

With the redeemed almost taken to Him in the Rapture of the Church, "the prince of darkness" was about to step forward to "seek and devour" those without Christ. People's very souls needed protection through the perfect blood of the Sacrificial Lamb, as has been prophesied in the Bible hundreds of years ago. Mankind and everything on earth would soon have no choice but to complete those prophesies in a way that would lead to the blinding of mankind except for God's "elect."

Blind eyes in blinded times, because the world would believe the lie, and the liar! They would believe that great deceiver, Satan himself!

There's so much to tell, and so much explaining to do! So many things went on to shape things up to where they are now, and so many things went on at one time to develop things into what they are now! As I look back, I now understand it needed to be that way in order for God's plan to unfold this way! His plan was always in place, the stage has always been set, propelling us into the "Battle of the Ages!"

Always know and try to understand that it's sometimes, or often times, strange to us how God achieves His divine purposes! We don't understand the things He uses or the placement of certain people in specific positions. I mean, who would have thought that a play, a drama about Christ's martyrs, could or would be used by or for either side in the plan?

Sometimes a picture is worth a whole lot of words, but it can be used to prove solidarity and resolve for the cause of "right" and the good and faithful righteous cause of Christ. On the other hand, (the far, far left hand), Satan used his power and influence to eliminate any possible advancement of the work of the *Martyrs of the Cross,* without attracting even more attention to Christ.

No, best let the people sleep! But, Satan is not in absolute control; Christ is! Mistakes are made, but God does not make them! Therefore, everything eventually backfires in Satan's face, and all goes according to Gods divine plan! Doesn't that just blow your mind?

It's been four and a half years since the incident at the little white church, and three and a half years since Christ came back for His Bride, the ones who were smart enough to be redeemed by His precious blood. Look around! The world has come to this! Who would have known? Who could have possibly thought it would be like this?

~

Day in and day out, this thing to do and that thing to do. *Eggs to buy, or were they too high in cholesterol, or was it sodium? Maybe just get a breakfast pastry or nothing at all.*

What about eating lunch and dinner? Who did you say what to, and why? What did you say the plans were for this evening, this week, this month? What was so important? Oh yes, I remember, it was the plans! Plans for this, that, and the other thing! Important this, that, and everything!

A year after the event at the church, it became blatantly obvious. All those things, all those plans, all those "important" things revealed their complete insignificance!

In a moment, in the twinkling of an eye, like a "thief in the night," at an hour when you thought not, the Son of Man came, just the way He said He would! It had to be! It had to be because all of the prophesies have to be fulfilled, just like preacher Janus and other preachers said they would . . . the times I went to church.

You see, I wasn't like Mr. Canube, who went fishing, and I wasn't like the kids' mother or Ken who wanted nothing but to party all the time. I wasn't like Sam and Tina Harks, making war and fighting to the tune of uncontrolled self-indulgence.

No, I was the "lucky one!" I was there! I was where I should have been! I was in church being who and what I should be! Mom said I should be in church, so I was in church! Social circles said I should be in church, so I was in church! Be around the right people, they said. It will influence your life.

Remember me, I was the one at the beginning of this book, on the way to church. I was the one noticing Mr. Canube, and Sam and Tina Harks in all their misery and the misery they produced for others. I was also privileged to hear preacher Janus' wonderful sermons! But, of course it was unknown to my family and friends that I ignored or rejected them all, while pretending . . . while pretending!

So why are *you* here? You think just because you're sitting here reading my story instead of recounting your own life before Christ came for His Children, that you're safe and forgotten? Read all about it! This is my life, this life, and that life. It's this time period, and that time period. It's this place, and that place . . . no problem! You're safe, remember? You're innocently reading. It doesn't relate to you or your loved ones. Right? It has to be right! Right?

Wrong! So very, very wrong! This Rapture thing has affected us both and all our families and friends who didn't go.

Why didn't I listen? Why didn't you listen? Instead of talking to you, I could be in Glory with Christ and my loved ones right this very minute . . . instead of talking to you! Man, oh man . . . .. what a horrible trade off!

Yes, I hear you! You're rightfully groveling because if you had listened, really listened, if you had the faith and acted on it, you wouldn't be sitting there reading this book. You wouldn't be living in this horrible time of tribulation under the rule of the antiChrist! You'd be living everyday in the presence of the Eternal God!

I know you! Yes I do too know you! You were in church that day! I saw you! I'd seen you there a couple of times before, so instead of just reading, tell me your story! Oh, I get it! Just visiting, or maybe you'll say, "No I wasn't just visiting; I was a member of that church!"

Big deal! It doesn't matter, does it? It's obvious now that you were all show like I was! I was there! I saw you that day, the day of the play, when the "nicely suited" men first became obvious to us . . . and probably to the world . . . so quit lying to me! You're no safer or immune than I am! You ask, "What does that mean?" Are you gonna tell me again that you were a member of that church?

It doesn't really matter now, does it? Neither one of us can talk high-and-
mighty, holier-than-thou now, because now because we're both liars! We're both hypocrites! We put on a show, but it wasn't enough . . . and now we're *not* enjoying Gods eternal peace, love and rewards!

240

You had your chance just like I did . . . endless times . . . over and over! We could have listened to the "Romans Road to Heaven" and heeded it; but no, that was too much trouble! We would have had to submit ourselves to God, so we walked over the Cross instead of stopping at it, admitting we were sinners, and repenting. Why was it so hard, what could have been so incredibly difficult about admitting we were sinners, lost and without God in our lives?

Stop denying it! You knew it then, I knew it then, but believing on Jesus, that He died for our sins, would've put a cramp in our style, right? We heard it and heard it and heard it. We "prayed" but did God hear us? Did we pray that simple sinner's prayer? Well, did we?

I sound bitter? I SHOULD! I was only sixteen years old then and *you* knew the truth! **I needed you, dear reader.** Oh, so you say that I wouldn't have listened to you just like I didn't listen to Pastor Janus, or Granny, or anybody else? I guess we'll never know for sure, will we, because *you* never witnessed about Christ to me. *You* might have been the one to harvest the seeds the other planted in my soul! That's right! *You* might have been the one!

Funny huh? I mean with you "missing" the Glory Boat just like I did. Guess we were both stupid, huh?

I'm confused. The Holy Spirit? What's that? It's been so long since the Holy Spirit filled the churches! Used to be the Holy Spirit restrained evil . . . now, well . . . I guess He's dealing with folks one-on-one . . . maybe still beckoning us to repent .. . . to not take the mark!

Maybe we are hearing from the Holy Spirit. Maybe He's letting us feel such deep remorse because we could have made things right with God through Jesus. Yes, Jesus, the One who holds the rightful position of intercessor to the Throne of God through the shedding of His perfect blood for our sins.

You're so smart . . . so prove me wrong! Go ahead and prove me wrong. That's right! We're both in this together! Again I'll tell you, we both missed that Glory Train along with so many millions of others who had their own agenda to follow!

Oh, for the grace of God to pour down on us! Oh, to be led to Christ by the Holy Spirit, to be filled with the Holy Spirit, to listen to His voice as He ministers to us each day! What a joy to have the Holy Spirit work on our hearts . . . to pull at our heartstrings!

Now, we must be willing to die as martyrs for God. And we will probably die as martyrs if we don't take the mark!

Remember how things sped up that last year before Christ returned for His children? Remember the rapture of the church and how things changed? Oh, there was mass chaos, but then it became so peaceful on Earth. Everyone seemed so glad when the "man of peace" was stepped forward and took control. Things were supposed to be so wonderful and prosperous, just like we were told they would be, at least for the first three and a half years! Oh, sure, there were the "seals" opened by the Lamb, who was found worthy to open them to redeem mankind! Yes, and what about the trumpets that God ordered His angels to blow? The bowl judgments were something else, weren't they?

Now I've had to grow up really fast! I'm not even twenty-two yet and I've been through so much, I feel and look sixty!

Oh hey, thanks for agreeing with me . . . it was so very kind of you! In case you didn't know, all this hasn't been so "youth defying" on you either! **You, reader,** *look like some mangy, scraggly old dog that should have been put to sleep to take you out of your misery years ago!*

O.K., so we're both right! I've told part of the story as I lived it and know it. Now, tell me the story of your life and the events, as you know them. You might as well tell me. I have nothing but time until my death or the Glorious Appearing of the Lord . . . whichever comes first! Don't want to? Not ready yet? **Tough! Tell me anyway!**

Chapter 27

Dear reader, tell your story

Narrator: You, reader, should narrate this segment
Location: You must be in hiding, unless you've taken the Mark of the Beast
When: Sometime ACR

We encourage you to vent your creativity by becoming part of the book here. Go ahead, tell what it has been like for you, having been not taken with Christ at His second coming!....
...

Go ahead! Get started! This isn't fair...We've been doing all the talking. You're in this with us...so now you tell us what these Tribulation Days are like for you...think...what are you going through?

Chapter 28
Condition: Miserable

Narrator: Mr. Canube
Location: Unknown…In hiding
When: well into ACR

*M*y name is Mr. Canube, and I could tell you a few things just to brighten and excite your misery! My story is most interesting. Why don't you ask me to tell you what I know?

"Mr. Canube, please tell us your story," you ask.

Okay, then, I'll just do that!

Mine is not as imaginative perhaps as yours is, reader, but I did write notes in my daily journal, to be sure! At least I won't feel the need to make up a *bunch of babble* like you just did! I do believe you should know that nobody believes your nonsense, so **maybe you should just go back to reading!**

I'll tell it from a little farther back. After all, I'm a little older and I noticed the "winds of rapid change" long before this young fellow who has been rambling incessantly up to now . . . and before your own ramblings!

Let me stop here for a moment if I may. Maybe I should apologize for starting our conversation so harshly and with such insults. ***Reader, I do apologize.*** Will you please forgive me? I'm just so hungry, tired, and miserable. As you know, it's just so hard to witness all God's wrath on mankind in addition to the torment we receive daily for not taking the mark.

Begging your indulgence, I will start again to share circumstances and events in my life as I perceived them.

My name? You want to know my name? I just told you my name! My name is Mr. Canube. Again, my name is Mr. Canube! My first name is not important so please don't ask again! Would you please try to remember my name when you refer to me or address me... please?

Oh, there I go again! I'm just brutally blunt when I'm so hypoglycemic. My body has a terrible affect my mental functions, what with all these chemical imbalances such as constantly low blood sugar. Here we go! Let's try this again!

As a child, young man, and young adult, I had always heard, "The Lord is coming, the Lord is coming soon to get His Children!" At one time or another, I also tried that church scene. I found it to be okay at times and bothersome at others. When trouble came, I found solace in the bottle and sometimes in drugs rather than "Holy Rolling."

On the rare occasions that I did attend church, I faked my way through the service and couldn't wait till it was over so I could get out in the open . . . just beyond those sanctimonious doors. My mind was almost always on other things . . . all kinds of other things . . .while the service was going on. Mostly, I had my mind on my stomach!

Hey, and what about all those huge fish I wasn't there to catch and eat, or the golf game I wasn't there to play, the beers I wasn't drinking, and the women I wasn't chasing?

Well, evidently none of that mattered! When my little boy was run over by a car, he spent weeks in the hospital before he died. My other kids and I were so emotionally drained. All I could do was blame God, blame my wife, and blame myself. Nobody wanted to be around me, and I certainly didn't blame them for that!

I'd been drinking, like I said I before, but now I felt I really had a reason to indulge. After all, hadn't it been proven that you only go around once?

Soon after, my wife, whom I really did dearly love, left me. About

246

six months passed and she was diagnosed with a rapidly progressing, terminal cancer. Six weeks later, she was gone . . . she was gone!

My wonderful, wonderful, beautiful wife was gone and there was no chance to work things out . . . no chance for reconciliation!

I didn't hate her, I need you to understand, reader, I really didn't hate her! I just couldn't live with myself because of the loss of my son and because *I'm the jerk I am!*

Any way, with them gone, I blamed God more than ever! I knew some of the signs of the times. I saw them unfolding rapid fire! Again, I just stubbornly refused to get ready, to get my life and soul ready to see Christ!

Now, I desperately want to see Him! I want to see my wife and little boy, my other loved ones, and friends who either went to the Lord before the Rapture or in the Rapture! I want to be sure I'll see other friends I have or people I know in Gods Kingdom!

Martyr! Is it true that I must now die a martyr's death in order to fulfill all that I wish for? This is what some people keep saying including the young man who's with us now!

Yes! I put it all together, fortunately in time! I didn't take the mark. I wanted nothing to do with the mark of the great liar, the one who seeks to destroy and devour all souls.

Don't get me wrong! I almost gave in many times! He was so hard to resist, so easy to believe. Over and over I actually wondered if he really was Christ returned! He fooled me, then he didn't, he fooled me, then he didn't, over and over, but I refused to take his mark!

Many did though, and still many, many more are daily.

You know very well, just like I do, that those who take the mark of this *"Christ wannabe"* are doomed to eternal damnation and everlasting separation from God! There's no getting around it! The plan was simple. Submit to the will of the Father through the act of a simple prayer. I should have done it!

"Father, I know I am a sinner. Please forgive me. I know that Jesus is the Christ, the Messiah and came to Earth to be born a virgin birth, live a perfect life and be put to death by a lost and dying world because of their disbelief and their fear.

I believe He arose on the third day, and was and is the only person to ever do that of his own free will.

I believe that just asking forgiveness of my sins is not enough, I must believe on the deity of Jesus, and I do.

I believe John 3:16

"For God so loved the world that He gave His only begotten Son, that whosoever believeth on him should not perish' but have Everlasting Life!"

I believe Jesus is alive and well, and sitting at the right hand of the Father!

I believe You, Lord, when You say this is all it takes to become one of Your children and will now get to be with you in Your holy, perfect presence when I die!
I thank You for this right now!

I should have done it …I should have done it …I should have done it!

That's all would have taken! I knew that! I was too arrogant, procrastinated too much, or was too self absorbed.

After all, there's always tomorrow, or I was too busy being what I now know to be haughty. Bow a humble, submissive knee? Get away from me! I doubt you'll ever see me do that! *That's what I said, that's what I thought!*

That bunch at this church or that one was just as lost and confused as I was! They were not a bit better than I was. At least I didn't get all dressed up on Sunday morning and pretend to be somebody I wasn't! At least I was for real! That buncha phonies!

What'd I get for thinking so much...for being so smart?

Well, guess what? Now they're gone to be with the Creator of the Universe and I'm stuck here with the master of everything wrong, everything bad, the master of everything evil and deceitful.

I made a choice. I made a choice, then another, and another, and another. My choices were all wrong! Now I can't buy or sell anything. I can't take care of anything or anybody, let alone myself! **We're all going through this great tribulation period together, because you made very similar decisions!**

I'm starving, I stink so badly I can't stand myself, and I can't bathe without breaking into someone's house. I can't do that because I'll probably get caught and be imprisoned. I can't allow myself to be captured, because in these days, you can't be imprisoned without the mark, which they give to you automatically. I would have no "rights" to reject it. I would be a "criminal element", therefore, I would reap the *"benefits of the New World Order"*; because without the mark, I can't be traced and tracked. My entire life history, every purchase or benefit, even imprisonment, would then be monitored by the system installed by the abominable one.

He is slick, is he not? The persona, the controlled coincidences, the charm, the control, brilliance and power! Why, you can almost worship this man-god. Many did from the first, and still do!

The *lucky ones* seemed to go about their lives normally when all this chaos started. They're the ones who reaped so many benefits, like fine homes and cars that were better than they ever imagined or bought for themselves because things became so right, so peaceful, and so prosperous.

It was so normal and explainable, too! I mean, it was necessary for safety and freedom to implement all those safeguards, starting with the ones that brought about the "**controlled incident**" at that little white church, then other places soon after.

First like a trickle, then a little splash, then a full tidal wave

Martyrs of the Cross, Martyrs of the Cross, Martyrs of the Cross!

Christians everywhere became totally engrossed in a great revival of Christianity; and the government became totally obsessed with stopping the cause of Christ, and terrified of creating what they knew and feared most, *Martyrs of the Cross*! I mean the government wanted to stop a cause, not create one bigger and "better" than their own!

Many were giving their lives freely as martyrs for Christ-about three hundred thousand precious people per year, which breaks down to about eight hundred and fifty people every day! Those people, as it is written in God's Holy Word, will each receive the martyr's crown.

We didn't hear about them, did we? I mean, come on! That's a lot of people to die day after day after day after day. How come we heard so little about one or two or a small handful and only every once in awhile!

No government cover-up there! Oh, no! There couldn't be! Not our government! **Sound the wakeup bells! Sound the wakeup bells!** None sounded, or at least not many, and the ones that did sound weren't loud enough . . . weren't strong enough, and it was too hard to fight the government!

It wasn't in the plan to beat them as a whole because this is Satan's world. No, it wasn't in Gods plan for man to go to battle against man or against Satan for this cause at this time.

Care must be taken. We must not think too small about the unfolding events of those days-the few years prior to Christ's return for His Body, the church!

After the government changed and started moving so rapidly into their evil agenda, so noticeably towards the new, one world government, many new laws were put in full force. Safeguards (some good, some bad) were supposedly created in the name of protecting us against terrorism, both foreign and domestic. Definitely a worthy cause, huh?

Why didn't we see this coming? Prayer removed from the schools, the Ten Commandments out of all government buildings, at least at first, then removed from the public square. Oh, yes, they found ways to ban them from parks and businesses, and no more license plates with anything religious on them.

Think I'm full of baloney...DON"T YOU?

SNAP to ATTENTION!!!

Gideon Bibles could no longer be freely placed in hotels and motels across the nation! More and more, we saw the open acceptance of wiccan and pagan practices. It started with the easing in of tolerance and the acceptance of lifestyles different from our own-different from what God permits.

We should not have freely accepted, especially not to the point of sacrificing our own morals and values, both personally and in our thoughts that this sort of behavior is really not that bad, and is even acceptable. Yes, it was wrong. It was even more wrong to promote those things as not being wrong.

What do you want me to do? Start telling you all the things that are sins? There is already a book for that...it is called "The Holy Bible, aka God's Holy Word".

Stop right there! I am in no way-promoting sin practice! Sin is sin and is an abomination! People do have a propensity, or yearning, or desire for sin. We must allow our perfected spirit to win this battle against sin as many times as possible. I could give you the details about sin's consequences but you are adult enough to know where this is going!

People of all varieties of sins need God in their lives. "For all have sinned and come short of the Glory of God". "He who is without sin, cast the first stone". "Go, and sin no more".

How can you witness and teach and influence a person, if you critically judge them, and as the Bible says, "the mote is in your own eye"?

Love the person, in understanding that Jesus came **not** into this world to condemn it (John 3:16 and 17), but through belief in him, people could be saved. Do you believe in him? Do you really? Did you ask Him into your life? Did you not only ask him to come into your life, but also submit to Him so He can come in, and work with you and through you?

I really can ask some tough questions, can't I?

One of those sins people are battling over is homosexuality. I am not trying to right-justify homosexuality or adultery or idolatry or any other sin, but you should know that none of those sins will keep a person out of God's Kingdom. The only thing that will keep a person out of Heaven is Blasphemy of the Holy Spirit, which is not believing in the Lord Jesus Christ as our messiah, our redeemer, our personal Savior.

I almost feel compelled to apologize to the modern day legalists, but really can't, because it is written in God's Holy word …so I fully believe it!

As Christians, we are not to treat homosexuals any different than we do heterosexuals, we are all sinners until we accept Christ as our personal Savior...then we are sinners saved by His miraculous Grace. Our main job in life then is to stay in prayer, study the Holy Word and do the works of the Father, spreading the Good news of Jesus Christ! These people, as well as all people , whether saved or lost, need our witness, for strength and for encouragement and for knowledge of what this life is all about and how to live it best and most Righteously, and more importantly, to teach knowledge of the importance of the life to come!

~

Sorry about becoming sidetracked …you and I were on a discussion about these Post-Rapture Days. Different became acceptable through the efforts of a few, to the point that it became commonplace.

That's how those changes came in. Not all at once, but a few changes at a time inched in, then gained, gained in momentum. They constantly tested the social waters to see what and when new mind-set techniques would become increasingly acceptable.

It wasn't just that they refused to turn their lives over to Christ that was so bad, it was their decision to worship the evil one as if that was a good thing. True, it's gone on for many centuries, but never as bad as it is now . . . never on such a worldwide scale.

They filled our children's minds with lies. The theory of evolution was spread and then enforced as a "calculable possibility." That's a trick from Satan, himself. Lie to the children, mislead our children, so they grow into adulthood believing man is so smart. Oh, yes, he's been able to put the pieces of the puzzle together to eliminate even the remotest possibility that God, not coincidence or evolution, started the chain of events that lead to the creation of man. They purposefully leave out the **Law of Biogenesis**, which states that **life comes from life.**

Nothing else can create life. Man has never and will never be able to create life, no matter how smart he thinks he is, even today! Cloning is not creating life, as much as they want to deceive us into thinking it is. It's a fraud, a copy, but it proves that man does not have the power to create something from nothing. Only God can do that!

If you give a clever cardsharp a deck of cards, he can do many incredible tricks with them. If you give a skilled magician a few prepared props, he can amaze you to no end performing mind-defying tricks.

Scientists must also have something to start with . . . like a pre-planned set of circumstances to develop, using things they may have mixed up or scientifically formulated; but they started with life, because a living cell is life.

They cannot create that first cell, nor will they ever be able to. Heat, light, the elements, and the chemicals and compounds they use, were created and allowed to exist by God. How did they come into existence without certain ingredients, provided by God, light, air, and the materials it took to make their microscopes and other tools, also provided by God, and with the aid of gravity and other laws of physics, as provided by God?

If you live in reality and attribute everything in existence back to the Big Bang, you'd have to believe that all matter was in one huge massive chunk. Then for some reason, which you think you can explain, that chunk explodes into something called a "universe" (just where did this universe thing come from?) and all life eventually starts on it's own from there.

So, where did the chunk come from and where did the universe come from? Where did the life for the first cell come from and how was it protected so it would eventually flourish? Yeah, go ahead and answer those questions for me . . . because no one else could . . . because they couldn't and because they can't.

These things and others that really ticks me off is the garbage I was taught in school by teachers who should have known better! There should have been a teacher revolution! They should have refused to teach this horrible nonsense to our children, whose impressionable minds searched for answers, searched for the truth. They trusted their teachers! They believed their schoolteachers would tell them the truth! How could they when they were so miserably liberal they didn't even believe truth existed! Truth was relative, they told the children! Relative to what?

When the parents questioned those teachers, the teachers said they were required by law to teach possible alternative answers to get young minds thinking! What rot! Either way, they didn't tell the children they had the answer because they didn't have the answer! They said they told the children that they would have to come up with what they considered to be the answers for themselves! Can you believe it? I mean, can you believe it? They said there were no answers except those the children invented!

Baloney! I was there! I remember it well, and their little game messed me up for years! They had this picture depicting the "theory of evolution" on the wall in my social studies class. When asked what it was, they said it explained where man came from and how it had been proven that he "evolved!" They then talked "knowledgeably," about the "search for the missing link." Once found, all the pieces of the puzzle would be in place and man would know all about where he came from.

I don't know about you, but it made me feel that probably my parents were wrong with this "religious" stuff.

They refused to give any speculation as to how all this related to what we learned in church, as if that "theory" was not even in the equation; as if, at best, "evolution" was reality and Christianity was just a far out, antiquated theory!

Same thing in my science class! Same thing, only more of it. Science teachers tried, unsuccessfully I might add, to actually prove how all this was "reality!" And they did it without one shred of scientific proof!

I always had a nagging desire to prove what the Bible says about creation! How could I even attempt to prove it when we weren't allowed to even mention God?

Now, with all I know to be truth, all that hocus-pocus was a waste of my time, and nothing more than an attempt to brainwash me! Thank God He pulled me through all that mind-devastation and made me see reality for what it is! I just wonder how many millions of people bought into that devil-manipulation they called education! How many were not smart enough, too stubborn, too narrow-minded, too brainwashed to see the truth . . . to see that those they trusted were liars!

~

Now then, about those TV shows made especially for children .. . . you remember them, don't you? There were all sorts of "innocent wizardry" used to "mind-lavish" the children! It was enough to watch those TV shows-the endless barrage of cartoons and the movies that were supposed to "acceptable for kids!"

On second thought, I hope you didn't watch them. If you did, how much of that stuff did you believe was good and wholesome, just plain fun, and mind stretching? How long did it take for you to soak up all the messages embedded in those shows?

My Lord, my God, how did we allow society to diminish to this? No more "under God" in the Pledge to the flag because it offended one man. Oh, somebody came up with that just to remove God from His rightful place in the American culture, and the Supreme Court of the United States passed the buck by refusing to hear the case. Naturally, it came back again and again because the same guy was offended until the court caved in and sided with secularized tolerance. It was just like everything else! In time, it was easy to pass it into law.

Thing is, when these things got in, they stuck! The powers that be that could have taken a stand, and could have said it was too hard to fight those issues because they were etched in the history of this nation. The "good" people that would take a stand were too few and far between, and became fewer and fewer as morality and good Christian sense got watered down more and more.

Workplaces were not a place for worship or even speaking about God. More and more workplaces placed restrictions and guidelines on prayer and discussion of religious oriented topics, which brought about the passage of the Occupational Religious Encumbrance Laws, (OREL), in five BCR. In simple terms, they state that an employer must not discriminate against, among other things, race, ethnic background or religious affiliation.

That was okay . . . all seemed well and good, but then they added that employers didn't have to tolerate religious symbols, materials, or conversations of any kind while workers were on the time clock. This was odd, wouldn't you think? On one hand, the employer couldn't discriminate against people for religious affiliation, while on the other hand, stating that employers were not required to honor those who were Godly minded, with any sense of favoritism or even tolerance. Employers had the right to demand that potential employees either sign a waiver of their right to religious freedoms or stand the possibility of not being hired. Employers could sue for relief in civil court under breach of Federal Labor Laws. Now read about the first part of OREL again. What did I miss here? Oh, it was more beaurocratic hullabaloo.

Many trucking companies systematically forbid their drivers from having religious materials in their trucks. Mills and plants, factories and retail shops then forbid their employees from bringing religious materials onto the premises. Such offenses were punishable with termination and possibly stiff fines. That was not the end, though. It went on to become criminally prosecutable to do so.

Those applicants who made it known during pre-employment interviews that they were preachers or even more than moderately interested in religion were considered "NO HIRES." The interview was immediately terminated and the resume was tagged "FILE 13." That meant the file was "trash canned (but not before information was sent to a government database)!"

At first, this seemed to stem from "uphill" or "up the ladder." The guy had to do what the guy said he had to do! Go far enough uphill, and where do you wind up? Government! Always the government! Where does government get its power? From the people! How does the government get its power to dictate such laws, "downhill?" Lazy, apathetic, or non- committed people who forgot that they were the government! That left a minority of the people who would manipulate at a whim, because they knew they were just too hard to stand up against or too much trouble.

So the laws changed to silence the few, and it rolled downhill to us. We had to abide by the law and conform, had to keep silent to the point that eventually we were part of the conformity and could no longer identify its vile incorrectness.

That's how preachers used to preach and teach! What happened? Is the truth no longer the truth? Did the truth suddenly change or cease to exist? Don't you realize that what the powers that be (and yes, there

IS a conspiracy!) want you to think. If it's on TV or radio, it's all right to indulge your mind or your children's minds in!

What about the next satan-supported television or radio shows? The last one was okay; this one wasn't that much more shocking or sacrilegious, so it's probably all right, too!

Promote any form of sex out of the bonds of marriage?

Not okay!

Promote the sacrilegious!

Not okay!

That's like making light or fun of Christianity, as if there's no God, or God is powerless, irrelevant, unwilling to take a stand, or make a move, or God just ignores us. Sound familiar? Believe me! God DOES NOT ignore us!

It's not okay!

Promote wrong over right, or justification for wrong actions? Not okay!

I once heard that if you didn't take a stand for *something,* you'd fall for *anything!* This is surely misquoted from what probably was, in reality, a very fine saying. It should have been, "If you never take a stand for what's right, you'll always take a fall for everything!"

A lot of those laws and rules of business were first enforced at the federal level on government jobs. You know, they used that old smoke screen, "separation of church and state" time after time, again and again. It wasn't in the Constitution. The Supreme Court made it up so we would all worship the secular state, which means we would worship nothing! Suddenly the no-so-all-powerful state was in competition with the all-powerful Creator!

It then rolled downhill to include state jobs, and county and city jobs. Then, if it was enforceable by the government, it had to also be enforceable over civilian jobs. All it took was a lawsuit or two and a few smart lawyers who knew how to getting the media on their side, and there we were . . .the new, irreversibly secular nation.

And after all that, we still had our freedom of religion, as guaranteed under the Constitution. Well, at least we used to have it . .. . nice wasn't it? To be able to exercise it or not!

As you know, in these Post-Rapture days, that privilege has been long-gone! The trick now would be to just try implementing or enforcing that kind of "right" and see what happens!

Get with the program! Heads roll when people try that now; and I mean . . . really roll!

As most Christians now know, this was brought on, in large part, by the ultra liberal movement. Yes, that movement was liberal for everything, of course, but so highly defensive about defending the nation against terrorism. Oh, and guess what? It became the popular thought pattern that religious activity, religious people, and people who believed in doing the right and moral things in life were subversives. They were a danger to society, especially if they would give their very lives and freedoms for the cause of Christianity!

The government trembled at the thought of mass martyrdom, even more massive than what they were already covering up! My God (uh oh, mustn't say the "G" word)!

Even more, they couldn't let the people think the moral right wing crowd couldn't be controlled! After all, the world and its grand future were at stake!

Surely they thought that to quash a few little "insurrections" like the one at the little white church would create just a few, unnamable and insignificant martyrs. That wasn't a big problem for the government. It was for the good of society . . .. in the best interest of the citizens, and proof they had things under control. They knew so little about "cause and effect and the creation of a powerful counterculture!"

Now, here I am! I'm one of the "untaggables!" There's no microprocessor in my forehead or in my right hand!

All this sounds so self-pitying, doesn't it? Well, I told you all these things the way I did so you would see reality through the eyes of so many others

This life, even in these Post-Rapture days, is just too unpredictable. Predictable, yes, but unpredictable all the same! Torturous, even in their type of "freedom." Unbearable, but we must press forward and spread the word of the Living God for those who are still untouched by the mark of allegiance to the evil one.

We must offer them a glimmer of encouragement, and never give up. Don't give in to the lie. In these few remaining days of ours, we must remain true to the faith, we must continue to fight in His name.

A portion of this fight was manifested in the play. It's now become about us, the Christian martyrs of the near future, with its cause of extolling the righteous cause of martyrdom for the love of the true and Living Christ, rather than eternal damnation!

As I believe Christ would want it, peace and love to you, dear reader. I pray you did not take the mark and now reluctantly, but in a sense, also eagerly await the finality of martyrdom for Christ on this side of life eternal.

You know that all who are alive on earth right now missed that greatest of days, the Rapture of the Church . . .three and a half years ago. God be with you, instead of the antichrist now!

Chapter 29

Fire and Brimstone

Four years ACR
Narrator: Unknown
Location: Unknown
Rationale: This person obviously had a conversation with you sometime in the past.

Remember the story about Tiny that I told you? You remember; it was just before he died. Yes, it was the story of the confrontation with Scontee and his cronies at Mr. Lands' house. Well . . .

Okay, okay, you're right! My wife says that if I'm going to tell that story, I need to keep it as accurate as possible, so here goes. I do tend to exaggerate just a little, but we all need our heroes, don't we? I mean, Tiny did save the day for many people that at that showing of the play. He helped them stay alive-if one could consider staying in this world the same as being "alive."

You must remember, though, that while the world considers someone dead, if that person died in Christ, he is more abundantly alive from then on! What this world considers alive is really dead compared to the reality of eternity with Christ is!

The question is, did Tiny do those people a favor that day or not? I was there. Did he do me a favor with the heroics he actually performed that day? He saved my life along with so many others, but the question again is, did he do us a favor?

Yes! Tiny was a Christian, and he went on to fight more physical battles against the evil foes for a short time. You might say that Tiny and that group of people should have freely died for Christ that day at Mr. Lands' house. Truthfully, some did die, but others walked away!

Does Christ expect us to willingly stand there and die in this world even if we can, at that particular moment, defend our mortal bodies? Isn't that a bit like the person who says, "Oh hey, Christ, look at me! Look what I did for you or in your name! I died for you or I suffered for you!"

It was righteous for the perfect Lamb of God to do that for us, because it was all part of God's plan for our redemption, but it's not right for us to do this because all our righteousness are as filthy rags!

If called upon to do so, it's righteous to give of ourselves in suffering or dying for the cause of Christianity, but to not defend oneself or ones loved ones when given the opportunity is unwarranted! God instilled in each of us the desire to remain alive as this world sees alive to be! To do otherwise would be catamount to walking up to a person and saying "I am a Christian and I want to die a martyr's death, so please proceed to torture and kill me!

Basically, I am saying that for Tiny to defend himself and those people was the right thing to do. Later, when Tiny was captured, he was not given that option, and he died willingly, graciously, and with great dignity as he was witnessing not of himself, but of our Living God!

I know when you last spoke with me, I was telling you about the tragedy at the little white church I attended as a sixteen-year-old boy. I told you about how Pastor Janus, Granny, and many others were martyred that day. Remember how bitter I was? I was mad at the world . . . I mean ready mad!

Want to hear a really strange story? *I* was the one who witnessed to Tiny at the little white church the day the massacre occurred! Tiny had just brutally killed our brother in Christ, my friend Paul Plank. I witnessed to Tiny and he dropped to his knees and said the sinner's prayer.

Tiny was saved that day, and is now in the presence of the Lord. He was killed about three months before the Rapture. I, on the other hand, was never truly saved, so I'm still here. I had heard the sinner's prayer probably hundreds of times and had a few versions of witnessing approaches and a couple of versions of sinner's prayers memorized.

I said the sinner's prayer enough times as we had heard it, but I never put my heart into it. You can say the Pledge of Allegiance every day of your life and still be a subversive or terrorist. If it doesn't mean anything because it's just words . . . it's just words. That's what that prayer was to me . . . just memorized words!

I saw it work on other people, especially folks with broken hearts and all. In fact, I saw it work many, many times. I was willing to stop the carnage at the little white church that awful day at just about any cost! It seemed hopeless, but of everything in the universe, witnessing was all I had that could even remotely be used.

Who would ever have figured it? A lost person saved by a lost person's witness! A good friend once told me that God can even use lost people to achieve His desired results. How many times have you seen that happen?

Anyway, Tiny gave his soul to Christ, then he stopped the total slaughter of almost everyone at that church. He saved my life and the lives of so many others. And still, I didn't give my heart and soul to the Lord. He Raptured His church four years ago and I finally figured it out, thank God, or I would have been blinded by the antiChrist and my soul would be damned to the lake of fire for eternity!

I'm now sorry for all those nasty insults I threw at you, reader! It really isn't your fault that I'm here and wasn't Raptured with the church! Most of the time I was in the presence of other "unsaved" people! I

263

witnessed other "runners from Christ" often.

All those excuses! All those really stupid, lame-brained excuses! Well, weren't they lame-brained?

Here we are, four years after the rapture and look at what all we've been through. No, I'm not being bitter towards you, because you obviously have your own problems! I just miss my family and you miss your family. I've endured man's wrath and terror and you've endured as much as I have. Many times I've narrowly lived through God's fury. You have too!

Choices to make! Choices to make! Made the wrong ones, didn't we? Well, at least we'll be with Christ sometime . ... within about three years! That's as long as we hold true to Him! All we have to do is stay true to Him! I know, that was easier back then . . . so way, way back then before the Body of Christ was taken to meet Him in the clouds!

The scorching heat, the starvation, the thirst! That awful thirst! The running, the hiding! The daily loss of our friends and loved ones is so hard to bear. It's so hard to watch them go through this!

All the things we wish we could do for them . . . I know you do just like I do! Now, everything is out of our hands, except to stay alive to be witnesses for Christ!

While some may think this odd, I do not resent this. I endure willingly and gladly for my Savior! I can still only imagine what He went through for me! He suffered the weight of the sins of the whole world! Only believe! Only trust Christ this very day, this very moment! That's what I heard, that's what it seems we both constantly heard!

We didn't heed it, though. Four horrendous years ago!

Now at least I know that my Savior may consider me to be one of His martyrs! Now I also realize that I may not die as a martyr, but I'm truly living in these Tribulation days as a suffering martyr for Him!

Although I suffer for Him, I may not die for Him, but possibly, or conceivably may live until His Glorious Appearing.

Which is the third time Christ comes to earth . . . His second return! I may actually be here at that time . . . when He begins His thousand-year reign!

All Glory to God, since we missed the Rapture, and didn't rise in the air to meet Him, didn't see Him, we still may live to see His return, this time in all His Glory to rule the earth for a thousand years!

The down side is we may not live that long! We may bleed and die as martyrs, our heads cut off before then! My friend, don't be afraid if that happens! It's truly not a down side, the conclusion of life on this earth, as you know it!

Sing proudly God's praises, even as man does what he chooses to you, for there is only just so much man can do! Immediately after, you or I will be with Jesus, having carried out His blessed purpose!

We'll be with our blessed loved ones, resting in Christ, and will later receive the martyr's crown that we'll gladly place at our Saviors Feet! We'll then return to earth with Him at the Glorious Appearing to rule with Him for a thousand years! After that, Satan will be loosed for a short while. Then he and all his angels, his followers, those who didn't receive Christ as their personal savior and all that took the Mark of the Beast-will receive the second death. They will be cast into the Lake of Fire that is truthfully written of in Revelations. Christ and the martyrs will watch as they receive their eternal "reward."

~

Do you think the horrible torment inflicted on humanity since Christ Raptured the Church are awesomely horrible and difficult? Be careful how you answer that question! No sir, you absolutely must NOT become part of that!

Why did so many preachers water down the Word of God before Christ's return for His own four years ago? It became popular to theorize that people had changed, so you had to be sweet like honey to reach them.

As a preacher of the Word, you had to be a diluter. Whether you knew the truth or not, people kept changing and couldn't or wouldn't listen to any more "old school" preaching . . . like that Fire and Brimstone stuff!

True, they did need to get people in church, but didn't they notice that people needed to quench their spiritual thirst on "the truth, the whole truth, and nothing but the truth?"

I wish I'd heard preachers who weren't so insecure. Behind closed doors they were so concerned about delivering a soft and gentle message. They should have been concerned about following the Holy Spirit and telling it like it is . . . or at least like it was until the Rapture occurred! We, the members of their congregations, were entitled to the truth!

The masterful preachers were too few. They could deliver the eternal message, then offer the salve to help them not "burn like fire." Those preachers looked out for their flocks. Those "sheep" needed to know what could be in their future

~

.

It's too late for millions of people, but for millions more it's not too late, even in this post-Rapture world.

It was easy back then. All a person had to do was realize that they were a sinner-which is part of being led to Jesus through the Holy Spirit, ask Jesus for forgiveness for their sins, and acknowledge Jesus as their Savior! Sorry about only using "his."

Now, in these horrible post-Rapture days, you must ask for forgiveness of your sins and you must NOT TAKE THE MARK of the antichrist. That's right, DO NOT TAKE THE MARK of the false one who has always deceived the world with his lies; the one who would have all people worship him as the messiah, the savior of the world!

He is not! Do not take the mark! Whatever you do, do not take the mark! Suffer and die-you, your children, husband or wife, mother and father-whoever was left here and not taken in the rapture!

No matter how hard it is for you to see them suffer, or go without food or clothing, heat in the winter, air-conditioning in the summer, do not take the mark! No matter how desperate they are for just a drink of water, medicine for their sores, or bandages for their broken bones they receive from the "authorities," do not take the mark!

DO NOT panic, DO NOT give in, and DO NOT take the mark! It doesn't matter how great they make it sound . . . if you just take the mark and lead your loved ones to receive the mark, all will be well ...they say

Wrong! Don't do it! Remember how hot eternally the Lake of Fire is!

You must somehow become a Christian. You may live through the Tribulation and the Great Tribulation-that's a total of seven years-or suffer as a martyr and live through the seven years, or die during that time as a

martyr for Christ!

~

Now you know why I was so bitter when we first spoke. Now you know why I called you all those names. Now you're going through the same thing.

The three great things I've learned in the six months since we last spoke with each other are really very basic. First, it's okay for me to be angry with myself because I didn't give my heart and soul to Christ and didn't go with Him in the Rapture, but I can't be bitter with myself or other people because, like so many others, I had my chance!

Second, being proud and completely willing to serve Him partly out of fear is good, but what's better is serving Him because of my love and adoration for Him! He's so mighty that if people didn't love him, the rocks and the mountains would still love and worship Him! He created them! We might not be able to understand it, but whoever made us so almighty that we would understand?

Remember the story in the Bible about Mary and Martha? Jesus was visiting them, and Martha was busy running around the house doing things for Jesus. Mary was at his feet, crying and worshipping Him. Martha became upset because she was doing all the work and felt that Mary should be helping. Jesus let her know that Mary was by far, doing the better thing.

Worship Him! Praise Him! Honor Him! Live for Him! Work for Him!
This book is about working for Him, yes it is…but don't ever take your eyes off the cross in worship of Him! This fuels you up so you can do His work!

Praise God!
Praise Jesus!
Praise the Holy Spirit!

Ponder…meditate…and let Him permeate!

The third great thing I learned was that I thought I would surely have to die a martyr's death in order to be with the Lord. You left before our discussion with Mr. Canube was over. After all the insults I've thrown at you-and as you could tell, I didn't know much of anything about what I was talking about-I can't say I blame you!

I may not die before the Glorious Appearing of Christ. You knew that and Mr. Canube was nice enough to tell me that little bit of truth! Not everyone who's alive during the Tribulation will die!

I just certainly wouldn't want to be a follower of the antichrist, no matter how much they try to sweeten the deal! You see, what I found out is, you have to meet face to face, or head on with reality at one time or another! I had every opportunity to do it before and didn't! Everybody has to face reality at one time or another, because life is brief . . . it doesn't last long!

Many people think they can outlast such an ominous confrontation, but they can't! Nobody ever has and nobody ever will! Not me, not you!

We can all be grateful for what men like Tiny did that day in the short time he had left on this earth! He helped keep me alive . . . perhaps long enough . . . to hopefully see me become a Christian! For some incredibly stupid reason or another, I didn't repent before the Rapture, but at least I'm alive now . . .. and I'm a Christian now.

I can finally be a true witness for Christ . . . the witness that I should have been all along . . . leading people to Him and all His glory so they can spend eternity with Him. I should have been doing this before the Rapture, but I couldn't because I wasn't ready for it myself!

You know, I sometimes think that I would have been with Him now if I'd been smarter and opened my heart to Him. God only knows how many other people would have gone in the Rapture instead of being in this terrifying torment with me or instead of caving in and taking the mark. They'll spend eternity in the Lake of Fire.

My decision, or indecision, was responsible partly for the eternity of many, many souls will spend eternity!

As I said, decisions, decisions!

Chapter 30

Your mind will be avenged

Narrator: Unknown
Location: Different locations
When: Shortly ACR

Lord and Savior, Jesus the Christ, Lord and Savior, Jesus the Christ, Lord and Savior, Jesus the Christ!

*R*ocking back and forth, rocking back and forth .. . . all day . . . everyday . . . that's all she does.

"Lord and Savior Jesus the Christ," she says, all day . . . everyday. That's all she says.

You would have thought she was autistic, but she wasn't.

The Rapture affected her so much. When her stepfather was suddenly taken that day, her whole life changed. She was so into her stepfather! She loved him so much!

We were in a family comfort group immediately after the Rapture, you know. It was one of those groups where family members of Raptured individuals get together and air out their feelings, discuss what they think happened that day, what they think will happen next, and try to sort the whole thing out. It was just a way to just try to cope with it all.

Well, support groups seemed to help, especially when they were giving their theories about instantaneous death and vaporization of people's bodies due to radicals or terrorist attacks with their weapons. I mean, the government came right out and admitted they have weapons that will do that. Have you never heard of "Microwave Weapons?"

Other weapons they had could target the general structure of a specific DNA, then tap a couple of times in some technical way on a computer keyboard, and the New Ultra Filtration & Absorption Device, or NUFAD as everyone called it, could do the rest. Supposedly, it's some new government defense technology that's ultra-sonic, ultra-wave or ultra-something.

Then they said that radical militants, radical Christians, or terrorists got their hands on it and unleashed it on mankind. It's strange how the government put them all together to come up with RCMTs, our terrible new enemies. Everyone was told to be on the lookout for 'Radical Christian Militant Terrorists.' That about summed it up in a neat little package . . . didn't it? It covered anyone who would take a stand against them, anyone who would even think about taking any stand at all or, for that matter, anyone who would discuss the idea taking a stand, whether pro or con. The only folks left were those who didn't care, didn't want you to care-the ones who looked for someone to lead them and finish off those who did care.

My fourteen-year-old daughter started gazing. She wouldn't say anything, she would just gaze at whoever was speaking at the moment.

There were other theories too, you know! There was the one about the aliens from outer space, but that one had been around for centuries . . . all that stuff about UFOs and aliens mating with our culture for this reason or that reason. Then they tried making us believe that aliens were just arriving because of SETI, the agency that for many years sent strong signals into outer space looking for extra-terrestrial life. According to that theory, they found it, and it doesn't think in ways we could ever have imagined.

Anyway, they tried to convince us that they'd abducted all those people to populate their dying culture because they're so far advanced that their procreation numbers are down. They can't reproduce at a pace that's fast enough to keep up with their declining population-as if the same thing didn't happen all over Europe for decades. What a load of hooey!

My daughter would just shake when she heard all this theoretical stuff. I thought about not taking her back and almost didn't, but when we weren't at one of those meetings, she seemed so withdrawn and would constantly mumble, "I have to know, I have to know."

We'd both know soon enough. Someone brought a Bible to one of those meetings and started quoting from it. It was quite terrifying to me . . . I mean, all that stuff just couldn't be real and it wasn't new. We could freely access it for so long and didn't pay it any attention. We heard God this and Jesus that, but wasn't life really too full and too complicated without adding the confusion of "religion?"

I don't know, I just don't know! I don't know what happened that day that I lost my little twin stepsons and my husband. I want to know. I desperately want to know, especially with Clarissa in the state she's in now. In a way, I wish that religious theorist hadn't been invited to speak that day.

It's probably all right to consider a spiritual perspective, but it sent my Clarissa right over the edge! They got so deep into their perspectives on Jesus, the Messiah, and all the stuff about the Rapture that day . . . . and all she does now is rock back and forth and say "Lord and Savior, Jesus the Christ." I put her on medications, but they either put her to sleep or she's totally out of it saying the same thing. The only difference is her words are slurred.

I remember what they said that day. They said we all missed that great and wonderful event, the Rapture of the Saints. They said they had missed it too, and talked about martyrdom for Christ. It was frightening to hear them say stuff about people getting their heads chopped off . . . my goodness, the tales they wove that day!

Clarissa appeared to be at some kind of breaking point, and instead of those meetings helping her, they sent over right over the edge. Now I want to be part of this new movement that will stop this rubbish once and for all before it gets into everybody's head. What nonsense! How dare they come up with such fantasies and try to get all those people to believe it! I want to make them pay for what they've done to her. I need a belief, and I believe what the government is telling us about the radical Christians!

"My Lord and Savior, Jesus the Christ, My Lord and Savior, Jesus the Christ, My Lord and Savior, Jesus the Christ!"

Did Clarissa discover something I didn't understand or was unwilling to investigate? Am I looking for easy answers when there are none?

I had no idea that my daughter had found the truth-her Savior, Jesus. I didn't know that it overjoyed her and terrified her at the same time. She understood that her stepfather and stepbrothers had been caught up in the Rapture. She wasn't out of it! She was actually "in it." Clarissa had zoned into the knowledge, fear, and admonition of the Lord. He was dealing with her just as he had dealt with others before her. He left Saul blind for a few days, then restored his sight when he professed his faith in Jesus as the Messiah. The Lord was dealing with Clarissa in a special way.

First, she had to get in tune with the Lord in her mind where there could have been a million reality checks. Realities . . . like what took place that day, where her daddy and brothers went . . . and accepting those things on faith, something I, her agnostic mother, could never do-like a leap of faith! Reality . . .like what was in store for the world and for the people who weren't Raptured. What would happen to them? What would happen to me-her too-busy-to-believe mother-whom she loved so dearly?

What would happen if her faith wasn't strong enough or wasn't enough on its own? How could she make it to her dad, her stepfather, and brothers now? How could one little girl, just barely a teenager, make a difference?

Hey, remember this! WITH GOD, ALL THINGS ARE POSSIBLE!

The main thing Clarissa knew during the times I was searching, accepting the wrong things, and rejecting the right things, was that she *had* to stay focused. She had to stay focused on what? She knew . . . she had to stay focused on what the Lord told her was the key thing-the fact that her Lord and Savior is Jesus the Christ! He is her Lord, He is her Savior, He is Jesus the God-man, and Christ the Messiah, the Redeemer, God the Creator of everlasting to everlasting, and all things natural and spiritual!

I had so many questions and I wanted answers immediately! I didn't want little hypotheses for answers; I wanted the truth. I didn't understand why this happened to my Clarissa. Other people at the focus groups didn't go over the edge like she did.

First, there was the one we don't talk about, then my husband and twin sons disappear, and then Clarissa lost touch with reality. She might have been a woman, but this was beyond enough! It was best to leave Clarissa in the hands of a sitter and make the best of the evening hours.

Information expansion was the profile of the day.

Easy enough to do! Just melt in and partake of it! Had she lost her mind too? She had always considered herself to be a moderately intelligent woman at the least, but with all this information . . . lies . . . misinformation, and the misinformation of the intellectually ignorant, I could find myself at the end of my life real quick if I'm not careful. After all, it's now the law.Zero-tolerance for refusing to conform . . . for the non-conforming. Refusing to conform . . . Non-conforming to what?

I could have answered all of her questions. I mean, where was she when I was trying to tell her? Didn't she listen? She thought it was okay to accept the new One World Government and it's leaders. She thought is was okay to accept not just whatever they said, but what they taught and preached about their New World Order religion. The key was the word "order." It was their order that was the key to safety and security . . . and they also offered the solace of rightful revenge!

Right! Full!

Yes, she wanted plenty of both! She would avenge what those radicals did to Clarissa's mind! "The one they didn't talk about" would be avenged! Her husband and twin boys would be avenged! The time was near . . . the world had fallen apart, not at all like it was prior to the year one BCR.

She looked back on her life before the Rapture of the Church. She worked, came home, cooked, cleaned house, occasionally spent time with her husband and kids, and got ready for bed and another day. Her husband did his things . . . you know, a few "honey do's," his hobbies, and sometimes sports-you know, guy things.

He tried talking with her about Jesus, over and over again. He would throw around a few thoughts about religious stuff and then it was off to bed, "sweet dreams, honey," and all that stuff.

How do you change people and not affect free will? That was a major question for God. The answer was probably just by letting events unfold, as they always do; but don't take me as an authority on that subject. You can put that question to God if and when you see Him. I do know that God intervenes in the affairs of men from time to time, as He sees fit.

Some of those interventions are called miracles.

Miracles . . . that's what was needed. Beautiful, sweet Clarissa needed a miracle from God. Her mother wasn't praying for her, and most of the people in the focus groups weren't either. She had prayer, though. Many fine Christian people were praying for her . . . and for her mother.

Her mother definitely needed prayer, especially for what she got herself into. She didn't have to try very hard to get herself into the ISD. By then they accepted just about anybody with a left-wing hatred for right-wingers. She wanted to vent her frustration and anger so much that she quickly worked her way into the position of left-hand woman to Mr. Scontee. Such irony! Her brother, the man they called Brother Danny, was greatly responsible for Scontee being in the position of power he was in.

Chapter 31

I.S.D.

Narrator: Unknown
When: Sometime starting BCR and going into ACR

Well, she and Scontee became very close very fast, mostly because he realized she was Brother Danny's sister. Besides, they both had the same like things in mind-the death and destruction of the Christians!

She had been real close with Brother Danny and, unlike many siblings, they actually got along, enjoyed talking to each other, and enjoyed the tight bond that most children in a family don't enjoy. Indeed, theirs was a rather unique brother and sister friendship-one that broke from the weight of that last straw, her daughter losing all semblance of reality... as it were.

Scontee was a nobody, a nothing cog in a nothing wheel. Things were just beginning to shape up after those tumultuous elections. Those radical leftists were just beginning to feel their oats a bit what with their newfound freedom to take freedoms away from everyone . . .. and easily enforce those changes. For his own personal reasons, Scontee wanted to be part of what he saw shaping up. You could call him a visionary, if you don't mind stretching the term that much! Everybody is right at least sometimes, and this was his time to be right. Things were shaping up even more radically and even more quickly than he had hoped.

There was a problem though. He started out the same way he did when he worked for the far right radicals, as his clique called them. He was less than a lackey, a paper shuffler and paper pusher! He'd been thinking about the way he was treated for quite some time, but at least the benefits of hearing about the mildly mean things they were doing legally to those "rad-rights" made his job easier and more tolerable.

He'd often listen to those tales, as the storytellers would laugh up a storm . . . a storm of exhilaration and exhaustive excitement for him. He let his imagination run wild as incredible scenes played out in his mind; and at least in his head, it wasn't a pretty picture.

Then came the not-so-pretty picture of Brother Danny. Brother Danny had put together the bold plan for the demise of his own wife, that angelic Sister Brenda. He did it using his power of influence-not that it took much, with the boys at the brand new ISD. They were bored, restless right from the get-go, always looking for some really quick "clear to go" action, as they liked to call it.

Brother Danny was the ticket. Their eyes glistened with rampant excitement as they clung to every word he uttered. He toned down, looked around, and whispered as if to say, "Let's be very quiet so nobody will hear." It got them to hunker down and listen intently, focusing ever so keenly on the meaning of every word he spoke. Then he would get excited about part of the plan, jump back and start slamming his fist, then break into what looked like a charismatic dance.

Oh, yes, her brother, Brother Danny, was quite the character all right, or maybe I should say all left! Before he took off for what he called greener pastures, they were totally captivated, and ready, willing, and able to carry out his plan. Who would have thought Sister Brenda was so important? She was just a housewife to most people, but Brother Danny convinced them she was the igniter of the bomb that had to be de-fused. What a blood-rushing thrill it would be for the ones that not only pulled the plug, but at the same time got such great practice in their "art," along with justification to further their "well-intentioned" exploits!

Too bad they didn't know about the chain of events their little "cog in the-wheel," with his panic-driven compulsion to rub out Sister Brenda, would unleash!

It was time for Sister Brenda to come home to Christ! She had completed her life's work, and now she could take leave of her life on earth and come home to Him totally unsupervised by Brother Danny.

Brother Danny, God *will* deal with you! Oh reader, God did, but not yet. God used those events for His Glory! As it was written, "Those that live by the sword shall die by the sword," and Brother Danny was no exception. He had to have lots of living by the sword under his belt until it was his time-and for the same reasons that caused the downfall of power-hungry warlords.

Word of what had happened to Sister Brenda spread to both far-left circles and among the Christian circles. The events that followed were both amazing and totally repulsive, at least to anyone who had what used to known as a sense of decency. Problem was that it was no longer called that or even thought of that way, at least not by the forces that were in control. No, their new motto was "I don't see and I don't care."

That meant murder was acceptable. They could get away with murdering the "right" people. They were left justified, just as their new phrase signified. Right Justification was obviously outlawed, and that left only left justification for the straight out, immediate, and complete exoneration for those who committed the right kind of murders!

Brother Danny, what did you do? Scontee became your lead man, so to speak. In other words, he was more than willing to take the chance and take control of the capture, torture, and execution of your wife. It's correct to assume they all got what they wanted. Brother Danny got rid of his righteous wife and she got to go to her Jesus. The guys at ISD got their adrenaline flowing. Leftists all the way up the ladder, and I do mean ALL the way up, saw to the institution of their "World Institutionalization of the New Way of Life (also known as WIN). It was slingshot forward into forced implementation at near warp speed! Only the losers, the current enemy, the radical rights, didn't prosper by what Brother Danny helped put in motion.

The next thing we knew, Scontee was a hero. I know that odd

things were taking place everyday, and we often don't know what gets those things started. It doesn't matter if they're odd or not odd, they just happen. I mean, who knows what it took to get that horrific imbalance of power in place? Oh yes, it was that man with all the charm and charisma- (what we now call "negative charisma") -that started the ball rolling so all the pieces could fall in place.

Scontee was a hero? Who would have ever thought that Scontee would amount to anything? Well, the fact is, I would say he never did amount to anything and, even worse, he amounted to less than nothing!

With the rapid implementation of the new laws, his work didn't involve much risk-taking. If there was even a debate on Capitol Hill about those new laws, those in favor blamed the whole thing on filibustering for the benefit of partisanship!

End of story? Not a chance!

Partisanship on the part of right-committal became pacifist moderated, both for personal safety and for popularity (they were afraid to take a stand for conservativeness). They knew the polls would soon reflect their like-mindedness with their constituents.

Was it a risk, what Scontee did at that little white church? No. Not really! Brother Danny even set that scene up. He knew about it through his church circles and was well aware of the mood and mind set after the unfortunate demise of Sister Brenda. He just knew that the logical next step in this "order of things" was to make a statement of incredible impact, one that displayed their power, unchallenged authority, cunning, and willingness to follow through.

And he did so with the attack on the little white church; and what made it especially tasteful to the power palate was the *Martyr's of the Cross* play they were putting on. Oh, that play was just what they needed because it displayed martyrdom for what the far left called religion. They were wrong! It was martyrdom for the love of our Risen Savior!

Scontee now had more unchallenged power and authority than he ever imagined he would have. He had nothing in mind but to use it as harshly as his imagination allowed . . . and that was a lot! Brother Danny didn't want that position. He just wanted to be the right-hand man, the man behind the man, the man that no one knew was the real brains behind it all! That's why he participated in the "incident" at the little white church, where he had the pleasure and privilege of showing his sheer brutality. Brother Danny was the one who threw Granny out of the window to her earthy demise!

There was just one catch to all this. Scontee got everything he ever wanted and more. He began to think of the damage Brother Danny could do to him, to what he almost considered his own regime. He let these thoughts fester like a painful, huge boil. Scontee knew that Brother Danny had far more of what it took to stay in his position than he did. There was only room at the top for one man, and Scontee knew that Brother Danny was a shoe-in for that spot if he wanted it. It was time to protect his authority and hopefully the time to do so hadn't passed.

There was something missing. Scontee needed a pasty, someone who would take the fall for everything that went wrong. Tiny was still alive, and Scontee couldn't think of a better person to play the part. All he had to do was find him. One way or another, he would make sure that Tiny would pay. Oh, he would pay dearly for being a Christian, because of all the things he did to Scontee, personally, and because of what he did after he "gave his life to the Lord."

Well, Scontee almost lost control of his command after Tiny carved that lovely smile on his face at the little white church. Now, Scontee was determined to kill Tiny and ruin everything he now stood for. He could do the "ruining" part even if Tiny wasn't found. It was the killing part, that sweet revenge, which involved setting up Brother Danny!

Brother Danny didn't know Tiny like the rest of the ISD knew him. He didn't know of the danger of coming face to face with an almost invincible force that was filled with so much rage that he liked nothing more than to brutalize anything living, especially Christians! Scontee, however, knew that Tiny was the same, except he was working for the ones he wanted to help, the ones he had joined . ... the Christians.

Plan in motion!

Scontee had a conference with Brother Danny, told him about the imminent danger that Tiny posed and the urgent need to eliminate that threat! Brother Danny was more than willing to participate . . . no, let me re-phrase that . . . he wanted to capture and personally abolish every atom of Tiny's being from this earth . . . but only after endless days of torture. Scontee was satisfied. Parts of the plan were thought out well enough.

Word had it that after the meeting at Mr. Land's house-which was when Tiny unleashed on the ISD for the second time-that the evil and cunning Brother Danny set up the near-perfect trap for Tiny. He had been a rather insincere member of that bunch of Christians, not being a Christian, himself...just pretending to be one so he could make money from being the pastor of his church before joining the ISD. If there was a way to protect his ISD brothers from imminent danger, he would, even if he had to give up his own life. Brother Danny knew that Tiny believed in martyrdom. He knew he wasn't concerned about prolonging his life on earth.

Ball in motion! Scontee would get two for the price of one! Brother Danny and Tiny would both be gone and there would be no more fear of harm from either of those potential party poopers. Yes, Scontee had superiors, but he didn't always recognize them as such, because he pictured himself someday rising to an all-powerful position, with everyone being his pawn to rule.

Scontee didn't know that wasn't going to happen, though. There was a man who was already set aside for that position, the man the Bible told us was the antichrist. From before the foundations of time, God knew that "the man" would set himself above everyone else and derive great power from the abominable one, Satan.

What I didn't get was why Satan would even bother with this

pawn, the antichrist, to try to rule the world. What's the point of a phony messiah? Maybe he didn't think he was a phony. Maybe he was trying to be the real thing.

The answer, well it's time for a good old-fashioned lesson based on truth! God is the only being from everlasting to everlasting. Even God's angels are not from everlasting to everlasting, they were created, so therefore they had a beginning, as did satan. He was not a being from a reproductive process, which God monitors and blesses. But Satan had the same delusions of grandeur he's had for eons. You see Satan was a created being. Remember that his name was Lucifer and he was God's most beautiful creation . . . and he knew it . . . but that wasn't enough for the old boy. He wanted to set himself above God, the Creator, because he was, and still is, so vain that he thinks that he should hold the highest position of power. How utterly and absolutely stupid!

Lucifer rebelled and became the leader of the army of fallen angels- those who also rebelled against God, who wanted power equal to God's power. His name, Satan, is from the old Hebrew, -Ha Satan-, meaning The Accuser, or The Adversary.

These have been pretty good reasons not to become vain, proud, and boastful, have they not? We must be careful lest we fall into the same or similar traps that snared Satan. None of those things can set you in a positive light or make you look good to others. They only make you think they do, and then where are you? I'll tell you, you are in your own little isolated world where nobody thinks as highly of you as you do. You can't get power with people that way. You must be honest and sincere with them, and care about them. Don't set yourself above them like Satan keeps trying to do with God. The Lord is always just, and will make sure your haughty spirit leads to a fall and your pride results in destruction.

Anyway, Satan really wants to be God's superior and the antichrist to be the superior to Christ. What an idiot! But there's a little more. God said there would come a time when Satan would no longer be able to visit Him in heaven. Remember how he always went to God accusing us of this or that . . . like he did with Job? Remember he told God that Job only loved Him because He gave him everything he wanted. Well, God knew Job would pass that test.

Now, if Satan can't enter heaven, he has to have someplace in which to dwell. Enter the antichrist . . . a warm body in which to hang out and torment the world, especially believers.

SO,

If Scontee wasn't *the* antichrist, he was at least willing to be very high in the pecking order for him. His plans for the Christians were steeped in the same type of evil, and so far his newest plan worked. The ISD set Tiny up using the chaos that accompanied the capture, arrest, and torture of a hundred and thirty Christians.

Tiny knew he might be able to secure the release of those children of God. What he didn't know was that he was the golden prize all along. During his one-man rescue attempt, word had it that Brother Danny somehow gotten the drop on Tiny. Then, word leaked back that Brother Danny stupidly got greedy and thought that he could get Tiny away from the protection of the ISD and take him somewhere to have fun relentlessly torturing him.

Scontee's plan had been simple. Tiny would take Brother Danny out and the ISD would take Tiny out. Oh, they might lose a few ISD agents, but they would hopefully be rid of all the Christians they had in captivity as well!

Didn't happen that way, though.

As I was saying about the rumor that came back, it was told that Brother Danny had been able to take Tiny down, with the assistance of about twenty agents. Only one of the twenty agents came back alive, and his story was chilling, or most civilized people would have found it so. Of course, in reality, Tiny had achieved his own release, which brings me to a stopping point in the story because it's very difficult to explain what happened.

Okay, bear with me now, because I'm trying to tell this without all the flamboyant adjectives it really deserves. I worry that you'll think I'm telling it in some way as to over sensationalize what happened, but I'm not. You must understand, it's just the way it happened. Cut it out, stop worrying! You are right, I may use some pretty descriptive words, but in this case there aren't enough sparkling adjectives in anyone's vocabulary to add to the beauty of what Tiny did that day!

Go ahead and paint your own picture. I simply can't do it justice. Oh, trust me, this is one of those rare events in the history of mankind that no amount of words could describe. You've heard many times that a picture is worth a thousand words? Well, I'm not sure I know which of those thousand words to use, but I'll give it try . . .

The one man that came back was broken in pieces and barely resembled a human being. I heard the reason he was allowed to live and leave that gruesome scene was just so he could tell "the powers that be" what happened, and to distract them into believing the plan was a success. Maybe they would find some degree of satisfaction in Tiny's death and stop killing so many of the brethren.

I heard tell that among the other acts Tiny accomplished that day, he also killed Brother Danny and, in the end, allowed himself to be so severely injured that he bled to death. But Tiny didn't die until he had deeply wounded or killed every man there except the last man, the one he wanted to tell the story. Believe me, it was no picnic for him, either. The pain that last man must have endured was unspeakable! Fortunately for him, Scontee was a "humane" individual and eased his torment.

Yes, I guess you know what that means! It was too bad that man wasn't a Christian when he died. The torment he endured was a rose garden compared to what came next . . . and next . . . and next . . .. and next. His 'end life torment' had been a rose garden

285

We don't even want to go into what "next" involved, for "vengeance is Mine saith the Lord," and He had plenty of vengeance all lined up, for all eternity!

Well, "word had it" and reality …were two totally different ways of understanding what happened next. As I understand it, Scontee took that man's life not because he was being merciful about his suffering or pain, but for the pure joy of doing it. The man had recanted his original story I just told you, and had decided to spill his guts about what really happened.

Reality . . .

The ISD found out where this was all going down, they got there late, Tiny was bleeding to death, and they were going to have a little fun. They got out their switchblades and four of them hacked at the big guy's neck. You got the picture now? They hacked through what seemed to be super-tough tissue, slinging blood all over the place until they cut his head off!

Oh, it was ISD party time! Instead of spending time mourning the loss of their brave fallen comrades, the ISD held a three-day party to celebrate all the carnage! This was a party . . . well, the likes of which you and I would never consider having ourselves. I certainly hope you wouldn't. I know I'm definitely not like that in any way, shape, form, or fashion!

When the party finally ended, they got down and dirty, like getting down to the business at hand, or doing what good, radical leftists do. It was the old, *me, me, me, me* . . . the great big, important *me*-first policy, and if you don't like it, I'm sure there was something they would do about it if they found out! (THEY WOULD HAVE YOU KILLED!). Who's next?

Reader, you don't think that's right? You don't think it's right to be a radical leftist? Well, who knows, you might be their next target!

Plain and simple, everything had been Scontee's way or the highway! No more Tiny and no more Brother Danny, although no one knew for sure where Brother Danny was. No one knew if he was severely wounded or if he was dead. Nobody but me, I know he was dead . . .just kidding…in reality, I don't even know how Brother Danny played in the carnage, but I do know that his body wasn't found there or anywhere else for that matter.

So, at headquarters, the I.S.D. partied those three days with Tiny's head used as either the brunt of a joke or at least in plain sight at all times. No, it was definitely going to be Scontee's way or the highway from that point forward-the highway to the grave that is! He would even dig a grave especially for you, reader, if he wanted to, just to be certain there was one more rad-right in his way!

Scontee kept gaining power and was very extremely close to the top (and you know what that meant). He instituted policies and gave orders that escalated and intensified martyrdom for Christ, which had the opposite effect that he wanted it to have.

What he really wanted was to kill a whole bunch of Christians and scare everybody else so badly that they wouldn't dare become one. In effect however, he rallied a call to arms of the praying, Word-spreading Christians, and for the continued production of *Martyrs of the Cross* to spread Christianity to more and more unsaved souls. Fight the good fight. Submit to Christ and witness constantly until Christ calls you home. If you're martyred for the cause, celebrate and praise His Holy Name!

All prophecies fulfilled and all things in place, the God of the universe said to Jesus in his own divine words something to the effect of, *"The time is now to bring your Bride home. It's time for the marriage supper of the Lamb."*

I started to say that He said, *"Behold, go get My children,"* but I think He probably didn't have that second sentence in there because I doubt that our Savior needed to be told twice! He loves us so greatly that I believe He was en route the very instant God spoke it.

Well, it happened . . . that awesome and miraculous event, that indefinable event, the Rapture of the Church. The dead in Christ rose in the air to meet Him, then those living and on earth were taken up and met the others in the clouds. The King of kings and Lord of lords accomplished it, and the world was quickly heading towards what would appear to be an era of peace. The key word is "appear."

Several astonishing events had to take place first, including the attempted invasion of Israel by the " Bear of the North ", Russia, and it's allies. This is miraculously defeated, then the quick rise to power of a very persuasive man, the " man of peace, the antichrist ", the Christ's Power and Glory wannabe!

Enter Scontee!

Oh no, Scontee wasn't the antichrist! He was just an antichrist wannabe! He had listened so intently to Brother Danny expound on Christianity and "religions." He had heard him talk so much about so many worldly things, with all his delusions of grandeur, he thought he was the man for the job. Satan, however, had other designs!

Chapter 32

Clarissa's Family

Narrator: unknown...Thought to be ISD agent sympathizer of Christians

So, I guess I had better tell you more about Clarissa and her family. We left off a about them a chapter or two ago, but it is time now for you to understand how things had gotten the way they were for all of them.

Clarissa's mother, her stepfather, and stepbrothers experienced deep emotional turmoil after the horrible death of Clarissa's sister, Carla Aglar. The media claimed she was murdered because of the sheer madness of fundamentalist Christians. Healing was a slow process . . . one that drove Clarissa's mother far away from God.

At a family meeting, they agreed not to talk about her . . . it was the best way to go for emotional healing to take place. After that meeting, Carla was referred to as "the one we don't talk about . . . and only if they had to mention her at all. Carla and Clarissa were daughters by their mother's first marriage. Her first husband, James Aglar, had been a Christian, like her second husband, but he was killed while on a visit to dangerous areas of the Middle East. That was a few years before her second marriage.

They knew he was a Christian. He was also one of the first people kidnapped and beheaded in the Middle East for political reasons. They also had a message to the Christians: **"Stay out"!** It all happened right before they came to the United States to start a war here. (Of course, the Loosey Lefties used it to promote their "crackdown" on the Radical Rights.)

Some said they had a just cause for attacking America. Others said they started a war that would never end until one side or the other was destroyed. Whatever their reasons for the attacks, they used it to expand their political purposes to include so-called political "survivalism!"

After the beheading of James in the Mid East, and after the brutal death of Carla at Crazy Tom's Sandwich Shop, life became a little fuzzy for Clarissa's mother. Her second husband, Tom Edwards, the man who owned Crazy Tom's Sandwich Shop, was a very good and decent man who loved the Lord with all his heart. Tom tried talking with his wife, as did Clarissa . . . sometimes quite often. The twins, Tom's boys by his first marriage, which ended suddenly at the little white church, also tried talking with her.

Clarissa's mother wasn't the only one who'd lost a spouse to horrible violence. It was Brother Tiny who ended Tom's first marriage when he snapped a woman's neck. It happened to be Tom's wife. Indeed, it happened just a moment before that teenage boy witnessed to him, and just minutes before Tiny fell to his knees, asked Christ into his life, and became a Christian.

You might say that Brother Tom had every reason to be resentful and angry, but God used that man and those circumstances in powerful and wondrous ways. Tom was a loving and forgiving man, a lesson he had learned early in life. He had to forgive the newly saved Brother Tiny, and he chose to love him as a brother in Christ.

Some said that Tom and Clarissa's mother got married too soon after the deaths of their spouses. Yes, he knew her for over a year through Carla. He believed she was a good woman in need of Christ. Since Tom was a Christian and Clarissa's mother wasn't, Tom knew they would they be unevenly yoked; but Tom didn't feel they would be unequally yoked for very long.

She was a loving mother and, as with all non-Christians, she needed God's guidance, the prayers of Christians, and the continued examples of good Christian people. Tom had felt that the love of believers, their prayers, and watching their lives would be enough to help her see the truth. Tom also knew that the Holy Spirit was constantly tugging at her at a time when she was enduring the loss of her husband and daughter to such heinous deaths. Besides, she still couldn't understand why radical Christians had killed her beautiful Carla, if they really did, and why Middle Eastern radicals had killed James.

Now, she was at her wit's end. Her second husband and the twin boys had mysteriously disappeared with millions of others worldwide. All the conjectures at the focus groups were hard to take, as was Clarissa's new "habit" of rocking back and forth saying "Lord and Savior, Jesus the Christ" all the time. The two combined, plus not being firmly rooted in the Word of God, made Clarissa's mother snap. The world has gone nuts and she is going to join them!

She found herself at the bottom at ISD where she could vent her frustrations and newfound taste for violence with no need for remorse. When Scontee noticed her, she quickly became his prime prize.

A short time after becoming Scontee's left-hand woman, something strange happened. Brother Danny showed up at her door one morning while she was getting ready for work. She hadn't seen Danny for about a year and a half, to maybe two years. She never called him Brother Danny, she just called him Danny. After all, he was her older brother!

Anyway, Brother Danny showed up knocking at her door and told her that Scontee had mistreated him. He also told her about Scontee trying to have him killed by Tiny. Did he stop there? Not a chance! He told her that Scontee was into serious meanness against those he considered his enemies-which meant almost everyone. What was really strange was Brother Danny describing himself as a saint who no one except the cruel and evil Scontee would want to harm. Did she understand how Scontee had so successfully deceived her?

Then Brother Danny told her hat Scontee had ordered the cruel and needless death of her precious Carla and had put out the word to have her first husband killed, which he did not do. Scontee had done a lot of things, but he didn't have a thing to do with James' death.

When she got to work, Scontee was already there, plotting his next evil moves. She entered his office smooth as silk, so nobody would suspect her motives. She wanted to question him, because she was still in disbelief that he had done those awful things to her loved ones. She didn't have to go far with her quizzing because Scontee was quite the cocky guy. He knew very little of failure or defeat except what Tiny had taught him!

He told her that he had personally designed the plan for her brother's murder. He was sure it was slow and torturous for him. In fact, he got so excited about it every time he thought about it that he absolutely could not control himself! He told her that Brother Danny was a bad man and he just wanted to see him annihilated-so he made it happen!
He assured her that everything she had found out was true, except for the part about her first husband . . . but he would be more than happy to take credit for that, too!

Then he explained that the only reason he let her enjoy the luxury of advancement to left-hand woman was so he could gloat a little more. He wanted a constant reminder that he was THE man, and thanks to her, he had those reminders in spades! He had gone far beyond the old-fashioned, self-assured man to become an egotistical and evil murderer!

Too bad for him! Nobody ever found Brother Danny's body, so they just figured he had been totally obliterated by Tiny, which was not impossible to believe! There were two critical things that Scontee underestimated. First, his belief that Brother Danny was really dead. Second, that Clarissa's mother would be afraid to change her focus of vengeance ...and therefore wouldn't.

Dumb moves!

She kept her walkie-talkie on the whole time she talked with Scontee, and Brother Danny, trying to remain unrecognized, at least for the time being, was dressed as a hobo on top of his good clothes, and was hanging around, pretending to be goofing off, about a quarter of a block away. When she said the code phrase, he came barreling into ISD headquarters-a bad deal for Scontee. Oh, sure, all the guys at ISD recognized him as soon as he shed the hobo garb. All of those creeps remembered how much they liked and respected him.

Scontee spotted Brother Danny just as Clarissa's mother pulled out her service revolver. Scontee turned pale as a corpse, even before he actually became one! Well, at that point, you would think there would have been a whole lot to say, but there really wasn't.

She shot him! It was that simple. She shot him right between the eyes . . . point blank!

He died and immediately went to a real and burning hell! There really isn't anything else to say about the death of that IDIOT. Case closed. He's dead …he's gone …goodbye from Earth …good riddance!

With Brother Danny's influence, nobody batted an eye or flinched a muscle towards Clarissa's mother for "smoking" Scontee.

Chapter 33

Open the Pickle Jar

She was completely exonerated for the murder of Scontee . . . I mean on the spot exoneration. Those guys were just a bunch of hoodlums who happened to like Brother Danny.

Now there was a party for the "untimely exit" of Scontee. Clarissa's mother wanted to leave the party early, to check on Clarissa, but every time she tried, the other members of ISD would press her to show them again how she got the quick drop on Scontee! Again and again, she explained what happened until it was after seven that night. It was great!

Now, she really had to go. She wanted to check on Clarissa, get her night- things done, wind down before going to bed. She also had to prepare for another day.

She said "adios" to the guys, and headed towards home, feeling really good about her accomplishments for the day when ...

Suddenly there were blue lights! Blue lights were everywhere! Blue lights seemed to keep passing her. She wondered what was going on? Sirens were screaming the sound of alarm! She seemed to be surrounded by them! Was anybody she knew hurt? Was anybody she knew in trouble? Was it another one of those Christians?

Good! Let them hurt for all the grief they had caused her!

Perhaps that was a bad second thought. Come to think of it, what had she just learned? Scontee! Didn't all or most of her pain originate from him in one form or another? How many of those agents had helped? Which ones were there? Which ones had been there in the near past when they were hurting someone she loved, unknown to her?

More sirens . . . more blue lights . . . and more thoughts . . .

What if other people's pain counted as much as hers? What about those people? What possible harm had they done?

All this going on way too close to her house, where Clarissa and

her sitter were supposed to be safe. Please let Clarissa be all right! Please
. . . please! To whom did she make that request?

She turned the corner . . .

Couldn't breathe . . .

Heart stopped,

Cold dead . . .

Gurney . . .

Body . . .

Sheet . . . Blood . . .

What else do you want to know?

She poured it on . . . hit that gas pedal as hard as she could . . . .
she was getting close . . . people had to move out of the way . . . she didn't
care!

Oh no, my baby . . .

Oh no, my precious baby!

Hot metal . . . brakes couldn't take much more . . . she slid
sideways again . . . didn't care . . . she would have the ripped the car's door
off it's hinges to get to that bloody sheet

Stop right there?

Whoever you are, you'd better get out of my way.

Don't mess with me! Oh my baby . . . oh my baby . . . mommy's
right here! Oh my baby!

The world was spinning wildly . . . fast . . . too fast!

Suddenly . . .

On the ground eating grass . . . why?

Dirt in eyes . . . couldn't see . . . didn't matter . . . . had to get back
up fighting to get to the bloody sheet.

Handcuffs . . . no . . . no . . . no . . . why . . . why?

Danny . . . Danny . . . no, don't take my gun!

What are you doing Danny! It's Clarissa, Danny. Danny, please,
quit laughing. Why are you laughing?

Suddenly her face was throbbing, with pain! Horrible pain!

I'm falling, help me. Somebody catch me!

Her head was spinning, and there was dirt in her mouth. She had to shake it off, but she was handcuffed.

Ambulance leaving . . . no siren!

Come back, bring her back!

Danny, let go of my hair, Danny, you're hurting me! Danny, why are you looking at me that way? Why are all these guys from ISD looking at me that way and laughing?

Ow! Lord Jesus, please help me! What did I just say? They were right! They were right that Jesus is the only answer!

Danny, what's on the back of that truck? What is that thing? No! I know what it

is . . . I have sent plenty of people to it.

Leave me alone! Danny, why are you doing this?

Danny, everybody, Christ truly is the Son of God! Please let me go so I can tell you about it! I want to live so I can learn more, so I can help more!

I get it now!

I know what all those people I killed and helped kill were trying to do. They were just trying to live for Christ! They weren't radicals on a rampage. . . . we were!

Danny, all of you, wake up, please! Wake up!

We can't do this! You mustn't do this!

This scene was so familiar. I have seen so many other people do the same or similar things that I did! I couldn't believe it was happening to me this time! I couldn't believe life was so short, and then it was my time, it was really my time, not someone else's time. My time was nearly up and I wasted it so!

Please, Lord, give me one chance to make an impact on those people for you! Please, Lord, please grant me just this one last request,

I beg you. give me one chance, just one … to try to get through to these people for you.

She had only one shot at this.

God granted her last request.

She had seen this happen many times before, because she had been the one on the scene doing those things to other people, and now it was her brother's turn to do them to her.

I had to make the best of the very little I had!

"Joy, why did you want to make this happen?" Brother Danny asked. "My sister, Joy isn't having much "joy" right about now, is she?"

"Danny, why?"

"Why? You ask why? I'll tell you why, sis! Do you remember my niece, your daughter, Carla? Yes of coarse you do! Do you remember that first husband of yours, James Aglar? Yes, of coarse you do! Well, it appears that I didn't like the way things turned out at that church that day," Danny gloated. "You see, sis, I was there! Yes, it was just like Scontee told you a few hours ago . . . right before you plugged him right between the eyes! It wasn't Scontee who put together that little show. It was fun!

"I wanted credit for it, but for the time being, it was okay to appear to be just a side-liner, just one of the men under Scontee's command, just in case anything went wrong and there was big trouble to follow. Afterwards, when it became popular sport, Scontee got greedy.

"I told him it was time to give me the credit he owed me! He was the slick one, always thinking he was playing me. All along, I was calling the shots and directing the fire where it worked best, for the most effectiveness on the annihilation of the Radical Rights. Hey, I even came up with that phrase! Did I get any glory from it? No, of course not! All the guys knew, though, didn't you, guys?"

Everybody there started whooping and hollering and in one form or another, confirming what Brother Danny said.

"Anyway, I was the one that got the thrill of throwing that little old lady out of that window at that little white church! Hey, excitement like that you just can't buy! You had to there! Sort of like the "high" I'm getting right now, knowing what I'm about to do to you.

"Danny, what about Clarissa? Please, what about Clarissa?"

"Clarissa? Oh yeah, Clarissa! Well, I'll tell you about Clarissa, but first I need to tell you about what's her face, oh yeah, 'the one we don't talk about,' your used-to-be daughter, Carla."

"Please Danny, please tell me you didn't have anything to do with her death."

"Okay. then, I didn't have anything to do with Carla's death.
 Just kidding!

I had everything to do with it! It was my scheme . . .I set it up! I told Scontee where to find your precious Carla, told Scontee that through her we'd find your second husband, that Edwars guy, and he would lead us to Tiny. What we didn't know was that they would be together. You should know that if things hadn't been so botched by Scontee at that man's house in Chattanooga, you never would have known the 'displeasure' of being married to old Edwars!"

"You hated him that much, Danny? Why? Why did you do it?" she cried.

"Scontee called me from that house to ask for more directions on proceeding once they thought they had secured the house and its perimeter. I told him, in no uncertain terms, to make sure to "off" Edwars along with any others they chose to kill.

I knew, I just knew Edwars would be trouble. I just didn't know how. Well, part of how was that my stupid sister married him! I would have come back and done him in myself, but Scontee got really power greedy just a bit quicker than expected.

"Danny, I can't believe you did all those awful things! What's wrong with you?"

Wrong with me? Nothing's wrong with me! It was Scontee who was wrong! Oh well, I guess all of us are due one mistake in our lives, huh? Scontee's biggest one was thinking that old Tiny had killed me.

I'll even tell you about that in a minute, because I like the pleasure of prolonging your departure a teeny bit. It will make telling this story later a bit more pleasurable!"

"Pleasurable? Danny, are you so sick in your soul that you find all this pleasurable? And what happened to Carla? Tell me, Danny!"

"Okay, I'll fill you in on Carla! She's dead! I did it! Ha, Ha! Well, let's just say that Scontee had a heart for that one! He was going to let her off the hook. I persuaded him to have her knocked off. I was in the decision room for that one, too! I told those clowns from ISD to do that job and bring her head back to us. I was going to mummify it, but they messed up as usual and only gave her a "Chinese Necklace.""

"You killed my Carla, Danny, you killed my Carla, no, no, no!" she sobbed violently! The more she broke down, the more Danny kept gloating!

"Hey there, hey there, calm down now, it gets even better! Who was Clarissa's missionary daddy? What was his name? Wasn't it James Aglar? Yep!

Did that one too!

That thing about beheading sound familiar? I hope so! It was becoming popular in the Middle East, so I just woke up one morning with a whim to do 'ol James in. Anyone Radical Right enough to be a missionary, sis, had it coming; and you know you deserved better than that! I did have his head mummified. You want to see it?

She closed her eyes and started to pray. There was nothing she else she could do. Her brother was lost to the evil he clearly worshiped.

"Hey guys, go get that big pickle jar I keep in the back floorboard of my car, and be careful. If you drop it, your head will be in the next pickle jar!"

"Oh Danny, oh Danny, oh Danny, oh Danny," she cried.

"Calm down sis, it won't hurt you! I can't say the same for what's in the back of that truck over there, but nothing in that pickle jar will hurt you!"

They all started laughing and mocking her. One of the ISD goons brought the covered pickle jar to Danny. Then he made her look. He held her head in a headlock and then they forced her eyes open with their fingers.

None of those people had really liked her. They had just acted like they did because she seemed so close to Scontee, and they were afraid of ticking him off. They knew what he was capable of, and none of them wanted to be set up by him. Now was the time to be loyal to Brother Danny and pretend to like him, for safety's sake! Besides, they had gotten reasonably good at such charades, out of what had become necessity.

With her head in the grip of an ISD agent and her eyes forced open, she had to look; and what she saw was grotesque. The head was deformed, unnaturally discolored, and wore a permanent pained but peaceful gaze .... at least that's what she thought. Then it really hit her. James! She recognized him even though no one else, including his own mother, would have. She had loved him so much. She identified all his features, and it broke her heart to see him this way. She sobbed even more violently.

"Break this up, break this up sis," Brother Danny said as he cleaned her face, her tears, and running nose with his handkerchief. "Your head will be in its own pickle jar and will look very much like his by this time tomorrow!

Why, I just had one of those great ideas of mine! Why don't I put you head in there with his? Then the two of you can be together again! How's that?"

A few of the ISD agents groaned, a few laughed.

"There, there now, isn't that all better? Let's take a little walk, and we'll talk about that other daughter of yours, Clarissa! I'm sure you want to know about her now don't you? I don't know if we have time or not, or maybe I should say, I don't know if you have time or not! The little toy in the back of this truck is waiting impatiently for us, so we'd better talk fast!"

As much as she wanted to know about her sweet Clarissa, she knew this was the only time on earth left for her to witness, and through all her pain she felt that this was the right way to finish her life. She broke out witnessing to the same things she had heard her sweet Carla witness to. She witnessed to the things James talked about until their marriage union was broken by death. During his brave work for Christ, he had witnessed to her.

Then there was her beloved Crazy Tom. He was such a hoot! What a sense of humor! He had such novel ways of witnessing! Always so interesting, but she still never really bought it! Then he was gone too!

Gone in the Rapture of the church . . . gone with the redeemed of Christ! There was no way that wasn't real. Too late, she accepted the truth too late! Too late? She could still breath- for a few moments, and she would leave this world working for Christ! She would leave whatever happened next to her body, soul, and witness in His capable hands, to do with as He saw best.

Danny said she was too dangerous to keep alive, too dangerous for him and for the entire ISD because of her natural vulnerabilities. He knew that someday she would discover the truth and try to "light him up!" In the mean time, he thought she would do irreparable harm to the ISD and the New World Order. Her death would end any worry about those possible scenarios.

She witnessed!

Her witness during those last fleeting moments of her life was stronger and more effective than the witnessing of most people during their lifetimes. She had more knowledge through her husbands, through her Carla, and through everything she had learned about Christ all her life. She spoke of love, compassion, and willingness to sacrifice. She talked about asking forgiveness of sins and of not taking the Mark of the Beast, if they hadn't already.

This newly saved woman talked on and on, even as they walked her up the steps at the back of the flatbed truck . . .. and as they uncovered . . . a French Guillotine that had been well used during the 1700s. They bent her down, shackled her hands and bolted her head into the monster device!

She kept witnessing! "Please make your heart right with God! Join with Christ in heaven! I will, and my hearts desire is that I'll see you all there! We'll be able to walk the streets of gold together, sing His praises before Him, walk with Him and love Him in his presence!"

They raised that hideous blade and one of her "friends" from ISD held the rope that kept the blade in place. Her brother, Brother Danny, got her attention as she was squirming to get her head up so she could see the people she was trying to help one last time.

"Sister, oh my sister, there was one more little tidbit of information that I believe you desired? You wanted to know about that little daughter of yours?

"Yes, yes, please, yes . . . tell me . . . tell me please, before I die!

"I will grant you your last request! Your daughter is . . . "

The blade raced to her neck irretrievably fast, entered the soft flesh, then meat, then bone as he said, "Safe!" Did she hear his last word? Did she have to learn the truth in the Glory life?

"Somebody open the big pickle jar!"

Chapter 34

intrusion at YOUR door!

Matthew 5:10-12. "Blessed are they, which are persecuted for righteousness' sake: for theirs is the kingdom of Heaven. Blessed are ye, when men shall revile you, and persecute you, and shall say all manner of evil against you falsely, for my name's sake. Rejoice, and be exceeding glad: for great is your reward in Heaven: for so persecuted they the prophets which were before you."

Matthew 5:14, 16. "Ye are the light of the earth: A city that is set on an hill cannot be hid. Let your light so shine before men, that they may see your good works, and glorify your Father which is in Heaven."

Where's your Heart? Are you still here, **reader**? I see you! We talked about this, didn't we? You were instructed. No, you were ordered, in no uncertain terms, to have nothing to do with this book! You were told and shown what would happen if you persisted, and yet you willfully disobeyed a direct, lawful order from the ISD.

What's on your mind?
Shut up!
Doesn't matter now!
You've been caught!
Go to the door before I bust it down!
I'll come into your house or business, or anybody else's . . . anytime I want . . . in the name of security . . . and without a search warrant or any other warrant of any kind . . . even without the need to show probable cause!

How? Easy! It's called the "Patriot Act." Never heard of it? It covers a broad spectrum of legal intrusions! Remember when the banks started requiring a special thumbprint on checks if you cashed one at a bank in which you didn't have an account? Even the grocery stores and check-cashing places required a fingerprint. You asked about it and were told what it was all about.

Then what about those Biometrics? Technology is a hoot, isn't it?

You're under arrest.

You have the right to remain silent.

Yeah, you know the routine!

Up against the wall and spread 'em!

I'm going to cuff you again, now!

You should have learned the first time you were arrested for reading this book! Weren't you warned about the consequences of reading this garbage?

Quit whining! Nobody cares about lawbreakers like you! It's people like you that make it rough on everybody else! You see, reading illegal materials that incite others, like this book, are derogatory to the needs and advancement of society! You know this though. You've been told and warned.

Hey! Where's your "necklace?" I want to see your "necklace" and I want to see it now! Remember what I told you about the "necklace?" We know everything you "readers" do and we know everything you read!

You say that our "savior" is really the "man of perdition" as spoken about in that Bible you've read? You must know, as I do, that this world was in such a state of utter turmoil that we had to unify and come under "his" will, or this world would have faced complete destruction! You must surely know this, yet you blaspheme his name and the "goodness" that he has accomplished. You say you don't believe in him? You say you don't believe he is God, or the Son of God?

What's that you just said? You love Jesus? Is that what I heard you say? You say there was a Rapture of Christ's children and you and I were

306

not in it? Well, you now know you were wrong not to repent and have since given you life to Him? You say you will never "serve two masters", God and Satan, because God doesn't allow it? You say you serve the God of Abraham, Isaac, and Jacob, and the Christ who suffered and died on the cross for your sins and my sins .. . . if I will believe?

Why are all your loved ones and "friends" coming out of their houses? You ask why they're trying to talk you into rebuking God? Quit shouting profanities at them like "God is Great and His power is endless" and "His justice is righteous and swift!"

You've been leading people to the Lord? You admit you have been illegally talking this religious stuff to people, and trying to teach them how to be saved and spend eternity in Heaven? You freely admit this?

You know this is not the Dark Ages when people could get away with doing that, when they didn't receive any kind of punishment for it. Thank goodness for us that we know the "truth," that those people didn't do as much damage as they could have if they'd exercised their freedom and were nearly as excited as you are right now!

If they had, our battle would have been harder. Instead, we found them "sleeping", and we slipped this New World Order into place . .. . right under their noses. And now there's absolutely nothing they can do about it!

We now control everything and they control nothing. After all, wasn't the world begging for someone to come to power . . . someone who could control the chaos and confusion going on? You Christians thought it was Al-Quiada, and Muslims, and terror organizations all over the world! Well, from our viewpoint, it was, but it even more so was our need to subversively eradicate the Christians and Jews!

We used the mayhem and madness of those groups to gain, inch by inch, the same overwhelming control that we now clench tightly in our fists!

What about you loved ones? Well, we better not catch them reading this book, "witnessing," participating in unlawful "religious assemblies," or doing anything else illegal as per the "Treachery Laws." And, if they refused our mark of allegiance on their right hands or in their foreheads, they will see and get closely aquatinted with what you now see in front of you!

Don't be afraid of him that can only destroy the body and not the soul?

Well, that would be me! I'd say that you and all the rest of those religious zealots and fanatics had better be afraid!

Do you see what I see? Yeah, you HAVE seen it before! That time I arrested you for reading this book! And now you say you've been witnessing to anyone and everyone that would listen? You looked out of the window at the jail and said, "Oh my God, oh my God, Oh my God!" Now you get to "witness" what happens to people like you, the "oh my God people."

Please don't do this, you beg? You shout, "be strong in the Lord" to your loved ones as they scream and cry for you? Have mercy, you beg? I am having mercy. I'm having mercy on this world by taking you and all others like you out of it!

Walk up those steps or I'll drag you up them!

That's the beauty of this system! A few thousand of these Mobile Eradication Devices and, per unit, we can separate scores of heads from their bodies each day! Sooner or later we're bound to eliminate all Christians, either by killing you off or by scaring you into accepting the mark!

Up the steps you go! You want a hood? You know it really doesn't matter to me whether or not you take the hood! If you want all these people you know to see the look on your face as that shiny blade races through your neck, then I'll allow that. No problem! Now bend down and put your head into the locking device! Head in? Fabulous! Got you locked in tight now!

Witnessing right up to the end, huh? Witnessing to the people who are now reading this book and other Christian books, and to people reading the Bible.

You're telling them how it didn't have to come to this, how you and they could have gone in the Rapture, aren't you? You're telling them how you and they didn't really believe in it, and you believed all the malarkey the world had to say. You believed us when we discredited Christ, and His followings and teachings, but now you do believe with all your heart and are willing to die for it! Is that it? Great! That makes my job much easier!

You're telling them to keep reading, to not set this book down until they're convinced they've been saved by the blood of Christ . . . that they're really redeemed, really Christians bound for heaven, and in one accord with God? You're telling them to keep reading, and if possible, you'll tell them about heaven and being in the presence of God? You're one strange Christian, you know? How do you think you will accomplish all that?

I want to see your head in that basket over there! I want to see your head talking after it's severed from your body! I want to see your head telling anyone who will listen!

I can't wait to see that one! In a few moments, I'm going to see your body over there . . . on my right . . . and your head over there . . . on my left . . . in that basket!

When your "dead head" starts talking, I got a feelin' somma those feets a gonna start walkin'.

Well, I liked that! Let's do another! When your head starts a hummin', your friends'll be a runnin'!

All right, all right, no applause, please! So I'm no poet! I'm just a poor old Christian basher, underpaid and overworked. What's a guy supposed to do? I need some relief from the grisly labor of Decontaminating Society! Hey, who's next? The next person who's caught reading this book?

Oh, by the way, tell me more about how you'll tell anybody anything when the doing gets done, you know when your head thumps into the basket! You admitted you were the reader and now you're the victim. When this is over, you'll become part of the book! Yeah, right! I'd like to see that happen!

Now, on with the show!

This is where I always get the most excited, even with all the "amputations" I've done! *Head in . . . straps secure . . . basket in place! Now be a good little martyr for Christ and just* die! **Now, where did I leave that release rope?**

What's that you are trying to say? Still trying to witness?

Oops! Oh, No! I slipped and I had hold of the rope . .. . until it slipped! What's that you say . . . head? I can't hear you!

Chapter 35

Opening of the Fifth Seal

And now as your soul enters heaven, now martyred, beheaded; YOU join YOUR earthly mother, father, sister, brother, son, daughter, aunt, uncle, grandmother, grandfather, friends, family-all so greatly missed for what been perceived as so long ago ....but now, with full understanding, you know it was in "the twinkling of an eye!"

What a reunion! It's a reunion YOU never would have thought possible, because YOUR love for all people, all creations, and all heavenly beings, is so magnified, so abundant as to engulf every person, ever!

Martyrs for Christ.

Revelation 6:9.

And He (Christ, the worthy One, the only One in the universe righteous enough to open the Seals) had opened the fifth seal. "I saw under the altar the souls of them that were slain for the word of God, and for the testimony, which they held . . . slain for the word of God, and for the testimony which they held . . .

...slain for the word of God, and for the testimony which they held

Revelation 6:10.

How long, O Lord? "And they cried with a loud voice, saying, how long, O Lord, holy and true, dost thou not judge and avenge our blood on them that dwell on the earth?

"Judge and avenge our blood."

Revelation 6:11.   How long O Lord?

"And white robes were given unto everyone of them, and it was said unto them, that they should rest yet for a little season, until their fellow servants also and their brethren, that should be killed as they were, should be fulfilled."

They must wait until all their fellow servants (servants being the key word) and brethren (brethren being Christians, not necessarily servants), that should be killed as they were, (martyred for Christ . . . beheaded) should be fulfilled. The last person to be beheaded for Christ's sake must arrive in Glory before Christ's final and completing vengeance can be released upon His enemies, Satan and his follower, can occur.

Revelation 20:4.   AFTER . . . AFTER . . . THE LAST MARTYR!

"And I saw the souls of them that were beheaded for the witness of Jesus, and for the word of God, and which had not worshipped the beast, neither his image, neither had received his mark upon their foreheads, or in their hands; and they lived and reigned with Christ a thousand years."

Lived and Reigned with Christ for a Thousand Years! The Millennial Reign of Christ . . . begins at the end of the seven-year Tribulation . .. .

...BUT ...

V: 5

But the rest of the dead lived not again until the thousand years were finished. This is the first resurrection.

...UNDERSTAND!

"This is the first resurrection," refers to the resurrection of the beheaded martyrs. . this we know because . . .

V: 6

"Blessed and Holy is he that hath part in the first resurrection; on such the second death hath no power, but they shall be priests of God and of Christ, and shall reign with Him for a thousand years.

WHO SHALL REIGN WITH GOD FOR A THOUSAND YEARS?

Revelations 20:4.

" . . . The souls of them that were beheaded for the witness of Jesus, and for the word of God, and had not worshipped the beast, neither his image, neither had received his mark upon their foreheads, or in their hands."

YOU CAN'T WORSHIP THE BEAST IF IT ISN'T HERE YET! THE BEAST ISN'T EVEN KNOWN UNTIL THE START OF THE SEVEN-YEAR TRIBULATION

THEREFORE ". . . the souls of them beheaded" MUST REFER TO THE TRIBULATION MARTYR'S! Therefore, the first resurrection referred to here is the resurrection of the martyrs for Christ who were martyred during the seven year Tribulation

...ALSO. .

The sixth verse again, says,
"Blessed and holy is he that hath part in the first resurrection, on such the second death hath no power"

...What is the second death????

Revelations 20:14

"And death and hell were cast into the lake of fire."THIIS IS THE SECOND DEATH. AND WHOSOEVER WAS NOT FOUND IN THE LAMB'S BOOK OF LIFE WAS CAST INTO THE LAKE OF FIRE.

Notice that there was a period at the end of that sentence. That means that whosoever was not found in the Lamb's Book of Life was cast into the lake of fire. PERIOD! End of story! It may not be popular in these changing times. People are different now than they used to be . . . and all that stuff. People don't like to hear that kind of talk . . . and a thousand other excuses.

...But . . ..

NOBODY REVISED THE BOOK OR THIS PART OF THE

SCRIPTURE TO ACCOMMODATE THE SO-CALLED CHANGING TIMES
OR SO-CALLED CHANGING PEOPLE!

Get this straight! Nothing has changed! You heard me! Nothing has changed! God is the same yesterday, today, and tomorrow, and the Bible says the same thing and means the same thing! And the other thing that hasn't changed is the condition of man's soul!

The meaning is simple. If you leave out, selectively omit, or ignore that part of your scriptural learning or scriptural teaching, you must be doing something wrong, something dangerous, and something ungodly! You are soft soaping the Inspired Holy Word of God!

Does your Bible say something different than mine? If so, you'd better be looking around for a King James Version of the Bible. Compare again! I sound a bit sarcastic?

For the love of those around you, in your sphere of influence, read it like it is, understand it the way it was intended, and witness as the Holy Spirit, not your fear of rejection, dictates! Jesus bore witness of His Father in heaven . . . and His sheep heard his voice. Now for the sake of the people in your sphere of influence, pray about it, tell it like it is, keep telling it like it is, and leave the rest to the sweet Holy Spirit!

And from His Holy Word . . .

Revelation 21:4. "And God shall wipe away all tears from their eyes; and there shall be no more death, neither sorrow, nor crying, neither shall there be any more pain; for the former things are passed away."

Revelation 21:10-27.

"And he carried me away in the spirit to a great and high mountain, and shewed me that great city, the holy Jerusalem, descending out of heaven from God.

"Having the glory of God; and her light was like unto a stone most

315

precious, even like a jasper stone, clear as crystal;

"And had a wall great and high, and had twelve gates, and at the gates twelve angels, and names written thereon, which are the names of the twelve tribes of the children if Israel.

"On the east thee gates; on the north three gates; on the south three gates; and on the west three gates.

"And the wall of the city had twelve foundations, and in them the names of the twelve apostles of the Lamb.

"And he that talked with me had a golden reed to measure the city, and the gates thereof, and the wall thereof.

"And the city lieth foursquare, and the length is as large as the breadth; and he measured the city with the reed, twelve thousand furlongs. The length and the breadth and the height of it are equal.

"And he measured the wall thereof, an hundred and forty four cubits, according to the measurements of a man, that is, of the angel.

"And the building of the wall of it was as of jasper; and the city was pure gold, like unto pure glass.

"And the foundations of the wall of the city were garnished with all manner of precious stones. The first foundation was jasper; the second, sapphire; the third, a chalcedony; the fourth, an emerald;

"the fifth, sardonyx; the sixth, sardius; the seventh, chrysolyte; the eighth, beryl; the ninth, a topaz; the tenth, a chrsoprasus; the eleventh, a jacinth; the twelfth, an amethyst.

"And the twelve gates were twelve pearls; and every gate was one pearl; and the street of the city was pure gold, as it were transparent glass.

"And I saw no temple therein; for the Lord God Almighty and the Lamb are the temple of it.

"And the city had no need of the sun, neither of the moon to, to shine in it; for the glory of God did lighten it, and the Lamb is the light thereof.

"And the nations of them which are saved shall walk in the light; and the kings of the earth do bring their glory and honor into it.

"And the gates of it shall not be shut at all by day; for there shall be no night there.

"And they shall bring the glory and honor of the nations into it.

"And there shall in no wise enter into it any thing that defileth, neither whatsoever worketh abomination, or maketh a lie; but they which are written in the Lamb's Book of Life.

Revelation 22:1-5.

"And he shewed me a pure river of water of life, clear as crystal, proceeding out of the throne of God and of the Lamb.

"In the midst of the street of it, and on either side of the river, was there the tree of life, which have twelve manner of fruits, and yielded her fruit every month; and the leaves of the tree were for the healing of the nation.

"And there shall be no more curse. But the Throne of God and of the Lamb shall be in it; and His servants shall serve Him;

"And they shall see His face; and His name shall be in their foreheads.

"And there shall be no night there; and they need no candle, neither light of the sun; for the Lord God giveth them light; and they shall reign forever and ever.

Chapter 36

The Last Martyr

Narrator: You, Dear Reader ...You wrote this!!!

May God bless you richly in all aspects of your life. May He abundantly keep you as you now read the rest of the story . . .

HAVING FREELY GIVEN YOUR LIFE FOR CHRIST AS HE AWAITS YOUR ARRIVAL.

... YOU   ARE .. . .

THE LAST MARTYR . . .

Sights and feelings upon YOUR arrival in YOUR Heavenly Home . . .

*I*n God's abundant love we rest in total peace and absoluteness. Absolute what?
Absolute everything that is ...There's no part way, no second best, no inkling of discord. No in-between beauty, no in-between highs in the Lord!
YOU are forevermore in the presence of the pure Love of the

universe. No! Wait! It goes beyond that! It transcends the universe. This universe, as complex, huge, and marvelous as it is, doesn't even minutely compare . . . it's too miniscule!

To say that God is Love is such a strong understatement as to almost not even say it at all!! The constant emotional state of being in His presence is too awesome to even try to describe.

Such beauty . . . such understanding of compassion in a way YOU never before could.

Things of Beauty! Things of Love-Beauty! Things are not as they were and things are not gauged the same way.

"Things" valued are trivial, not as before.

Money and trade are not the issue of value.

That's what He told us, not what He tried to tell us, but what He DID tell us!
Not the love of things and possessions, because YOU already owned everything that matters through Him!

It was the love of serving Him, and the love of serving our fellow man that held real value. It was the compassion, helping one another, lifting one another up-He told us this, did He not? Forgiveness and Mercy, especially when not asked for.

Through our perfected eyes we see His and our kingdom, as now we are . . . Joint Heirs with our Lord and Savior.

Beauty indescribable, as only through our eyes that are here, can comprehend in it's **magnificence and grandeur** . . . as never imaginable until in our presence we now Behold!

YOUR heavenly home is truly Love-Beauty. IT ALL IS!

YOUR God is Love-Light-Beauty in a way no man could have ever conceived.

This home is perfect, as never was able to be told through mortal's words. For in all the thoughts, in all the syllables of all the words of every language, there is that distinct difference between man and God, including the former fallible manner of communication.

"I thought I said **this** *but you somehow heard* **that** *instead."*

Letters of alphabets, syllables, phrases, conjectures-unneeded and beyond the mideavaley antiquated here.

Language, Thought, Pure Thought, and Thoughts that are totally Pure and Loving of all Things for their worthiness to be Loved. Not for the sake of being a selfish possession, even for the selfish possession of a memory. We love it because God loves it, and we love it as God loves it, especially here, where we are consumed by those things of God's presence of all and in all.

<u>Joy unspeakable!</u>

–

<u>Love unspeakable!</u>

<u>Beauty unspeakable!</u>

<u>Harmony unspeakable!</u>

<u>Understanding unspeakable!</u>

<u>Light, as man could not understand. Love . . . Light . . . God . . . . All the same.</u>

Not light as we saw and understood before ...a Light spoken of but never even vaguely realized in truth and understanding. This light is Light, the energy of Love energy that penetrates the very fibers of the body, the soul, the mind, the being . . .

Rejoicing . . . Rejoicing!

Peace, Sweet Peace that should have touched onto YOU, dwelled in YOU, but was never because it in this exalted completeness only can be all-engulfing!

We, who were persecuted and were beheaded for the honor of His allowance, enjoy now this awe-filled Sanctity.

Oh, to do it all again, but magnified millions fold more!

Oh that they would hearken and listen!

Oh that they would have listened!

Oh that YOU had done more. Oh that YOU could have! Not only that we answered for as much at His Great Judgement Seat . . .

The Judgement, the review of our lives . . .

Where mourning was far deeper than YOU had ever known . . . mourning for the lost opportunities.

Lost opportunities, lost opportunities, lost opportunities . . .

Not taken, not seized. Lost!

What that we had seized those moments, that even just one more person, known,

That we knew...or not...would be here with us now-.instead of suffering **Eternal Damnation!   Eternal ...Eternal ...Eternal ....**

We forgot to tell them, were afraid to tell them, missed them, ignored them, and didn't know them . . . out of sight, out of mind. They are not now out of sight or out of mind.

WE SO TERRIBLY MISS THEM!

Our Savior, in whose presence we abide, will perfect this within His perfect plan! He is the Word and the Word is with Him and the Word is in Him.

~

Now YOU meet and rejoice with so many millions of other *Martyrs for Christ*, and *beheaded Martyrs for Christ* ...who one at a time had their life's labors for Christ on Earth come to a close, but not their work.

For in Christ, their work lives on
For in Christ, they live on . . .
In Heaven . . .

It was peace, rest, ease, comfort, beauty, incomparable love excitement, with all in perfect harmony.

The perfection of perfection itself, as could only be known in this life...itself!

This *REAL* life ...in Heaven . . .

As if this is the way it was, the way it should have been, the way it was always to be.

The things considered to be ...the *real* world ....are now known to be the things YOU thought were real.

The places and things YOU imagined as spiritual or "on the other side," are the things that were truly the reality after all. The reality YOU didn't see is more real than the one you DID see. And you were told . . .

"For we know in part and we prophesy in part. But when that which is perfect has come, then that which is in part will be done away. When I was a child, I spoke as a child, I understood as a child, I

thought as a child; but when I became a man, I put away childish things. For now we see in a mirror dimly, but then face to face. Now I know in part, but then I shall know just as I also am known. And now abide faith, hope, love, these three; but the greatest of these is

LOVE

Reality magnified!

Millions of times more real than any reality YOU thought YOU knew.

Then, YOU saw reality as with blinders on, through a foggy glass in a dark room. Hallelujah, it is known as it is written! All praise, all honor, all glory to the Living God almighty!

IT WAS INDEED, ALL FAITH, ALL FAITH! ALL FAITH! All FAITH! ALL LOVE, ALL COMPASSION, AND ALL THIRST FOR HIM!

Eternally Perfect communications here.

Perfect sight, to see objects large or small, but to see all things with the beauty of love and the love of beauty in them all!

We look back with no other eyes and hearts, but to wish we could have understood and conveyed it as we do now, this sweet reality that no man in his earthly confines could ever do!

The things we see, the way we see them, and the heart we see them through!

As never could be imagined or expressed!

YOU are at rest with Him, and so YOU are in the ultimate living state!

YOU have the *glorified consciousness!*

Rest from all prior forms of turmoil, which plagued all mankind from the first sin!

YOU realize that YOUR former life was stricken with that disease, and do now sympathize.

It was ours and it still is theirs that inhabit the Earth-that disease, sin, unto death!

Our souls were saved unconditionally and eternally, setting us free from condemnation through the Lamb's Perfect Blood . . . the Lamb's Perfect Blood!

The sin disease that kills every person's body, unexceptionally, cannot enter HERE!

Here, the blood of the perfect sacrificed Lamb engulfed it and removed it from the sight of The Lord God Almighty, .as far as the east is from the west, through our atonement by forgiveness through our prayers by our blessed intercessor, Jesus, the Christ.

We, the ones that. ...not we ourselves ...but that He bestowed on us as deserving, because of our fruits and our love as far as we could know it, and because of the sacrifices to the degree of beheading for the sake of the righteous and true cause of our Worthy Master. Wearing in all humility the white robes He bestowed to us and placed upon us.

We are His martyred saints who rejoice gleefully for our choices and our willingness to serve Him, do upon His loving command, wait the while (He spoke of) for his vengeance on those inhabitants of the earth-the ones that have been, still are, and will continue their wickedness until **that day sure**....The Final Judgment.

He will justify our wait!

Fear was ...*until the moment just past the beheadment, for the reality known.*

Justifiable at the total state!

Inbred within us, the desire to remain within the cloudy and sinful state, the flesh, but yet, even still, through love beyond the then norm, and not through stubbornness or haughtiness, we did willingly submit, even unto our lives themselves!

Unto Him *YOU* did commit *YOUR* spirit, even as He did unto His Father, our Father, as *you* were adopted unto Him by faith through the blood of perfection, the Lord Jesus Christ!

YOUR soul does rejoice exceedingly, beyond any mortal understanding. It compels YOU into this amazing and awesome exceeding gladness for this beyond absolute perfectness. YOU now and forever inhabit this wondrous state, this Heavenly Home!

All should have seen His all-powerfulness!

We no longer vision or envision, but see Him,

face to face.

His might and power were there and are there and are everywhere.

In all things good,

In all things truly beautiful,

In everything that is kind,

gentle, and forgiving,

in all things magnificent, wondrous,

and created to be our spectacle.

They are in every miracle!

They weren't fabrications of YOUR mind, they were possessions transferred by His great and boundless love!

Miracle realities, majesty realities from the Omni-loving God!

Hosanna to the Highest!

Lovingly gifted to YOU and more so except for the limits YOU allowed upon Your faith! …YOUR faith!

These things are His Essence. . . they are His Persona. Let the wise hear and understand.

Where He is, there we now are also!

As He prepares for battle, as the angels of Heaven prepare for the near-conclusion of the Battle of the Ages,

Glory and Honor encircle His Righteousness constantly.

Without the self-righteousness of the religious harlotry of the boastful and the proud-

Not worthy, Not worthy!

Their works are as filthy rags!

Work through His Love is gain, but only through Him!

Only through prayer and supplication did one and does one disperse of all but the truth.

Enter now, as I did, as straight is the road and narrow is the door in which YOU enter herein. Beauty is in everything here, as eyes could never behold before. Divide and partake of the Holy Word!

His battle is worthy. His cause is just. The reward is overpowering in its blissful majesty.

As it was written, "…and let your life be an unselfish witness of Him, helping others to meet us there!"

Eternal of Eternal of Eternal!!!

He is victorious**, the Worthy One, the Worthy One!**

The wicked created one, no longer in Heaven and soon to be vanquished from even the approach to The Throne, no longer to accuse man that he has infested with his sin-infection.

As He said it would be, so it is on earth. Forty-two months remain until the final pre-millennial Battle of the Ages. Then it will be...

As it was written in (Rev. 20: 1-3)

"And I saw an angel come down from Heaven, having the key of the bottomless pit and a great chain in his hand. And he laid hold on the dragon, that old serpent, which is the devil, and Satan, and bound him for a thousand years, and cast him into the bottomless pit, and shut him up, and set a seal upon him, that he should deceive the nations no more, till the thousand years should be fulfilled: and after that he must be loosed a little season.

(Rev. 20: 7-9).

"And when the thousand years are expired, Satan shall be loosed out from his prison, and shall go out to deceive the nations which are in the four quarters of the Earth, Gog and Magog, to gather them together to battle: the number of whom is as the sand of the sea. And they went up on the breadth of the Earth, and compassed the camp of the saints about, and the beloved city: and fire and brimstone came down from God out of Heaven, and devoured them

After which...

As it was written in (Rev. 20: 10)

And the devil that deceived them was cast into the lake of fire and brimstone, where the beast and the false prophet are, and shall be tormented day and night forever and ever.

As it was written, (Rev. 20: 4). .

"...And I saw the souls of them that were beheaded for the witness of Jesus, and for the word of God, and which had not worshipped the beast neither his image, neither had received his mark upon their foreheads, or in their hands; and they lived and reigned with Christ a thousand years.

We, the beheaded Martyred Saints, shall live and reign with Christ for that thousand years"

We shall reign with Christ Jesus forever and ever.

As it was written, (Rev.22: 5),
And there shall be no night there; and they need no candle, neither light of the sun; for the Lord God giveth them light: and they shall

reign for ever and ever.

~

Romans 8: 18 'For I reckon that the sufferings of this present time are not worthy to be compared with the glory which shall be revealed in us'.

Romans 8: 35- 39 Who shall separate us from the love of Christ? Shall tribulation, or distress, or persecution, or famine, or nakedness or the sword? As it is written, 'For Thy sake, we are killed all the day long, we are accounted as sheep for the slaughter.' Nay, in all these things we are more than conquerors through Him that loved us. For I am persuaded, that neither death, nor life, nor angels, nor principalities, nor powers, nor things present, nor things to come, nor height, nor depth, nor any other creature, shall be able to separate us from the love of God, which is in Christ Jesus our Lord.

The End

Thank you for reading Martyrs of the Cross, I hope it has been a blessing for you, as it has been for me.

Please give your heart and life to Jesus
PLEASE MEET ME THERE!

About the author:

Martyrs of the Cross, Passion for Christ, was written by Larry Skelf, who has
 lived in the Chattanooga Tennessee, and Rossville, Georgia for most of his life.

Mr. Skelf was saved by God's wonderful grace when only about seven years old, while attending Vacation Bible School at a satellite church of a rather large church, Highland Park Baptist Church, he adds,{ "don't forget the miracles God works in those little Vacation Bible Schools, they are well worth the effort!")

He has a wonderful, loving wife, Debbie, and five terrific kids, and several fabulous
grandchildren.

Martyrs of the Cross has been a five and a half year journey for Mr. Skelf, starting while a member of a small church in Rossville, Georgia.

Mr. and Mrs. Skelf had the opportunity to watch a Life of Christ Passion Play in Townsend, Tennessee, and while there, caught the fire and passion for writing, producing and directing dramas that had to do with our Lord.

While driving the streets of Birmingham, Alabama frequently, as part of his job, and while assigned a teaching role in the church he attended, called "Reality Check", Mr. Skelf was inspired by God to write the first version of Martyrs of the Cross, and thankfully, had a supportive pastor who allowed the first presentation of the play. It was a very simple play, but God's anointing was on it and it was a tremendous blessing.

The play was repeated again, this time while attending Jones Memorial Baptist Church, in Rossville, and again, God's anointing was on the play. Eventually, Mr. Skelf answered God's call in his life to write a book... Martyrs of the Cross-Passion for Christ, and several other versions of the play, Martyrs of the Cross, as well as a version of The Life of Christ Passion Play. Mr. Skelf currently serves his Lord in the capacity of Adult Sunday School teacher and radio Evangelist author and speaker.

More information can be obtained from the website, **WWW. Martyrsofthecross.Com**

A Martyr's Last Prayer

In this moment
I recall the dismal day
When you gave your life for me
Now, unto you Father, I pray.

In this moment
I recall your endless suffering
As the Lamb's blood was shed on Calvary
Releasing us from Hell's fierce sting.
In this moment
I recall the joyous hour

Salvation burst the chains bounding my heart
Rescuing me from Satan's horrific power.

In this moment
I ask you, Lord
Cast your strength into my soul
As I give my life for you
For precious is a Martyr's reward.

In this moment
I cast my soul into your hands
As I escape the grip of evil's hatred
You open the golden gates to the Promised Land.

In this moment
You now comfort their hearts
Remind them of your endless love
Let them all live for you
So we can join again, never to part.

Stacey Smith

Miracles do happen. They happen intentionally, purposefully and for a reason or reasons.

My God is real, and he answers prayers. When God answers your prayers, don't just thank Him, but ask yourself occasionally, why it you think it was that He answered your prayer. Most of the time, if not all of the time, you will come to one conclusion…so we can and will give Glory and Honor to Him and to use the answered prayer as a witness of Him and to acknowledge His great goodness and to allow an opening for a witnessing experience for Him.

The question is, do we do this? Do we take advantage of this wonderful opportunity He has given us, or do we even take the time to even thank

Him?

Following is a wonderful testimony of answered prayer from a wonderful young lady, the model for the cover of this book. Stacey, it is obvious God has many works for you. Stay tuned to Him and receptive to Him, always willing to witness our Savior!

Reader, please do the same. It is my prayer. Reader, if you have a testimony you would like to share, please be our guest to do so on the internet at

This one miracle, just this one (I say each time) meant the world to me...literally!

Everyone has had a near death experience. On December 31, 1994, I was involved in a tragic event. It was New Year's Eve night and I was going to a lock-in skating party. My friend's and I were supposed to stay the night at the rink. At least, that is the story I told my mom. My friends and I all met at the skating rink around 7:00 p.m. We skated around for awhile. One of my friends told me she had heard of a party we should go to. We all agreed to leave the skating party before they locked the doors to go check it out. If we had known the impending consequences, we all would have thought otherwise.

We decided to go a bar to pick up one of my friend's cousins. Being minors, we wondered how we were going to get inside. Amazingly, we walked into the bar without being questioned or carded. After we found him, we all got into his truck and headed to the party. I now realize how stupid I was to get inside a car with a potential drunk.

On the way to the party, we were stopped by the police. They did not see any liquor in the truck. The officer let us go without a ticket. There were seven of us crammed into the truck. Four of us were in the front; three were sitting in the truck bed. I was sitting in the front with one of my friends in my lap. The policeman did not comment on the fact that none of us had seatbelts on. At the moment, we considered ourselves lucky since we did not get a ticket, or worse.

When we got to the party, there were several drunks wandering around. We left almost as soon as we arrived. An angry drunk chased us out of the building with a shot gun and told us to get out. Needless to say, we all ran out. Afterwards, we decided to go to a friend's house to stay the night. One of the guys said he knew the person who lived there. On the way, we were stopped by the police again. We were stopped for having a headlight out. We were released again without a ticket. When we got to the house, no one was there. The guys decided to break into the house. They made it sound alright since they knew the person who lived there. We stayed there for about an hour, and then we decided to go to another party.

On our way to the party, we stopped at a convenience store for snacks and colas. As we were all getting back into the truck, one of the girls sitting in the back asked me if I would trade places with her because she was cold. Just as I was about to get out to switch, my friend (who was sitting in my lap) told her to stay back there because we were about to leave. I now realize that decision was a dramatic turning point in my life.. I had no idea where we were going. I hoped once we arrived, we would stay there the rest of the night. It was a cold, wet night.

As we were all having fun and snacking, I suddenly felt the truck being pulled to a sharp right and then to the left. I heard everyone screaming. Then, there was a brief silence and all I saw was lights. I felt the truck being airborne, and then it came crashing down. The truck rolled down a median three times. I experienced excruciating pain each time the truck toppled over. I remember praying to God asking him not to let me die. I was at the young age of fourteen. When the truck finally stopped turning, I was upside down. I asked God to please let it turn one more time so I could crawl out. I knew I would panic trying to get out of the truck upside down. The truck flipped another half turn. This is when I went unconscious for several minutes. When I came too, the vehicle was on its side. I climbed frantically up to the passenger window and climbed out. I was terrified the truck might explode or catch on fire.

When I landed on the ground, I remember being very sore. I looked up, and there was a lady standing there. I ran to her and she held me tightly telling me everything was going to be alright. I had a hard time catching my breath. I was hyperventilating as I ran up the hill to check on my friends. I found out they were all thrown out of the truck through the windshield before the truck started flipping. Several of them were thrown fifty feet onto the wet ground. Ambulances, police cars and fire trucks stretched for miles. I was put into a neck brace and told to relax. I did not see one of our friends who had been sitting in the bed of the truck. I panicked and asked where she was. I looked down the hill and there were several emergency caretakers surrounding her. Two of the people sitting in the back of the truck jumped out before the truck started tumbling. But, my friend wasn't so lucky. When the truck turned the first time, it hit her in the side of the head. It left her in a coma and paralyzed. This was the girl who asked me to switch places with her at the convenience store because she was cold.

When we arrived at the hospital, I found out I had a concussion and a hyper-flexed foot. I had a sever gash on my head. The doctors told me I could have seizures later in life because of the gash. I had to use crutches for two weeks. I have never had a seizure. Two years after the crash, I was diagnosed with diabetes. I believe this was caused from the crash. I have asked several doctors if this is possible, but none can give me an answer.

I am still amazed at all the miracles that night. The lady standing at the bottom of the hill when I climbed out of the truck was traveling in a church van. One of the passengers informed us how God told her to bring several blankets and pillows with her on their trip. I thank the Lord they were there when we crashed (around two o'clock in the morning). The firefighters told us if it had not been raining and the ground was not soft we all would have been dead. The soggy ground helped to cushion my friends when they were thrown out of the vehicle and it made the blows to the truck not as severe as it was turning. This was a gift from our Father. We had several warnings from God before we were involved in the crash. The police pulled us over twice, and a man threatened to shoot us at a party. We still insisted on going places we were not supposed to.

I still do not know what caused the crash. I thank the Lord for watching over us while we were out looking for trouble. I learned every action has a consequence. This may be the reason why I have diabetes today. My disorder reminds me each day where the road of destruction can lead. I must work diligently to stay on the right path with our Father. He gave me life by sacrificing his own Son on the cross. He owes us nothing. Yet, he graciously gave me life again during that horrible wreck. I am thankful our God is merciful. I am twenty seven years old. He continues to bless me and my family every day. My husband and I work hard to live for the Lord and to teach our children about our Father's unfailing love.

Stacey Smith